PERFECT STRANGERS

"Excuse me," Gabrielle said hopefully to the large redheaded man, "but would you please point out Colin Douglas to me?"

If the man heard her, he made no sign.

Gabrielle frowned, cleared her throat and spoke again. "I said, which one of these men is Colin Douglas, my betrothed?"

Finally the man turned his attention to her. "Colin? Is that who ye be looking for? Colin?"

A grin twitched at the corner of his thickly mustached lips. "Och! dinna look so worried. Ye'll be kenning it all soon enough, once we reach the keep."

"Are you saying my future husband will be disappointed in his wife?"

"I'd not be worrying about that right now if I were ye," the giant confessed. "Truly 'tis the least of yer concerns."

PERFECT STRANGERS

REBECCA SINCLAIR

ZEBRA BOOKS
KENSINGTON PUBLISHING CORP.

ZEBRA BOOKS are published by

Kensington Publishing Corp.
850 Third Avenue
New York, NY 10022

First Printing: March, 1996
10 9 8 7 6 5 4 3 2 1

Printed in the United States of America

"The good ol' law, the simple plan.
That they should take who ha' the power,
And they should keep who can."
>   —A popular Scots Border Ballad

". . . the brave Connor Douglas,
Who is both fierce and fell,
He willna give one inch o' ground,
For all the devils in hell."
>   —A more popular Scots Border Ballad
>   . . . Connor Douglas disagrees.

Onε

London, England
February 1603

Sitting on the edge of a hand-embroidered set-tee in Queen Elizabeth's starkly furnished sitting room, Gabrielle Carelton awaited the meeting Her Majesty had called last night. It was to begin a mere five minutes from now.

Gabrielle tapped her toe impatiently on the carpeted floor. Her full silk skirt rustled as she shifted uncomfortably on the settee. The movement encouraged a spirally black curl to fall forward over her right shoulder. The settee looked to be a fragile piece, and Gabrielle always worried that the delicately spindled legs might someday collapse beneath the burden of her weight. Yet it thus far had proved to be a solid, trustworthy piece of furniture.

Commanding an impromptu, private audience with one of her ladies was not Elizabeth's customary practice, especially so early in the day. Everyone at court knew Her Majesty was a notoriously late riser. So why had Elizabeth done so?

Gabrielle wondered. Why today? And, more importantly, why with *her*?

A noise in the corridor outside snagged Gabrielle's attention. Her green eyes jerked upward, fixing on the oak door. A distinct metal-against-metal hiss announced the door was being unlatched from without.

Gabrielle's pulse accelerated. Why, she wondered again, had Elizabeth called this unexpected audience? A troubled feeling settled in her stomach like a ball of lead, for she was about to find out.

The dark hair at her nape prickled with nervous anticipation. Her stomach fluttered, her breathing shallowed. Somewhere deep down inside, Gabrielle Carelton knew she was not going to like this audience with Elizabeth. Nay, she was not going to like it at all.

Bracklenaer Castle, Scots Border
February 1603

"What do ye mean I'll nae like it? Och! mon, dinna be sitting there deep in yer ale, grunting vague, one-word answers, and staring intae the fire as though it holds the key to some great mystery. What that hearth holds is hot coals, ashes, and flames, but naught else." Ella Douglas gave a toss of her head, sending her hair swaying like a thick bolt of dark-red velvet to her tiny waist. Despite the heat emanating from the dwindling fire, the great hall was dark and cold and damp at this hour of the night. Shivering, she pulled the woolen plaid closely about her shoulders and scowled down at her cousin. "As always, ye're being a fine muckle evasive, Connor. Will ye please just have out with it? Tell me exactly *what* it is I'll nae like hearing, then *I'll* be telling *ye* if I like it or nay."

Connor Douglas ignored the girl. Instead, he stared broodingly at the fire in question, his gray eyes narrow; it was hard to tell which was hotter, his glare or the fire it was fixed upon.

The Black Douglas.

Connor shook his head and lifted his heavy pewter mug. He took a long, deep swallow of the tepid tasting ale.

The nickname "The Black Douglas" had been given to him as a bairn by his father as a parody of the real Black Douglas, Connor's ancestor James Douglas, notorious friend of Robert the Bruce in the 1300s. As Connor grew older, however, the tag signified more than his long black hair and craggy good looks. It was also a clear warning that, like James, Connor Douglas was also in possession of a fierce Scots temperament.

Connor's reputation was long, tawdry, and only partially earned. Some said he surpassed in bravery and daring even the infamous Alasdair "The Devil" Graham. Connor disagreed. Oh, aye, he'd launched his share of successful raids and trods against Scots and English Marches alike in his twenty-eight years, but no more frequently or more cleverly than any other Border reiver he knew. The Devil had finally wed and settled down in his tumultuous ways, and mayhap that would explain why everyone was suddenly so interested in *him*, Connor Douglas concluded. He'd grown up in this country, knew the landscape and its inhabitants well. The people who lived in this wild, uncertain wilderness that was known as the Border between England and Scotland needed a figure around which they could spin their yarns and write their ballads. Connor Douglas had been picked for that dubious honor seemingly by default.

A sudden sharp pain in his right ankle diverted Connor's attention to his cousin. Ella's dainty size was deceiving; Douglas blood pumped hot and strong through her veins, as was evident now in the scowl that pinched her coppery brow and the way her gray-blue eyes sparkled with impatience.

With his free hand, Connor reached down and rubbed his ankle. It smarted mightily where she'd just kicked him.

"Are ye planning tae answer me within me life-time," Ella asked stiffly, "or should I go catch a wink of sleep whilst I still can? Connor, do ye ken what time it is? All ye've said in the last hour since ye so rudely woke me up is that ye've something tae tell me that I'll nae like hearing. Truly, Cousin, I'm tired of watching ye gulp down ale while I poke and prod the words outta ye. I've done all but reach down yer throat and yank the words out with me fists—and dinna be thinking I've nae thought aboot doing exactly that, for I have!"

Connor grunted. Aye, he'd a feeling she was right. He didn't realize how much ale he'd drunk until now, when he tried to shape his mouth around the words that ran blurrily through his mind. His lips felt oddly numb, his tongue over-sized and fleecy. Even his vision was muted. The great hall—and Ella—looked oddly fuzzy around the edges. His voice, when it came, was slurred. It took great effort for him to ask, "So what's stopping ye, lass?"

"The obvious." Her shrug was brisk.

"That being . . . ?"

"We both ken that ye'll ne'er tell me yer news,

or whate'er it is yer wanting tae say, until ye're bloody good and ready. There's nae a thing I can say or do tae change that."

"Yer a smart wench, Cousin."

"Nay, I be only a Douglas," Ella stated, her chin inching up proudly even as she gritted her teeth and swallowed back a yawn. Dear Lord, the hour was late. Why wouldn't Connor simply tell her what he'd dragged her down here to say and be done with it? The suspense was eating at her already frayed nerves. "Connor, please . . . !"

"I'm thinking, lass! Ye see, 'tis nae that I dinna want to tell ye. Would I have awoken ye if such was the case? Nay. 'Tis only that . . . och! I'm unsure *how* to say it."

"Bluntly would be a ver good start, methinks."

Draining the mug of ale, he set the container aside on the floor near his chair leg, then linked his fingers over his hard, flat stomach and returned her stare with a level one of his own. The subject he was about to broach—bluntly—had the power to sober him up a wee bit. His voice wasn't as slurred when he said "Afore a fortnight is out, I shall wed."

Ella stared at him for a full minute. "I dinna understand. It took ye the better part of an hour tae tell me *that*?" Her frown deepened as she shook her head. "Nay, there maun be more tae it. I know it, can feel it. Do tell me what yer *nae* telling me, Cousin."

"There be twa things, actually." Connor scratched his darkly stubble-dusted chin, his gaze never leaving Ella's. "First, my bride-tae-be is promised tae another."

"Who?"

"Colin."

"I dinna like the sound of this already."

"Ye need nae like it, Ella. The decision's been made, the plan set intae motion."

"So ye're going tae steal yer brother's intended, is that the way of it?" she asked flatly, and he nodded. She muttered a hearty Gaelic swear beneath her breath. "Heavens above, Connor, when are ye going tae let the past go? What's done is done. It canna be changed."

"Mayhap. But it *can* be avenged." Connor gritted his teeth and the muscles in his cheeks and jaw bunched tight beneath his swarthy skin.

"Ye were right aboot one thing, Cousin. I dinna like hearing this." Ella began pacing in front of the smoldering hearth. "Ye said there were twa things," she added cautiously. "Much as I'm sure I dinna want tae hear it, I maun ask what be the other?"

"The lass is English."

Ella's eyes widened and her cheeks went pale. "A S-Sassenach?" she stammered. *"Ye're wedding a Sassenach?* Connor Douglas, are ye out of yer mind?!"

"A Scotsman?" Gabrielle gasped. While she'd have liked to blame too-tight corset lacings for her sudden light-headedness, she knew better. It was the Queen's disclosure that had knocked the breath from her lungs and made her head spin. At the mere *thought* of wedding a heathen Scot, she shuddered visibly, her horrified gaze on the monarch. "You want me to marry a . . . a *Scotsman?!*"

"I do." Elizabeth nodded vaguely. She was standing in front of Gabrielle, who was still seated atop the settee and at the *unfair* disadvantage of having to crane her neck and look upward to meet with the Queen's gaze. Knowing the woman, Gabrielle could have sworn Elizabeth had planned their positions this way. "You've no objection to carrying out an order from your Queen"—one of Elizabeth's pale eyebrows arched in silent challenge—"do you?"

"I—" Gabrielle swallowed hard, her mind racing. She shook her head, trying to clear it, but her thoughts were too jumbled and chaotic.

Surely Elizabeth was jesting. Aye, that had to be the explanation. Anything else was untenable!

With a quick glance, Gabrielle assessed her sovereign. In the last six years of service, rare was the time she'd seen the aging Elizabeth look more serious. The blood pumping through Gabrielle's veins felt as cold as mountain water. "An order?"

Again, Elizabeth gave that clipped little nod.

Gabrielle gulped and rubbed her palms together nervously. Had she ever felt so trapped? Aye, once. When she was six years old, two of her cousins had cornered her against one of the rose trellises in her mother's garden. The boys had chanted nonsensical rhymes about her plain looks and teased her unmercifully about her even-then burgeoning weight. Gabrielle had tried desperately to get away from them, but they wouldn't let her pass. It wasn't until she was in tears and screaming for her father that the boys, either bored or fearing reprimand, finally gave up and wandered away . . . no doubt to find some other poor soul to torment. Though the incident had occurred fifteen years ago, it was still fresh in her mind.

She bit her lower lip, the sting of pain yanking her back into the present. It was a fact that if her Queen ordered her to marry a Scot, then marry a Scot she must do. Her family had always been loyal supporters of the English Crown.

Still, was there not *some* way of dissuading Elizabeth? If so, Gabrielle could not think of it; her mind was still too numb with shock for her to be able to concentrate long on anything, let alone a plan to escape Elizabeth's dictate.

Marry a Scot? Lord in heaven, what had she ever done to deserve such a horrendous fate, Gabrielle wondered. She glanced down at the fingers—short and thick, the skin ruddy from a recent washing, the fingernails bluntly cut and serviceably short—she now twisted nervously atop her silk-clad lap. The answer, when it came, hit her like a slap across the face.

Robert Devereaux, the second Earl of Essex.

A friend only, she and Robert had spent much time in each other's company since he'd come to court. Oh, Gabrielle was careful to make sure they were never alone, but apparently that didn't matter. In a court prone to rumor, much like any court in any kingdom, the latest gossip to be bandied about—was that Gabrielle Carelton and Robert Devereaux were carrying on a lusty affair behind Elizabeth's back.

When the rumor had reached Gabrielle, her reaction had been to tip back her head and have a hearty laugh. As if a man like Robert Devereaux would be interested in a heavyset, plain-looking woman like herself. Not bloody likely!

Through the shield of her lashes, Gabrielle snuck a look at Elizabeth. The Queen didn't look amused. It would seem the rumor had finally reached Elizabeth's ears. Gabrielle was surprised it had taken so long.

How had Elizabeth received the tidbit of misinformed news?

Gabrielle could well imagine!

Elizabeth had always been a self-centered woman who demanded to be the center of attention—both inside and outside the castle walls. As she'd aged and what little harsh beauty she had started to fade, her desire for attention—and especially *male* attention—had blossomed into an obsession.

What Gabrielle hadn't considered—until now, *until it was too bloody late!*—was how much it would sting Elizabeth's pride to have it publicly displayed that her latest suitor—whom Elizabeth seemed more interested in than those many gentlemen who had come before him—was distracted by a woman as unattractive as Gabrielle Carelton.

Gabrielle's gaze had dipped again to the fingers she twisted atop her lap. Her eyes rose slowly, meeting Elizabeth's. If there was a trace of sympathy in the Queen's face, she couldn't find it.

Gabrielle's hopes plummeted. "Would Mariella Rose not be better suited for such an"—she hesitated for a beat—*"honor,* Your Majesty?"

"I considered her, aye, but in the end it was obvious that you would best suit my needs."

"But why?" Gabrielle couldn't help but prod for information.

"Unlike Mariella, you've a trace of Scots blood in your veins, lady. That suits my objective perfectly."

" 'Tis but a very *small* trace."

"But a trace all the same. 'Tis Maxwell blood you have in you, is it not?"

"Aye," Gabrielle admitted reluctantly. The relationship was one any Carelton worth his name admitted to only under extreme duress. "I don't understand. What has the shadier part of my lineage to do with—?"

"Everything, dear lady. Absolutely everything."

Sweeping aside her nightdress and robe—the occasional times Elizabeth rose early; she did not dress until shortly before noon—she took a seat next to Gabrielle on the settee. Reaching over, she took Gabrielle's hand in her own.

Behind her back, some in court referred to their sovereign as The Ice Maiden. Never having had occasion to touch Elizabeth before, Gabrielle had always disregarded the term. Now, however, she thought the nickname well suited to the Queen. Elizabeth's fingers were very long, delicately shaped, enviably slender . . . while her skin was colder than a pane of glass during a roaring winter blizzard.

Elizabeth gave Gabrielle's fingers a squeeze that Gabrielle assumed was meant to reassure and encourage. In truth, it did neither. "You've not been with me long," Elizabeth said, "surely not as long as some, but you've been one of my ladies long enough to know the troubles I currently face. The Borders between Scotland and England are in a severe state of turmoil . . ." She rolled her eyes heavenward and sighed tiredly. Again. "As your protector, provider, and friend, I ask for your help in settling those savages down."

"And as my Queen . . . ?"

"I demand it."

" 'Tis a heavy task you ask of me. I'm not entirely sure how I, simply by marrying a barbaric Northerner, can accomplish it."

"Rest assured I do not expect so much of you. To tame the Border single-handedly simply would not be possible, especially for a mere woman. However, your marriage will be a start by uniting two of the most powerful families on either side of the Border. 'Tis my hope that an alliance of this nature will settle one of the fiercest blood feuds the Borders has ever seen. A feud, I might add, that has recently been reborn with a vengeance, and which gets worse by the day."

"Your Majesty, surely you are not suggesting—?" Gabrielle's words clogged in her throat and her heart skipped a heavy beat. While she'd thought herself shocked before, now that the heat of realization was starting to seep in, Gabrielle realized that was nothing compared to her present feelings. "I've misunderstood," she said, her voice a hoarse, cracked whisper. "Aye, that must be it. Surely you don't intend to marry me to . . . *a Douglas!*"

"A Maxwell? Ye're wedding a *Maxwell?* I'd wondered before, Connor, but now I be certain. Ye've flipped yer kilt, and that's that."

"I'm as sane as e'er, and I ken exactly what I be doing, Cousin."

"Nay, ye dinna. If so, ye'd nae even be *thinking* aboot marrying intae such a foul, disreputable family." Ella's eyes flashed as she lashed out again, kicking Connor's ankle, this time even harder. "Maxwells! Och!" She shuddered and huddled more deeply within the plaid. "God rot 'em all! Sweet Jesus, Connor, dinna tell me ye've forgotten the Maxwell is the ver same family we've had a blood feud running with for near three centuries?"

"Hold yer tongue. How many times maun I tell

ye, 'tis unbecoming for a lady tae speak in such a manner," Connor growled as he again reached down to rub his throbbing ankle. Damned if the girl hadn't kicked him in exactly the same spot. Och, but his cousin was a strong one! And then there was that dagger-sharp tongue of hers. Connor doubted it even crossed Ella's mind to keep her mouth shut when there was something on her mind she thought needed saying—whether it needed hearing or not. It was no wonder the girl, at the past-marriageable age of sixteen, remained unwed. Only Ella seemed to question why this was so. The answer was apparent to everyone else. What man in his right mind would take to wife a wench who, in speech and deed, proved more of a man than her mate?

Connor shook his head and forced his thoughts back to the conversation at hand. "I've forgotten naught, and well ye ken it. Least of all have I forgotten what rabble the Maxwell be. Howe'er, I can also see what is happening around me. The times are changing, Ella. Slowly, but changing all the same. Now that young Jamie has come intae his own, he is determined to test his mettle by settling the Border. That Ice Queen in England seems equally determined tae help him." He glanced at his cousin. Their gazes met and warred. "Use yer head, lass. Ye maun see all the changes taking place. In the last year alone hundreds of Borderers have been hanged or beheaded in Edinburgh and London. Punishment is coming faster, getting harsher, fiercer, and maun more frequent. Mark me words, the time for reiving and feuding is coming tae an end. Sooner, methinks, than most expect. When that happens, the Douglas will*na* be losing his head over past grievances but respected for stretching out his hand in peace *a'fore* it is demanded—or, worse, lopped off."

"Ye plan tae accomplish all that simply by stealing your brother's intended and wedding a Maxwell?" she scoffed.

"The wench is a Carelton, Ella. She's got a mere drop of good Scots blood in her. But nay, I'm nae so foolish as tae think a mere marriage, even tae a distant relative of the Maxwell, can accomplish so much. What I do think is that such a union will be a ver good start when the Border ways come tae a head."

"That 'mere drop' of Maxwell blood running through her veins makes her a Maxwell in my eyes, Cousin," Ella said angrily. "Were I ye, I'd nae be surprised if the rest of the clan Douglas feels maun the same. Och, tae think a Maxwell will be living here in Bracklenaer, roaming its corridors at will. . . . Ne'er, *ne'er* did I think I'd see the day. Ye were dead right. I dinna like this idea of yers, Connor. I dinna like it a wee little bit."

"I'm nae o'erly fond of it meself, but at least I ken the rewards. As for a Maxwell living in Bracklenaer . . . as I said, the wench is a Carelton, soon tae be a Douglas. Rest yer mind on it, Ella, and think on it this way: How long do ye think she'll actually be living at Bracklenaer?"

Ella frowned and shook her head. "I dinna ken."

"The bride was reared English tae the core, Ella. How many years has she spent lounging in the Queen's court? Four? Six? Ten? I dinna remember exactly, nor does it matter. What *does* matter is that all the while the lass has been pampered and protected, waited upon and coddled. I dinna ken what she looks like, nor does it matter, but in me mind I picture her as fair, delicate . . . and ver weak of constitution, the way English women tend tae be. Now tell me, how long can such a one survive this harsh climate of ours? One winter? Twa? No more than that, I'd wager. If I'm lucky, she'll live long enough to provide me with an heir, and that shall be long enough for me, but I shan't count on it."

Ella's gaze narrowed thoughtfully. Her expression cleared and a trace of a grin tugged at one corner of her mouth. "Methinks that by the next Day O' Truce—slated for this coming spring, is it nae?—yer Sassenach bride will be resting 'neath good Scots soil, and ye'll be a widower."

"A poor, bereft, sorely *grieving* widower," Connor corrected her with a matching grin. "Oh, aye. 'Tis exactly what I am counting upon, don't ye ken?"

The weather is . . . atrocious. Especially the winters. I'll be lucky to live out the year.

The remembered words echoed through Gabrielle's head. She'd spoken them less than an hour ago to her Queen. As expected, they'd had precious little effect. Once Elizabeth made a decision, there was never a chance of changing her mind. Elizabeth had decided that Gabrielle would wed Colin Douglas, and Gabrielle had been coerced into conceding that, as a loyal subject to the Crown, there was naught she could do but yield to her sovereign's demand.

Like it or not—and like it she most certainly did *not*—Gabrielle was journeying to Scotland to marry a stranger. A dreaded savage. A Northerner. Except for her great-great aunt, she'd no

Scots ties. She'd never even met a Scot, although she'd heard perfectly horrible tales about them. The prospect of meeting one now, of *marrying* one, was infinitely unappealing.

Every miserable rumor Gabrielle had ever heard about the brutish Scots bombarded her now. The men, she'd been told, wore rags, drank more heavily than they swore, and had a penchant for beating their womenfolk—not to mention one another—when they weren't out pilfering the English countryside . . . or the *Scots* countryside for that matter, since they seemed to have no preference from where they plundered and stole. The women were said to be harsh-looking, harsh-mouthed, and filthy. The terrain on the Northern side was said to be rough, craggy, and strenuous to traverse, and the food there gruesome and unpalatable.

Gabrielle closed her eyes, groaned, and wished to God that she had more time. But she didn't. Elizabeth had tersely informed her that she would be leaving for her new "home" within the hour.

Gabrielle's head spun. Everything was going so fast! She barely had enough time to pack her belongings. Not that there was much to pack.

Planting balled fists on her ample hips, Gabrielle glared down at her half-filled trunk. For the last quarter hour she'd been haphazardly tossing everything she could think of into it. She still had room to pack more, but pity take it, there was no more to add. Her wardrobe was of fine quality, thanks to Elizabeth, but sparse, her material property equally as meager. Except for her clothing, there was only one other possession she'd rather die than leave London without: the necklace her mother had given her when Gabrielle was but an infant.

Like a hummingbird, her mind flitted, no more taking the time to perch on one thought before swiftly taking flight and fluttering on to the next.

Would what little clothing she owned be warm enough to see her through the rest of the harsh Scots winter? What would Scotland be like? Was it truly as rough and wild as its inhabitants?

Last, but by no means least, dare she think of her future, and of her forced marriage to Colin Douglas, the estranged twin brother of the infamous Black Douglas?

The Black Douglas.

The nickname of her betrothed's brother sent a chill icing through her veins. Gabrielle shivered violently. Bad as the situation was, it could be worse. She could be marrying *Connor* Douglas, a man whose reputation for ruthlessness, cunning, and daring—not to mention blood-lust and vengeance—was well known as far north as Kintail and as far south as London.

Were *Connor* the Douglas she was being forced to wed . . .

Nay, she could not, *would not* think about it.

Besides, The Black Douglas was the least of her concerns right now. Her intended was *Colin* Douglas, *not* Connor. Elizabeth had been most adamant about that, and Gabrielle most thankful. There was no time to waste worrying about something that would never be. She had enough to worry about, thank you very much. Her departure. Her imminent marriage. Her acceptance into a clan of foreigners who no doubt would hate her on sight.

Gabrielle chased that last thought out of her mind. She'd deal with the certain hostility when it came, and not a second before.

Slowly, she cast a last, wistful glance about her chamber. Had she forgotten anything? A night-gown? A corset? Nay, she saw none of those. Even her precious silver hairbrush and mirror were tucked securely away. With her belongings packed, the starkly furnished chamber looked depressingly empty.

Her sigh was one of resignation as she slammed the lid of the trunk closed. Her fingers trembled as she belted the two leather ties that would, hope-fully, hold the trunk shut throughout the rigorous journey ahead.

Two clipped knocks sounded at the door just as she was securing the last buckle.

"Enter!" Gabrielle called out, distracted.

The door was pushed open by a tall, thin, dark-haired young boy.

"Rumor has it you're off to Scotland and a hus-band," the boy greeted her with annoying jovial-ity. Only his dark eyes shimmered briefly with a glint of sympathy for her predicament.

Gabrielle nodded tightly. Here, once again, was proof that at court, gossip traveled faster than a runaway carriage. No doubt there were more than a few confidants of the Queen who'd learned of Gabrielle's upcoming nuptials long before she herself had been told!

"Are you ready, m'lady?" the boy asked.

"W-what?" Gabrielle asked, jarred from her thoughts.

"I asked if you were ready to go."

Gabrielle swallowed hard. There was a tightening in her throat, chest, and stomach. Her voice cracked as she replied, "Aye, as ready as I'll ever be."

Two

They traveled for two weeks before entering the far north country that was known as the Borders. The craggy mountains and wild landscape was unlike anything Gabrielle had ever seen.

Gabrielle's aching body—especially her tender and bruised backside—was all too aware of every jostling mile she spent atop this shaggy-looking nag the Scots called a horse.

While with the Queen's men, they'd stopped at inns that Gabrielle had thought shoddy. A week ago she'd been transferred to the care of her future husband's men. Apparently the Scots didn't believe in inns—or *beds* for that matter. At the end of each impossibly long day of travel, they simply stopped, usually in a small clearing, and dismounted for the night. They cooked in the open and slept on cold, hard ground sheltered by nothing more than a big woolen strip of cloth. Or, in Gabrielle's case, her cloak. Long into the nights she'd lain awake, her sore body feeling every jutting lump of sod beneath her, her mind toying with images of the inns' lumpy beds that she'd sneered at but now longed for mightily.

Last night it had rained.

She'd hoped that Colin's men would be sensible enough to seek shelter. They hadn't. Like the seemingly endless string of nights before it, they'd slept under the cloud-strewn sky.

A more miserable evening Gabrielle could not remember ever spending. By morning, she was drenched. The men had allowed her to change clothes from the trunk of her meager possessions they'd secured atop a rickety wagon.

A warm, blessedly dry dress had helped. However, the only cloak she owned was the one she'd used for cover from the rain during the night, and the thick woolen garment had soaked up the rain like a sponge. She had wrung out as much of the moisture as she could, but it was a poor effort; the cloak remained saturated. Unfortunately, she'd no choice but to wear it. The air was too nippy and the wind was too strong for her to dare ride on without even its damp protection.

At midday her eyes started watering and she began sneezing. Her legs and arms and spine felt sore. Her head was fuzzy and her temples ached with a dull throb. She'd caught a cold. As if the weeks of travel hadn't been bad enough, now she would have to endure more of them while sick!

If she wasn't so loyal to her Queen, Gabrielle might have surrendered to the temptation to curse Elizabeth's soul.

As a distraction, she scanned the men about her. A shudder rippled down her spine. A scruffier, rougher looking bunch she'd never seen. Six years of court life had accustomed her to well-dressed and equally well-scented men.

As day compared to night, this motley crew sported scraggly beards, and thick, hairy legs exposed beneath sleep-wrinkled kilts. Deadly broad-swords hung ever ready at their hips, slapping against their muscled thighs as they rode. The plain steel hilt of daggers peeked out from the tops of their boots.

She felt as if everyone was staring at her. Well, that might be a *slight* exaggeration, she conceded. Still, the majority of men riding horseback both in front and behind her certainly were casting surreptitious, assessive glances her way.

Gabrielle's chin inched upward. Her spine stiffened resolutely as she moved in bone-weary time with the horse beneath her. Let them stare if they so desired. What did she care?

If spending half a dozen years in Elizabeth's demanding service had done nothing else, it had hardened Gabrielle to curious stares. After all, it was well known Elizabeth liked to surround herself with handsome men and women; among them Gabrielle had stood out like a lump of coal amid a bevy of exquisitely cut diamonds.

Aye, she was as much used to stares, and the occasional rude comments that accompanied them, as she was used to not showing a trace of response to either.

Outwardly.

Inwardly, her reaction was another matter; she felt dismal, discouraged, and embarrassed by her looks, for she knew that was the reason the men stared. Not for the first time did she wonder why people insisted upon forming a first impression by appearance alone.

The men seemed not to be a very chatty bunch. When they did talk, their speech was thick and guttural, most of their words incomprehensible to Gabrielle.

Was her husband-to-be among this ragged-looking group? she wondered. The question had been circling her mind for a week, her curiosity intensifying by the day. Surely if Colin was here he would have made himself known to her. Wouldn't he?

Gabrielle sneezed and wiped her nose with the hem of her still-damp cloak. There was only one way to find out if Colin was indeed part of the group, she decided finally.

Gathering up her courage, she edged her horse into step alongside that of a large, redheaded man. Her nose wrinkled. The man smelled as though bathing was a ritual to be practiced but once a year, and then, only if forced!

"Excuse me," she said hopefully, "but would you please point out Colin Douglas to me?"

If the man heard her, he ignored her.

Gabrielle frowned, cleared her throat, and tried again. "I said, could you please tell me which of these men is Colin Douglas, my betrothed?"

Finally, the man turned his attention toward her.

Gabrielle swallowed hard. Perhaps she should not have bothered him? He didn't look pleased to be yanked so abruptly from whatever thoughts were traipsing through his mind.

His voice, when it came, was gravelly, thick and angrily tight. *"Nach eil mi a'bruidhinn Beurla?"* he muttered hotly under his breath in his native Gaelic. Louder, he said, "I dinna ken what ye be saying. If ye canna speak slow and plain, lass, dinna speak at all."

The man might have had trouble understanding *her*, but except for whatever he'd muttered in Gaelic, she understood the rest of what the man said all too clearly.

She scowled darkly at his dismissive tone as well as his words. Her own expression and tone hardened when she said, a bit more loudly and a bit more slowly, "I asked you where Colin Douglas is. Can you point him out to me?"

"Colin?" One shaggy red brow cocked high. Was it her imagination, or did Gabrielle see a glint of amusement flicker in his eyes? She was unsure; the emotion came and went too quickly for her to interpret it. "Is *that* who ye be looking for? *Colin?*"

She nodded. Was the man daft? Who else would she be looking for, for heaven's sake?

While Gabrielle wasn't sure what sort of reaction the man would give her, the one he settled upon shocked her to the core.

A grin twitched at the corner of his thickly mustached lips. As she watched, he tipped back his shaggy red head and let loose a loud, deep, rumbling laugh that drew the attention of more than one of the riders nearby. They craned their necks, looking at the man with surprise. Hadn't they ever heard him laugh before?

Gabrielle gasped and winced at the booming racket. The man's mount seemed equally shocked. As though it was also unused to hearing laughter originating from its master, the horse whickered nervously and sidestepped in surprise.

She'd barely enough time to maneuver her own horse away before the two could collide. Pursing her lips, Gabrielle's frown deepened. " 'Twas a simple question, sir. I fail to see what's so funny."

"Aye, lass, that I'm sure of," he said, barely suppressing the laughter that could still be heard rumbling in his thick, gruff voice. "Och! dinna

look so worried. Ye'll be kenning it all soon
enough, once we reach Brack— er, the keep.
Hmmm, methinks by then, I'll still be the one
who's laughing, whilst ye'll be scowling a muckle
more than ye are now."

What an odd thing to say. Surely he was not
crass enough to be inferring . . .

Gabrielle felt a blush heat her cheeks. She
thought of her size, of her plain features, and felt
the familiar trickle of self-consciousness seep into
her bloodstream.

With fingers that trembled only a bit, she used
her free hand to fist the cloak more tightly beneath her chin. "Are you trying to say that my
future husband will be disappointed when he sees
the woman he's to marry?"

"*Och! chan eil thu luath!* I told ye, *speak slowly.*
That accent of yers is thick, and I'm having the
devil's own time understanding ye."

Gabrielle complied, but only because she was
so anxious for an answer. "I asked if you think
Colin will be disappointed in me."

"I'd noe be worrying aboot that right now if I
were ye. Truly, 'tis the least of yer concerns."

"I don't understand."

"Nor did I expect ye tae. Yet. Ye'll ken the way
of it soon enough. And when ye do, methinks
ye'll wish ye dinna."

Gabrielle sighed and shifted in the saddle. All
this riding was making her backside and thighs
sore!

The man's words echoed through her head.
They were not comforting, if only because he
hadn't given her an answer. No matter how hard
she tried not to, she couldn't help but wonder—
and worry—what Colin's reaction would be once

he saw her. If his heart was on set on one of the tall, slender, beautiful women she'd left behind at court, he was destined for disappointment.

Her thoughts and emotions spiraled downward. Sweet Jesus, if she didn't distract herself soon, she would scream! That in mind, Gabrielle cast a side-long glance at the man. He'd moved his mount away and was staring ahead blankly.

"Excuse me," she said, slowly and precisely, as she again guided her horse closer to his. He sighed deeply, glanced at her, and frowned in annoyance. Since that seemed to be his normal temperament, Gabrielle took no offense. "You said something before, in Gaelic, that I didn't understand . . . ?"

"Chan eil thu luath?"

"Aye, that's it." She smiled. He did not. "I don't speak the language," she explained. "Could you tell me what it means, please?"

"Aye. It means that yer nae ver swift." He scratched his thickly bearded jaw, nodded, and shrugged, as though he found it an apt transla-tion. If he realized he'd just insulted her, it didn't show in either his manner or expression.

Gabrielle sat back in the saddle as if she'd just been slapped. Indeed, her cheeks smarted and burned as though the blow had been tangible.

Fuming, she clenched her teeth around a most unladylike response and, after shooting him a hot glare, mimicked the man by jerking her attention forward and forcing herself to stare straight ahead.

What she saw did not improve her mood.

The hustle and bustle of London was long be-hind them. They were now in the open, rough, and ragged countryside known as the Borders.

A more hostile and unwelcoming terrain

Gabrielle had never seen. The area was called the Cheviot Hills. To her jaded eye, the seemingly endless ridges of hills looked more like small mountains.

What they lacked in height they made up for in steepness, she soon discovered. The tangled ridge of moorland was cut with valleys and gulleys that ran every which way. How these men knew where they were going was beyond her comprehension; one hill very quickly began to resemble the one after it. And the one after that.

Gabrielle tugged the hood of her cloak up over her head to shield her face from the whisk of the strong breeze. Her surroundings were as dreary as her mood. Desolate and bleak, the hills stretched on for what looked like an eternity.

So did her future.

"What are ye doing, Ella? Ye've been standing in front of that window half the day staring at naught. Did ye forget there be chores still left tae be done?"

"I've forgotten naught. The chores will get done, Cousin. Eventually. Ye needn't worry, the evening meal will be ready on time."

"Ye still havena told me why ye're staring out the window," Connor reminded her.

"I'd think it obvious."

Connor shook his head and sighed. Women were a constant source of confusion. Why they *thought* what they did, *said* what they did, *did* what they did . . . Och! but it rarely made a grain of sense to him. Figuring out the fairer sex was a job for much better men than himself, he'd concluded years ago.

His cousin, Connor had also concluded, was a stranger lass than most. A frown furrowed his brow. Mayhap it was time to find Ella a husband? God knows she was over the age for it. Let whomever the poor fellow ended up being deal with her; she was ever an annoyance and frustration to Connor!

"Nay," he said finally, " 'tis not obvious. Why dinna ye tell me?"

"I'm waiting for yer bride tae arrive. What else?"

He blinked hard, his frown deepening into a scowl. "Why?"

"Och! mon, but ye can be dense sometimes. While ye may not be the least bit curious about yer future wife, *I* maun certainly am. I want tae see if she looks the way ye said she would."

"She'll look like a Sassenach. 'Tis what she is."

"Aye, I ken that well enough. But will she be as tiny and frail as ye think? And if so, how do ye plan tae get an heir from her? The hardest part of winter is fast upon us, Cousin. What if she doesna survive until spring?"

"Then we shall bury her in true Scots tradition," Connor replied matter-of-factly. His broad shoulders rose and fell in a negligent shrug. "Whether she survives the winter or nay, the end result will be the same. Maxwell and Douglas will be united by marriage and the feud tempered, at least somewhat. Meanwhile, me dear brother will have been cheated out of having accomplished the feat. Dinna ye see, Ella? The marriage will have served its purpose no matter how long—or short—a time the wench lives. Oh, I admit I'm hoping tae get an heir from this, howe'er I'm nae so foolish as tae be counting upon it. I'm of a mind an heir would simply be a nice reward for all the trouble I am taking tae fetch the lass."

Ella glared at him from over her slender shoulder. Were she closer, she would have kicked him, he was certain of that. Hard. Connor made a mental note to tame her of that unladylike habit *before* finding her a husband.

"Now I be kenning why they call ye The Black Douglas, Connor," she said tightly. "Have ye no heart? No soul? No compassion whate'er? How can ye speak so indifferently of burying yer own wife?"

"She's nae me wife yet," he reminded her coolly. "Right now we're talking aboot naught more than putting tae her final rest a lass who is a complete stranger." Connor lifted his chin and scratched the underside of his jaw as he regarded her thoughtfully. "Tell me something, Ella. Exactly when did *ye* start troubling yerself o'er the welfare of a Maxwell?"

"Hmph!" Ella quickly shifted her attention back to the window. Her lips parted, her intent to voice a hot retort, but the words evaporated off her tongue as quickly as they came.

A sudden commotion outside jerked her attention past the cold pane of glass. "Ye'd best brace yerself, Cousin," she said. The rest she called out over her shoulder as she raced excitedly toward the door that led out of the great hall. "Methinks the complete stranger in question willna be such a stranger come nightfall. Yer wife has arrived!"

So this *is how the Scots build a castle,* Gabrielle thought . . . only because it was all she would *allow* herself to think at the moment.

She sneezed, wiped her nose, and tried not to notice how the gesture smarted; Lord knows what damage she'd done to her poor nose with a day of blotting on coarse wool; she only hoped the tip of her nose wasn't as red as the soreness there implied.

Her puffy, watery eyes focused on the castle and its various buildings. She had no idea what purpose the latter served. She sniffled, then bit down hard on the inside of her cheek to keep in check any outward reaction.

The castle was tall, square, hulking. The drizzle of rain darkened the stone to a discouraging shade of grayish black, backdropped by a sky that was cloudy and gray and equally as dismal looking.

There was no comparison between this place and the grand castle she'd left behind. Nor would she attempt to compare the two. To do so would only make her cry, and that was something Gabrielle stubbornly refused to do. Especially in front of strangers.

And speaking of strangers . . .

Was it her imagination, or were there more of them now than there'd been but a moment ago? Nay, it wasn't her imagination at all, there *were* more.

The group's arrival had caused a disturbance in the day's routine. Men, women, and children abandoned what they were doing and, unmindful of the cold, drizzling rain, straggled out of the thatch-roofed buildings situated protectively close to the keep. Their stares were open and curious, the brunt of them stopping on Gabrielle.

Ah, now stares she was used to. And the whispers . . . Gabrielle had no doubt as to the subject of these people's hushed, excited words.

She noticed that the man she'd spoken with earlier had at some point sidled up near her horse. Of them all, his stare was the most intense, the most curious. A twitch of a grin tugged at one corner of his bearded mouth, and a glint of amusement shimmered in the eyes almost hidden beneath bushy red brows. He looked to be waiting for . . . something.

Ye'll be kenning it all soon enough, once we reach Brack— er, the keep. Hmmm, methinks by then, I'll still be the one who's laughing, whilst ye'll be scowling a muckle more than ye are now.

The man's words haunted her, gliding through Gabrielle's mind like a ghost floating over a misty glen. She shivered violently and buried herself deeper within the folds of her now only slightly damp cloak. The gesture served a dual purpose. The harsh, scratchy cloth also effectively muffled a duet of sneezes.

She was about to learn just what he had meant.

Her heart skipped a beat, then hammered to life with double speed. A heavy feeling settled like a chunk of lead in the pit of her stomach. Suddenly, Gabrielle thought she could live quite happily without that knowledge. She was certain that whatever she was on the verge of learning, she was not going to like it.

"Och! Cousin, will ye please hurry up? 'Tis nae polite tae keep yer future bride waiting."

The voice, soft and delicate and as light as a fresh springtime breeze, drew Gabrielle's attention to the door of the keep. Running down thick stone stairs was a girl of about sixteen. At least Gabrielle *thought* it was a girl.

Trews encased the creature's thin legs. A baggy leather jacket, with a faded yellow tunic beneath, hung from her shoulders, disguising the form beneath. A sword, smaller than the type the men around Gabrielle carried, hung from the girl's waist.

Gabrielle frowned. It *was* a girl . . . wasn't it? Truly, it was hard to tell. Squinting, she looked again, harder, as the figure raced energetically across the carpet of wet grass separating them. Aye, it was a girl all right. The features were too delicate, the cheekbones too high and smooth, the mouth too full and pink to be those of a boy. Yet at first glance, if not for that unbound, wild shock of long red hair flying out from behind her, Gabrielle would have sworn the girl was a boy.

The girl skidded to a stop next to Gabrielle's horse so quickly she almost tripped and landed on her backside for the effort. Gabrielle eyed her warily.

The girl's eyes were bright blue, fringed by enviably long, thick coppery lashes. Her gaze was straight and direct as it met Gabrielle's.

Settling small, balled fists on her hips, the girl cocked her head to one side. A frown furrowed her brow as her gaze raked Gabrielle's face, then, one copper eyebrow quirking high, dipped to scan over her cloak-hidden figure.

"Are ye sure ye've Maxwell blood in ye?" she asked bluntly.

"None that I'd willingly admit to," Gabrielle answered with equal terseness.

"Hmph! Ye dinna look like any Maxwell I've e'er seen."

A hint of a smile curved Gabrielle's lips. "I'll take that as a compliment."

"Take it any way ye like, ye still dinna look like a Maxwell." The girl's attention turned to the man at Gabrielle's side, and she demanded of him, "Gilby, ye great lug, are ye ver sure this is the right wench? Are ye absolutely certain? Mayhap there was a mistake? 'Twas nae doubt night and hard tae see. Methinks ye may have picked up another—?"

"Nay, Ella," the man called Gilby replied gruffly, "there's been nae mistake. This is the one."

Ella pursed her lips. Her frown deepened to a scowl. If the way she kicked at the ground meant anything, she wasn't pleased by Gilby's reply. "Well, there's naught for it, then. She'll have tae do." She glanced behind her, and her expression lightened. Lifting her voice, she called out, " 'Tis aboot time ye got out here, Cousin. The first person tae greet yer future bride should have be *ye*, nae *me!*"

"And so it shall be, lass. Though somehow I'm doubting 'twas a proper greeting ye came out here tae give the wench."

The girl had the decency to blush, even as Gabrielle shifted her attention from Ella to the possessor of that deep, rumbling voice.

Gabrielle's breath caught in her throat.

He had shaggy black hair—the color at least three shades darker than her own—and sharply chiseled features; she wouldn't call him *handsome* exactly, but his craggy features were intriguing. His shoulders were impossibly broad, his chest wide; the latter was partially exposed by the untied laces of a cream-colored tunic. Gabrielle tried not to notice the dark, springy curls that peeked up from the separation of fabric. Tried not to, but did nonetheless. Her attention dipped. His stomach was flat and tight, banded by the folds of a black-and-gray plaid kilt.

Her gaze strayed lower still, and she swallowed hard. The man's legs were bare, the bands of muscles playing beneath the tanned flesh tight and powerful, rippling as he walked. His stride was long and confident.

The man was fast approaching. As she felt his gaze sharpen, volleying keenly between her and the girl, Gabrielle buried her face in her cloak and let the coarse material muffle another sneeze. Huddled in the voluminous folds, she instinctively leaned back in the saddle, as though to put as much distance between them as possible.

It was a silly, childish reaction, she knew, but one she couldn't check. For no reason besides his appearance, the man frightened her senseless. An unwelcome thought flashed through her mind, and she swallowed back a groan. If this dark, ominous figure was Colin Douglas, supposedly the more amicable of the legendary Douglas twins, she hoped never to have the misfortune of meeting his brother, The Black Douglas!

The man stopped beside Ella. The two glared at each other for a second before simultaneously shifting their attention upward . . .

To Gabrielle.

Gabrielle had felt herself an unattractive eyesore many times at Queen Bess's court, but never had she felt it to the extent she did at that moment. For the first time all day she found herself grateful for the cloak; adjusting it slightly, she was able to make the dark fabric hide the blush that stained her cheeks as she met and held her future husband's gaze.

His eyes were a piercing shade of gray, his gaze as intense as his expression.

"Since I dinna think me cousin has given ye the proper greeting she claims, I shall be the first tae do so." He bowed at the waist—a brisk, jerky motion—and as he straightened said, "Welcome to Bracklenaer, Lady Gabrielle Carelton."

While it rang a bit stilted, his greeting nevertheless seemed sincere enough. Gabrielle sneezed, sniffled, then tentatively lowered the cloak until the dark cloth sagged limply beneath her chin. "Thank you, m'lord, I . . ." The words clogged in her throat. Her voice went flat as an ice-cold sense of dread washed over her. "Did you say Bracklenaer?"

"Aye, mistress, I did."

"But that is not possible. Bracklenaer belongs to—"

"Connor Douglas," Ella supplied, then giggled behind her hand.

Over the pounding of her heart in her ears, Gabrielle barely heard the girl, or Gilby's burst of much harsher laughter.

While she would have liked to think it was the cold that made her head feel heavy and foggy—*perhaps bringing on a most unpalpable hallucination?*—Gabrielle knew better. This was no hallucination. The man had not been joking when he'd greeted her to Bracklenaer, nor had Ella when she'd proclaimed the keep's owner.

Connor Douglas?

The Black Douglas?

Dear Lord!

Her blood ran cold. Surely the dark-haired man who stood so proudly and confidently next to her horse could not be . . . ? Could he?

Fisting the cloak beneath her chin in a white-knuckled grip, Gabrielle swayed unsteadily in the saddle as she tried to absorb this news. Her head spun and her thoughts spiraled downward. If there was a breath to be had, her too-tightly-laced corset refused to allow her to find it.

His gray eyes narrowed, his gaze assessing her keenly, waiting for her reaction.

That reaction was not what it would have been on a day when her body didn't ache from tiredness and burn with fever. Her vision was watery, blurry, and there was a distinct blackness around the edges that alarmed her. She'd never fainted in her life, yet she'd an uneasy feeling she was about to do exactly that.

Blinking hard, she shook her head. Instead of making the blackness clouding her vision abate, the gesture served only to enhance it. This would never do! She bit down hard enough on the inside of her cheek to taste the sharp, salty tang of her own blood. That helped clear her head, but only a bit.

Gabrielle didn't know what she was going to do; she knew only what she *wouldn't* do. She wouldn't, couldn't, faint now or she would be lost. She needed to stay conscious, if only for a little while, while there might be a chance—a slim one, aye, but a chance all the same—to set this most inconceivable situation to rights.

Struggling to keep her senses sharp, Gabrielle tightened her fingers around the reins until the strips of leather bit into her skin. She'd ridden this horse for too many weeks to count and knew it well. A nudge of her knees set the nag off and running.

What should have been a brave, daring escape was cut humiliatingly short.

Two steps. That was all the ground the horse was allowed to cover before Connor Douglas casually reached out and snatched the reins from Gabrielle's hand. With a flick of his wrist, the horse came to a halt.

The quick stop came perilously close to tumbling Gabrielle out of the saddle. The blackness was back, edging her vision, but she was too embarrassed and angry to pay heed to it.

Her attention jerked to the side and down. The glare she leveled on Connor Douglas was hot enough to ignite a bonfire. "Let go of my horse."

" 'Tis nae yer horse, 'tis mine."

"I'll not argue over wording with you, sir! I demand you let go of those reins and let go of them *now!*"

"Why? Ye dinna ken which way tae go."

"I've a very good sense of direction. I'll figure it out."

"In yer condition? Ha! Nay, lass, aboot all ye'll do is get yerself lost in the forest and die of the fever." His frown was dark and stormy as he scratched at the stubbled underside of his jaw. "Or mayhaps ye're going tae deny ye're sick? I suppose ye could try, but dinna fool yerself intae thinking I'd believe it. Yer nose is swollen and red, and yer bloodshot, watery eyes speak for themselves."

Ella nudged her cousin's side and whispered loudly enough for Gabrielle to hear, "Poor Connor. Mayhap not e'en *until* winter?"

His reply to the cryptic remark was a noncommittal grunt.

Gabrielle swayed and again bit the tender inside of her cheek. This time, the sting of pain didn't help. The blackness was edging in, growing strong, tunneling her vision until all she could see was Connor Douglas.

It was the one thing on earth she did not want to see.

"Obviously there has been a mistake," Gabrielle said, mirroring the words someone had spoken earlier. Her thickly clouded mind wouldn't allow her to remember who or when. Was it her imagination, or did her voice sound slurred, oddly distant? Nay, it was not her imagination, that was how her ears perceived it.

Her limbs felt weak and shaky. She had to grip the edge of the saddle hard, until it cut ridges in her fingertips, and even then her seat remained wobbly. Still, it was either that or tumble in an ungraceful heap at Connor Douglas's feet.

"There's been nae mistake," he said evenly. "Ye're exactly where ye're supposed tae be."

"Nay, I am not even close," she replied stubbornly, and realized it was getting more and more difficult to force her tongue to shape words. The blackness was racing in quickly now. Even the easiest thought flowed through her fevered mind like water, refusing to freeze and solidify. "My destination is Gaelside, castle of *Colin* Douglas. *Not* Bracklenaer."

"Och! lass, I ken yer destination well enough. Do *ye* ken that ye're aboot to faint?"

"I most certain am *not!*" Gabrielle replied hotly. She then proceeded to do exactly that.

The blackness swept over Gabrielle, the strength drained out of her body. Her limbs felt heavy yet at the same time light and limp. Her eyes flickered shut of their own accord. Her head dipped, and her chin collided with her cloak-covered collarbone.

The saddle beneath her shifted. Nay, that was wrong. It was not the saddle that shifted, it was herself . . . shifting out of it.

Dear God, she was falling!

With what little consciousness she'd conserved, Gabrielle commanded her body to do something, anything, to stop herself from falling. While her body would have loved to obey, tried to even, in the end, it simply couldn't. Her arms, neck, and legs felt as if they'd been weighted down by chunks of lead; no amount of mental coaxing could shake off the heaviness and make them move.

Gabrielle groaned, or at least tried to. To the best of her knowledge, no sound left her tight, dry throat. Reluctantly, she realized that her only hope now was to be totally unconscious before she hit the ground, and therefore saved the embarrassment of falling at this arrogant Scot's—*The Black Douglas's!*—feet.

Just as she was about to pitch out of the saddle, she felt an arm slipped behind her waist. Another slid quickly beneath her knees. Both were as thick and hard as a tree limb.

Had Connor Douglas caught her? she wondered, even as the blackness came up, threatening to swallow her completely.

"Umph!"

The sound came as though from a distance, echoing in her ears as she felt him take on her full weight.

The last thing Gabrielle heard before unconsciousness overtook her was Ella's soft, melodic laughter. "Pampered and delicate of constitution, did ye say she'd be? Dainty and frail? Methinks ye've misjudged yer future wife, Connor . . . in a fine muckle maun ways than one!"

Three

News on the Borders moved faster than Kinmont Willie slipping out of Carlisle Castle.

The first messenger arrived at noon.

Connor and Gilby were in the great hall, sitting at one of the tables lining the wall, drinking ale and debating which would happen first: the Kerrs pilfering Bracklenaer, or the Douglas pilfering the Kerrs. Deep in conversation, neither noticed the hesitant-looking man who was led into the room by a serving wench, the latter's arms were piled with fresh rushes and sprigs of summer-dried heather.

The girl cleared her throat. "M'lord," she said, her knobby chin jerking briskly in the stranger's direction, "he's come tae see ye. Says he bears a message."

Stopping in midsentence, Connor's gaze left Gilby and shifted to the stranger. The man was wearing the gray of the Douglas, but the plaid was embellished with thin strips of blue; the sight left no doubt in Connor's mind as to from whom the message came. "Dinna stand there staring, mon. Come o'er here, give me yer message, and be done with it.''

The man approached the table. His eyes were narrow as his attention volleyed warily between Connor and Gilby.

Connor considered offering the man a drink, then decided against it. There was no need. The stranger hadn't traveled far to get to Bracklenaer, nor would he have far to travel home. Instead, he took a sip from his mug and regarded the man sharply from over the rim.

The stranger shifted his weight from foot to foot, obviously eager to deliver his message and quit the keep, the sooner the better. ''M'lord, I've a message fer ye from—''

''Me brother,'' Connor supplied for him. ''Aye, I ken that well enough.'' His gaze dipped, lingered for a poignant second on the man's wearfaded kilt, lifted. From the corner of his eye, Connor noticed that the wench was taking her sweet time spreading the rushes over the floor. Eavesdropping, no doubt. ''Ver well, mon, say what ye've come tae say and be quick aboot it. I've business tae attend.''

The man cleared his throat and sucked in a deep breath before starting. ''M'lord, Sir Colin Douglas of Gaelside, Duke of ''

''Och! mon, I ken who me brother be,'' Connor interrupted impatiently. ''Can ye nae skip that part and get directly tae the message?''

The man hesitated. Now that the words he'd been carefully rehearsing during the hours it took to travel between castles were not to be spoken, he seemed unsure of how to proceed.

''Mayhap if ye simply sum up Colin's threats?'' Connor prompted the man helpfully.

The stranger nodded, yet he continued to hesitate.

Connor ignored the way Gilby gulped back a laugh along with a deep swallow of ale, and prodded, " 'Tis doubtful Colin would send ye here without the obligatory threat of murder and mayhem in retaliation for stealing his future bride. Aye?"

"Aye!" The man's rigid posture relaxed a wee bit, and this time his nod was enthusiastic.

"Did he threaten tae steal the lass back?"

"Aye!"

"That sounds typical of Colin. Did he also say I'd live tae regret the hour our mither gave us birth?"

The man frowned slightly. "Well, nay, nae in so many words exactly . . ."

"But the implication was there?"

"Maun than there, m'lord."

"Were there naught other more specific threats he sent ye here tae relay?"

"Just one more, m'lord."

"And that is?"

"Methinks this one may nae be a threat so much as a warning."

Connor shrugged and motioned with his hand for the man to continue. The wench, he noticed absently, had abandoned her pretense of spreading the rushes and heather; she'd taken a seat not far away and was now listening openly, eager to snare a tidbit or two of gossip.

"All right, mon, what be me brother's warning, then?" Connor asked, checking his impatience.

"I am tae tell ye specifically that he will slice off yer . . ." The man gulped, his gaze skipping to the wench then back to Connor. "Er, that is tae say, he means tae relieve ye of a certain part of yer anatomy if ye so much as lay a finger on the beautiful and fragile Lady Gabrielle Carelton."

Gilby and the serving wench laughed heartily, until even the huge dogs that stretched lazily in front of the hearth picked up their heads, ears perking as they looked around to see what the commotion was about.

Connor, who had lifted his mug and was in the process of downing the rest of the ale, felt the yeasty liquid clog in his laughter-tightened throat. He choked and sputtered. "Beautiful and fragile?" he asked when he was finally able to catch his breath. A warning glare at Gilby and the wench toned them down to snickers. "Colin said that?"

"Aye, he did," the man replied hesitantly. "I dinna see what's so funny aboot it, though."

"Nor will ye, unless me brother has suddenly become smart and crafty and accomplished his threat tae steal the lass back."

"And we all ken that the chances of that happening," Gilby interceded, "are aboot as good as me being crowned King of England in that dour old puss's place. Ha!"

Connor slammed his empty mug down on the table and released the chuckle he'd been suppressing. His attention returned to the messenger. "Do ye have instructions tae take back a reply?"

He shrugged warily. "I have nae instruction *nae* to."

"Ver good. Ride back to Gaelside and tell me brother . . ." Connor pursed his lips and scowled thoughtfully. "Aye, tell Colin that I said tae use what little brains God gave him and cool his hot-blooded heels for once. The Lady Gabrielle was rightfully stolen, and no March Warden on either side of the Border can argue that point. 'Tis no fault of mine if me brother canna keep proper track of his belongings, don't ye ken? The lass is in my care now, and in my care she shall stay. Howe'er . . ." A shrewd grin tugged at one corner of Connor's mouth and his gray eyes gleamed as he rubbed his hands together in anticipation, "tell him that if he willna listen, and he's truly of a mind to rescue the"—ahem!—"beautiful and fragile lass, he's welcome tae try." His gaze narrowed on the messenger. "Whate'er ye do, mon, dinna forget tae tell him that last part."

"I'll nae forget."

"Good." Connor gestured toward the door to the hall. "What are ye waiting for? Be off with ye. Ye've an important message tae deliver."

The man nodded briskly and turned toward the door. He reached the arched stone doorway, then stopped. Looking back over his shoulder, the man paused for a beat before saying in an oddly timid tone, "M'lord, rumor has it that ye and but fifty men crept intae Caerlaverock, whisked away two dozen of the Maxwell's beasties and half that again in prisoners, without e'en disturbing the laird's sleep. Rumor also has it that Johnny Maxwell wasna aware of his losses until the next morning when he sat down tae break his fast . . . but the table stayed empty. One of the prisoners taken was his cook." A spark of admiration flashed in the man's eyes. " 'Tis quite the tale of daring . . . if it be true. Is it?"

"Tell me, do ye believe e'ery rumor ye hear?"

"W-well, nay," the man stammered. "Howe'er,

I've been hearing a fine muckle of rumors aboot
The Black Douglas of late. E'eryone at Gaelside
is curious tae ken how many of them be true and
how many be so maun talk."

"I dinna see that it matters. True or nae, people
believe what they will." Connor forced his shrug
to look negligent as his attention shifted. He
waved to the wench, indicating she should fetch
more ale. She stood and retrieved his and Gilby's
mug, then quickly disappeared around a corner
at the opposite side of the hall, heading down the
dimly lit corridor that led to the kitchen.

There was no need to glance at the doorway
to see if the messenger had left; the man's
bootheels echoed on the stone steps leading
down to the ground-floor entrance.

Connor glanced at Gilby and sighed. "Dinna
ye think it a wee bit strange?"

"The message?" Gilby asked.

"Och! nay, that was expected. Colin is Colin;
'twould have been odd if he'd *nae* made any
threats. What I be talking aboot are these . . .
these *rumors* going aboot."

"Ballads," Gilby corrected easily, "is what they
are now. They were rumors only for a short time
before someone paced them and put them tae
song."

"Rumors, ballads, whate'er they be, they're be
a fine muckle strange."

Gilby shrugged. " 'Tis the way o' things. Ye
dinna need me tae tell ye that Borderers are wont
to write ballads and tell tales, the taller the better."

" 'Tis nae the rum— er, *ballads* themselves that
bother me, Gilby, 'tis their subject matter. Ye
should ken better than maun that there's naught
extraordinary about me. Why this sudden atten-

tion? Why waste prose on me and my nae so daring but really quite ordinary deeds?"

The Douglas's first in command thought about this for a moment. "Now that The Devil is wed and settled down to raising his bairns, they've naught left to sing about him but lullabies. Ye have tae admit, Connor, ye *did* ride on Caerlaverock exactly as the mon said."

"But nae with fifty men!"

"Aye," Gilby agreed, "with twenty. Which is e'en more daring than accomplishing the deed with a mere fifty."

"Methinks 'tis a good thing me brother's men dinna ken that or they'd have me canonized."

The thought made Gilby laugh. The sound bounced off the hard stone walls of the hall like resonant claps of thunder.

The serving wench returned, and gave Gilby an odd glance as she set the two fresh mugs of ale in front of them. Just as she was about to turn away, Connor reached out and gently grasped her wrist, stopping her short.

She glanced down at him, puzzled. An impatient light shimmered in her eyes, and it was obvious she was anxious to get back to the kitchen and finish telling the other servants what had just transpired in the hall.

"Has the lass come 'round yet?"

She nodded her dreary brown head. "Aye, m'lord, aboot an hour ago."

Connor let go of her slender wrist and sat back in surprise. "An *hour* ago? Why dinna anyone come and fetch me?" he demanded.

"She asked us nae tae disturb ye."

"Nae tae disturb—?! Saints alive, wench, dinna I tell ye to get me the second she awoke?" Connor's scowl was dark and fierce. He'd lifted his mug to take a deep sip, but the girl's words stopped him short. He set the mug back down on the table hard enough to make a goodly portion of the foamy contents spill over the side, down his hand, and onto the scarred oak tabletop.

The girl opened her mouth, shut it, then opened it again. Her gaze shifted briefly to Gilby, but she found no help there. This time when she spoke, her lower lip trembled, and her voice was weak and edged with hesitancy. "A-aye, ye did, but . . ."

"Tell me something, Alice. Do ye now obey a Carelton's orders over my own?"

Alice's eyes widened and she shook her head vigorously. "Nay! Ne'er!"

"Then why was *my* order nae carried out, whilst *hers* was?"

"I-I—"

Alice was saved having to answer the question by the sound of more footsteps stomping on the stairs outside the hall. They grew louder instead of softer, indicating an approach instead of a retreat.

The relief in the girl's eyes was tangible. When Connor gestured tightly for her to leave the room, she did so without a trace of reluctance.

"A messenger, m'lord," a gruff male voice announced from the arched doorway. "From King James."

Connor lifted his mug, his fingers tight around the handle. He drained two thirds of the tepid contents in a single gulp, all the while wondering how many more messengers were to come, and how much worse the day was destined to get.

* * *

"Will ye nae be a good lass and open yer mouth a'fore the broth spills all o'er the covers? As ye nae doubt can see, me hand isna so steady as it once was, and I've nae desire tae be changing the bed simply because ye're tae sick and tae stubborn tae open yer mouth."

Gabrielle sat back against the pillows cushioning her back from the hard wooden headboard. "I keep telling you, madam, that I'm not *that* sick. I'm perfectly capable of feeding myself. Give me the spoon and I'll happily prove it to you."

The old woman laughed; to Gabrielle's sensitive ears, it sounded more like a harsh cackle, harder and colder than the stone walls off which it bounced. "Och! 'twas a good try, lass, but nae good enough to slip past the likes of me. Now, open yer mouth."

Gabrielle clenched her teeth together stubbornly and shook her head. The gesture made her head pound, even as she eyed the old woman speculatively.

Mairghread was the old woman's name. At least that was what the woman had claimed, loud enough to make Gabrielle wince, the instant she had regained consciousness, before she could even open her eyes. The woman had been sent by her nephew, Connor Douglas, to nurse Gabrielle back to health. Judging by the tone of that stern voice, *nothing* would stop her from doing exactly that.

Gabrielle had pried open heavy, gritty eyelids and found herself staring up into a stern face that resembled nothing so much as a juicy apple that had been set to dry under a hot summer sun and left out for days too long. Beneath a cloud of unruly, wispy white hair, the woman's features

were wrinkled and crooked, sloping to the left.
From the bridge down, her nose leaned toward
her ruddy left cheek. That side of her mouth
drooped, while her left eye was nothing more
than a slit. With the exception of an unnaturally
bulging blue eye, the right side of the old
woman's face looked normal.

Mairghread was glaring at her.

Gabrielle held the woman's attention for a second, then her own dipped with silent defiance to
the spoon. Mairghread was right, her gnarled old
hand was shaking badly, threatening to tilt the
spoon's contents onto the blanket at any moment.

Gabrielle sniffed the air tentatively. There was
a whiff of faded lavender scent clinging to the
old woman, the mossy scent of rushes strewn over
the floor, and above all that . . .

Her stomach muscles clenched around a hungry grumble. Her mouth watered. Compared to
the dry, overcooked rabbit meat and thick, tasteless porridge the Douglas men had been feeding
her for weeks, this savory-smelling bowl of soup
seemed a veritable feast!

Gabrielle almost opened her mouth to accept
the offering. Almost. The only thing that stopped
her was the streak of Carelton pride that pumped
hot and sure through her blood. While she still
had an ounce of strength left in her body, she
would not lie here and be fed like a helpless babe.
By God, she would *not*.

"Och! lass, stop being so stubborn," Mairghread chastised in that ancient, crinkly voice of
hers. "Pride is all well and good . . . in its proper
place. Howe'er, it willna fill an empty belly, put
strength back in yer muscles, or add color tae yer

cheeks. Oh, aye, starving yerself may strip ye of a few maun needed pounds, but 'twill do naught to get rid of the fever raging through ye. Only eating and keeping up yer strength can do that."

"Then give me the spoon," Gabrielle said tightly, "and I'll take your most wise advice."

"Nay, lass," the old woman replied equally as firmly. "Connor told me tae nurse ye, and nurse ye I shall"—her right eye narrowed until it was almost as small as the left one; both glinted with sharp blue fire—"e'en if it kills the twa of us. Mark me words, lass, I'll nae have ye worsen and die whilst I'm caring for ye. They'd like that tae much. Och! I can hear them talking now, God rot 'em. 'Daft auld Mairghread's gone and done it again.' Aye, 'tis what they'll be saying aboot me. If I let them by nae taking proper care of ye."

Gabrielle shifted restlessly against the pillows. A pair of sneezes left her sniffling and watery-eyed. Instinctively, she took the cloth the old woman pressed into her hand. She wiped her eyes, then blew her nose.

"A-again?" Gabrielle asked tentatively. Despite her sore, dry throat, she gulped.

"Isna Ella always telling me that I prattle on tae much? One of these fine days mayhap I'll listen," the woman muttered to herself. She gave a shrug of her humped shoulders. The broth cupped in the still-poised spoon came dangerously close to spilling over; miraculously, only a drop splashed atop the cover spread over Gabrielle's chest. Louder, she said, "Dinna pay attention tae an old woman's ramblings. Just open ye mouth and eat this fine tattie bree a'fore it gets colder than the Hebrides in winter. Ye need something warm inside ye to fight the chill a fever leaves inside the bones, don't ye ken?"

Gabrielle's gaze lifted, meeting and holding the old woman's.

There was something in those mismatched blue eyes, something Gabrielle couldn't quite put her finger on. Guilt? Supplication for a second chance? Fear of being ridiculed yet again? All were emotions Gabrielle was uncomfortably familiar with. Seeing them mirrored in the old woman's eyes caused warm fingers of sympathy to wrap around her heart reluctantly, softening what had been a very hard first impression of Mairghread.

Holding the old woman's gaze, Gabrielle slowly, deliberately parted her lips and allowed the old woman to deposit the spoonful of soup in her mouth. The rich potato and broth concoction, laced faintly with dill and a spice she couldn't identify, melted like butter on her tongue. It coated and soothed her sore throat as it slid down to be welcomed heartily by her empty stomach. She must have been more ravenous than she'd thought, for that stomach immediately growled, demanding more.

" 'Tis delicious," Gabrielle remarked, surprised. Had she not been told Scots food was inedible?

After a heartbeat's suspicious hesitation, the old woman's eyes sparkled with yet another duet of emotions. In those ancient blue eyes, Gabrielle thought she spotted a flash of admiration and appreciation.

The old woman gave a brisk nod. "Of course it is. A fine muckle may disagree, but I be telling ye, ye'll nae find a better tattie bree this side of the Trossachs than that which Siobhan Maxwell brews."

Gabrielle quickly swallowed another mouthful of soup. "A Maxwell?" she asked, shocked. "Bracklenaer's cook is a *Maxwell*?"

"Aye." The old woman's thick white eyebrows pinched together in a thoughtful scowl. A fresh ripple of wrinkles ridged the leathery skin of her forehead. "Well," she corrected, "a Maxwell begot on the wrong side of the hay, if ye catch me meaning, but she's a Maxwell all the same. Mind ye, me memory's nae what it was when I was eighty, so I could be wrong, howe'er I seem tae recall Connor saying Siobhan was the first prisoner he stole when last he raided the . . ." She muttered a Gaelic term uncomplimentary by tone, *"Maxwell,* and that the beasties he chanced tae gather up and bring home were but a bonus compared to the lass's fine cooking. If ye think her tattie bree delicious, ye've a real treat in store. Siobhan makes a haggis that'll melt on yer tongue and make ye swoon. Or," she added with a crooked grin, "do ye only swoon for the likes of The Black Douglas?"

Gabrielle felt her cheeks color, and purposely ignored the latter question. "Haggis?" she asked as she used a dry corner of the cloth to wipe daintily at her mouth. "What's that?"

The one that answered was not Mairghread's old, crackly voice. Oh, nay, just the opposite. This voice was young and deep and husky. Thoroughly masculine, thoroughly familiar.

"Methinks 'tis an answer best saved for *after* the dish has been tasted."

As though the mention of him had conjured

the man up, it was the voice of The Black Douglas.

Gabrielle's breath caught in midsniffle. Her watery eyes widened, her gaze jerked to the doorway.

It was nearly dusk. Yesterday's downpour had returned in a fine drizzle, spitting from the cloud-strewn sky. The last shards of daylight were hazy and gray. Murky shadows gathered in the doorway where he stood. A sconce had been lit somewhere down the hallway; the vague, flickering, yellowish-orange glow backlit Connor Douglas's husky frame, emphasizing the breadth of his shoulders and chest, highlighting the silky blackness of his hair.

Gabrielle realized her mouth must have sagged open, for without warning she found another spoonful of soup deposited on her tongue. Unlike the others, this one tasted bland. She had to force herself to chew the soft potato, and coerce her tight, sorer-than-ever throat to swallow it down. The mouthful landed in her belly like a warm chunk of tasteless granite. She lifted a hand to stop Mairghread, who was in the process of repeating the gesture, and hoped she was the only one to notice that her fingers trembled. "Nay, no more, please."

"Ye're full? So soon?" the woman asked. Gabrielle heard a note of amusement in the old woman's voice. "Odd. Ye were eating maun heartily only a wee moment ago."

"I've lost my appetite." Try though she did, Gabrielle couldn't drag her attention away from the figure that loomed like a dark silhouette in the doorway. While she couldn't see his eyes, she could feel his gaze roaming over her like warm fingers. "It must be from . . . aye, 'tis from all this talk of haggis, I'd wager. Truth to tell, the mere name sounds revolting."

Mairghread placed the spoon in the bowl, her attention shifting between Connor and Gabrielle. Her right eye narrowed shrewdly. "Mayhap 'tis nae the soup ye've lost yer appetite for, but this tired auld woman's ramblings." She gave an exaggerated stretch of her back, her free hand kneading at a cramp that fisted in the base of her spine. For all the attention the younger two occupants of the room paid her, she might as well not have bothered. "Connor," she said, drawing her nephew's gaze as she held the bowl of soup out to him, "be a good lad and finish feeding yer lady, will ye? Judging by her size, she's used to eating a fine muckle more."

Connor nodded and took a long, confident step into the room. Three more and he was standing beside Mairghread, and towering over the side of the bed upon which Gabrielle lay.

Gabrielle swallowed hard; her throat felt raw, as if it had been rubbed with the gritty side of a stone. Instinctively, she pressed herself back against the pillows. A minute ago the bedchamber had seemed adequately roomy, yet now it felt crowded and uncomfortably small. It was The Black Douglas's presence that brought about the change. His large, prepossessing body ate up the space until even Gabrielle felt small and insignificant. It was an odd feeling, that. While her years serving Elizabeth had acquainted her with feeling insignificant, feeling physically small was something she'd absolutely no experience with.

Connor took the bowl from his aunt's gnarled, shaky hands, and waited while the old woman pushed her thin body from the chair. More than one age-brittle bone creaked loudly in protest. The woman's posture was stooped; the top of Mairghread's wispy white head came only to the middle of her nephew's chest.

Gabrielle nibbled her lower lip and wondered if her own dark head would clear the shelf of those impressively broad shoulders . . . ?

After one last glance, split between Connor and Gabrielle, Mairghread nodded briskly, then turned and ambled out of the room, closing the door behind her. She didn't look back.

Gabrielle sneezed, sniffled, then wiped her eyes and nose on the cloth. Distracted, it took a second for the reality of the situation to seep in. Sweet Lord, she was alone in the chamber with none other than The Black Douglas. Her heartbeat accelerated, heating the already fevered blood in her veins. She shivered and yanked the blanket up protectively close beneath her chin.

"Cold?" Connor asked as he eased himself onto Mairghread's recently vacated seat. The wooden chair legs groaned beneath his weight.

"Aye, a bit chilly," Gabrielle lied. Her shiver had nothing to do with the damp night air and everything to do with this man's commanding presence. However, there was no reason *he* should know that.

"Then Mairghread was right for once. 'Tis maun soup ye be needing tae warm ye up on the inside and chase away those fever chills." Gabrielle watched, transfixed, as he dipped the spoon into the soup, coming up with a hearty mouthful. Compared to the gnarled old hand that had so recently held it, Connor's big hand dwarfed the spoon handle until the utensil looked sized for a child. "Here ye go, lass. Eat up and get well. The preacher willna wait fore'er, don't ye ken?"

"If you're thinking . . . Oh, nay, I will *not*—!" Her words were cut short as, seizing the opportunity of her open mouth, Connor shoved the spoonful of soup past her lips. He used the bowl of the spoon to not only catch the drop of broth that trickled down her chin but to also nudge her gaping mouth shut before more broth could spill out.

Gabrielle chewed swiftly, barely noticing that the once-tasty soup now had the flavor of clay. A wave of irritation swept though her. Oh, but it was difficult to suppress the urge to finish what she'd started, and tell this heathen exactly what she thought of him and his impatient preacher.

She swallowed down the soup and was in the process of opening her mouth to vent her mounting ire . . . only to find she had no breath left in her lungs to vent it with. Her breathing had paused just beneath her hammering heart when Connor plucked the cloth from her hand and wiped the residue of broth from her chin.

Gabrielle stared at him. The gesture left her speechless. Nay, that was wrong. It wasn't the gesture that stunned her so much as the *gentleness* with which he'd accomplished it.

While The Black Douglas was known for many things, consideration wasn't one of them. Was it possible the rumors and ballads about this man were wrong? That he wasn't in truth the heartless, barbaric monster they all painted him?

Gabrielle suppressed a groan. Dear Lord, she must be sicker than she originally thought to even be considering such a notion. Was this not, after all, the same man who'd flagrantly—and much too easily, as far as she was concerned—stolen her, his brother's fiancée, right out from under the other man's nose? Was this not the same man who claimed it a rightful theft, the same man who'd then boldly bragged about marrying her himself?

Aye, it was. But, Gabrielle found all of those misdeeds hard to remember when the feel of Connor's strong, cloth-covered fingers gently skimming her jaw still lingered and tingled in her veins.

"Here, lass, swallow down another bite. 'Tis good and hearty fare, just the thing for a sick wench." He'd dipped the spoon back into the bowl and now held it close to her tightly compressed lips.

Gabrielle shook her head. She was wise enough this time not to open her mouth to voice the protest that itched at the tip of her tongue.

Her attention had been locked on the closed door at the foot of the bed. It now lifted to his face.

From a distance, his eyes had looked . . . well, merely gray. Up close, she saw that there was nothing "merely" about them. The irises *were* predominantly slate colored, yet now she noticed they were also flecked with intriguing shards of brilliant blue. The darkness of his eyebrows, and the uncommonly long, thick black eyelashes, contrasted sharply, complementing and enhancing their color.

She shook her head to clear it, ignoring the way the gesture set her temples to throbbing anew. "I'll not be marrying you, Connor Douglas, so get that notion out of your head right now."

This time, Gabrielle was prepared. She kept her teeth clenched together as she talked, giving him no opportunity to shove more food into her mouth.

Connor frowned and looked vaguely disappointed.

Gabrielle gritted her teeth until her jaw hurt almost as much as her pounding head. Did he truly think her so stupid that she would fall for that trick more than once? If so, the man had a good deal to learn about Careltons and their intelligence . . . not to mention their stubborn determination!

"Right now me main concern is nursing ye back tae health. What's done is done, and canna be undone. What happens after ye're well will happen. There's naught ye can do aboot it. Ye're . . . er, a robust lass, I'll grant ye that, but nae more than a lass all the same. If I chose to wed ye, there's nae a thing ye can do to stop me."

"That's where you're wrong. There are *several* things I can, and *will*, do," Gabrielle replied tightly, even as her fevered mind scrambled to think of what even one of those things might be. "You realize that . . ."—*ah-ha!*—"that Elizabeth will have your head when she finds out what you've done, do you not?"

"Elizabeth isna *my* sovereign, she's yers." Connor replaced the spoon in the bowl, then sat back in the chair, his shrewd gray gaze never leaving her. "And aye, the messenger she sent this afternoon did mention something aboot separating me head from me shoulders, but I paid the threat no heed."

She sucked in a quick breath. The Queen had sent a messenger? And The Black Douglas had blatantly ignored the threat the messenger carried? Was the man insane?! Did he not know that, while Elizabeth could ignore much, never could the woman stand to be ignored herself?

"What about your young king?" Gabrielle asked, and winced. Even to her own ears, her voice sounded weak, shaky, lacking its previous conviction. "Methinks James will be equally displeased with what you've done."

A reckless grin that made Gabrielle's heart skip a beat tugged at one corner of Connor's mouth. "Och! but there's the luck. Ye're right aboot him nae being pleased, but I've gotten him angrier in the past. Jamie threatens only a fine." When she regarded him suspiciously, he shrugged and added, "His messenger arrived as the Queen's was leaving, and shortly a'fore twa sent by the March Wardens. Squeezed in between those was a messenger from the Maxwell. Er, I think that be the order. Truth tae tell, I dinna remember exactly, there were so many messengers coming and going. 'Tis been a busy afternoon."

That even one messenger had come was music to Gabrielle's ears. Surely with so many protests and threats The Black Douglas would *have* to let her go now.

Wouldn't he?

Her gaze raked his face; Connor's features were ruggedly carved, his expression decisive. A glint of persistence shimmered like liquid gray fire in his eyes.

An uneasy feeling prickled along the nape of Gabrielle's neck. The Black Douglas looked more determined than ever to keep and wed her.

She shuddered. This would never do!

If she must wed, she would obey her Queen

and marry the man Elizabeth had chosen for her.
She would marry Colin Douglas, the nicer of the
Douglas twins. It was a much more tolerable fate
than the alternative: being espoused to the man
about whom horrible Border ballads had been
written, the man whose nickname mothers on
both sides of the Border used as a threat to make
their children behave.

The seed of a plan sowed itself in the back of
her fevered mind. It was a shaky plan, daring and
risky, with little chance for success. Still, she'd
nothing to lose by at least *trying*.

Her gaze shifted to the bowl The Black Douglas
cradled in one big hand. Her smile was as wide
as it was forced as she asked sweetly, "Might I
have more soup now? 'Twould seem I'm hungry
after all."

What Gabrielle thought but did not say was that
strength was one property she'd need in abundance if her plan, tenuous though it was, had
even a marginal chance of success.

Strength, and a lot more courage than she
thought she possessed!

Four

"Say that again. I couldna have heard ye right, lad."

"Ye heard correctly. Early this week, the Black Douglas stole Colin Douglas's bride right out from under his twin's nose."

"Och! I dinna believe it. Where? *How?*"

Short and well-toned lean, Gordie Maxwell had a thick shock of unruly red hair that he now impatiently combed all ten of his fingers through. His bootheels clicked against the hard stone floor as he paced in front of the hearth situated to the left of his father's desk. "In Dumfrees. As tae the 'how' . . . well, methinks the younger Douglas twin shall be a fine muckle embarrassed for many fortnights tae come when word gets out of how easily his bride was snatched from him. Connor simply had his men replace those of his brother's at the place where the transfer of the lady from the Elizabeth's men tae that of the Douglas's was tae take place."

"And the Queen's men dinna ken the difference?"

"If they had, wouldna the Lady Gabrielle be at

Gaelside now, nae Bracklenaer? Yet Bracklenaer is precisely where she be. Nay, Da, they dinna ken the difference. To a Sassenach, one Scot be the same as the next, ne'er mind the minor discrepancies in a mere two Douglases. 'Twas in Douglas hands they were ordered tae relinquish the lass, and in Douglas hands she *was* relinquished."

"The *wrong* Douglas's hands," Johnny Maxwell pointed out tightly.

"Aye," his eldest son agreed, "but rumor has it the lass wasna aware of that fact until recently."

"How on earth could she nae ken who'd taken her?"

"She's also Sassenach, Da," Gordie said and shrugged, as though that explained everything. In a way, it did.

"Och! this is nae good news, Gordie. Nae good a'tall." Johnny rested his elbows atop his desk, cradling his weathered forehead in his palms. "I kenned that Connor Douglas is bold," he sighed, "but . . . guddle me, I ne'er thought he'd do something like *this!*"

"They dinna call him The Black Douglas for naught."

"Aye, and well I'm starting tae ken it," Johnny moaned. " 'Tis a blessing and a curse, that nickname . . . a might fearsome reputation goes hand in hand with wearing it. Many's the Black Douglas of yore who were shown respect nae for their merit but simply because of the tag. This time howe'er . . . aye, methinks this time be different. Methinks this time, the lad they call The Black Douglas is out tae carve himself a status equal tae none. A fame that, in the end, shall stand above all others." His black eyes narrowed, clouding over with an ill-tempered memory,

Johnny grudgingly added, "Any respect the lad is shown has naught to do with a mere nickname, but 'tis well earned."

Gordie, who'd been standing by the long, slit-shaped window, turned his head and stared at his father as though he'd never seen the man before. "Earned by deeds such as his latest ride against Caerlaverock? Dinna tell me ye've so soon forgotten that!"

"Forgotten? Ha!" Johnny's laughter was as harsh and dry as the weathered skin that stretched taut over his harshly carved cheekbones. He sat back in his chair, his shrewd gaze lifting and falling slowly as he assessed his son. "Och! nay," he said, waving the thought away with a gesture of his hand, "the Douglas's raid is nae more forgotten than 'tis lived down—which is tae say 'tis neither. If I had tae guess, lad, I'd wager young mithers will be singing that dreadful Border ballad aboot the episode long after we're both deep under this country's fine soil."

"Have a care, Da, ye're beginning tae sound as though ye admire him," Gordie growled accusingly.

"Mayhap I do."

"Nay!"

"*Aye!* How can I nae? Oh, aye, I'll admit 'twas a time I'd nae small reputation of me own, but that was when I was maun, maun younger. E'en in me prime I'd nae have dared aught so bold against a family so strong, a family I'd a centuries-auld blood feud with. Yet The Black Douglas dares that and, with his latest escapade against his twin, maun. Kidnapping the Lady Gabrielle threatens tae bring down upon his head the wrath of both young James *and* that sourpuss old Bess. One doesna have tae *like* what Connor Douglas does tae admire his guile and daring for doing it, don't ye ken? Och! lad, stop scowling and shaking yer head at me."

"I dinna believe I'm hearing this, and from me own da nae less! Are ye going tae let a Douglas, *any* Douglas, get away with stealing a goodly portion of Caerlaverock's beasties and tae many prisoners tae count?"

"O' course not."

"But ye just said—"

"That I admire Connor's daring, naught else." A slow, sly grin tugged at the corners of Johnny Maxwell's lips as he linked his fingers together and rested them atop the generous hill of his stomach. "I dinna say a word aboot nae seeking me revenge. Och! lad, we be Maxwells! Revenge is in our blood. We couldna stop seeking it—especially against those God rotten Douglases—any maun than we could stop breathing."

Gordie returned his father's grin. "Now, *that* I'm liking the sound of. Tell me, what do ye plan tae do?"

"Weeell . . ." Johnny's smile broadened. "Naturally I've filed a bill with the March Wardens against The Black Douglas. It shall be heard on the next Day O' Truce. I admit I'm sorely grieved tae loose Siobhan—och! that wench was a mighty fine cook!—but I'm nae so foolish as tae think we'll be getting her back any time soon, if e'er. Yer mither and sisters are already busy weaving us new blankets tae replace the ones taken by The Black Douglas. There's naught else that can be done aboot the raid, nae *legally*, except the obligatory counterattack, which we've already planned." Johnny shrugged and lifted his right hand palm upward in a gesture indicating he was helpless to do anything more, which indeed he was. About that matter. He swiftly turned the conversation to a matter he *could* do something about. "Now that I think on it, mayhap The Black Douglas's latest escapade be nae so bad for us after all."

"Meaning . . . ?"

"Meaning 'tis well kenned that a Maxwell's blood runs thick and strong, our loyalty to each other unmatched. Nae matter our differences, we always defend our own."

Gordie frowned and cocked his head to the side. "Aye, so ye've taught all yer sons since we were bairns. I dinna ken how any of this has tae do with Gabrielle Carelton, or getting revenge on Connor Douglas."

"Think a wee bit harder." When Gordie showed no indication that he knew what his father was talking about, Johnny pillowed his elbows on top of the desk and leaned toward the young man, his gaze locking with Gordie's. "Did ye nae just tell me The Black Douglas is in possession of a misbegotten guest in his keep? A guest who, unless I be wrong, and I dinna think I am, would rather be anywhere but Bracklenaer?"

"I did," Gordie acknowledged.

Johnny nodded. "Mind ye, ordinarily I'd nae care. Howe'er, as luck would have it, the guest in question happens tae have a drop of Maxwell blood trickling through her veins."

"*Only* a drop," Gordie reminded his father firmly. "Have ye nae said often enough that 'tis an ancient indiscretion we dinna admit tae?

Something that happened in the past and was meant tae be forgotten?"

"Aye, that I have. And so 'tis. Yet, like it or nay, the fact remains that Gabrielle Carelton *is* a Maxwell. Och! lad, the maun I think on it, the maun I like it. This could work in our favor quite nicely! Do ye see where this all be leading?"

Gordie's frown deepened, then just as suddenly disappeared. "A Maxwell takes care of his own," he repeated softly, seemingly to himself. Louder, as realization dawned on him, he said, "What sort of kin would we be if we dinna lift a finger tae get the poor, sweet lass away from her arch enemy, the Douglas?"

"Poor kin, indeed!" Johnny agreed, then laughed. His fist slammed down hard on the desk as he used his other hand to wave his son closer. "Come, sit. Methinks there's a need to alter our original plan a wee bit. We need to craft the plan for a retaliatory raid that will overshadow e'en The Black Douglas's swiftly growing reputation. A plan that will . . . er, how should I put it? Oh, aye, a plan that will finally reunite us with our dear, long lost Carelton kin . . ."

A bolt of lightning cut a jagged streak through the sky, flashing a brilliant, blinding shade of silver. The immediate, bowling roar of thunder was so violent it shook Bracklenaer's centuries-old stone walls.

Gabrielle winced, her ears ringing. Did she hear the bedchamber's door rattle in its hinges, or was the phantom sound a product of her fevered imagination? There was no way to be sure. Between the alarming rattle in her chest, the deafening claps of thunder, and the rain that lashed harshly at the bolted shutters, it was difficult to hear much of anything.

The pillow beneath her head was damp from her perspiration, and her inky hair clung to her sweat-beaded brow and neck. Sweet Jesus, she was hot! Her bones ached from the inside out as she restlessly kicked the sheepskin and Douglas-gray kilt off her. The chilly night air had no more washed over her body than she commenced shivering. Violently. With a groan, she yanked the coverings back up and huddled beneath them.

Mairghread had come at dinnertime and spooned more broth, this one with a thick lamb base, into her. All hopes of regaining her strength and escaping this place had fled by that time. She might be a Carelton, and therefore stubbornly determined, but right now she felt as weak as a day-old kitten. She would be going nowhere for a while, and well she knew it. It was bad enough that her stomach refused to hold much of the rich broth the old woman insisted she eat. After a few spoonfuls, Gabrielle had shaken her head and turned her head away. In seconds, she'd fallen asleep.

When she finally awoke, it was to a dark, empty bedchamber. The smoldering embers in the hearth gave off precious little light. No one, it seemed, had seen fit to rekindle them.

A quick scan of the room told her that Mairghread was gone. The only sign that the old woman had been there at all was the goblet of what Gabrielle presumed was wine sitting on the table beside the bed.

Clutching the covers close, she struggled to sit up, then took the metal goblet and lifted it to her lips. Her eyes were watery, her temples throbbed, and her mouth felt drier than the Cheviot Hills in summer. A sip of cool wine would sit well right now and do much to improve her flagging spirits.

Gabrielle tried to sniff the contents, but her nose was too stuffy. Thirsty, she took a deep sip. A fit of coughing tore through her body as she choked the stuff down. The fiery brew coated her tongue like molten lava, scorching a path down her already gritty and sore throat. Stinging tears dripped hotly down her cheeks, splashing unnoticed on her forearm as she coughed and gasped and wheezed for precious breath.

That was not wine. Oh, nay, nothing so bland. That was a large-size helping of strong Scots whisky. The liquor had been mildly diluted with water and lemon, yet neither could take away its sting. Had her sense of smell not abandoned her, Gabrielle would have recognized the pungent fumes immediately.

Gradually the sting on her tongue started to fade, as did the burn in her throat. A warm, not entirely unpleasant glow swirled in her nearly empty stomach. The heat seeped outward, radiating throughout the rest of her body like the ripples of a stone tossed in a calm lake.

Another clap of thunder rattled the shutters. Last night's storm had returned with force; slashing rain and wind settled around Bracklenaer like a dark, heavy blanket.

Gabrielle sneezed and gave a half-hearted sniffle. Truth to tell, it was a blessing the weather hadn't been this bad last night. If she was sick now and all she'd been exposed to was a bit of rain, who knows how ill she would have been after spending a night tossing atop the hard, wet ground amid a storm of this magnitude!

This time it didn't cut through her as harshly as before. Oh, nay, just the opposite. Now that her tastebuds had been shocked into accustoming themselves to the potent brew, she was surprised to discover that the wicked concoction was actually quite tasty. More delicious still was the sweet, hot feeling of relaxation that seeped through her veins, warming the chill from her bones even as it eased the stiff aches and pains in her muscles.

Gabrielle grinned. What would Elizabeth say if she saw her charge now? She pictured the old woman's tightly compressed lips puckering as Elizabeth glared disdainfully down the thin, rigid line of her nose. It was a glare that had brought high-powered men from all over the world to their knees.

The Queen, however, was not here to chastise or to glare, thank heaven. That was just as well, because the whisky worked wonders, and with amazing swiftness. While her aches and pains weren't completely gone, they weren't nearly as pronounced or troublesome as they'd been a few moments ago. Her cough had subsided, her sinuses had cleared a bit, and the pounding in her head had diminished. Except for the vaguely bitter aftertaste, the whisky was a miracle potion! Why wasn't this brew being hawked as a fever remedy on every street corner in London?

She lifted the goblet and took another drink of whisky, even though her thirst had passed. As any good Carelton could tell you, if one of anything worked well, two would work better . . . and three better still.

Gabrielle set the goblet aside and lay back

against the pillow. She stifled a yawn with her fist and arched her spine, stretching tentatively at first, then, when her muscles didn't cramp in protest, more expansively. Aaah, but that felt divine.

Another clap of thunder boomed.

Gabrielle gasped, startled, remembering suddenly that summer had come and gone, and that the day—rather, it was night now—was anything but clear.

Rain and wind flailed at the castle's thick stone walls. A bolt of lightning illuminated the sky like the sparkling blade of a newly polished dagger. The silvery flash came and went in a blink.

The mattress rustled as Gabrielle pushed herself to a sitting position. Mayhaps another sip of whisky wouldn't be out of order? Heaven knew the unexpected jolts of thunder had made sure the effects of the first three wore off with alarming speed. While she'd been aware from the instant she awoke exactly where she was—Bracklenaer, home of that thieving Scots heathen known as The Black Douglas—only now did that knowledge really begin to penetrate her fever- and liquor-dulled mind.

She swallowed hard, and in that same instant became aware of something else. Keenly aware of it.

She was no longer alone.

The fire had petered out; smoldering embers did naught to brighten the room beyond a dim glow that hovered only a foot away from the hearth. But did she really need light to know there was someone clinging to the shadows, watching her? Nay. Gabrielle felt the heat of an unseen gaze move over her.

"Mairghread?" she called out uncertainly. It

was not the old woman, Gabrielle would bet the Queen's crown jewels on that.

Cloth rustled. The sound of a bootheel clicking atop stone that echoed between harsh bursts of thunder sounded ominously loud. Near the door, where the shadows clung and twisted like thick London fog, there was movement as the intruder stepped forward.

Gabrielle sneezed, then sniffled loudly and squinted at the form. Her heartbeat quickened.

The intruder was tall, broad, as undeniably virile as it was male.

He took another step forward, which brought him a mere stone's throw away from the bed. Any doubt Gabrielle had harbored fled like leaves scattering before a brisk autumn wind.

The intruder was The Black Douglas.

Gabrielle wasn't surprised. Nor was she pleased. Her spine stiffened and her chin inched upward. She faced him squarely. The flutter of alarm tickling the pit of her stomach was forcefully suppressed. "Skulking around in the shadows now, are you, Douglas? Haven't you ever heard of the term 'knock'?"

" 'Twill be a cold day in hell afore I'll knock on me own bedchamber door, lass."

The words slid through Gabrielle much the same way the first sip of whisky had only moments before. Shocking at first, then radiantly hot. This time the warm, breathless tingle of response that rippled through her did not come from a manufactured source. The Black Douglas's deep, husky voice was all too real, as was her tumultuous reaction to both it and his nearness.

The temptation to huddle protectively beneath the covers was strong. The proud Carelton blood—smeared by only a small taint of Maxwell—that pumped hot and fast through her veins was stronger still.

Her shoulders squared instead of slumped as her green eyes narrowed. Her gaze pierced the darkness, meeting and warring with his. "Your bedchamber is otherwise occupied."

"Aye," he said, and took that final step, his attention never leaving her, "and well I ken it. Mairghread's found her bed and I be on the way to finding another for meself. I wanted to check on ye first, though, to see how ye fared."

"I fare—" She sniffled and, for lack of anything else available, tried as inconspicuously as possible to wipe her nose on the sleeve of the white linen nightgown she only now realized she wore. Who had changed her into the garment? She was afraid to ask for fear he might tell her. "I fare well, thank you. As you can see, I'm getting better . . . getting better—" *achoo!* "—getting better by the . . . by the—" *sniffle, sniffle, achoo!* "—by the minute."

Lightning and thunder splintered the night.

It was a minor disturbance compared to the tension crackling throughout the bedchamber.

" 'Tis cold and damp in here. Nae good for a sick woman." He turned, his long strides carrying him to the hearth. Fresh kindling and logs had been stacked beside it. He used the former to rekindle the fire, the latter to stoke it until it blazed.

That done, Connor straightened and went back to the bed. The máttress crunched and sagged beneath his weight when he sat down on the edge of it. A frown creased his dark brow as his gaze drifted over the chair that, earlier, his aunt had pulled close to the bed. Why had he not sat there? His frown deepened to a scowl when he realized that, for one of the few times in his life, he didn't have a ready answer.

Sitting on the bed had not been a good idea . . . Connor realized a split second too late. The curve of Gabrielle's hip was a mere fraction away from brushing his outer thigh. Even through the thick wool of his kilt, he could feel her fevered heat seeping into his skin, into his blood.

Connor angled his head, looking down at her. The color in her cheeks was high. From the storm? From her fever? Or from the same awareness that was suddenly coursing through him, hotter and faster than the lightning that streaked through the sky outside?

As he watched, her attention shadowed his. Her gaze shifted to the chair, then back to him. One black eyebrow arched in a silent question.

It was a question he'd asked himself, and one that Connor registered with only a portion of his mind. The crux of his attention, much like his bedchamber, was otherwise occupied. While the lass was heavy of build and plain of features, she had the most captivating eyes he'd ever seen. Crisper and clearer than a meadow in early summer. Would her eyes crinkle at the corners when she smiled? Would the green depths sparkle like shards of sunlight glinting off a tumultuous sea?

It was not something Connor would be discovering any time soon. The lass was *not* smiling now. Exactly the opposite. It was a glare she'd fixed on him, and fixed on him hard. As for sparkling . . . well, the only shimmer of emotion he could detect glistening in those pretty green eyes of hers was one of sheer annoyance.

He drew in a measured breath, releasing it with equally forced leisure. Connor hesitated. His frown deepened as his chin lifted and he angled his head to the side. His eyes narrowed as he inhaled again, this time slowly, assessively. One dark brow shot high in his wide forehead as his gaze raked the wench. "If I'm nae mistaken—and when it comes tae this," he added carefully, "believe me, lass, I ne'er am—'tis the scent o' the best Scots whisky this side of the Teviot that I'm smelling. Ye wouldna happen tae have been tiddling . . . would ye?"

Gabrielle averted her gaze to the flames crackling in the hearth at the foot of her bed. Her shrug was implausibly tight. "Tiddling?"

"Drinking."

"Oh. Um, well, I *may* have had a sip or two of the brew Mairghread left by my bed," she replied evasively. "But I'd not call that 'tiddling.' "

Connor reached out and grasped the goblet. Half the contents were gone. He lifted it to his nose, inhaled deeply. A grin tugged at one corner of his mouth. " 'Tis a toddie."

"There, you see? I *told* you I wasn't drink— er, tiddling."

"Lass, this toddie has double the normal portion of whisky in it. Did ye nae notice that when you drained half of it?"

"Now that you mention it, I did think it a bit potent," she agreed.

Connor's grin broadened. She hadn't lied and said that she wasn't the one who'd drank it. For some reason, that pleased him. He leaned to the side and started to set the goblet back down on the table but changed his mind. "Here, now be a good lass and drink up the rest. There's nae better cure for the fever that's making yer cheeks ruddy and yer eyes o'er bright. Go on now. *Slainte a var!*"

Gabrielle sneezed, sniffled, then accepted the goblet with shaky fingers. And what, she wondered, would The Black Douglas say if he found out the color in her cheeks and sparkle in her eyes had precious little to do with her fever . . . and everything to do with him?

The silky heat of his body seeped through the woolen plaid and sheepskin beneath, through the thin linen shift to caress her hip. She only wished she could blame her too vivid awareness of this man's closeness on the whisky she'd consumed! But her conscience wouldn't allow such a deception; instead, a small, nagging voice inside forced her to recognize the thought for the feeble, worthless excuse it was.

Gabrielle lifted the goblet to her lips and foolishly inhaled. The fumes assailed her immediately, making her eyes sting and water. Wrinkling her nose, she held her breath and took two hearty gulps, leaving only a quarter of the goblet's contents. Her mouth and throat were much too numb now to notice the whisky's passing as it slid smoothly down to the warm pool gathering in her stomach.

She started to pull the goblet away from her mouth. To her surprise, Connor reached out and, with the tip of a index finger, tilted it so the remainder of the liquor flooded into her mouth.

Gabrielle choked down the rest of the drink, glowering at him all the while. Outrage simmered to her core, swift and strong and hot. As if his forcing her to finish the drink wasn't humiliating enough . . .

God blast it, the heathen was laughing *at her!*

Well, mayhap not laughing exactly, but he was undoubtedly smiling. Small creases shot out from

the weathered corners of his sharp gray eyes. Two
more bracketed his sensuously thin lips. Since she
could detect only those few laugh lines, Gabrielle
guessed that The Black Douglas wasn't a man normally given to laughter. Pity. The gesture softened
his harshly sculpted features and made him ap-
pear quite attractive in the soft bath of flickering
orange firelight.

Gabrielle swallowed hard, twice, wrinkling her
nose at the sharp aftertaste of whisky and lemon
on her tongue. Good Lord, what had gotten into
her? Had she just thought this man devilishly attractive? And had she truly been on the verge of
smiling back at him?!

She had, on both counts.

It was the whisky. Aye, that explained it! The
potent brew had gone straight to her head and
addled her normally good sense. She seized on
the excuse. What other reason could there be for
so blatantly uncharacteristic a reaction?

Lowering the goblet, she opened her mouth to
say something.

What might those words have been?

It was something Gabrielle was destined to always wonder about . . . for in the same instant
Connor reached out and, with the pad of his
thumb, wiped away the amber drop of whisky
clinging to her chin.

The contact was shocking.

Thunder echoed outside, a distant rumbling
now that the storm had begun to abate. Rain continued to batter the glass windowpane. A log in
the hearth shifted, rolled, popping and snapping
as it volcanoed up a spray of sparks.

Gabrielle was oblivious to it all. Her attention
had tunneled inward, until she could notice noth-

ing beyond the warm, rough feel of Connor Douglas's thumb whisking over the much softer, sensitive flesh of her chin.

The drop of whisky had been absorbed almost immediately by the battle-calloused tip of his thumb, yet his touch lingered and disturbed, soothed and burned.

Her gaze lifted, locking with his. Was it her imagination, or were his eyes a shade darker than she remembered them being only a few short minutes before?

"Ye need rest," Connor said finally, his voice oddly low and thick. As he spoke, he turned his hand and stroked the line of her jaw with his knuckles.

A vague nod was all she could muster. Truly, she thought herself lucky to manage *that* much. It was taking the brunt of her concentration not to give in to the hot, basic instinct that clawed away inside her, an instinct that demanded she turn her head a fraction and bask in the serene warmth and strength of his hand caressing her face.

She started to close her eyes, started to turn her head into the wonder of his touch despite her determination not to . . .

"Rest," Connor said, as if only in repeating the word did it finally soak into his mind, along with its meaning. He yanked his hand away, cleared his throat too loudly, and bolted to his feet. He took the goblet from her slack fingers and placed it back on the small table beside the bed. "Aye, lass, rest. 'Tis exactly what ye need. And lots of it."

In three long strides, he was at the door. He stopped, glanced back as though he was about to say something, then shook his dark head, opened the door, and left.

Gabrielle sneezed and sniffled, all the while trying not to notice how large and empty the bedchamber suddenly felt. At the same time, she tried also not to notice the way the side of her face felt cold without his touch, the outer curve of her hip oddly chilled without his body heat to warm it.

Tried not to, but did.

Even the fire that The Black Douglas had coaxed into blazing in the hearth could not warm her in those two areas.

Her attention still on the door, Gabrielle tugged up the covers and fisted them tightly beneath her chin. The liquor formed a hot, liquidy pool in her stomach; like a stone cast in a calm lake, it sent warm ripples throughout the rest of her body.

So why, she wondered, even as she huddled beneath the covers and lay back against the pillow, did the left side of her face and her hip refuse to be warmed?

Five

"Wake up!"

The words hissed out of the velvet black night, playing on the edge of Gabrielle's sleep-clouded mind. Muttering beneath her breath, she sniffled and rolled onto her side.

Something—*a hand?*—nudged her. Sleepily, she tried to swat it away.

A Gaelic curse warmed the damp night air. "I'll give ye this . . . while ye dinna *look* like a Maxwell, ye sure the devil *sleep* like one."

The nudge was back, only this time it came in the form of a jostle. A very firm, very insistent jostle. Fingertips bit into the tender flesh of her shoulder. Gabrielle winced.

Grudgingly, Gabrielle allowed herself to be shaken awake, and in so doing abandoned quite an interesting dream. In it, a craggily handsome Scotsman with shaggy, glossy black hair and piercing gray eyes was sitting on the bed beside her. Oh so closely beside her. She'd not seen Connor for over a fortnight now, leaving her to the care of his aunt and assorted guards, and the dream had been so tantalizingly vivid that—

"Och! lass, will ye please wake up? Yer maun tae big for me tae pick up and carry. Nae that I'm foolish enough tae try, mind ye, I ken me limits."

"Who . . . wha—?"

"She speaks. 'Tis a miracle!"

The sarcasm wasn't lost on Gabrielle, whose eyes snapped open in response. Blinking hard, she squinted at the inky shadows until she was able to pull into focus the vague shape squatting beside the bed. The size and shape was unmistakable, as was the shock of brilliant red hair that, even in this inky darkness, couldn't be missed. "Ella?"

"Aye, and Mairghread is o'er on the other side."

Gabrielle stifled the half yawn, half cough that rose in her throat and turned her head. Her vision was quickly adapting to the darkness; making out the thick, stooped shape of the old woman took only a fraction of the time it had taken for her to recognize Ella. "What is wrong? What has happened?"

"There's nae time tae explain," Ella said. "Here, put this on."

"Do it quickly." Mairghread's aged voice cracked with urgency.

"Aye, lass, ver quickly. There's nae a second tae waste."

Ella shoved something—a pile of clothes from the weight and feel of it—into Gabrielle's arms. If the feel of the coarse material hadn't told her the quality of the clothes she'd just been handed, the stench of them would have. Her nose was still stuffy, but not *that* stuffy! The previous owner's smell lingered, seemly woven into every thread of the coarse fabric.

Gabrielle's first instinct was to drop the bundle

of clothes and demand to know what was going on. But, no she knew that would not be wise. She was woefully out of her element on this side of the Border, forced to trust in strangers. She could only hope her trust was not unfounded, that those who lived here would keep her safe until she learned the ways of things herself. It went against her nature and better judgment, but there was no help for it; she was, after all, among strange people whose strange ways were completely alien to her.

And then, too—and more important—now that Gabrielle was fully awake, other sounds intruded over the harsh rattle of Mairghread's breathing.

The angry rumble of men's voices.

The thudding thread of feet stomping hurriedly to and fro.

From outside, the icy rasp of steel raking steel.

It was the last sound that trickled down Gabrielle's spine like a drop of melting snow. She couldn't tell from which direction any of it came, she only knew that the ruckus was close. Too close. Was there even time to pose a question?

"Light a candle so the lass can see what she's aboot," Mairghread hissed.

"Nay, I dinna dare it."

"What we dinna dare is tae tarry here o'er long. Use yer head, Ella. Without light, how much longer will it take for her tae put on unfamiliar clothes in the dark?"

By her tone Gabrielle knew Ella grumbled something uncomplimentary. After a brief hesitation, the redheaded girl lit the candle beside the bed. Gabrielle stifled a sneeze with her fist and blinked quickly against the sudden light. Her gaze volleyed between the two Scotswomen. Their wor-

ried expressions encouraged Gabrielle's already
hammering heart to beat in double rhythm.

Dropping the bundle of clothes onto her lap,
Gabrielle quickly sorted through them. There
wasn't much. A pair of men's trews, a baggy beige
tunic, soft leather boots that looked three sizes
too large. If there were undergarments, she
couldn't find them. Nor did she waste time asking
for any. The way Mairghread watched her with
keen impatience said time was of the essence.

For once not overly conscious of the rounded
figure beneath the white linen folds, Gabrielle
yanked the nightgown over her head and tossed
it to the floor. She shivered when the cold, damp
night air hit her flesh like a vigorous slap. The
tunic felt rough against her skin as she tugged it
over her head, the trews rougher still—and a
good deal tighter!—as she yanked them up over
her hips.

She was right, the boots were far too large. For
her size, her feet were small; they fairly swam in
the leathery depths. The tunic stretched tightly
across her breasts, and the trews felt uncomfortably snug, provocatively revealing. She tried not
to notice the ripe aroma clinging to the clothes,
and now to her.

"I'm ready." Dressed, Gabrielle stood and
faced the women, her concerned gaze touching
briefly on the scabbard hanging at Ella's side, and
the leather-wrapped hilt peeking out of it. Mairghread had come around to the other side of the
bed while she was dressing, and now stood beside
her niece.

Remembering Ella's argument about lighting
the candle, Gabrielle licked her forefinger and
thumb and doused the wavering teardrop of

flame. Perhaps it was a trick of light and shadow, but she could have sworn she saw a glint of respect in Ella's eyes an instant before the dim glow was abruptly extinguished.

To her aunt, Ella said, "Margie, ye take one of her hands, I'll take the other." More harshly to Gabrielle, " 'Tis maun important ye dinna let go, no matter what ye see or hear. Do ye understand?"

Gabrielle nodded, forgetting for an instant that neither woman could see the gesture in the dark. "Aye," she whispered. "I understand."

Mairghread grasped her left hand, Ella her right. Even in the dark, the feel of each was unmistakable. On one side, her fingers wrapped around leathery skin and brittle bones, on the other enviably slender fingers and skin that felt softer than the inner petals of a rose.

The softer, seemingly gentler hand gave an unexpected, and not at all gentle, yank.

Gabrielle stumbled into step behind Ella. She winced, her shoulder smarting as she strained at an awkward position to make sure the same impact wasn't put on the older, more fragile bones in Mairghread's hands.

"Where are we going?" Gabrielle whispered as they inched their way in the dark toward the door.

"Outside, where 'tis safe." It was Mairghread who answered.

"Excuse my ignorance, but it doesn't sound like outside is a safe place to be right now." Gabrielle tried to swallow back her alarm. The men's voices had grown louder, the sound of rushing footsteps and scraping steel closer. Were these two women insane that they would purposely seek to go out into that uproar?!

"Because ye're Sassenach, we excuse maun," Mairghread replied. "Keep in mind, ye dinna yet ken nae the ways of the Border, lass. Trust us, 'tis a fine muckle safer tae be *outside* Bracklenaer's walls than trapped *inside* should Johnny Maxwell—God rot 'im!—have his way and capture the castle."

They reached the door. Ella made a sharp, hissing sound through her teeth, indicating they should stop whispering between themselves. Only once the girl was positive the other two would obey did she slowly lift the latch and ease the wooden panel open a crack.

A sliver of sconcelight cut a swath through the opening, slicing over the floor even as Ella pressed her face to the crack and scanned the hallway. Something else intruded in the room as well: the thick, cloying aroma of burning wood.

Gabrielle's breath snagged in her throat; she had to concentrate hard not to give in to a bout of coughing. Good heavens, they were burning the castle! Nothing in all her years of training in Elizabeth's court had prepared her for anything like *this!* A surge of panic swelled inside her, almost overwhelming her. Almost. As though reading her mind, Mairghread's bony fingers tightened, clasping Gabrielle's hand in a painful grip. The bite of the old woman's fingers was painful but oddly comforting and enough to still her panic. For the moment.

" 'Tis clear," Ella informed them from over a delicately molded shoulder. "Come, we maun hurry. If I ken Johnny Maxwell, 'twill nae stay so for long."

Ella slipped through the door, with Gabrielle close on her heels. While Gabrielle had worried about Mairghread keeping up with the two younger women, she found out quickly that her concern was misplaced. The old woman might be stooped and crooked from age, but there was nothing wrong with her legs; she hustled along the hallways as fast, if not *faster*, than both of them, more times than not bumping into Gabrielle's back as though urging them to a quicker pace.

The smell of charred wood was growing stronger. Since her nose was still stuffed, Gabrielle wondered exactly how potent the odor really was. Just as quickly she decided it was a question she'd no desire to have answered. She was frightened enough, thank you very much! A sneeze tickled her nose; she turned her head and trapped the brunt of it with her shoulder, grimacing when her mouth and nose came into contact with the smelly, grimy cloth of the tunic.

They didn't head toward the central staircase, as she'd somehow expected, but instead turned down the hallway and headed away from it. Gabrielle didn't question Ella. Not only didn't she dare risk talking right now—the sounds of fighting were too uncomfortably close—but no matter what the girl thought of her, Gabrielle was certain that Ella would not put herself and her aunt in jeopardy of being taken prisoner by going toward the enemy instead of away from them. Obviously the girl had a plan. Gabrielle had no idea what that plan could be . . . except to get out of the keep and away from the clutches of Johnny Maxwell.

Johnny Maxwell.

Gabrielle grunted softly, derisively. The man was a distant relative. A dirty, murdering scoundrel, if her family's stories could be believed. She'd been taught from the cradle that the link between families was as fragile as it was unfortunate, a humiliating indiscretion to be ignored and admitted to only when cornered. It simply wasn't in their nature for a Carelton to acknowledge any Maxwell as his kin.

Still, the truth remained that they *were* blood relations.

The irony of finding herself being dragged out of Bracklenaer by a Douglas, who was trying valiantly to get her *away* from the "enemy" Maxwell, was not lost on Gabrielle.

The mystery of where they were heading was soon solved. Like any good Border castle, Bracklenaer had more than one exit. The one Ella led them to was through an overtly masculine bedchamber. Rather, more precisely, into a dank, musty-smelling tunnel concealed behind one of the wide oak bookcases flanking the chamber's inner wall.

The sound of voices and footsteps receded as Ella eased the passage door shut behind them. The noise was replaced by the rhythmic plink, plink, plink of water dripping in some hidden puddle. The end of Ella's scabbard occasionally grazed the wall. Small, unseen claws scratching against the cold stone floor.

Rats? Gabrielle wondered, and grimaced. She swallowed back a cough, ignoring the way her fingers shook as they tightened around Mairghread's. Her free hand did not so much as flinch; so careful was she not to alter her grip on Ella's hand, not wanting the younger girl to sense her weakness.

Silently, the trio inched their way through the

tunnel. The cool, damp air felt clammy against Gabrielle's fever-heated skin. By the time they reached the opposite end, and the faint trace of silvery moonlight that slanted in through the narrow opening, her breathing was swift and shallow, her nerves frayed.

At some undefinable point, the voices had started again. They were even louder now. So was the distinct clashing of swords.

"Where are we?" Gabrielle asked when Ella came to a stop. She'd spoken in a whisper, yet the cavernous depths of the tunnel snatched her words, tossed them repeatedly off hard stone, making her voice echo and sound louder than it actually was.

"Do ye remember when ye rode to Bracklenaer?" Ella asked.

Not a pleasant memory, that, and recalling it now scratched at a sore spot within Gabrielle. At the time she'd thought to be arriving at Gaelside, the men accompanying her that of her future husband, Colin Douglas. Being reminded of The Black Douglas's duplicity rubbed her raw. Her voice, slightly nasal from her cold, went hard as stone. " 'Tis not something I'll soon forget."

"That's as it should be," Ella replied, her voice edged with pride. "Bracklenaer is a breathtaking sight at first glance. E'en at second and third and . . . Ooch! ye've gotten me sidetracked. Where was I? Ah, aye, in front of the main gate, across the road, there be a thick patch of trees and bramble and rocks leading intae the woods. Do ye remember seeing that as well?"

Gabrielle thought for a second, then nodded. "I think so."

" 'Tis where this tunnel empties out, where we be now."

"Where do we go from here?"

It was Mairghread, behind her, who answered. "As soon as the way be clear, deep intae the woods where the Maxwell canna follow."

"You run away and hide?" Gabrielle didn't mean to sound demeaning, she was merely surprised. What she meant, however, turned out not to matter. From the way Ella's slender back stiffened and Mairghread's bony hand tightened painfully around hers it was obvious that was exactly the way they'd taken her words. If she could have bitten the statement back, she would have, but it was too late now. God's blood, she'd just insulted the two women who were trying to keep her safe! She wouldn't blame them if they fled into the woods and left her here to fend for herself. That would teach her to talk before thinking in the future.

"Since ye be Sassenach," Ella said oh so calmly and coldly, "and dinna ken the way of things, I'll forgive yer ignorance. *This* time. Be thankful ye dinna say that to me cousin, lass. Connor isna so patient nor so generous."

"I know. I've heard the ballad."

"Which one?" Mairghread cackled softly.

Ella glared the old woman into silence.

The end of the girl's scabbard rasped against the craggy stone as she peeked through the opening. The nearest voices had begun to dwindle. "Och! Margie, 'Tis Willie O' Nill's Tom out there banging swords with Gilby."

"Nay, it canna be. He's a mere bairn," Mairghread said.

"At fifteen summers, he'd nae like hearing ye

call him that, I'll wager. 'Tis his first time riding, methinks, and he's nae a ver good fighter. Gilby is going easy on him."

"Fifteen already, is he? Och! but still so young."

"Ye forget, Margie, Connor was o'er a year younger when he went on his first night raid."

"Yer cousin be a fine muckle different, lass."

"Ye dinna need tae be telling me— Och! that's got tae hurt."

"What happened?" Mairghread asked, excited.

"Gilby just nipped the bairn's shoulder."

Still holding Gabrielle's hand, Mairghread stepped past her and to her niece's side. "Move o'er, I'm wanting tae see this."

"Who is Willie Oh Nillis Tom?" Gabrielle asked, confused. "And what the devil sort of name is that?"

Ella stepped back, next to Gabrielle, giving her aunt enough room to look out the opening. She leaned close to Gabrielle's ear and whispered, "Willie O' Nill's Tom," she said, pronouncing the name slowly, precisely, "is Tom, Willie O' Nill's son."

"Wouldn't it be simpler to call him Tom?" Gabrielle asked. The logic made perfect sense to her, but not to Ella, if the way the girl shook her head was anything to judge by.

"Methinks ye're wrong, Margie, she'll nae be an easy one tae teach. Like all Sassenach, she thinks ver illogically." Ella sighed and turned her attention back to Gabrielle. Her voice edged with forced patience, she asked, "Have ye any idea how many Toms there be in these parts?"

"Er . . . several?"

"Aye. Several *dozen*. 'Tis a ver common name."

"Oh. I see," Gabrielle said, and stifled a sneeze

with her shoulder. She was lying, she didn't see a thing, but she wasn't going to admit it after Ella's last comment; her pride still smarted.

"If yer tae live here, lass, the least ye can do is ken our names. 'Tis so easy e'en a bairn could master it."

"In that case, it should give me no trouble."

Ella grunted. In the dim, silver glow of moonlight, the girl's deceptively delicate features tightened into an expression that said she doubted a hated Sassenach—one with Maxwell blood running through her veins to boot!—would be able to understand anything Scots, even something so simple.

"Willie O' Nill's Tom is bleeding maun fierce," Mairghread hissed from the tunnel's opening. "Methinks Gilby is merely playing with the lad before finishing him off."

Gabrielle's mouth went dry, her eyes wide. She could be wrong, but what she'd first thought was tension electrifying the damp night air now felt like something else entirely. It felt like excitement. Aye, that was it. That was the emotion she felt emanating from the two Scotswomen.

Many were the blood-filled, hair-raising tales she'd heard while tucked safely away in Elizabeth's Court of the atrocities that transpired on the Borders. She'd listened with mild interest to all the stories, even had a daring dream or two about a few, yet Gabrielle had not put stock in a single one. Surely only in fable could such folk as the rough, bloodthirsty heathens known as Borderers exist.

Or so she'd thought.

Then.

While warm and safe in London.

Now that she was here, now that she was caught amid a bloody battle and felt the two Scotswomen's morbid excitement at witnessing the destruction, she was forced to reassess her opinion. God in heaven, even the *women* here took pleasure from seeing an enemy's blood let! It was a staggering realization.

Gabrielle's back came up hard against the wall. The stone chaffed into her skin beneath the tunic, but she barely noticed the bite of pain.

Every word of every story had been *true*.

Her horrified gaze volleyed between Mairghread and Ella. If they'd felt fear before, it was apparent neither felt it now. Both had dropped Gabrielle's hands and were now jostling each other, squirming to get a better view from the tunnel's narrow opening. Their enthusiasm was palpable, as real as the surge of disgust that made the muscles in Gabrielle's stomach clench and her knees so shaky and weak.

Gabrielle gritted her teeth, stifling a half groan, half cough in the back of her stinging throat. What had Elizabeth done, sending her here? Didn't the woman know what kind of land, what kind of *people*, she was sending her faithful lady to live among? What kind of *heathens*? Oh, of course Elizabeth knew. Twice while Gabrielle was in her service she remembered the Queen traveling to the Borders in unsuccessful attempts to tame them.

The clang of metal hitting metal startled Gabrielle out of her disturbing thoughts. She tried to gasp, but couldn't. Perhaps it was the tightness of the trews, the raid, the fever, the realization of exactly how much her life had changed . . . Whatever the cause, she suddenly found that she could not pull even the smallest of breaths into her lungs.

Her empty hands closed into white-knuckled fists at her sides, her nails creasing painfully into tender palms.

If she couldn't make herself force in a breath soon, she was going to faint. The last time she'd fainted, she landed smack in The Black Douglas's arms.

Gabrielle closed her eyes and sent up a silent prayer. Thinking of Connor now was the *last* thing she needed to quell her panic . . . she realized too late. His harshly carved features, inky black hair, and piercing gray eyes stabbed through her memory. The world around her seemed to recede and tilt in the background. The earth beneath her was solid, she knew, yet it felt like the planks of a ship, pitching and swaying sickeningly beneath her feet.

"Och! I dinna ken a lad's lanky body could hold so much blood!"

"Aye," Ella whispered in agreement, "yet still he fights. Methinks Gilby will end him by skewering him through the belly. What thinks ye?"

"The throat," Mairghread said with grisly enthusiasm. "Gilby will give the lad a second grin and send him tae hell. It be maun quicker, albeit a good deal messier."

"Methinks it canna get messier. Look at the blood! 'Tis all o'er. E'en Gilby is covered in it, as is the ground and—"

Gabrielle grimaced when her stomach churned, lurched, then convulsed with a heave.

Fresh air.

Aye, fresh air! Gabrielle seized on the thought. She had to get a breath of fresh air, had to get it soon. Already her vision was getting familiarly dark around the edges. Thanks to the memory of her arrival at Bracklenaer, she knew exactly what *that* meant!

Gabrielle's gaze went to the opening, past the two women huddled there, locking desperately on to the midnight sky and the icy drizzle of rain that fell from it.

Her feet felt leadened as she lurched forward. Her hands were shaking almost as violently as her knees as she settled her palms atop each woman's shoulders, clenched with a strength she'd not normally have given herself credit for possessing, then parted Ella and Mairghread as though they were double doors.

The women were apparently too shocked to protest. Or Gabrielle too desperate and too intent on her goal to notice if they did.

She was only a few short feet away from filling her burning lungs with much-needed fresh air.

Gabrielle didn't burst from the narrow opening so much as stagger and lurch from it. The rain pounded the top of her head, splattered her face and neck and shoulders. Its icy drops accomplished exactly what she'd meant for them to: they made her shudder and suck in a long, deep gasp of blessedly fresh night air.

Hers wasn't the only gasp.

The two men, scarcely ten feet in front of her, came to an abrupt halt. Their attention jerked in Gabrielle's direction.

The one standing had to be Gilby, for she remembered the big redhead as the man who'd brought her from the inn in Dumfrees to Bracklenaer. That meant the other one—much younger and lighter of hair and complexion—the one on whose stomach Gilby had a booted foot planted and was standing over, the one he was about to lunge the point of his sword into the chest of, must be Willie O' Nill's Tom.

Once his surprise at seeing her had worn off, and it did so with alarming swiftness, Gilby raised his sword and prepared to strike.

Later, Gabrielle would regret that she'd no time for thought or deliberation, but only one throbbing heartbeat of time in which she was forced to take immediate action.

Six

Connor bit down on the inside of his cheek until he tasted the sharp tang of blood on his tongue. He was hoping the sting of pain would distract him, stop him from laughing.

It didn't.

He shifted his thoughts, tried to concentrate on the lingering odor of smoke, on how much work it would take to rebuild the small portion of the first floor that the Maxwells had torched—and luckily, the damage was minor. That plan didn't work very well, either; he could still feel a grin tugging at the muscles in his cheeks, tempting him no matter how hard he tried to suppress it. Oh, aye, he knew this was not a laughing matter. Yet things could be worse and, grave though the situation might be . . . well, it was comical the way Ella flailed her arms, stomped her small feet, and otherwise used her whole body to reenact the account she breathlessly narrated.

How much of what his cousin said was actual fact, Connor didn't know. Yet. Nor was there any way to discern it. Until Gilby regained consciousness, he'd only Ella and Gabrielle's version of the

mishap to go by; he wasn't sure about the Sassenach, but he did know his cousin was wont to
stretch the truth a wee bit if it suited her purpose.

"It all happened so *fast*, Connor! We snatched
Gabrielle the way ye asked, and the three of us
made it tae the tunnel without mishap. E'erything
seemed tae be going smoothly. Until we reached
the end of the tunnel. One minute, we were waiting until 'twas safe tae scoot intae the woods and
join the others, the next . . ." She shook her
head, sending the tight red braid swaying against
the curve of her bottom. "Ye should've been
there, should've seen it. 'Twas so much blood!"

"Aye, and yelling," Gabrielle added with a nod
of her dark head as she watched Ella pace in front
of the fire blazing in the great hall's hearth. The
half dozen hounds, usually asleep at this late
hour, scrambled to their feet and tipped their
heads as though sensing and reacting to the
young woman's agitated excitement.

"Dinna forget the swearing," Ella reminded
her.

"Good heavens, how could anyone forget it?"
Gabrielle replied with a shiver. "I think there was
more cursing than yelling," she told Connor, "if
you can believe it. Never have I heard such language before. M'lord, I blush just remembering
it."

One dark brow cocked as Connor glanced at
Gabrielle. In the crackling firelight, her cheeks
looked flushed with excitement; his shrewd eye
couldn't detect even a hint of a blush. For her
first raid, he had to admit that she'd held up
quite well. Admirably so. His glance volleyed between her and his cousin. " 'Tis nae surprising,"
he decreed finally. "Gilby was hurt, of course he

swore. 'Tis what men do in such situations. I've been kenned tae—"

"*Gilby?!*" Ella and Gabrielle exclaimed in unison.

Gabrielle waved a hand, indicating that Ella should continue the story.

Ella gave a toss of her fiery red head and abruptly stopped pacing. Planting her fists on her hips, she glared at Connor as though he'd lost his mind. "Nay, Cousin, ye've got it wrong. Whilst I dinna doubt that Gilby cussed—God's truth, I dinna remember, so maun happened so fast—'twas *Mairghread* we be talking aboot."

It took a second for the full impact of what Ella said to sink in. When it did, Connor found himself grinding his teeth together in order to keep his jaw from sagging in disbelief. "Margie?"

"Aye."

"Mairghread Douglas?!"

"Aye!" they echoed.

"Who else have we been jabbering aboot?" Ella asked smugly. " 'Tis what we've been trying to tell ye, Cousin. *She* be the one who did all the cursing."

"And quite a bit of it, too," Gabrielle added. "You should have heard what she called your man's mother! 'Tis not fit to repeat, and even if 'twere, 'tis simply not physically possible!"

Clearing his throat, Connor's narrowed gaze shifted to Ella. "After the swearing was through, what happened?"

"She attacked Gilby."

Gabrielle nodded. "Aye, jumped right on his back, she did. And clung to him like a she-cat. 'Twould have been a comical sight were the circumstances not so dire. Your man, Gilby, dropped his sword in the struggle—she had her arms wrapped around his throat and he couldn't breathe. By the time he managed to shake her off, the boy had already recovered his own sword."

"From there," Ella added with a grimace and shiver, "the situation became maun unpleasant."

"*Maun* unpleasant? 'Tis possible?" Connor asked, surprised. From what he'd heard, the situation couldn't get worse. Nay, that wasn't true. The Maxwell might have been successful in stealing Gabrielle from him, that would have been a good deal worse.

"Aye," she replied gravely. A few red curls had come free of the plait, curling softly against her cheek and brow. Ella swept them behind her ear, crossed her arms over her stomach, and again began pacing in front of the hearth. The hounds whined and scooted out of her path as far as their leashes would allow. "But that isna how Gilby got hurt."

"Nay?"

"Nay." It was Gabrielle who answered. Ella merely snorted in agreement, gave a toss of her fiery red head, and picked up her pace in front of the hearth. "His back will no doubt be sore come morning, but I don't think he was hurt when Mairghread jumped on him. The second he saw her flying toward him, he dropped his sword and put his hands up for protection. I was already outside the tunnel. Ella tried to grab your aunt and haul her back into the tunnel when she followed me out, but the old woman is amazingly quick. 'Tis lucky for your aunt that Gilby was unarmed by the time she reached him. Ella says he wields the blade expertly, that you and he learned to fight together, and that he's almost as good as you."

"Aye." Connor sighed and raked his fingers through his inky hair. The story was getting more convoluted by the moment. More and more he wished Gilby would regain consciousness, and regain it soon, so that he could learn precisely what had happened without female embellishments and melodramatics. "But I still dinna understand how—"

"Don't rush me, m'lord, I'm getting to that part," Gabrielle admonished saucily. "At the same time Gilby was dropping his sword and Mairghread was cussing and pouncing on him, the boy Willis Tom Something, was fumbling for his own blade and gaining his feet. 'Twas he who wounded Gilby."

Connor had suspected as much, and wondered why the devil the two women hadn't told him this in the first place. He decided it best not to quibble. If he knew nothing else about women, the Black Douglas knew that it didn't pay to rush one into telling a tale they were determined to tell at their own leisurely pace. Not, that is, unless one wanted a longer story, a story enhanced beyond credibility. "So that was when Margie was taken by the Maxwell?"

"Er, not exactly, m'lord."

"I ne'er said she was taken by the Maxwell. Did ye say so, Gabrielle?"

Gabrielle sneezed twice, sniffled loudly, and shifted her gaze to the flames snapping in the hearth as her fingers toyed with the hem of her tunic. The trews suddenly felt embarrassingly snug. So much had been happening before that she'd had no time to care about the tight fit. She had adequate time to care now. Especially when Connor Douglas's gaze gravitated to her, trailed slowly, slowly over her legs, his gray eyes darkening to a mysterious shade of midnight blue. "I-I don't think so, no," she muttered finally.

Connor gritted his teeth. Except for the ticking of a muscle in his jaw, and the way his hand closed in a fist around the arm of the chair, his demeanor remained as neutral as his voice. It wasn't easy. The sight of Gabrielle Carelton's legs, indecently encased in snug trews, had caused an odd tightness in his chest, constricting his breathing and wreaking havoc with his heart rate; the sight was an uncomfortable distraction. He forced himself to look away and focus on his cousin. "So now ye're saying she wasna taken by the Maxwell?"

"Did I say *that?*" Ella asked.

Her tone was much too sweet and innocent for Connor's liking. It took a good portion of his self-restraint not to bound out of the chair, grab Ella by the shoulders, and shake the rest of the story out of her. Where was Mairghread? Who had taken her? Which way had they ridden off, and how long ago? He must learn these things before a rescue attempt could be launched. If only Gilby hadn't been wounded. A man would have told the story *while* they rode to the old woman's rescue, and done it in a far less dramatic fashion.

It was Gabrielle who finally provided the answer he sought. Leaning forward and pillowing her elbows atop trews-encased thighs that he refused to look at again, she confided " 'Tis your brother who took Mairghread."

"Nay!" Connor roared.

"Aye!" Ella confirmed. "Ye may nae have seen

him and his men, for they stayed in the back, but
I did. Sassenach though she be, the lass isna lying,
Cousin. Colin rode with the Maxwell on Brackle-
naer this night."

Connor was out of the chair in a beat, and furiously matching step with his cousin in two. The
dogs strained, reaching the end of their leash.
"Nay!" he repeated so loudly that the family
shield hanging over the hearth threatened to fall
to the floor. His voice bounced off the hard stone
walls, echoing around them with all the force of
a close clap of thunder. " 'Tis a lie. A Douglas
would ne'er ride with the Maxwell. Nae e'en
Colin would dare such an insult."

"Ne'er say ne'er, Cousin. I ken what we saw. As
for what Colin dares . . . Och! mon, have ye forgotten the lad is e'ery bit yer brother? E'ery bit
a Douglas? Whether ye care tae admit it or nae!
What would ye have done were the situation reversed, and *he* had stolen *yer* bride? And dinna
be telling me 'nothing,' for I'll have none of that
nonsense. I'll tell ye exactly what ye'd have done.
First ye would have ridden over tae Gaelside and
confronted that unruly cousin of mine, then ye
would—" Ella's tirade was cut short when Connor
shot her a silencing glare.

He stopped pacing abruptly. A thoughtful scowl
furrowed his brow. What *would* he have done were
the situation reversed? Was it not obvious?

"I'd have reacted in the appropriate fashion,"
he replied finally, determinedly. "I'd have stolen
me bride back."

"Aye! Canna ye see? 'Tis exactly what yer
brother was aboot."

Connor muttered a thick Gaelic cuss under his

breath. "Where Colin failed, however, I would have succeeded."

A slow grin tugged at the corners of Ella's mouth. "Aye, and well I ken it. Nae doubt they'd have written yet another ballad aboot The Black Douglas, tae."

"Methinks they'll be writing ballads of a different nature once Margie is done with the Colin. There's never been any love lost between them, and methinks this will make that rift wider. I almost, *almost*, pity me brother. I wager he'll be pounding upon the door, begging us tae take the auld woman back within a fortnight."

"Ye're o'erly generous. My guess would be half that time."

A pair of sneezes drew their attention to Gabrielle.

Gabrielle's cheeks heated as she sniffled and shifted position, the bench beneath her feeling suddenly hard and uncomfortable under the intensity of their stares. She tried to glance away, but her attention settled on Connor, and his gaze, sharp and gray and piercing, held hers ensnared.

"Ye should be thanking yer lucky stars me brother wasna successful this night, lass, or 'tis in front of Gaelside's hearth ye'd be warming yeself right now."

Gabrielle stared at him mutely. Had she heard right? Had he said she should be *thankful* not to be rescued from The Black Douglas? She shook her head, thinking that only an insane woman would feel so.

Then again . . .

Perhaps her own sanity should be questioned? Although she'd rather die than admit it, Gabrielle felt a tiny shred of relief that the fire warming her emanated from the huge stone hearth at Bracklenaer. All things considered, it was not a rational response. Perhaps it was caused by her fever? The unexpected excitement of the night? The nauseating charred scent that lingered in the air making her stomach churn and her head spin? While all were flagrant lies, any was better than the truth . . . that the heat of Connor Douglas's gaze boring into her muddled her mind, warmed her cheeks, and made her heart pound at an alarmingly fast rate. What it did to the pattern of her breathing and the stability of her knees was beyond description.

It was Ella who voiced the thought that had just occurred to Gabrielle. "The poor lass looks confused, Cousin. And who can blame her? She's Sassenach. She canna understand the way of things here, maun especially how a woman can be thankful *nae* tae be rescued from The Black Douglas's infamous clutches."

Gabrielle's back stiffened. Her chin tilted at a proud angle, and her shoulders squared. Green eyes narrow, she returned Ella's gaze with a level one of her own. "Don't be so hasty to judge. I know precious few Englishmen who wouldn't be out right now trying to get Mairghread back. Yet the two of you sit idly in front of a fire, joking about her capture. Aye, you're quite right in saying that I find all of this most confusing."

"Nae harm will come tae me aunt, lass. Dinna worry aboot that. Remember, Colin is her nephew, tae."

Connor's thick, deep voice trickled down Gabrielle's spine like a drop of sun-warmed butter, melting the rigidity of her posture. Her gaze shifted to him, and she regretted the impulse immediately. The flames in the hearth snapped and popped, the muted light played in a soft orange haze over his harshly carved features. Softening planes, emphasizing angles. His hair was tousled; a thick, silky black strand curled appealingly against his brow. Gabrielle's fingers closed into white-knuckled fists. Unfortunately, the bite of her fingernails digging into her palms wasn't the distraction she'd hoped it would be. She still longed to lean forward, to reach out and smooth that errant strand into place. The urge was as tempting as it was strong. Frighteningly so.

Her voice, when it came, sounded a pitch huskier than usual, even considering the state of her stuffed nose and sore throat. "You don't know that. From what I've seen tonight, blood relations means precious little to you people."

"There ye be wrong." Connor had stopped pacing; he now stood a mere foot away from her. Small and insignificant weren't feelings Gabrielle was accustomed to experiencing, yet again she noticed that with The Black Douglas's virile body towering over her, it was exactly how she felt. "Blood kinship means *e'erything.* 'Tis why I can say with such certainty that Colin willna hurt Margie."

"And yet—"

"M' lord?"

An intrusive fourth voice cut Gabrielle's words short. That was probably for the best. Judging by the determined set to Connor's hard, square jaw, and the decisive glint in his sharp gray eyes, winning an argument with this Scotsman would be akin to Queen Elizabeth accepting a man's proposal of marriage. In other words, it simply wouldn't happen.

Their attention shifted to the woman who stood framed in the arched stone doorway. She was tall of stature and heavy of build. Her blond hair had been worked into a plait that trailed down over a beefy shoulder; the ends grazed her matronly thick waist.

"What is it, Siobhan?" Connor asked. "Has Gilby awakened?"

The woman nodded. "Aye, m'lord. And 'tis surprised I be that ye dinna hear him all the way down here. He came 'round yelling aboot what he plans tae do tae Will O' Nill's Tom when he gets his hands on the poor lad." She shook her head and clucked her tongue. "He's nae shut up since."

Connor tipped his head back and laughed.

Gabrielle shivered; the sound was like black velvet—smooth and rich and dangerously appealing. It sent a tingle through her blood that both baffled and warmed her.

" 'Tis good tae hear," he said to Siobhan. "Naught else could assure me as well that the mon will indeed recover."

"Oh, aye, he'll recover," Siobhan said, then snorted and rolled her eyes. "That is, if he stops thrashing aboot and pretending he isna wounded. Och! but he be a stubborn one. Why, he'd nae more opened his eyes when he tried tae crawl out of the bed. It took me and twa others tae hold him down, and all the while he kept muttering something aboot getting dressed and hunting down Tom afore dawn. The knowledge that a mere lad wounded him seems tae have pricked his pride."

"As well it should, especially when the lad in question is a Maxwell. Dinna look so concerned,

Siobhan. I'll go up and see him. While I'm there, I'll have a talk with Gilby and see tae it that he takes care of himself whilst he heals and make sure he gives ye nae more trouble. Meanwhile . . ." Connor had started to walk toward the door, but he stopped, hesitated, then turned back to Ella and Gabrielle. His gaze quickly raked the former, then narrowed and darkened as it lingered assessively on the latter. "Ella, take Gabrielle back tae her room, please. We dinna want her tae get sicker from exhaustion, and 'tis been a maun eventful night."

That said, he spun on his heel and followed Siobhan out of the room.

Gabrielle listened to the sharp click of his bootheels on stone. They slowly faded as he ascended the stairs leading up to the bedchambers. When she could no longer hear them, she turned her attention to Ella, who had plopped down on the bench across the table from her. "What about Mairghread?"

The girl frowned. "What aboot her?"

"Isn't it obvious?" Gabrielle countered, surprised. "Ella, the old woman must be rescued. Immediately."

A spark of mischief lit her blue eyes, but her voice remained calm and neutral. "If there's any rescuing tae be done, 'tis up tae me cousin tae do it. We be women, and as such 'tis nae our concern."

"I beg to differ. It most certainly is our concern. At least 'tis mine. If I'd not run out of that tunnel when I did, none of this would have happened. Mairghread would be here, sound and safe."

"That be true enough, there's nae arguing it."

A frown pinched Ella's brow as she glanced at Gabrielle slyly. "What I fail tae understand is why ye should be caring aboot what happens tae Margie . . . ?"

Gabrielle shrugged tightly. "I suppose you could say I feel somewhat responsible for her current circumstances. Also . . . Ella, the woman was most kind to me earlier. I'd like to repay her kindness if I can."

"And exactly how would ye go aboot doing that?"

"By rescuing her myself if there's no other way."

"Well, guddle me," Ella muttered, then shook her head. Her laughter was soft and musical. "Lass, ye dinna e'en know where Gaelside is!"

"True," Gabrielle acknowledged thoughtfully. Her gaze had dipped to the fists clenched tightly atop her lap. It now lifted and boldly met Ella's. A sly, challenging grin tugged at her lips when she added, "But *you* do."

Seven

There was but one thing that could make the women who worked in Bracklenaer's kitchen cleave to their quarters, no matter how great the temptation to stray and snatch juicy bits of gossip. Only one thing that could make the hounds chained to the hearth cower and whimper. Only one thing that could make the men of clan Douglas—hard, strong men who'd fought in many battles and ridden hard on many a midnight raid, men reputed to be the most stalwart on either side of the Border—cast wary, restless glances among themselves.

That thing was The Black Douglas when angered.

Connor wouldn't have said he was angry. Och! nay, he'd bypassed that tame emotion when, upon leaving Gilby's chamber, one of his men tersely informed him that Ella was missing. He'd sailed smoothly into raw fury when an immediate search unearthed no sign of Gabrielle Carelton. A sentry, whose breath smelled ripe with the pungent fumes of whisky, had been quizzed and admitted to seeing what he'd thought at the time were "a damned gonnie-looking pair o' kelpies" spiriting themselves away from the castle.

There had been no kelpies, of course. What the man had actually seen was Ella and Gabrielle riding away from Bracklenaer as though the devil himself was nipping at their heels.

From what the sentry could discern, their direction could be none other than Gaelside.

The white-hot, sizzling sensation that pumped hot and fast through Connor's blood made "angry" seem as docile as a sunswept knoll of grassland.

In five minutes he'd shrugged into his jack and strapped a saddle onto a rugged stallion whose shaggy coat was as black as his owner's mood. Five more minutes saw him galloping hard across the ragged countryside, his ire mounting with each jostling gait.

That Gabrielle Carelton would do something so irresponsible, rash and, put quite simply, asinine, he could almost forgive. Almost. The lass was Sassenach, after all, fresh from the pompous ways of Elizabeth's court, sheltered and protected from the harsh realities that were part of Connor's everyday life. He didn't expect her to know about, or to defend herself against, the wild ways of the Border and its people. A woman such as her couldn't begin to guess at the grave danger she'd put herself into.

Ella, on the other hand . . .

Och! it would take Connor far longer to forgive his cousin for her impetuousness. If he ever forgave her at all, and he had his doubts about that.

What could Ella have been thinking?! She *knew* the land and it customs as well as he did. Only a fool, an Englishman, or a Maxwell wouldn't understand how risky it was for two women to be out riding at such a wee hour. The black velvet sky sported only a sliver of a moon; it was a fine night for riding, and Connor had no doubt many neighboring families had taken full advantage of it.

His fingers gripped the reins so tightly his knuckles smarted and throbbed. His knees must have unwittingly dug into the stallion's sides, for his horse whickered and sidestepped in alarm.

Connor's breath caught and a shiver of pure ice trickled down his spine when he imagined Gabrielle and Ella encountering a group of reivers on their way to or from a successful night's ride. Gritting his teeth until his jaw ached and his temples pounded fiercely, he forced his thoughts away from that course before it could be brought to its natural, and highly unpleasant, conclusion.

With a flick of his wrist, Connor guided his mount around the dark silhouette of a leaf-bare birch tree. The lighting was dim, but that suited him. The Black Douglas had no need for illumination; he could traverse this land with his eyes closed. The rough, craggy landscape was as familiar to him as every weather-parched crease in his aunt's forehead.

There was a stream a quarter mile to the north. Connor turned the stallion in that direction, hoping his usually good intuition held true and that the women had indeed stopped there to rest before traveling on to Gaelside.

It was a risk, he knew, to waste time, veering off the set path to find out if such was the case, but a risk he deemed worth taking. Ella might be as acquainted with the countryside as himself—she was a Douglas, she could ride for hours without tiring—but Gabrielle Carelton was different. The Sassenach might not be as slender and delicate as he'd thought she would be, but that didn't mean she was used to traversing such a harsh, unforgivable landscape. She wasn't. Her bottom and thighs were pleasingly soft and supple . . . not the unsightly, hard-muscled limbs of a woman used to riding for extended periods.

Aye, a Sassenach like Gabrielle would surely require regular breaks from riding. And what better place to rest than where the horses could graze at their leisure and sip upon crisp, mountain-fed water?

He heard the gentle gurgle of the stream before his horse cleared the dense patch of trees. Squinting, he made out the twisting, snakelike form. The water babbled at a docile pace, its surface suffused by the few streaks of silvery moonlight that managed to sneak past the latticework ceiling of branches and leaves.

The air was thick with the acidy tang of the spent storm, a fragrance that mingled with the smell of horse and man. The temperature had dipped; it was cold enough for Connor's breath to turn to vapor. A drop of rain that had gathered in the cup of a leaf slipped free, splattering icily on the top of his head.

Connor hadn't expected to be lucky enough to spot the women immediately and therefore was not disappointed when a quick scan of both sides of the stream bed told him that he was alone. He saw no indication that the pair had passed this way. Then again, he also saw no indication that they hadn't. The woods were thick, the narrow, twisting stream a few miles in length; they could have stopped at any point.

In which direction should he go?

The decision took only a second to make.

Instinct having served him well in the past, Connor gave the stallion a nudge with his knees and guided the horse along the eastern bank, still heading in Gaelside's general direction. His narrowed gaze studied the wet ground, paying particular attention to the muddy patches around puddles. He looked for hoofprints: the ground was certainly wet and soft enough to hold an impression.

The search was frustrating and slow, an irritation to his frazzled patience.

As with the stream, he heard the women before he actually saw them. At first he detected only a vaguely out-of-place rumble that blended with the gurgle of crisp water trickling over rocks. The rumble magnified as he drew closer to it. Became louder, more distinct.

Soon the sound was recognizable as the hushed murmur of voices. Female voices.

A surge of relief washed through Connor. While he was still too far away to understand their words, their tones were reassuringly calm, suggesting both women were unharmed. His relief was short-lived. It soon melted away to a hot burst of fury when he thought of how very lucky the two were to make it so far unscathed.

Guiding the stallion to a nearby birch tree, he slipped down from the saddle and with an expert flick of his wrist tethered the reins to a low-hanging branch. He crept along the stream bank, his booted feet making nary a whisper of sound as he trod carefully over wet leaves and grass . . .

* * *

Ella paced in front of the stream bank while she and Gabrielle took turns inventing and discarding various plans to rescue Mairghread.

Gabrielle, ruminating on Ella's latest and most extravagant scheme, found her attention abruptly drawn elsewhere. Was it her imagination or had the damp night air suddenly become unnaturally cold? Why, she wondered, did the flesh at the nape of her neck feel so incredibly hot? The dark curls there prickled with sudden awareness.

Her gaze had been on Ella; it now jerked elsewhere. She scanned the stream, the bank, the dense patch of trees that sheltered both. Squinting, her gaze pierced the murky shadows where the scant moonlight could only partially invade.

Gabrielle spotted him in a heartbeat.

He was standing beside a birch tree, one padded, leather-encased shoulder leaning casually against the thick, scratchy trunk. His booted ankles were crossed.

The stance was very casual, blatantly male; it made his hips slant at a cocky angle, drawing her attention unwittingly down to the hem of the kilt, and the place where it grazed his sinewy thighs. The waistband hugged the flat, hard plane of his stomach.

He stood close. Oh so close. Only a few short yards of wet ground separated them.

Swallowing hard, Gabrielle's gaze lifted, tracing the wide breadth of his chest and shoulders, the thick trunk of his neck, the hard-set line of his jaw. Higher.

Was it the fury emanating from The Black Douglas's eyes that made her mouth and throat feel abnormally parched? Surely it was that and not his physical closeness, or the way she thought she could already feel the heat of his body radiating through her masculine attire, caressing the soft skin beneath.

The strength in her knees seeped abruptly away. Standing became a study in concentration; she managed the feat through sheer force of willpower alone. Her heart raced, slamming an erratic beat against her rib cage. The crisp night air soughed in and out of her lungs, clearer now that her sickness had passed. It was rich with the fragrance of fresh rain, pine, leather . . . and the enticingly unique, masculine scent that was Connor Douglas.

Connor's gaze never left Gabrielle, although his words were meant for his cousin. His voice—the tone deep and rich with barely suppressed fury—was pushed through tightly gritted teeth. "Get on yer nag, Ella, and ride back tae Bracklenaer."

"Connor?" Ella spun around, her blue eyes wide with surprise as her attention jerked to Connor. Hugging her arms around her slender waist, she regrouped quickly. "Cousin, 'tis dark!"

"Aye, and 'tis sure I am that ye noticed that fact when ye stole the horses and rode from Bracklenaer. Ye managed tae get this far with only a sliver of moonlight to guide ye, ye can make yer way back with the same. Och! Ella, dinna try tae look so defenseless, for I'm nae so foolish as tae believe it for a second. Ye ken this countryside almost as well as I do, ye'll nae get lost."

"Nay, Connor, don't. 'Tis not safe!" Gabrielle cried. "What if she gets lost or, worse, what if the Maxwells are still skulking about?"

"Ver good questions, lass. Howe'er, should ye nae have considered the answers tae them *afore* leaving Bracklenaer? Dinna fash yeself aboot me cousin. Ella can use the sword hanging at her side." His hand brushed at his shoulder, and he thought of the small, hairline scar that marred the skin there, a scar that was the direct result of that same sword tip grazing him years ago, when his cousin's temper was particularly foul. "Aye, she can use the weapons well. I taught her meself. She'll come tae nae harm. And if she does . . . Och! for what she's done this night, I'm of a mind that she deserves whate'er fate awaits her." His attention shifted to Ella, and his eyes narrowed dangerously. "What are ye waiting for? *Be off with ye!*"

The furious determination in Connor's tone, the granite-hard square of his jaw, the dark shimmer of fury in his eyes . . . all combined to convince Ella that the wisest course of action would be to heed her cousin's grittily uttered instructions, and heed them posthaste.

After casting a quick, sympathetic glance at Gabrielle, she turned and approached her mount. The mare must have sensed Connor's temper, for the horse needed calming before she would allow Ella to mount her. The surge of sympathy she felt for the Sassenach lingered, disturbing her greatly as, ducking low-hanging branches, she guided her mount into the forest. It grated to feel anything, especially compassion, for a blood kin of the Maxwell. Yet how could she not? The poor lass was about to find out that, when it came to The Black Douglas's temper, the Border ballads had not exaggerated, they'd *understated* how deep it ran.

Gabrielle watched Ella go, and a strange sensation wadded in her stomach. She wanted to call Ella back, but didn't. Couldn't. She'd have needed breath with which to speak the words, and at the moment the feel of Connor's glare on her trapped the air in her lungs until they burned.

The adventurous spirit she'd felt tingle through her blood earlier had pinnacled with the idea of rescuing Mairghread; it now plummeted like a rock being tossed into the stream at her back as she watched Ella guide her mare toward the dense, shadowy line of trees. The girl's slender back was rigid and proud, the thick plait of red hair swinging saucily against her waist. Long after she'd disappeared from sight, Gabrielle thought she could still hear the soft, rhythmic thump of hooves treading over rain-soaked earth and leaves.

Then again . . . perhaps that was the sound of her heart throbbing in her ears? Nay, it couldn't be. The tempo of her heart was much swifter and irregular.

Sucking in a deep breath, she turned her attention back to The Black Douglas. In the thick play of darkness and scant moonlight, and in his current sour mood, the nickname seemed forebodingly accurate. Thick raven hair, harshly sculpted cheekbones, forehead, and jaw, gray eyes that gleamed out of the murky shadows, and a gaze that arrowed straight through her very soul . . .

Perhaps it was a trick of the night, a deception of moonlight and shadow, that made it seem like the rest of her surroundings blurred and drained of color, until Connor Douglas's piercing gray eyes were the only spots of color left in an otherwise pitch-black night.

He was staring at her, and staring at her hard.

Despite Gabrielle's resolve not to let him see how greatly his presence disturbed her, she couldn't hold back the shiver that iced down her spine like a drop of melting snow. His expression was expectant, as though he waited for her to say or do . . . something. Gabrielle shook her head, not knowing what that something could be. Shouldn't *he* be the one to make the first overture? After all, it was *he* who'd hunted *her* down and waylaid *her* plans. For that, the man owed her an apology if nothing else.

She waited for one.

It didn't come.

Instead, Connor crossed his arms over his firm, flat belly and asked tightly, "Are all Sassenach women as stupid as ye, lass?"

His tone was low and gritty, as harsh as the gaze boring into her. Gabrielle bristled. "You think it stupid to try to help someone who helped you? How strange. I think it natural."

He took a step toward her. Not a large one, yet it felt huge to Gabrielle. The night seemed to close in around her.

She took a counterstep back. By comparison the retreat felt small and feeble. Her heartbeat throbbed in her ears, so loud it blotted out the night sounds. As though from a distance, his voice came again.

" 'Tis maun stupid indeed," he growled, "when the helping in question could get ye killed."

Gabrielle retreated another step, even as he took another, more confident stride forward. He was closing the distance between them with alarming quickness. In another step she would be able to smell his musky scent, feel the heat of him seeping through the jack and trews and tunic, caressing the sensitive flesh beneath . . .

"There was never a chance of that," she countered, hoping her tone rang with indignation, knowing that her too soft, too breathless timbre didn't convey that at all.

"Nay?"

"Nay!"

"And what if ye and Ella had ridden upon a few stray Maxwells, or mayhap some that werena so stray? What then? How would ye have defended yerself, Gabrielle Carelton? *Could* ye have defended yerself?"

"I'm not so helpless as you seem to think, nor is court life so sheltered. I've learned my share of tricks to keep myself safe. The Maxwell would not have hurt me."

"Och! is that the way of it?" His laughter—loud, devoid of mirth—cut through the damp night air like a knife. The husky rumble sliced a warm path down Gabrielle's spine. "Nae matter how sternly ye did it, I dinna think that correcting their manners would have stopped a reiver from aught."

Like an expertly aimed arrow, the insult hit its mark. Gabrielle winced. She reacted on one part anger, one part instinct—hand lifting, open palm swinging toward his arrogant cheek—before she even knew she was doing it.

For a big man, Connor moved fast. Frighteningly so . . . Gabrielle realized only in retrospect.

Before she could blink, he countered the attack. His powerful fingers shackled her wrist, bringing her up short. Her palm was brought to a bone-jarring halt a mere fraction from blistering contact.

His grip was tight, but not painfully so.

Yet.

The glint in Connor Douglas's cold gray eyes as he glared down into Gabrielle's surprise-widened green ones said his restraint was hard won and, perhaps, temporary. His anger was tethered right now only by the utmost of self-control, a rein that could dissolve at any moment.

A muscle buried deep in the left side of his jaw ticked erratically. Like a magnet, her gaze was drawn to the stubble-dusted flesh there, inches from his sensuously carved mouth.

She sucked in a deep breath, only to find it was filled with the leather-and-spice scent that was Connor Douglas. She released the breath in a rush and watched, unnaturally fascinated, as it turn to a transparent, pale vapor that twisted and mingled with his.

The anger she'd felt only a second ago—*she had been angry, hadn't she?*—melted away to another, more confusing emotion. Dark and intriguing and mysterious, the sensation wove its way through her, so strong that it heated the blood pumping hot and fast through her veins, and made her knees feel weak and watery.

And what, exactly, was she feeling?

It was a grand question, that. Pity she'd no answer.

Gabrielle couldn't begin to describe the sensation because she'd never in her life felt anything even remotely like it. Well, nay, that was not entirely true. She'd felt something similar the time Essex, years ago, had kissed her in the Queen's gardens. The sensation then had been pale by comparison, the difference between a sapling struggling to stand next to a towering oak. Surely it was not the same . . . was it?

There was but one way to find out.

Gabrielle inhaled a shuddering breath, tried to ignore the enticing aroma it carried, and decided in a heartbeat that she did not want an answer *that* badly. If she let herself explore this strange and wonderful new sensation too thoroughly, she might trace it to its source, then be forced to give it a name. That would never do. Some things were best left unknown, a secret even from one's self. This was one of them.

Her lashes lowered, hooding her gaze as it slid down . . . over the thick trunk of Connor's neck, the broad shelf of his jack-encased shoulder, the firm line of his arm. She stopped at the place where his fingers were coiled about her wrist. That place felt molten; the flesh there burned and tingled in the most enigmatically splendid way. It was almost frightening. Almost.

Connor's attention shadowed hers. The muscles in his stomach tightened into a fist.

He should have let her slap him. Touching her, even if only to thwart her angry attack, had been a mistake. He'd known it the second his fingers grazed her wrist and he'd felt the warm silk of her skin whisper against his fingertips and palm. She was not small-boned; he could not circle her wrist and have his fingertips touch. She wasn't scrawny, all sharp angles and bones, like the other women he'd known. He liked that. Too much, he liked it!

She was full-figured and vibrant. The way her hips and thighs filled the trews was enticingly indecent. The way her breasts strained against the borrowed tunic . . .

Och! he'd never seen anything like it, and prayed to God he never would again. The tempting sight tested his resolve in ways it had never been tested before. Worse, for the first time in his life, The Black Douglas found his resolve lacking. And what, he wondered, would the Border balladeers think of *that*?!

The night air, heated by closeness and nerve-shattering contact, stirred against Connor's face. A waft of Gabrielle's oh so soft, oh so sweet and feminine fragrance drifted over him like a breathy sigh.

His gaze lifted, whisked over her mouth. Her lips were alluringly full and pink; as he watched, the tip of her tongue darted out, moistening the flesh there until it glistened in the muted moonlight.

Connor trapped a groan in his tight, parched throat. His tongue stroked the back of his tightly gritted teeth; Lord, how he ached to trace the gesture, to sip and savor what he knew without a doubt would be a thoroughly unique, thoroughly delicious taste of those sweet, sweet lips.

Jesus, Mary and Joseph, did the woman have any idea how desirable she was? E'en for a court-pampered Sassenach!

He frowned. Judging by the way she blushed to the roots of her silky black hair and, in a coyness he'd rarely seen displayed so openly in a woman, lowered her gaze to the scant sliver of wet ground separating them, he thought that perhaps she didn't. Incredible. But indeed mayhap true.

"I did not mean to worry you, m'lord," Gabrielle said finally, the words coming out in a soft and raspy rush, "or make you to ride out after us. Ella and I thought to accomplish our mission and return to the Bracklenaer before daybreak. We never thought we'd be missed. Please, I beg of you, m'lord, try to understand that we wished only to rescue Mairghread from the Maxwell."

Connor felt his anger chipping away. He tried to retain it—anger was a safe emotion; maun safer than the stronger one that threatened to override it. His tone softened a wee bit. "Yer motives are alien tae me, lass, yet I do believe ye."

Gabrielle nodded. Her voice, she was pleased to find, didn't shake nearly as violently as her knees. "The old woman showed me great kindness by nursing me through my sickness. It wasn't necessary, but she did it anyway. I sought only to repay her generosity by seeing her safely back at Bracklenaer. If I could. It seemed the least I could do."

Connor's grip on her wrist had loosened at some point. He didn't know when or why. His thumb now traced small, rhythmic circles against the pulse throbbing in the base of her wrist. He realized this fact only when he felt her quiver delicately beneath his fingertips. Her reaction was not caused by the cold, and well he knew it. Nor did the reciprocal shudder that coursed through him have roots in the weather.

His gaze lingered on her mouth. Her lips looked warm and moist, inviting. Would she taste as good as he thought she might? More importantly, since she was soon going to be his wife, was there a reason in the world to stop him from finding out?

None that he could think of!

Still, Connor hesitated. Very little space separated them. He'd only to lean forward, bend his knees a bit to accommodate the differences in their height, angle his head slightly to the side . . .

Like a piece of driftwood being swept away on a forceful current, Gabrielle swayed forward. The tips of her breasts grazed the rock-solid wall of Connor's chest even as her fingers wrapped around his sinewy upper arms in an attempt to regain her balance.

She gasped at the contact.

The sound was swallowed by Connor's mouth crashing down upon hers.

Her fingers tightened around his arms, her palms pressed against the coiled bands of muscle playing beneath the sleeves of his jack and tunic. Because of the padding it was impossible to feel his body heat against her hands . . . yet Gabrielle could have sworn she felt it anyway. And, oh, but it felt wonderful! Hot and enticing, his warmth seeped through the thick fabric separating flesh from flesh, into her palm, into her very being.

Her gasp melted into a low, throaty groan as she clung to him and went up on tiptoe. Her breathing had been shaky and shallow; it now took a deep, ragged turn . . . when she was able to suck in a breath at all.

The movement of his mouth on hers had started off gently, coaxing. Her shift in position pressed her lips more firmly to his, encouraging from Connor a lusty moan and a more hearty response.

One arm slid around her waist, and he shivered with desire as he hauled her to him. Och! but she was hot and soft, the generous curves of her body complementing to perfection the hard planes and angles of his. He could not remember any woman feeling this good in his arms.

The fingers of his free hand opened, raked through her dark hair. The strands felt like silk as they slid against his fingertips. He cupped the back of her head, tilted it to the side as his tongue skated hungrily over her lips. She opened for him with delicious readiness, and he wasted no time in plundering her mouth with his tongue.

She tasted good. Och! nay, she tasted far, far better than good. The best whisky in Scotland paled in comparison to the intoxicating flavor of Gabrielle Carelton's mouth. Connor felt drunk with a sudden, overpowering need that stunned him. The hand cradling her waist slipped downward. He cupped her bottom, his strong fingers gently kneading her through the trews. The snug trews hid nothing from his exploring hand.

Sweet Lord, even there she was temptingly, pleasingly soft and supple!

With a flick of his wrist, he pulled her hard against him. Her mouth swallowed his husky groan. Her breasts felt full and firm, pushing against his chest; the shape and feel of her burned through the thick leather jack, stamping an imprint into his skin that he'd a feeling would brand him forever. His tongue darted and probed and teased. He was shocked to feel her meet the passionate strokes measure for bold measure.

The woman was a seductress!

All thought of satisfying his curiosity with one simple kiss scattered from Connor's mind. There was nothing simple about this kiss, nothing simple about Gabrielle's unabandoned response. He'd expected her to be shy, perhaps even frightened and unwilling. He'd never miscalculated a woman and her response so drastically in his life!

What he'd wanted was but a quick kiss, something to tame his mounting curiosity and put the matter to rest in his mind.

What he'd gotten instead was an armful of wild, unrestrained passion.

Gabrielle attacked his senses in ways he'd never experienced, to an extent he'd never imagined possible. The sweet, fresh scent of her filled him. The silky feel of her hair slipping through his fingers, the warm pliancy of her perfectly rounded curves straining against his body, made him ache for something infinitely more intimate. The taste of her mouth left him parched, thirsty for a taste of all of her.

Her arms slipped around his waist, her hands splaying his back. She squirmed closer. Her hips pressed hard against his, her breasts rubbed against his chest. His breathing, what there was of it, went harsh and choppy.

Did the lass have any idea of how much he wanted her? Of how her untamed response was driving him insane? Did she care?

It took every last shred of Connor's self-control not to surrender to the sudden, unexpected urge to strip away the barriers of cloth separating them. He wanted—needed, *craved*—to feel her naked skin gliding beneath his open palms. Beneath his mouth and tongue. He wanted to touch and taste all of her. Now. So badly it frightened him. But not so badly that he would stop.

Releasing a shaky moan, he leaned into her until her spine bowed. Her curves cushioned his front as he deepened the kiss. She needed to feel the true extent of his desire for her, needed her to decide—now, before it was too late—to be sensible and stop this madness while there was still the time and ability to stop. The hardness between his legs said that the time for stopping was growing preciously short.

Gabrielle did not shy away, as he'd expected— hoped?—she would. Instead, she kept pace with the bold strokes of his tongue. In fact, her tongue made more than a few bold strokes of its own. Strokes that left him shaking and breathless.

Her hands stroked restlessly over his back— sometimes caressing, sometimes clenching around the leather of his jack in tight fists . . . always in ways that promised untold delight were the jack and tunic peeled away and his skin laid bare to her touch.

Connor shivered. A lightning bolt of raw sensation fisted in his stomach, rippling shockwaves throughout the rest of him when he imagined her fingernails raking over his ultrasensitive flesh. His head spun. His desire escalated, spiraling upward with soul-numbing speed.

She wasn't his wife. Yet. He should stop. So rationalized the small portion of his mind still able to cling to a tattered thread of sanity. Another, larger portion instantly countered the thought, reminding Connor that, while it was true Gabrielle was not his wife, she would be soon enough. This very night if he could manage it!

More importantly . . . had she even once, in either words or in deed, indicated that she wanted him to stop?

Nay, she had not!

Just the opposite. The way her temptingly full body wriggled impatiently against him, the way her warm, ragged breaths puffed like a sweet sum-

mer breeze against his cheek as she clung to him
and returned his kiss with an ardor that wanted—
demanded—more, encouraged his yearning to satisfy the mutual need simmering like liquid fire
inside them both.

An intense throbbing shot through Connor,
rocking him to the core. Och! how he wanted
her! Here. Now. In any manner she pleased. The
sanctity of marriage be damned; their legal joining was a negligible obstacle that would be reme-
died soon enough . . . after their physical one.

"Gabrielle," he sighed after easing the kiss
enough to whisper her name huskily against her
lips. Could she hear his heart pounding? She
must, for it was beating so loud and hard that
Connor could barely hear his own voice over the
racket. "What are ye doing, lass? Dinna ye ken
that ye're supposed to kiss like an innocent
maid?"

"I'll kiss any way you want for me to," she replied, her voice low and breathless, the pitch
equally as husky as his own, "provided you kiss me
like that again."

Connor's eyes snapped open. When had he
shut them? He didn't remember, didn't care.
Right now he was drowning in the most beautiful
gaze he'd ever seen, and he couldn't think beyond it. Her eyelids were passion-thick, the inky
lashes shielding eyes that were the tumultuous
color of the North Sea just before a storm; dark
green and vibrant, glazed by passion.

The sight evaporated whatever answer he might
have given.

He pulled back a little, his gaze raking her, taking in her whole face. Was the dim light highly
flattering, or had she always been this lovely and

he was only now noticing? Her cheeks were flushed, her lips full from his kiss, slightly moist, parted invitingly. A ray of moonlight snuck in through the ceiling of leaves; the silvery beam streaked over his shoulder and played on her hair, highlighting the curls clinging to her cheeks and brow until they appeared an appealing shade of rich blue-black.

Connor had not thought this woman ravishing on their first meeting. Nor did he think so tonight. However, at some point, for reasons he didn't dare examine too closely, his opinion of Gabrielle Carelton had slowly, with no concrete reason to be cited, changed. She'd never be a great beauty, to say otherwise would be a lie, yet she was easy on the eye in a way uniquely her own, a way that he found surprisingly appealing.

She wasn't the weak, frail English creature whom Connor had imagined weeks ago that he'd be saddled with. Rather, she had a sturdy body that not only adapted admirably well to the harsh Scots climate, but that also invited a man's touch and welcomed it without flinching.

While she'd proved she could be feisty enough when riled, Gabrielle normally displayed a mild disposition that he found at once gracious and intriguing. That she'd set out to rescue Mairghread equipped with naught but his harebrained cousin bespoke an innate kindness that her sometimes haughty Sassenach temperament was deft to conceal.

Aye, what she'd done was foolhardy in the extreme, he'd be the first to admit it. Yet her reasons were pure and unselfish. He did not have to like it, but how could he not respect and admire it? How could he be angry with her?

The answer was simple.

He couldn't.

Especially not when he was holding her in his arms, feeling her body strain against his, her warmth seeping through him as he looked into her beautiful green eyes. His tongue still savored the singular flavor of her.

Just one kiss. That was all he'd promised himself.

There had been dozens of Black Douglases before him; all prided themselves on keeping their word. A Border ballad had been written about *this* Black Douglas's trustworthiness. Connor had recently caught snatches of the verse when he'd overheard one of the kitchen wenches singing it under her breath as she kneaded dough.

With a remorseful groan, his lips again sealed over hers, his thirsty tongue probing and seeking out the rich, warm inner recess of her mouth.

For the first time in his life, Connor Douglas had made a promise he could not keep.

Eight

Stand up straight. I said straight! *Shoulders back. Oh, for God's sake, girl, suck in your stomach. You look like an overstuffed goose!*

The words, harshly spoken by Queen Elizabeth at a time that now felt like a lifetime ago, whiplashed through Gabrielle. The memory stung as sharply as the half-healed wound they'd created deep in her soul.

She flinched, instinctively pulling away from Connor's kiss, away from the confusion of his touch. He let her go immediately, and she wasn't sure if she should be happy about that or not. Her knees felt shaky as she staggered backward a step. Wet grass, moss, leaves, and pine needles crunched beneath the soles of her too-large, borrowed boots.

Gabrielle's size had been a constant source of irritation to her Queen, and Elizabeth wasn't shy about letting anyone within hearing distance know it. Why Gabrielle was allowed to remain at court, when her looks so disturbed her monarch, she could only wonder. She suspected pity had much to do with it, although, if pressed, she'd have to admit not knowing a single time when Elizabeth had allowed her actions to be guided by anything resembling such a humane emotion.

Gabrielle's gaze had lowered, her sight fixed on the top button of Connor's jack. It was made of horn, the disk dull and chipped. She tried hard not to think about the bands of muscle lying beneath.

Slowly, her attention lifted, locked with his. His eyes were passion-dark. At least she thought—*hoped*—passion was the emotion she saw in those piercing gray depths. As the memory of Elizabeth's words arrowed through her, however, leaving her breathless and numb, Gabrielle was suddenly unsure.

Was Connor looking at her with pity, or passion? And did it matter? Aye, it mattered a great deal! The uncertainty weighed heavily on her mind, for her reaction to him depended upon the answer.

If it was pity he offered, she wanted none of it.

If it was passion . . .

Gabrielle licked her suddenly parched lips. His taste lingered; the sharp flavor of his kiss was something she would savor in the lonely, sleepless nights ahead, no matter what had prompted it.

I'll kiss any way you want for me to, provided you kiss me like that again.

Had she really spoken such bold words? She had. More importantly, had she *meant* them? Aye, most definitely she had!

Gabrielle ached for Connor to kiss her again. Her body yearned to lean into his, press against his hardness, feel his heart beat against her breasts. Never had she experienced anything so wonderfully exhilarating. She had to fight the urge to take the hand he'd lowered to his side and put it back on her waist, her hip, the sensitive curve of her bottom. What she wouldn't give to feel the heat of his fingers burning through the material separating them, searing their powerful imprint into the tender flesh beneath.

The wants and needs raging through her right now were *not* those of a lady. Then again . . . Gabrielle's head was spinning with an abundance of strange desires and sensations, none of which had been constructed on ladylike foundations.

If nothing else, life at Elizabeth's court had provided her with a thorough education in the ways of men and women. Even if she hadn't participated, Gabrielle had observed it all keenly. And learned. She knew the intricate dance of courtship could be performed with a mere glance, a seemingly inadvertent flick of the wrist, the hint of a sensuously curved smile. In the right combination, all three could bring a man to his knees. She'd seen it happen time and time again.

While it was doubtful anything, especially a woman as plain-looking as herself, could bring The Black Douglas to his knees, that didn't hinder Gabrielle's thoughts from wondering. After all, she didn't want to bed the man, she only wanted to kiss him again. Please, just once more. Suddenly it seemed imperative that she know whether the hot, sizzling sensation she'd felt shoot like a bolt of lightning through her veins— a sensation that still left her feeling weak and tingly, that had made her toes curl into tight balls inside the too-large boots—had been her imagination, or if it had been caused by the feel of Connor Douglas's mouth moving hungrily over hers.

She'd a feeling it was the latter. Now, she sought proof.

In a move that would have left Elizabeth gasping at its brazenness, Gabrielle took a step forward, closing the space between them. Perhaps it was Elizabeth's harsh words, still ringing in her memory, that made her give a toss of her dark head and put a confident curve to her smile a second before she tilted her chin and sealed their mouths together.

She swallowed Connor's sharp exhalation of surprise, even as she leaned forward still more, leaned against him, leaned *into* him. The unfamiliar sensation she'd felt before was back, stronger than ever. It tingled in her blood and danced like frantic butterflies in her stomach. Her head felt light, her senses spiraled.

Ah, yes! She'd wondered, now she knew. There was no longer any doubt the sensation, whatever it was called, could be traced directly back to Connor Douglas, and the way his mouth opened over hers.

Unlike the last, this kiss was light, gentle. His lips whisked airily over hers with sweet promise, yet she sensed an underlying urgency.

Gabrielle splayed her hands over his chest. The leather of his jack felt soft and cool, moist from the rain, the wide chest beneath hard as granite. Her fingers closed around the material in tight fists as she tried to pull him closer. He went without even a hint of reluctance.

A moan escaped one of them.

Heat stained Gabrielle's cheeks a bright shade of pink when she realized the soft, plaintive sound had come from herself. It sounded oddly high, breathless and throaty.

Her moan echoed in his ears like the sigh of waves lapping at rocks. Connor shivered. His arms coiling around her waist, he hauled her hard against him.

She went willingly; her only struggle was to squirm, trying to get closer. It wasn't possible, although he found himself doing the same thing.

Feeling her against him wasn't enough. Connor wanted, nay *needed*, to be closer to her still.

Her arms wrapped around his neck, her fingers linking. Her breasts, so wonderfully full and firm, prodded against his chest as she returned his kiss with a voracious hunger that astonished him.

Trapping a groan in the back of his throat, Connor stroked and probed the sweet inner recesses of her mouth with his tongue. Milk and honey . . . aye, that was what she tasted like. His hands caressed her back in quick, restless strokes. His palms itched to peel away the barrier of cloth, to feel her skin beneath his fingertips. Restraining the urge wasn't easy, but surrendering would risk frightening her and having her pull away.

Such was a risk Connor was not willing to take.

Truly, he *had* kept his promise. He'd but kissed her once . . . och! all right, twice. But only to satisfy his curiosity. No matter how badly he might have wanted to, he would not have kissed her again.

And he hadn't.

She had kissed *him*.

Oh how that changed everything!

The gesture was so unexpected it knocked the breath from his lungs and at the same time toppled what little self-control he'd been able to maintain.

Without realizing what he was doing, Connor

scooped her body close and, bending, gently eased both of them to the ground. She made a hot, soft, heavenly bed upon which he cushioned himself. He lay half on her, half on the damp, moss-strewn ground.

His mouth left hers. Trailing tiny nibbles along the line of her jaw, he shifted slightly to the side and bent his right knee, nudging her legs apart.

Slowly, slowly, his leg lifted.

The top of his thigh rubbed intimately against her.

Her hips thrust upward, and she moaned. The sound was cut short by her sharp, quivering gasp.

Gabrielle's eyes were scrunched closed. Behind the velvet black of her lids, a burst of color exploded as her legs clamped tightly around the granite hardness of his thigh. Like the colors on an artist's pallet being washed away by a heavy rain, electrifying streaks of blues and reds and purples trickled together and merged.

"Do ye like that, lass?" he asked.

The moss pillowing the back of her head crunched when she nodded. "Oh, aye. Please, m'lord, do it again."

Connor gritted his teeth. The lass was a constant source of surprise. Her unexpectedly enthusiastic response was going to be the death of him! Feeling her body beneath his, feeling her squirming against the shelf of his thigh, created a sensation in him that burned like liquid fire. A sensation more intense than anything he'd ever known.

"Ne'er let it be said that The Black Douglas refused a lady," he growled . . . and did it again.

And again.

And yet again.

The muscles in Gabrielle's stomach tightened as she clung to him, moved her hips in time to the strokes of his thigh. Ah, sweet Jesus, she didn't know exactly what it was Connor was doing, or why it made her breathing accelerate and her nerve endings tingle, and at that moment she did not particularly care. All she wanted was for him not to stop!

Her hands strayed to the collar of his jack, her fingers slipping beneath. The cloth of the tunic felt scratchy against her fingertips as she slipped the jack, with its protective lining of heavily padded steel, over his shoulders and down his arms. He helped by shifting his weight from one arm to the other. All the while, his mouth, which had discovered the sensitive length of her neck, and reveled in the way she shivered and moaned, never left the heavenly taste of her skin.

In the past, Connor had always considered the loveplay before bedding a wench something to tolerate and provide as a courtesy to the lass. Oddly, as hard as his body was driving him to take this woman, he felt no rush. It was most strange, yet he had to admit that he could have continued to kiss and stroke and caress her until the sun came up . . . and not be bored with it or grow tired of it.

His right hand had been splayed over her waist; it now roamed over her in slow but fevered strokes. Her reaction to his touch was magnificently eager. When his fingertips grazed the temptingly full undercurve of her breasts, her shiver was as ardent as it was unrestrained. His mouth surrendered the salty-sweet taste of her skin for a moment before he groaned and reluctantly lifted his head to look down at her.

Gabrielle's eyes, which had been tightly closed, flickered open. Thick black lashes framed eyes that were dark green and passion-glazed.

Their glazes locked and held.

Her cheeks were flushed, her lips pink and puffy from his kisses. Her breathing was as ragged and choppy as his own.

Connor froze, waiting, wondering if she was going to stop him.

She didn't.

Instead, she surprised him yet again by blanketing the back of his hand with her smaller palm. Arching her back, she tugged his hand up, under the placket of her jack, until his fingers were splayed over the firm curve of her breast.

Their sighs came in unison, long and deep.

The bolt of sensation that shot through Connor was pure electricity. Och! but the woman was a bold one. Where most lasses hid their passion behind coy glances and subterfuge, Gabrielle Carelton bluntly let him know, in response if not words, exactly what she wanted.

The urge to strip away the material barriers between them became too great to resist. She wasn't going to stop him, Connor knew that for certain now. And, God help him, he was beyond stopping himself.

Grudgingly, he relinquished the intoxicating feel of her to go up on his knees and yank the tunic up and over his head. He tossed it aside and in an instant had spread himself on top of her again. The entire process took less time than for two heartbeats to melt together.

The damp night air should have been like a cold slap against his unprotected skin. If it was, Connor didn't notice. He had an uneasy feeling that the heat emanating from Gabrielle's full, lush curves could keep him warm for a lifetime. His left elbow levered the weight of his torso up, so as not to crush her. Pine needles and moss dug into his skin, but he barely noticed the nip of pain.

This time he grasped the folds of her tunic one by one in his fingers, then tugged upward. Inch by inch, her creamy skin was revealed to his appreciative eye.

"You're much too slow, m'lord," she said, her voice high and breathless.

His mouth went dry when Gabrielle batted his hand away, then, as he eased back to give her room, sat up. After shrugging off the jack, she yanked her tunic up and off. Both garments joined his, forming shadowy heaps on the damp, pine needle-scattered ground. Her hair floated down over her shoulders like a silky black cloud; after a tantalizing, split-second view, the strands artfully arranged themselves to conceal the portions of her voluptuous body that Connor ached most to see and touch and taste.

He groaned low and deep, reaching for her, only to falter. Her skin was pale and tender and flawless in the muted moonlight; he had no desire to see such perfection marred by scratches and bruises, yet that was exactly what would happen if he surrendered to the almost irresistible urge to push her onto her back and cover her body with his own.

He went up on his knees, shifted until he was behind her. His finger trembled only a wee bit when he scooped the bulk of her hair up and draped it forward over her shoulder.

He leaned into her, gasping when his bare

chest came into sizzling contact with her soft, naked back. A shudder rippled through Connor.

Like a rock being tossed into a summer-calm loch, tremors shivered through Gabrielle. His skin felt hotter than fire. His hands now flanked her hips, his fingers flexing tensely, digging into the woolen trews and the tender flesh beneath. Thick black hair coated his rock-hard chest; the strand tickled the skin between her shoulder blades and caused the most peculiar tingling sensation to burn all throughout her.

Her breasts felt heavy and full, the nipples rigid and overly sensitive from equal parts cold night air and sensuous anticipation. Gabrielle wanted to feel his hands on her there, feel the heat and pressure of his fingers and palms touching her. Her body ached for it so badly that she didn't think twice about seeking immediate satisfaction for the need. She reached down and loosened his hands from her hips, dragged them up over her waist. Higher.

The skin on his palms was battle-rough, but his touch was oh so very gentle. Gabrielle sighed her pleasure. The last thing she would have expected from The Black Douglas was gentleness. The hands that now cupped her breasts, the big palms that enticingly stroked her nipples, were rumored to have committed atrocious deeds. Feeling the way he touched her, she suddenly found that difficult to believe. Surely no man who could touch a woman with such tenderness could be as cruel as rumor said The Black Douglas was.

Rumor and truth. There was a difference. A large one.

While that difference had meant nothing to Gabrielle scarcely a month ago—she'd been as willing as anyone in London to believe the horrid ballads about this man; she'd had no reason not to—it meant a great deal to her now. For the first time, she wondered how much truth those Border ballads carried, and how much was pure exaggeration.

Connor's hands moved, and he began rubbing her nipples between his index finger and thumb, and Gabrielle abruptly lost the ability to wonder about anything at all. Anything, that is, except the white-hot excitement pumping through her. Anything except the way her mind was abruptly excruciatingly aware of every place where Connor's body touched hers, and every place his body *wasn't* touching hers—yet.

She was consumed by his touch; she couldn't think or feel beyond it. God help her, she did not *want* to!

Never the sort to throw caution to the wind, Gabrielle was astonished by her immediate, lusty response to this man. And exhilarated by it. More exhilarating still was the hungry, restless way his hands caressed her, as though he couldn't feel enough of her, wanted to feel more.

That the notorious Connor Douglas—heathen Scots Border reiver though he was—showed the obvious and intense desire to touch a woman whom Queen Elizabeth had likened to an "overstuffed goose" was heady knowledge indeed. It blotted out past pain—before now, an unimaginable feat—and filled Gabrielle with a warm, rich burst of satisfaction and pride. An undiluted surge of raw feminine confidence flooded through her.

The notorious reiver was kissing and nibbling the side of her neck, sucking patches of her flesh into his mouth and causing the most delicious pleasure-pain to sizzle inside her. Moaning softly, Gabrielle tipped her head to the side to give him better access, even as she tilted her chin up and cushioned the back of her head against the solid shelf of his right shoulder.

"How auld are ye, lass?"

His voice felt like a caress against her skin. "You don't know?" she asked.

"Should I?"

"Aye. You expended a great deal of effort, not to mention the risk you took, kidnapping me from your brother's hands. You've stated plainly that you intend to wed me in his place. Why you'd want to do that, I can't . . . nay, I *don't want to* know about. All things considered, I'd think you'd know all there is to know about me."

She could feel his lips move against her neck as he spoke. The feeling made it hard to concentrate on what he said.

"Truth tae tell, lass, I ken scarce little aboot ye."

"Then why would you—?"

"Ye were tae marry Colin and settle the feud between Douglas and Maxwell. I've nae liking for the latter, I admit. Howe'er, if 'tis tae be, and our stubborn monarchs insist that it shall, then *I* will be the one tae do it. That ye were Colin's bride was reason enough to snatch ye and wed ye. I'd nae idea what ye looked like afore ye stepped foot on Bracklenaer soil, and kenned less what sort of wench ye be. Nae did I care."

Gabrielle stiffened. "You kidnapped me and professed a desire to wed me *only* to thwart your brother?" Her blood ran cold as another, more potent realization stabbed into her heart. "Is that what this is all about, Connor? Are you trying to seduce me now for no other reason than to accomplish that goal?"

The idea caused a strange, fistlike tightening in Gabrielle's chest, traitorously close to her heart. She ignored the sensation as she waited breathlessly for his answer. It was a long, torturous time in coming. A time that she filled in with scrambled thoughts.

It all made sense now.

How many ballads claimed The Black Douglas was relentless? Too many to be ignored. When the man set his sights on something, whether it be lifting beasties from a rival family or wooing the charms from a hesitant maid, he did not surrender until success was his. He might change tactics, but he never cried defeat.

And if he'd set his sights now on wedding her? Aye, she thought, what then?

Gabrielle tried to swallow, but her throat was suddenly too dry and tight for it. If Connor pretended to enjoy touching her to melt her defenses and seduce her, would not such a seduction aid him in reaching his goal? And why, *why* did the thought hurt so very much?!

"Has a mon e'er bedded ye, lass?"

She should take offense at such a question. She did not. It was a legitimate query, especially when one considered the lusty way in which she had responded to his kisses and caresses.

What would Connor say if she told him the truth? That no man had even expressed a desire to bed her? That her experience extended only so far as one dry, chaste kiss shared, almost as if by accident, years ago, with one of Elizabeth's favorites? A kiss that had been initiated by the Earl of Essex but never repeated, nor had he ever showed a desire to repeat it.

Gabrielle frowned and inhaled deeply of the chilly, pine-scented night air. She had to fight the sudden, strong urge to reach for her tunic and cover herself. "Do you really need to ask? Isn't the answer obvious?"

"Aye, 'tis. And if only *because* of its obviousness, ye've overlooked one prime fact. Ye've naught to judge a mon's touch by but hearsay and suspect motives. If ye'd a mon had bedded ye afore, ye'd ken that desire this hot and strong canna be faked. I'll be the first tae admit there's aught a determined mon can do, but feigning desire for a wench who does not appeal to him isna one of them."

His mouth was back on her neck again, his hot breath puffing over her, his lips moving sensuously against her flesh; the feel set her senses on fire, chipping away at the hastily constructed wall of self-defense she'd thrown up around herself only a few short seconds before.

"I must have misunderstood, m'lord. It sounded almost as though you just said you . . . desire me?" The question was out before she could bite it back. Even if she'd had the chance, she doubted she would have. She wanted, nay, *needed* to know the answer. Her pride and self-respect demanded it.

His answer did not come in words, but in a gesture that was far more compelling.

Connor's hands had been cupping her breasts, but he'd forced them to remain unnaturally still. Slowly, slowly, they now slid downward, flanking her hips once more. His fingers curled inward, digging into her trews and tender flesh as he pulled that part of her body back against his.

Her bottom came up hard against his.

"Do ye feel that, lass?" he asked huskily as he ground his hips against her softness. The wisp of wool whisking against wool, of his kilt rubbing against her trews, sounded unnaturally loud.

Gabrielle shuddered. "Aye, m'lord, how could I not?"

"Exactly. But do ye ken what 'tis ye're feeling?"

"I-I'm not sure."

"Then I'll tell ye." His voice was low and oh so sensuously rough; it scratched warmly down Gabrielle's spine. "What ye're feeling is me body's reaction to ye. 'Tis the way a mon responds to a woman he desires beyond all rhyme and reason. The good Lord, for whate'er purpose, made sure a mon's physical response is tae natural and strong tae be controlled or denied. Howe'er, in all His wisdom, He gave us the ability to govern, nae matter how difficult it may be—and, truth tae tell, lass, with ye warm, luscious body filling me arms, 'tis maun difficult than I'd e'er kenned it could be!—what we do aboot slaking our desire." His pause was long and tension-thick, as though he debated his next words before daring to give them voice. "If ye asked it of me, I would stop now."

"And if I asked you *not* to stop?" she queried huskily. "What then?"

"Is that what ye're asking, lass?" His voice was deep and raspy. "Are ye sure?"

Gabrielle hesitated for one throbbing moment, then sighed long and deep and nodded. "Aye, 'tis exactly what I'm asking. And I've never been more sure of anything in my life. I like your touch, Connor Douglas. It sets me on fire and makes me want things I'd never dreamed were possible. If you've no objections, I'd like to feel more of it."

Her sudden humor was reflected in her teasing tone as she glanced at him from over her bare, creamy shoulder and carelessly tossed his own words from earlier back at him. "Ne'er let it be said that The Black Douglas refused a lady."

Connor laughed, deep and hard. He couldn't help it. The twinkle in her pretty green eyes was pure mischief, demanding a response, and that response was as strong as it was automatic. "Och, but yer Scots burr be a poor one, lass. 'Tis something you'll need tae work on."

"Aye, m'lord, I will. You can give me lessons later if you'd like. For now, however . . ." Her gaze narrowed, raking his naked torso and the color in her cheeks intensified even as her voice deepened seductively. "For now I've no wish to stay you from granting a lady's request. Lest you forget, you've a reputation to maintain."

Connor brushed his lips lightly over hers and whispered huskily against them, "Are ye planning to pen a ballad aboot this, lass?"

"Only if it proves worthy of writing about, m'lord."

The invitation in her soft, sultry voice was too great to resist. Connor kissed her fully as he adjusted their position and reached down to free his kilt. The plaid fell, draping over his naked calves in dark gray and black folds.

He pulled her willing body close as he shoved the bulk of the plaid beneath them. It made an adequate barrier to protect bare skin from the sharp bite of pine needles and scratch of wet moss, grass, and leaves.

Gabrielle twisted to the side and wrapped her arms around Connor's neck, clinging to him. Her tongue slid moistly, restlessly, over his lower lip. Her teeth nibbled the tender flesh there. She squirmed, pressing her breasts more fully against him, and inhaled sharply when she felt her nipples pucker and tighten still more.

Connor tasted warm and wonderful: the intoxicatingly rich flavor of his mouth all-consuming. Then, too, her nipples sent a sharp, tingle-burn throughout the rest of her body when he rubbed his chest against them. The thick pelt of inky curls tickled her in the most pleasurable way.

Gabrielle clutched tightly at fistfuls of his sleek, dark hair as she tried to pull his mouth closer still. It wasn't possible, but still she tried.

Connor's hands, which were again flanking her hips, shifted to duck beneath the hem of her tunic. The trews hugged her delectable curves like a glove; there was barely enough room to sneak his fingertips beneath the waist, yet he managed to find and use what little slack there was to his best advantage.

Gabrielle quivered and, her lips never leaving his, shifted so that she was on her knees facing him.

Connor eased the trews down. The curve of her naked bottom slid beneath his open palms. Lower. Over the creamy skin on the back of her thighs. Her flesh felt as warm and as soft as the velvety inside of a sun-warmed petal of heather.

The trews bunched around her knees. He wanted to feel more of her. Wanted to feel *all* of her. Wanted to feel it *now.*

With a flick of his wrist, Connor moved his hand to the inside of her thigh. She trembled beneath his touch, and oh but the sensation her reaction caused to bolt through him was incredible, like liquid fire sizzling hot and fast inside his veins. His heart hammered out a plaintive need that surpassed any he'd known before.

His mouth shifted its attention to her earlobe; he suckled it into his mouth and at the same time forced himself to temper the urgency raging through him as he lifted his hand. His calloused fingertips dragged ever so slowly over the sensitive skin of her inner thigh.

Her curiosity and eagerness had shocked him at first, but he'd adapted quickly. Now, Connor wasn't at all surprised when she automatically parted her thighs for him as his hand ascended higher still.

Her fingers tightened around his hair until he could feel the pull of it burning his scalp. There was, however, another, more compelling feeling that distracted his attention. It was the feel of her hips swiveling toward his touch in an age-old invitation.

His fingers moved ever upward along the inside of her thigh. The soft black curls there tickled and teased his fingertips, wisped softly, warmly across the back of his knuckles. His skin tingled and burned as his attention turned inward.

A soft moan whispered past her lips; the warm, moist waft of breath filtered through his hair and washed over the side of his neck.

He stroked her slowly, gently.

A shiver coursed down Connor's spine when he felt how hot and wet and ready she was for him. Her hips pulsated back and forth, matching the rhythm of his hand to perfection, urging it to increase.

He nuzzled her ear, then pulled back enough to watch her give a toss of her dark head, her silky hair shivering around her. Her eyes were closed, her soft features accentuated by the brief glitters of moonlight filtering down through the branches. The muscles in her thighs tightened and they closed firmly around his wrist. The movement of her hips increased and she moaned again, long and deep, as she rubbed against him.

The burden of restraining his passion, so unexpected and strong, was almost overwhelming.

Gabrielle's unbridled excitement served to increase his own. He wanted to push her back against the kilt, cover her body with his, claim her in a way she'd never been claimed before. And, God willing, never would be again! He wanted to make her his in the most intimate way. The need was raging inside him until he could think of nothing else but complete and total possession.

Only a few short minutes ago, Connor had offered to stop. Then, he would have, could have. Now it simply was not possible. With each thrust of her hips, with each feel of her dewy warmth against his fingertips, he knew he was beyond stopping. Her wild passion told him that Gabrielle knew it as well . . . and that neither of them wanted to see an end to such raw pleasure.

Swallowing back a groan, he slipped his index finger deeply inside her.

He heard her sharp inhalation. The fingers clutching his hair tightened painfully, but he didn't complain. Her hips went unnaturally still. After a beat, her inky lashes flickered up. Connor suddenly found himself staring down into passion-darkened green eyes. Eyes so deep and luminous they snatched away what little breath he had.

"M'lord, is that y-your . . . ?" Her words trailed off, even as the color in her cheeks heated to a vibrant shade of crimson-peach.

It took Connor a second to realize what she was talking about. Because of her unreserved response, he'd forgotten for a second that she was very much an innocent in the ways of physical love.

God in heaven, was she so innocent in the ways of a man and a woman that she thought . . . ?

Aye, he realized as he gazed down at her, that was exactly what she thought. He was torn between two equally strong urges; the first was to laugh, the second was to prove exactly how his ". . . ?" felt like when it moved inside her!

"Nay, lass," he said finally, when he had breath enough to speak. "Soon, but nae yet. 'Tis what I'm preparing ye for."

"Preparing me for? You mean there's"—she gulped hard—*"more?* You can make me feel better than *this?"*

She stared up at him with an innocent sort of amazement; her dazed expression and the hungry look in her eyes combined to warm a heart Connor had thought long ago frozen over.

"Aye," he murmured, "maun more. Relax, lass. Let me show ye."

Gabrielle did as he bid. She tried to relax. Tried, and failed. Her senses were soaring too high for that. A strange, burning sort of tension had settled deep inside her muscles, pulling them taut with white-hot anticipation.

Connor's hand started moving again.

She closed her eyes, arched her back, reveled in the tidal wave of exquisite sensation that washed over her. His strokes were long and deep and sure as he caressed her in places no one had ever seen before, let alone touched in such a gloriously intimate way. Her hips moved with the tempo he set, then her thighs tightened around his forearm, urging the pace quicker.

A choppy moan whispered past her lips when Connor dipped his head and whisked her nipple with his lips. Shaggy strands of black hair fell forward over his shoulders as his tongue made teasingly warm, moist circles around the rigid, rosy peak of flesh.

Gabrielle clutched at his upper arms, her fingers digging into his skin as she felt the muscles in her stomach, and lower, convulse with exhilarating pleasure.

She tried to pull him down atop her, wanting to feel the hard length of his body covering her, but he stubbornly refused. Instead, the strokes of his hand quickened, and he did something with his thumb that made all the sensations that had come before seem infinitesimal by comparison.

The tension that had flooded through her now centered, the crux of it focused on the juncture between her thighs. Another alien but highly pleasant sensation pooled inside her, gathering quicker than a wild sea storm.

"Dinna fight it, lass. Let yerself go," he murmured encouragingly as he quickened the pace of his hand to a dizzying speed.

The first spasms crashed over Gabrielle like waves breaking over rocks. She cried out in surprise and pleasure as the fierce undertow of sensation dragged her downward, threatening to

drown her in its fiery wake. Her cry melted into
a husky groan as her body convulsed and vibrant
strokes of color exploded behind her tightly
closed eyelids.

Her groan mingled with Connor's own as he
slipped his hand free and levered himself on top
of her. With his free hand, he guided himself into
her.

" 'Tis sorry I am tae cause ye pain, lass, but 'tis
the way a maid becomes a woman. Just a sting, I
promise ye. The pain willna last."

In one long, sure thrust, he shattered the restrictive barrier of her maidenhead.

Gabrielle gasped. Her fingernails bit into the
flesh on his shoulders and her body went rigid
beneath his.

She felt *perfect*, so very tight and wet and warm.
Despite his body's burning desire to move inside
her, Connor stilled, waiting with more patience
than he knew he possessed for the shock and
sting of the necessary pain to pass.

The pressure on his shoulders eased. Her open
palms stroked his back restlessly. Her index finger
traced a thick scar located just beneath his shoulder blade, a scar he'd acquired years ago on a
decidedly unsuccessful midnight raid against the
neighboring Kerrs.

Gradually she began to move tentatively beneath him, as though testing to see if more pain
was in store. When there was none, the movement
of her hips swiftly became bolder, more insistent.

Connor gritted his teeth, biting back a groan
as he began gradually to move inside her. She
met him thrust for hungry thrust, and the way
her body milked his pushed his self-control to the
limit. If he didn't slow the pace, and slow it

soon . . . och! no matter how good his intentions, he would not be able to last long.

Her legs entwined with his and her hands strayed downward. Over the small of his back. Lower. She sighed like a contented cat as she drew him deeper inside her still.

"Ah, yes, again," Gabrielle murmured, her voice as soft and amazed as the expression he found himself looking down into.

The muscles in Connor's stomach clenched when he felt her shudder beneath him, her inner muscles tightening spasmodically around that most sensitive part of his body.

His hands curled into white-knuckled fists around broken twigs, damp leaves, and the scratchy hem of the kilt. He picked up the pace, driving into her, his need for fulfillment suddenly so intense that his vision went blurry around the edges.

In a blinding rupture of sensation, the tension in his body gathered, then, when it was almost unbearable, burst.

Connor groaned her name as he thrust his hips forward, burying himself inside her as deeply as he could go.

Again.

And again.

It took far longer than Connor would have thought possible for the aftershock of relaxation to wash the tension out of his body. When it finally did, he shifted, lowering much of his weight onto the bed of her curves.

He nuzzled her ear with his nose. The soft, sweet fragrance of her filled him to overflowing, and he smiled with satisfaction when he felt Gabrielle's instinctive shiver of response.

He opened his mouth to say . . . something. The words evaporated unspoken off his tongue as relaxation surged into something stronger and more lulling. He was tired. Nay, exhausted. Yet in a thoroughly contented sort of way. Surely whatever he'd been about to say could wait a wee bit?

That thought in mind, he shifted onto his side, taking care to keep their bodies joined. Slipping one arm beneath Gabrielle's head, he coiled the other around her waist and pulled her close.

She felt warm and good in his arms. Her ripe, full curves fit the planes and angles of his body flawlessly. She snuggled against him, her cheek cradled against his shoulder.

As Connor let his mind and body come untethered, drifting naturally toward much needed rest, he was vaguely aware that he'd never felt such overwhelming protectiveness as he did right now for the woman who lay in his arms. His last thought before sleep overtook him was that making love had never felt so good and right as it did tonight, with this woman . . . and it never would again.

Nine

Two completely opposite sensations pierced Connor Douglas's sleep-fogged brain.

The first was that Gabrielle's warm, naked body was pressed against his own naked side in the most enticing way. Her head was pillowed atop his chest, the dark curls at the crown tucked beneath his chin and jaw, tickling his skin ever so nicely. She was curled into him in a way that suggested, even in sleep, she strove to melt her body right into his. Her left arm draped possessively over his waist. Her left knee was bent; the petal-soft inside of her thigh blanketed his hips in a deliciously intimate manner.

The second—not at all welcome—realization was that, at some point while he'd slumbered, someone had placed something that felt dangerously hard and sharp against the pulse beating sleepily in the base of his throat.

It was the latter sensation that jarred him awake.

His eyes snapped open in the same instant his right hand shot for the sword he'd laid atop the ground at his side. An increased pressure at his throat—only enough to draw a single hot drop of blood—stilled his hand. His fingers went slack, the moss scratching at palms and fingertips that had so recently slid over Gabrielle Carelton's silky, naked skin.

A glint of moonlight bounced ominously off the broadsword being held on him.

Connor's breath caught as he traced a slow path up the weapon.

Up.

Up.

Then up some more.

At this angle, the blade looked oddly asymmetric—too sharp at the tip, too thick at the hilt—and so very long.

The arm he'd wrapped around Gabrielle's shoulders tightened, even as his gaze settled, and settled hard, on the man whose lean fingers were wrapped around the leather-covered hilt.

It might have been a figment of moonlight and shadow, but Connor could have sworn Gordie Maxwell pulled back an instinctive fraction of an inch as their gazes met and warred. But in the space of a wink, the weathered creases shooting out from the corners of Gordie's eyes deepened and a cocky grin tugged at what little could be seen of his lips between his shaggy red beard and mustache.

Och! but this was *not* a good situation! Even if he could somehow mange to get to his sword before Gordie Maxwell slit his throat, Connor's problems would only be starting. At least a half dozen more armed and hardy-looking men stood in a semicircle behind Gordie. All were alert and watchful of the exchange playing out before them.

" 'One glance of the Douglas eye, 'tis said, can

turn a Maxwell foe tae dead,' " Gordie's grin broadened when, behind him, one of his men finished reciting the newest verse of the most popular Border ballad. "What say ye tae that, Douglas? Methinks the balladeers would be turning a different phrase if they saw ye thus. Or mayhap they were referring tae the fear ye inspire when ye've got yer clothes *on*? Truth tae tell, ye dinna look so fearsome right now."

" 'Tis the poor lighting," Connor growled, "or yer notoriously bad eyesight. If I'd me sword in hand, ye'd be spouting something entirely different. Like yer entrails o'er the ground after me blade sliced them out."

Gordie's laughter was rich and thick; the point of the sword tremored against Connor's throat. "Do ye think it, Douglas?"

"Nay, Maxwell, I *ken* it."

The force of his statement made Gabrielle stir restlessly against his side. Connor stilled expectantly, as did Gordie and his men. To their surprise, and Connor's relief, the lass did not awaken. He'd no desire for her to open her eyes and find her kilt-draped body being ogled by a ragged-looking band of reivers.

Connor's stomach muscles fisted when, as though following the path of his thoughts, Gordie's attention shifted to Gabrielle. The man's green eyes narrowed, shrewdly raking over what he could see of her form. And Gordie could see far too much of her body for Connor's piece of mind!

"The Carelton wench?"

Connor nodded tensely. "Aye."

" 'Tis nae the way I expected tae meet me long-lost relative."

4 FREE BOOKS

These books worth almost $20, are yours without cost or obligation when you fill out and mail this certificate.
(If the certificate is missing below, write to: Zebra Home Subscription Service, Inc., 120 Brighton Road, P.O. Box 5214, Clifton, New Jersey 07015-5214)

Complete and mail this card to receive 4 Free books!

YES! Please send me 4 Zebra Lovegram Historical Romances without cost or obligation. I understand that each month thereafter I will be able to preview 4 new Zebra Lovegram Historical Romances FREE for 10 days. Then if I decide to keep them, I will pay the money-saving preferred publisher's price of just $4.00 each...a total of $16. That's almost $4 less than the regular publisher's price, and there is never any additional charge for shipping and handling. I may return any shipment within 10 days and owe nothing, and I may cancel this subscription at any time. The 4 FREE books will be mine to keep in any case.

Name _____

Address _____ Apt. _____

City _____ State _____ Zip _____

Telephone ( ) _____

Signature _____
(If under 18, parent or guardian must sign.)

LF0396

Terms, offer and prices subject to change without notice. Subscription subject to acceptance by Zebra Home Subscription Service, Inc.. Zebra Home Subscription Service, Inc. reserves the right to reject any order or cancel any subscription.

A $19.96 value... absolutely FREE with no obligation to buy anything, ever!

ZEBRA HOME SUBSCRIPTION SERVICE, INC.

120 BRIGHTON ROAD

P.O. BOX 5214

CLIFTON, NEW JERSEY 07015-5214

"If I'd had me way, ye'd nae have met her at all."

Gordie shrugged. "She's a . . . er, fair buxom lass," he observed. Did Gordie's voice reflect appreciation or distaste? Connor wondered. He could not tell; the man's stoic expression and keen gaze gave nothing away. "She doesna look like a Maxwell."

"Aye, if ye ask me," grumbled one of Gordie's men, "she looks maun like a Johnstone."

"Who asked ye?" Connor growled. Wet moss and leaves crunched under bootheels as the man took a quick step back under the heat of The Black Douglas's glare. Again, Gabrielle shifted against Connor in her sleep, this time murmuring something unintelligible beneath her breath.

Gordie seemed unfazed by the exchange between Connor and his man. As though he was talking to himself as much as to Connor, he finally observed aloud, "She's for sure a deep sleeper."

"Aye," Connor grudgingly acknowledged, "so 'twould seem."

"Ye mean ye dinna ken it a'fore now?"

"And how would I be doing that, Maxwell? The lass has ne'er been sleeping when she's with me a'fore this."

Gordie's gaze narrowed, his green eyes darkening as his fingers wrapped more tightly around the hilt of his sword. The tip of the blade dug a wee bit more firmly into the tender skin of Connor's neck; he could feel another hot drop of blood trickle down the side of his neck.

" 'Tis sorry I am tae be hearing that, Douglas," Gordie said, yet in truth he sounded anything but. "A telling admission, dinna ye think? I wonder how 'twill sit with me da."

One of the men chuckled. When Gordie made no gesture to silence him, a few others joined in.

As the men's mirth died down, Gordie again directed the crux of his attention on Connor. Or, more accurately, on Gabrielle. The expression on the man's face was one of unabashed interest.

The muscles in Connor's jaw knotted. Not for the first time did he fervently wish he could reach his sword before his enemy slit his throat.

"The lass needs be woken. I'd do the chore meself, but I'm of a mind that ye'd nae like me methods," said Gordie, his voice far too calm for Connor's liking. "We ride in five minutes. We'll nae reach Caerlaverock a'fore sunrise, but if we ride hard, 'twill be less. Wake the lass and get her clothed, Douglas. Be quick aboot it lest I think ye need help."

Gordie bent and retrieved Connor's sword, which he'd kicked teasingly out of reach before waking Connor, then straightened and turned his attention on his men. He murmured something and the band stepped back a few feet, respectfully facing the opposite direction.

The men, Connor was quick to notice, remained within hearing distance, with Gordie Maxwell closest of all. One wrong move and the ragged-looking pack would be upon him in a moment—with the huge, deadly blade of more than one Jedburgh axe finding its mark in his body.

Connor raked the fingers of his free hand through his tousled black hair. Over the peaks of the trees, he saw the sky was beginning to brighten from forbidding black to a bleak, dull shade of gray.

Moss and leaves rustled when he shook his head in disgust. He was naked, unarmed. What kind of defense could he provide the lady sleeping with such sweet innocence against his side? A pathetically poor one, that's what kind. Wouldn't the Borderers who wrote those dreaded ballads not love to see The Black Douglas thus?

The way Gabrielle continued to sleep was a silent yet bitter condemnation. Even so deep in slumber, she curled against him like a child, instinctively trusting him to guard and protect her.

That he couldn't do either was grating to Connor's already chaffed nerves.

God's teeth, there was no help for it. With the Maxwell and his men waiting impatiently, he'd no choice but to do as Gordie bid and wake the lass up.

"Gabby?" He nudged her shoulder, all the while trying not to notice how soft and warm her skin felt beneath his palm. Her inky lashes flickered against her cheeks, but her eyes remained closed, her expression bairnishly peaceful.

"Gabby!" He nudged her a wee bit harder. "Och, sweeting, please, 'tis time tae wake up."

"Who—? Wha—?" The confused furrow between her eyebrows smoothed and she smiled warmly. "Oh, 'tis only you, Connor." With the back of her fist, she muffled a yawn. Connor swallowed hard when her wonderfully full curves pressed provocatively against him as she arched her spine and stretched. "For a moment I thought . . . well, I suppose it doesn't matter what I thought, does it? Is it morning already?"

"Aye, lass, almost."

"And what a wonderful morning 'tis. I feel so . . . so *relaxed.*" Her grin was wicked. "Truth to tell, m'lord, I think I could doze here in your arms for the better part of the day. What say you to that? Do you think 'tis possible? Never before have I felt so cherished and safe as I do right now—"

Her words stabbed through Connor like the finely honed blade of the dagger one of the Maxwell men had seen fit to appropriate from the cuff of Connor's worn leather boot while the latter had been sleeping.

"Now listen tae me, Gabby," Connor said, his voice stern as he cut her ruminations short, "and listen well. 'Tis imperative ye follow me instructions without question. Now, I dinna want ye tae fash yeself aboot it, but the fact is, we've . . . er, a wee bit of a problem. Ye need tae get up and get dressed. Quickly. Whilst they still be giving ye the chance tae do it in relative privacy. Methinks the Maxwell willna extend his generosity long; we maun accept it whilst we can."

Gabrielle gulped, her green eyes widening in alarm. "Did you say *Maxwell?!*"

"Good God, lass, will ye lower yer voice? Aye, 'tis exactly what I said. Maxwell." Connor had to hurriedly shield her eyes with his big hand when her horrified gaze seemed drawn to the area where Gordie Maxwell and his men waited. "Nay, dinna look o'er there, 'twill only upset ye. Trust me, 'tis a maun disheartening sight. Just do as I say and dress yeself quickly. I dinna like at all the way a few of those men were gawking at ye whilst ye slept. Those trews arena maun better, but at least they'll cover ye."

"Gawking?" Gabrielle asked, startled. Had she gotten no further than that part of his words? Connor wondered. Clutching the kilt modestly over her breasts, she sat up as gracefully as she could. With her right hand she swept the thick mane of love-tangled black hair back from her face until it tumbled silkily down her back. "Did you say some of those men were gawking? At *me?*"

Connor gritted his teeth. 'Twas no time for conversation, but he recognized the determined expression on Gabrielle's face and knew she would not rest until her question had been answered.

He set about doing so in the shortest manner possible. "Aye, a few were most assuredly gawking," he admitted grudgingly. "Me kilt is goodly sized, and 'tis thankful I be that I thought to toss some of it o'er us as we slept, but it's nae *that* big. There was a fair deal of ye tae gawk at, lass." A scowl creased his brow, and something in her eyes suddenly made speed lose a wee bit of its relevance to the strong, tightening fist of emotion—could it be jealousy?—clenching and unclenching in his stomach. Curiosity suddenly plagued his mind. "Now that I think upon it, lass," he added thoughtfully, "ye dinna sound like ye're offended."

"I'm *not* offended. Just the opposite, I'm quite flattered. I've never been gawked at before, and I must admit it's a most complimentary feeling. You Scots certainly have a very distinct criterion for physical appeal than the ones I'm accustomed to. Truth to tell, 'tis a welcome change." Gabrielle shook her head and, as though to herself, her voice a pitch higher than normal, repeated in surprise, "Those men were gawking. At *me.* Ha! What would Elizabeth have to say about *that?!*"

The grin that curved over Gabrielle's lips was full and appealing. He was captivated by it.

As though sensing Connor's distracted attention, Gordie Maxwell quickly interceded to remind both Gabrielle and Connor of his unwelcome presence. From over his shoulder, he growled threateningly, "Yer time is running short, Douglas. We leave in three maun minutes. Whether ye both be dressed or nae makes nae difference tae me. I maun admit, though, 'twould make an interesting sight tae see the notorious Black Douglas riding intae Caerlaverock as naked as the day he was born. Compared tae the other dribble I've heard sung of ye lately, methinks the ballads *that* sight would inspire may actually be worth lending an ear tae!"

Connor swore in Gaelic as he reached over Gabrielle and gathered up their clothes. He dumped them in a wrinkled heap in his lap, sorting his from hers as quickly as possible.

His fingers closed around the woolen trews he'd taken great pleasure in stripping Gabrielle of, and he swallowed back a groan. He remembered the way they clung to her hips and thighs, outlining every lush curve. How many stares would this woman's delectable body get with *those* on? A more important question was how far he could stretch his self-control. Could he hold his temper in check if any of the men who'd been ogling her tried to do so again, or worse . . . ?

His fingers clenched into fists around the wool as he thrust the trews at Gabrielle. Pushing the words through tightly gritted teeth, he said, "Och, dinna dally, lass. Get yerself dressed and do it quickly. Maxwells arena reputed for their patience."

"Then what *are* they reputed for?" Gabrielle asked as she accepted the bundle of clothes. Casting surreptitious glances at the men's backs, she yanked the tunic over her head.

"Ye dinna want to ken," Connor muttered as he pulled his own tunic on. The kilt would have to wait; at the moment, it was draped prudently under and around Gabrielle's naked lap. Connor had no urge to reclaim the garment yet. It would be just his luck to have one of the Maxwells choose such an inopportune moment to glance back at them. As far as he was concerned, they'd seen far more of Gabrielle than he was comfortable with.

Should any of the men try to ogle her while she dressed, Connor knew he would loose the tattered reins of his composure and challenge the man. Unarmed as he was, the outcome of such a skirmish was dangerously preordained.

Och! what good would he be to the lass if he was lying bleeding on the ground? For that matter, what good was he to the lass now?

Connor winced. Like the point of Gordie's sword had pricked the tender flesh of his throat, the last thought pricked his pride in a way he'd never imagined possible. Without realizing he was doing it, he fingered the scratch on his neck. The blood had begun to dry; the newly formed scab felt warm and rough against his fingertips.

Gabrielle had pulled on the trews and was in the middle of tugging on the oversize boots when a disturbance in the woods, quite close to the left of where the Maxwell and his men stood, drew her attention.

Gabrielle glanced at Connor, but he simply frowned and shook his head.

"Keep yer filthy hands off me, ye . . . ye . . . stinking *Maxwell!*" The feminine grouse was followed by a harsh, masculine grunt. "Ye think *that* hurts? Wait! 'Tis but a wee scratch compared to what I'll be giving ye if ye dinna unhand me, and unhand me *now!*"

"Ella?" Gabrielle and Connor sighed the name in unison, yet their voices held entirely different inflections; Gabrielle's was a sigh of relief, Connor's one of utter frustration.

Careful to still keep The Black Douglas in his vision—one could never, *never* trust a Douglas, even an unarmed one—Gordie shifted the brunt of his attention to the commotion. One eyebrow cocked in surprise when he saw a slender girl with flaming red hair being tossed, literally, out from behind a thick oak tree trunk.

Ella landed on her backside with a thump and a curse at the big man who strode casually out of the woods behind her. The big man stopped, rubbed his shin briefly with the calf of his other leg, winced, then went over to Gordie.

In less than a second, Ella was on her feet and furiously dogging his steps, a mere pace behind him.

"Oh, no." Gabrielle swallowed back a groan. That Ella was about to do something stupid was evident in the icy spark of anger in the girl's blue eye and the determined tightness of her jawline.

As Gabrielle watched, Ella swung back her foot and delivered to the back of the offender's knee another bone-jarring kick. The man howled, stumbled against Gordie, then quickly regained his balance and spun on his heel. His dark-green eyes flashed with anger as his right hand went for his sword.

Gabrielle didn't think about what she was doing, nor the consequences of doing it, she simply flung Connor's kilt at him, even as she sprang into motion.

It took four running steps to reach them. For a big woman, she'd enough Maxwell blood coursing through her veins to be unexpectedly quick on her feet.

By the time she reached Ella's side, the angry man's free hand was making an arch toward the girl's defiantly upturned cheek. Gabrielle stepped between the two in time to receive the brunt of the blow. The man's open palm collided painfully with her shoulder.

She staggered sideways a step under the force of the impact, grunting despite her resolve not to when a ripple of pain quivered down her arm and at the same time shot across her neck to lance through the other shoulder.

Her attacker was not tall, nor was Gabrielle short. They stood on eye-level, glowering at each other.

"Does hitting a poor, defenseless woman make you feel like more of a man?" Gabrielle demanded scornfully, ignoring the throbbing pain in her shoulder. Her hands, tightly fisted, were planted with defiance atop her hips as she glared into eyes equally as green as her own.

"*Defenseless?*" the man roared. A thick blue vein pounded in the center of his forehead, and the outer corner of his left eye twitched in time with it. "The bitch tried tae run me through with her sword when I found her. Then, after I finally wrestled the weapon away, she kicked me. Hard. *Twice.* I dinna call that defenseless!"

Gabrielle's gaze raked the man's sturdy body. "Are you a Maxwell?"

"Aye, Roy Maxwell, and proud of it!"

"Is it only you, or are all Maxwells afraid of being kicked by a girl? A girl who is," she hastened to add, "by your own admission, unarmed?"

The second the words had slipped off her tongue, Gabrielle knew that she should have resisted the urge and bitten them back. Baiting the enemy was never wise, especially when one had no means with which to back up one's words and, more importantly, the enemy in question was a seasoned reiver from one of the most brutal riding families on either side of the Border. By the time she realized her mistake, of course, it was far too late to correct it.

A pregnant pause hung heavily in the cool morning air; it was broken by the sparkle of Ella's laughter. The sound severed the tension and was quickly joined by more than one husky chuckle from the band of Maxwell men.

"Och! fancy that," Ella said in a taunting tone that made Gabrielle wince. Thanks to the men's encouraging reaction, the girl had apparently grown bold. That Ella was enjoying herself, Gabrielle hadn't a doubt. "A big, strong Maxwell afraid of being kicked by a wee lass such as m'self. Tsk, tsk, tsk. Yer da would be ashamed of ye, Roy, truly he would. And speaking of Johnny Maxwell . . . where is the auld brute?"

Roy Maxwell's attention narrowed on Ella. The vein in his forehead seemed to thicken even as his eyes narrowed to furious green slits.

Gordie, sensing his younger brother's mounting ire, answered before Roy had the chance.

"Last I saw, he was being slashed up by yer aunt's sharp tongue, lass."

"Ah, I see," Ella said, and nodded almost sympathetically. Almost. Her attention never left Roy. "Like father, like— *Eek!*"

Roy made a grab for Ella's wrist. The girl, however, was much too quick for him; she quickly stepped behind Gabrielle. Cursing under his breath, Roy tried to go after her, but Gabrielle squared her shoulders and took a sidestep to block him. A warm tingle of awareness along the right side of her body told her without glancing in that direction that Connor had put on his kilt and was now standing by her side. His presence comforted Gabrielle in ways she didn't dare try to understand.

"Leave her alone, Maxwell," Connor growled, and the words made Roy stop cold. "Gabrielle is right, the lass isna armed, she canna harm ye."

A change came over the Maxwell men. They were not chuckling now, nor even smiling. Instead, they regarded The Black Douglas with the sharp, wary eyes that a reiver of his stature and reputation deserved.

The previous tension returned in force; it electrified the early morning air until Gabrielle could have sworn she felt it crackle against her skin.

She glanced at Connor. Was it only an hour ago she'd seen this man's face relaxed, his eyes dark and sparkling with passion? Aye, it surely was. His expression was no longer calm, and the glint in his gray eyes would never be mistaken for passion as his narrowed gaze, sharp and piercing, assessively scanned the Maxwells.

Gabrielle swallowed hard and resisted the urge to take a step backward.

So *this* was the man whom ballads had been written about. It was her first real glimpse of the Border reiver side of Connor Douglas. Gabrielle knew she'd be lying if she said she didn't admit to feeling a shard of intimidation shoot through her.

She'd an inkling it was a feeling she shared with quite a few of the Maxwell men; two of whom, while they bravely stood their ground, shifted their weight uneasily from one foot to the other. Was it any wonder?!

Hard.

Cold.

Powerful, determined, and undeniably ruthless.

All those words and more summed up her impression of The Black Douglas. Even unarmed, his presence radiated strength and authority. Standing nearly a head taller than his rivals, his virile form, harshly chiseled features, and chilly gray eyes commanded attention, respect, and more than a little awe.

Gabrielle felt Ella squirm behind her. Reaching back, she swatted the girl on the bottom to get her to be still.

It was Gordie who finally spoke. "Enough o' yer bickering, they'll be maun than enough time for it later. Right now, we ride. As 'tis, Da and Colin should reach the keep hours sooner." He shifted his attention first to his brother, then to one of his men. "Roy, fetch their horses. Magnus, get some rope. Seamus and the rest of ye, stand ready tae tie them ontae their mounts. Hostages so distinguished dinna come 'round often. Take care that we dinna lose them."

The area was suddenly full of activity as the men hurried to do Gordie Maxwell's bidding.

Four of the Maxwell men placed themselves around the Douglas trio, guarding to make sure no chance of escape was available.

Gabrielle leaned close to Connor and whispered, "It doesn't look good for us, does it?"

"Nay, nae at all," he replied, his distant tone indicating his thoughts lay elsewhere. His gaze, she noticed, was still on Gordie Maxwell. His scowl was deep.

Gabrielle nibbled her lower lip and mirrored his frown. Oh, if only she could pretend she was unaware of who was to blame for this entire mess! Herself. Who else? If she hadn't been so stubborn, hadn't surrendered to what she felt was her moral obligation and convinced Ella to help her rescue poor old Mairghread . . .

A stab of guilt sliced through Gabrielle. "What will happen to us now, m'lord?"

"We'll be ransomed, of course. What else?" It was Ella who answered.

Gabrielle glanced back at the girl. "Ransomed?"

Ella nodded. " 'Tis when a family pays the person who stole ye tae give ye back, don't ye ken?"

"Aye, I think I, er, 'ken.' " Gabrielle's frown deepened thoughtfully.

"Spending any time amongst Maxwells isnae something tae be looked upon fondly," Ella agreed. Her tone softened; if she didn't know better, Gabrielle would have sworn the girl was trying to comfort her. "Dinna worry, we'll be with them but a short time, methinks. Gilby will see tae it the ransom is paid posthaste."

"Aye, for you and Connor mayhap."

The girl scowled at her. "Eh?"

"Until I wed, I'm a ward of the English court,

Ella. Nay, don't frown at me like that. I can see exactly what you're thinking, and I'll tell you right now, you're wrong. Elizabeth's purse strings are tighter than her corset laces. She won't pay so much as a shilling to get me back."

"But—"

Whatever Ella was about to say was cut short when Roy led the horses toward them.

The one named Magnus passed out strips of rope to the men who'd been standing guard. Gordie gave a brief nod, and the men stepped over to the prisoners and began tying their hands in front of them.

"Ouch! have a care, mon!" Ella snapped. "Must ye be so rough?" The man binding her was Roy; the fierce scowl that creased his brow said he was in no mood to be gentle.

Luckily, the guard who tied Gabrielle's wrists with the thick, rough, scratchy piece of rope was not so cruel. The knots were competent but the binding was not so tight as to cut off circulation to her hands and fingers. She chanced giving the guard a quick smile of gratitude, and was surprised when he blushed before turning hastily away.

Binding the women had been a chore easily carried out. Tying up The Black Douglas was something else again. Two men approached him warily for the task. Connor did not hold out his hands in resignation, the way Gabrielle had done; instead, like Ella, he kept his elbows locked and his arms held down rigidly at his sides. Roy had forced Ella's arms in front of her. The hard set of Connor's jaw and even harder look in his eyes challenged the men who'd approached him to do the same.

The two men hesitated, exchanging an uneasy

glance. Neither looked willing to commence the struggle it would undoubtedly take to get the ropes in place.

Roy was leading Ella—no, make that *dragging*—over to her horse when Connor, who'd been glaring at the two men standing nervously in front of him, shifted his attention to Gordie Maxwell. "Is this necessary?"

"Aye, 'tis." Gordie smiled coldly. "Ye're a slippery fox, Douglas, and well e'eryone on both sides of the Border kens it. Surely ye dinna think me so daft I'd let ye ride free! Were I in yer situation . . . untied, the potential for escape would be maun too great tae resist. 'Tis something I dinna dare risk."

The hard square of Connor's jaw lifted at a proud angle that was reflected by the glint in his gray eyes. "What if I offered ye me word I'd nae escape?"

"Do ye think I'd believe that?"

"Do ye have a reason nae tae? Is yer memory so short ye've already forgotten last winter?"

"I've forgotten naught," Gordie replied, his tone vaguely insulted.

Connor nodded briskly. "Then ye remember the Day o' Truce? Ye remember me taking yer word for repayment of fines owed for yer worst raid on Bracklenaer ever, when instead I could have demanded a pledge?"

"Aye," Gordie answered thoughtfully, "I remember. I maun admit, I've always wondered at yer reasoning, Douglas. 'Twas a foolhardy thing tae do."

"I disagree. Ye may be a Maxwell, and therefore me bitter rival, but ye're also a Scotsman, and Scotsmen are men of their word. As a rival, ye've proved yerself maun worthy of respect. Against me own men's advice, I trusted ye word then, and ne'er once did I doubt ye would pay the shillings owed in the spring, just as ye promised ye would."

"And pay them, I did."

"Exactly."

Gordie's frown deepened as he lifted his chin and scratched at the thickly red-bearded underside. His gaze raked Connor assessively, then shifted to the two men who awaited his orders. "Put the ropes away and let him ride free. But"— he glared at the two men to drive the point of his next words home—"ride close and guard him well. Seamus, ye ride close tae me newly discovered kin. If the mon even thinks about trying tae escape . . ."

The unfinished threat hung heavily in the air, more potent for what it *didn't* say.

As though he was displeased with his own decision, Gordie spun on his heel and faced his angry brother.

"Are ye insane?!" Roy roared. "He's a *Douglas! And nae just any Douglas, but The Black Douglas!*"

"Aye, I ken it, Roy, but there are things ye be tae young tae understand yet. For example . . ." Gordie's voice faded as he draped his arm around Roy's neck and led him away.

A different man than the one who had shackled her hands came up to Gabrielle and, taking her by the arm, guided her toward her horse. She put up no resistance. Truly, she was too shocked by what had transpired since Connor had awakened her to even consider it.

Ten

Dark and murky, the dungeon was located deep in the bowels of Caerlaverock. The cell in which Connor and Ella had been locked more than an hour ago was small and cramped. A narrow, slitlike window in the upper portion of the far wall—much too high to reach, even with Ella on his shoulders, Connor had been quick to discover—let in a modicum of midafternoon sunlight.

If he strained, Connor could see a patch of the sky. While the night's storm had dissipated somewhat, it hadn't entirely abated. Threatening clouds hung in the sky like thick, dark swatches of wool. The afternoon looked gray and dingy, as unpromising as his mood. The floor upon which he sat was as cold and hard as the stone wall against which he leaned his back.

The muscles around his heart clenched into a tight fist when he thought about Gabrielle. He'd not seen her since reaching the Maxwell stronghold, when he and Ella had been hauled down to the dungeon while Gabrielle had been taken . . .

Where?

He knew not, nor did he dare to guess at what

the Maxwells had done with her. A shiver coursed icily down his spine. The possibilities were too gruesome to contemplate.

Lord, how he wished he knew what was going on elsewhere in this cursed keep!

Unfortunately, the dungeon was situated too far below the ground floor for them to hear any activity coming from above. Connor was sure there was a good deal of noise and commotion going on up there somewhere, but the thick stones and mortar deadened any noise. And all of it centered around Gabrielle.

To distract his mind from unwelcome images, he concentrated on the sound of Ella's bootheels echoing crisply off frigid stone as she paced restlessly in front of him.

"Ye ken, of course, 'tis only thanks tae a Maxwell—may the devil roast the lot of 'em in hell for all eternity!—that a Douglas could find himself in a scrape such as this. I swear there's nae been a moment's rest for our poor, weary clan since those detestable Maxwells stole that ugly auld nag near on twa centuries ago!"

"Och! lass, ye dinna ken what ye're talking aboot. That horse was a prime specimen. 'Twas nae auld, nae ugly, and certainly *nae* a nag. 'Twas a maun fine example of its breed, well worth fighting o'er. Our ancestors were right tae want the beastie back at all costs."

"Dinna be such a simpleton, Cousin." Ella shook her head, gave forth a sigh of exaggerated impatience at the same time she sent Connor an indignant glance from the corner of her eye. " 'Tis our great-aunt Ailean I be referring tae," she explained with forced patience, *"nae* the fine beast lifted from Bracklenaer on the same midnight raid. The horse was recovered quickly enough. Nay, whilst the theft of the beastie may have started the feud, 'twas Ailean who kindled the grudge between Douglas and Maxwell by choosing tae stay and marry intae the hated clan."

"Had she a choice?" Connor shook his head and frowned. "If so, I dinna see it. Oh, aye, she could have returned tae Bracklenaer, but e'en if she did, how many Douglases do ye think would have wanted tae take tae wife a lass so obviously soiled by a Maxwell? Nae self-respecting one, I'll tell ye that for nothing. Nae doubt the safety of the bairn that Lachlann Maxwell had already planted in her belly weighed heavily on her mind, and her decision tae stay at Caerlaverock."

"Mayhap, but nae matter what the reason, I still think 'twas a foolhardy decision. One that, in its thoughtlessness, has caused her Douglas descendants—*us!*—enormous trouble and hardship e'er since!"

"Ella—"

"She was ne'er happy at Caerlaverock," a third voice interceded. "I dinna ken if that be any consolation to ye, but 'tis true."

Ella and Connor jerked their attention to the door, and the direction from which the voice had come. A window was embedded in the upper portion of the thick oak panel. The "window," such as it was, consisted of a small, lopsided square. The barred opening wasn't even large enough for Ella to shimmy through . . .

The shadows clinging to the window and the narrow hallway that lay just outside of it were complete.

"Who's there?" Connor demanded as he shoved himself to his feet. He took a step forward, positioning himself protectively between Ella and the door.

There was a beat of hesitation, and then the voice asked in an almost timid pitch, "Are ye The Black Douglas?"

Ella came up close behind Connor and whispered in his ear, "From the sounds, 'tis naught but a bairn."

He nodded, having already determined as much himself. He guessed the intruder's age to be between seven and nine years.

"Did ye hear me? I asked if ye be The Black Douglas." This time there wasn't a thread of timidity in the voice.

A layer of solid oak and handful of strong iron bars went a long way toward fostering false courage, Connor thought as he glared at both. "Aye," he growled finally, " 'tis what they call me, howe'er I'm nae, nor have I e'er been or claimed tae be, *The* Black Douglas. I'm but a descendant poorly nicknamed. Who be asking?"

An excited giggle drifted through the window, ricocheting throughout the cell. The high, sharp pitch made Connor wince as it reverberated off the bare stone walls. "Gordie said he'd done it, ye ken, but I dinna believe him. Yet here's proof! Imagine, the notorious Black Douglas safely locked away in Caerlaverock's dungeon." The boy paused long enough to giggle again; the sound was stifled, as though he'd muffled it with his hand at the last second. "Och! but is this nae a fine day for the Maxwell!"

Notorious, Connor thought, and gritted his teeth. How had one godforsaken exploit credited him with such a following? Not for the first time did he wish The Devil, Alasdair Gray, had remained unmarried; now there was a man whose reputation was earned by *many* deeds!

Connor, who'd let his gaze wander to a shadowy corner of the cell, the one where noises that sounded unpleasantly like small claws—*rats?*—scratching upon hard stone emanated, now refocused his attention on the door. Rather, he shifted his concentration to the boy standing in the murky hallway just outside of it.

A scowl etched deep creases between Connor's eyebrows. Could he turn this unexpected visit to his own advantage? 'Twas rumored a Douglas could be quite charming when he put his mind to the task. Given the proper circumstances, they could even go so far as to smoothly apply that charm in the direction of a hated Maxwell . . .

Gabrielle shifted upon the hard, narrow bench. Linking her fingers together, she straightened her spine, lifted her chin, and rested her hands atop the table in Caerlaverock's great hall. She doubted the gesture looked as casual as she intended for it to. Her insides were churning and, beneath the table where no one could see, her knees trembled against each other. Anxiety twisted in her stomach, gnawing at her from the inside out.

An untended fire smoldered lamely in the stone hearth to her left. Gabrielle felt none of its meager heat; the half dozen accusing stares, five from the men seated upon the bench opposite her, chilled her to the bone.

She recognized only Gordie Maxwell and his brother Roy. The eldest among them—she guessed his age to be at least two score older than

both Maxwells—sat between the two brothers.
The man's cheekbones, sharply carved above the
line of his full red-gray beard, combined with his
narrow forehead, weather-creased brow, and
short, stocky, solidly built frame stamped him a
Maxwell.

There was never a doubt in Gabrielle's mind
as to the older man's identity. Johnny Maxwell.
Father of Gordie and Roy. Laird of Clan Maxwell.
Owner of Caerlaverock. Who else *could* he be?

The remaining two men seated across from her
were strangers; she gave them only a brief glance
before forcing her attention back to Johnny Maxwell. At least her *physical* attention rested on the
Maxwell. Mentally, she was having a most difficult
time concentrating on anyone besides the sixth
man in the hall.

He stood next to the hearth, one broad shoulder resting negligently against the harshly chiseled stone. Gabrielle was very much aware of
when the sixth man's hands moved from hanging
limply at his sides to behind his back.

In two long strides he cleared the distance between them, moving to stand towering over the
head of the table. He was close enough that, were
she to move her elbow only a few inches to the
side, it would graze the rock-hard side of his
kilted thigh.

A chill skated down Gabrielle's spine. She need
not glance up to know the sixth man was staring
at her, and staring hard. She could feel his gaze,
and the feel of it was as troubling as it was confusing. Stubbornly, she refused to glance away
from Johnny Maxwell, even though her attention
wanted badly to stray.

She'd looked directly at him only once since

the two guards standing just outside the door had led her into the great hall. Even now, she thought she could still feel those odd, hot and cold shock waves rippling through her.

The man was tall and broad, with shaggy black hair that reached past the broad shelf of his shoulders and cold, piercing gray eyes. His cheekbones were sharp and well defined, his jaw hard and square. His lips were thin and sensuously carved. If one looked closely, one could detect a tiny dimple in the center of his stubble-dusted chin. Down to even that small detail, he was an exact duplicate of Connor Douglas.

A *duplicate*, Gabrielle reminded herself forcefully. A nerve-shatteringly accurate one, aye, but an imitation all the same.

The man, she soon realized, had to be Colin Douglas, Connor's twin. It was he who finally broke what was swiftly becoming a thick, tension-riddled silence. Not in words, but in deed.

From the sporran hanging at his waist, Colin took out a sheepskin pouch. With a flick of his wrist he tossed the pouch onto the table, where it landed with a rattle and clank directly in front of Johnny Maxwell. A few coins spilled out of the loosely tied opening.

Johnny Maxwell licked his parched lips and quickly plucked up the stray silver disks. He tucked them back into the pouch, then, with a sharp tug on the leather laces, tied it securely shut. "By all that's holy, I swear if there be so maun as a pence missing, mon—" His tone brooked no nonsense as he enclosed the pouch in his big fist.

" 'Tis all there, as we agreed," Colin interrupted. To Gabrielle's ear, his tone sounded too low, too even to be anything but offended at the insinuation he was trying to cheat his rival by a single coin. Oh, aye, he was a Douglas all right. "Count it yerself if ye dinna believe me. But be quick aboot it. I've a bride tae whisk back to Gael-side a'fore this day is o'er."

He looked like Connor, but he did not sound like him. Colin's voice was a pitch higher, and a good deal rougher; the timbre of it scratched down Gabrielle's spine like fingernails scraping slowly down a slab of slate.

Her heart skipped a heavy beat, then thudded to vibrant life. The echo of it, pounding loudly in her ears, sounded like repeating claps of thunder. She would have swallowed hard, maybe even have attempted to speak a protest, but she found she suddenly hadn't enough moisture left in her mouth for either. Flexing her fingers, she tightened them around each other until her knuckles were white and ached from the strain of her grip. It was either that or let these men see how badly her hands had begun to shake.

Pursing his lips, Johnny bounced the pouch in his hand, as though he could tell the exact amount it contained merely by hefting it and hearing the muffled jingle as the coins clattered inside. The frown that had drawn his bushy red eyebrows together eased, and a glimmer of respect darkened his eyes. "Ye're many things, Colin Douglas. A scoundrel and a rogue tae name but two. Howe'er, a cheat isna one of them."

Johnny's glance shifted to Gabrielle and his green eyes narrowed. He stood, then walked around the table, stopping at her side. His hand felt big and hot as he placed it in the crook of her arm and tugged her to her feet.

Despite her resolve not to, she felt her cheeks suffuse with color when all six men's attention shifted to focus exclusively on her. If she'd ever wondered what the prized goose displayed prominently on fair day felt like, now she knew. Gritting her teeth, she willed strength to flow into knees that felt watery and weak, threatening to buckle out from under her at any second as she stepped over the bench and stood beside Johnny Maxwell.

"As ye can see," Johnny said to Colin, "a Maxwell is equally as trustworthy. For payment in full, I present tae ye the Lady Gabrielle Carelton."

Gabrielle's gaze locked with Colin's. As she'd expected, his eyes were the same blue-gray shade as his twin's, fringed by a thick, dark sweep of inky lashes.

There, the similarity began and ended.

Even at his angriest, Connor's eyes glistened with an inner warmth and lust for life. Colin's gaze, on the other hand, was hard and cold, calculating and devoid of emotion as it swept her from head to toe. A humorless grin tugged at one corner of his mouth, a mouth that looked far too much like his twin's for her peace of mind. The way he looked at her sent a shiver down her spine.

She staggered forward a step when Johnny Maxwell splayed his big palm in the center of her back and nudged her forward. It took supreme effort for Gabrielle to force her knees to lock, thereby avoiding by a mere fraction the embarrassment of falling against the hard, chiseled width of Colin Douglas's chest.

Colin's gaze shifted dismissively, fixing on a point just past her shoulder. "Are ye sure 'tis the right lass ye're giving me, Johnny? Except for her green eyes and the . . . er, stockiness of her build, she doesna look like any Maxwell I've e'er laid eyes on."

"Aye, and well I ken it," Johnny replied. It grated on her nerves the way the older man sounded so proud of that fact. "Howe'er, ye need remember that a goodly dose of Sassenach blood o'er the decades has diluted her fine Maxwell lineage."

" 'Tis the lass Queen Elizabeth sent tae wed ye," Gordie Maxwell interjected. "Dinna doubt it, mon."

Roy nodded his shaggy red head in agreement and added gruffly, "Aye, that she is. With me own twa eyes, I saw her laying naked as the day she was born in yer brother's arms. If that doesna prove she's Gabrielle Carelton, nothing can."

A muscle twitched in the base of Colin's jaw. That and the darkening of his stormy gray eyes were his only outward reactions to Roy's admission. It was enough to make Gabrielle shift uneasily. Was her imagination running away with her, or could she really sense a swirl of anger churning just beneath Colin Douglas's outwardly placid surface?

Without warning, Colin reached out and coiled his fingers around her upper arm. His grip was bitingly tight. Gabrielle gasped sharply and winced. She tried to wrench her arm free, but quickly gave up when she was rewarded by a still tighter squeeze from his thick, powerful fingers.

"I thank ye for the help, Maxwell," Colin said, and nodded briskly at Johnny Maxwell. "Now that our business is concluded, I bid ye good day."

That said, Colin turned on his heel and, yanking Gabrielle in step beside him, headed toward the arched stone doorway leading out of the great hall. His bootheels echoed crisply atop the bare stone floor.

Gabrielle's spirits plummeted with each forced step that led closer to her departure from Caerlaverock. Her thoughts whirlwinded helplessly.

Connor was being held prisoner somewhere within these thick stone walls; if she allowed herself to be taken away, how could she ever hope to find him and set him free? Not that she stood a chance of being able to accomplish such a feat, she knew. How could she forget what had happened when she attempted much the same thing for Mairghread! Still, at least while she was being held under the same roof, she stood a *chance*, no matter how slim, of being able to liberate him. Away from Caerlaverock, she could do naught.

And what of Ella?

Gabrielle could not in all good conscience allow the girl to remain a prisoner of the dreaded Maxwell if she could in some way prevent it. Heaven alone knew what these ruffians would do to such a comely lass, especially a girl who was so close a relation to their arch rival, The Black Douglas.

Sweet Lord, she had to do something, anything, and do it quickly. *But what?*

The question had no more entered Gabrielle's mind when they reached the threshold. She wasn't a bit closer to coming up with an answer when she heard a harsh rumble echo out from behind. It was the sound of Johnny Maxwell clearing his throat.

The guards standing in wait outside the doorway stepped forward, blocking the exit.

Colin hauled Gabrielle to an abrupt stop.

The two guards who'd been posted there earlier had been joined by ten more. All had swords drawn, the sharp steel points aimed with deadly precision at various parts of Colin Douglas's anatomy. Gabrielle hadn't a doubt that at Johnny Maxwell's command they would not hesitate to use those weapons to slice both her and Colin Douglas to ribbons.

Colin let go of her arm and spun around to face his adversary.

Gabrielle seized the opportunity to take a few shaky steps away from the furious man. She didn't go far—she didn't dare, for she was very much aware of Gordie Maxwell's watchful eye on her—but she was careful to move far enough to the side as to be out of Colin's reach.

She felt the wall come up against her back, cold, hard stone grinding against her skin even through the tunic, and she sagged against it gratefully. Her knees were shaking so right now that they could not have held her upright for much longer without the support.

Colin, Gabrielle noticed only now that she was safely out of his reach, seemed ready to explode with fury. His complexion was ruddy, his eyes narrow and spitting hot gray fire as his gaze locked on Johnny Maxwell. If looks could kill, the older man would be sucking in his last breath.

"What is the meaning of this, Maxwell? Or did ye forget, *we had a deal.*"

"Aye," Johnny said evenly. "A deal made and met. Och! I can tell from ye expression that ye've forgotten exactly what the deal was." He stroked his gray-streaked beard and shook his head. "Tsk, tsk, tsk. Let me be reminding ye, lad. I agreed tae get ye the Lady Gabrielle in return for a hefty

sum of coins. As ye can see—" he hefted a thick,
calloused thumb in Gabrielle's direction "—get
the lass, I did. And that pouch Roy is holding
proves ye've upheld yer end and paid dearly for
the service. 'Tis where our deal begins and ends.
Leaving Caerlaverock . . . och! well, the matter
was ne'er discussed, therefore it canna be part of
our deal."

Everything happened at once.

Colin made to lunge for Johnny Maxwell.

The men at the table sprang to their feet, the
bench toppling loudly to the floor behind them.
Steel hissed against steel as swords were drawn
hastily from scabbards. Bootheels scuffed atop
stone as they rushed to Johnny's defense.

They needn't have bothered.

The guards barring the door were well trained;
they reacted instantly. In the blink of an eye, they
surrounded Colin, cutting off his access to
Johnny as well as any available route of escape.

The largest of the bunch grunted something
in Gaelic. To Gabrielle's untutored ear, the words
sounded like gibberish, yet in tone resembled a
dare.

As she watched, the man grinned threateningly
and pressed the razor-sharp tip of his blade
against the pulse throbbing in the base of Colin
Douglas's throat.

Confused, her gaze volleyed between Johnny
Maxwell and Colin Douglas.

What on earth was going on here?!

"Did ye hear me, lad?" a deep, gruff voice demanded. "I asked what the devil is going on here!"

Connor pressed his ear against the slats in the

oak door, listening intently to what transpired in the corridor outside.

Curse his rotten luck! In the past half hour, the boy—Simon, the lad had confided was his name, Johnny Maxwell's youngest son—had begun to warm to Connor and answer his questions. In a voice filled with a respect that made Connor more than a wee bit uneasy, the lad started to repeat the latest Border ballad being circulated about The Black Douglas. It was at that point when a guard, judging from the intruder's authoritative tone, had stumbled upon Simon tarrying outside the cell door.

Close to Connor's side, her head tipped as she also listened, Ella fidgeted nervously.

"Well?" the older voice asked. "Are ye going tae tell me what ye're aboot, or shall I fetch yer da and let ye try explaining tae *him* what yer doing down here? I'm thinking the Maxwell willna like hearing that his wee bairn was down here visiting such prized, nae tae mention *dangerous*, prisoners. What think ye of that, lad?"

"I, er, m-meant nae harm," Simon stammered. "I was curious and wanted but a peek at The Black Douglas, 'tis all. Gordie likes tae tell me the beast has fangs as long as my little finger and sharper than any blade. I was of a mind tae see if me brother is right. Besides," the boy added, and his voice took on a softly shrewd note, "if ye run and tell me da that I was down here, I'll nae have a choice but tae also tell him that the only way I was able tae get so close tae The Black Douglas's cell was because ye'd left yer post. I ken 'twas for but a wee dram tae quench ye thirst, and well I ken it that the prisoners couldnae get free nae matter how many guards were posted,

these doors be tae thick and sturdy. Still, I'm nae
so sure Da would agree leaving a Douglas un-
guarded, The Black Douglas at that, was a wise
thing tae be doing. What think ye on the matter,
Seamus? Mind ye, I'm nae squealer; I've nae wish
tae tattle on ye."

Connor and Ella exchanged a quick glance.

A pause was followed by a muffled chuckle. "Ye
be a crafty one, lad. I've nae a doubt that in the
years tae come, ye'll do the Maxwell and yer pack
of brothers proud. Aye, that ye shall. Meanwhile . . ." The man sighed heavily. "Weeell," he
said slowly, thoughtfully, "since ye already be
here, 'twould seem the damage is done. I suppose
there's nae harm in letting ye take a wee peek."

"Do ye truly mean it?" the boy asked excitedly.

"Aye, God help me, I do. After all, 'tis not like
Caerlaverock's dungeon is graced with such illustrious hostages e'ery day. Fact is, this dreary place
may ne'er see the like again. Besides, were I a
bairn such as yerself, I'd be doing me best tae
get an eyeful and slake me own curiosity. All right,
lad, come here. I'll hoist ye up on me shoulders
so ye can look yer fill, but as soon as I set ye
down, ye're tae scoot straight up those stairs and
nae e'en *think* of coming down here again. And
ye'll nae breathe so maun as a word of this tae
yer da. Do ye ken?"

"Aye!"

The man grunted something in response.

Connor and Ella moved quickly away from the
door.

In no time at all, Connor was again sitting upon
the cold stone floor with his back against the wall,
eyes closed as though he was dozing.

Ella pretended to recommence her pacing in

what little space was available on the shadow-strewn floor between her cousin's extended, ankle-crossed feet and the far wall.

Footsteps echoed in the hallway; they stopped directly outside the door. "All right, up ye go. Ugh! Ye're at least a stone heavier than the last time I hoisted ye. Shift a little tae the left, would ye? A wee bit more. Och! that's a good lad. Now, take a peek through those bars and ye'll be getting a rare look at the notorious Black Douglas, prisoner of the Maxwell. Go ahead, take a good look, Simon, and remember all ye see. Mark me words, lad, 'tis a sight ye'll be recounting tae yer own wee bairns one day, don't ye ken?"

Ella stopped pacing and, fists balled and planted atop the slender line of her hips, chin tilted proudly, she stared at the small, barred window.

Connor cracked his right eye open only enough to be able to glance at the window through the shield of his lashes. The shadows were too thick to distinguish much, but he glimpsed a pudgy face and a crop of bright-red curls just beyond the steel bars.

" 'Tis a woman!" Simon exclaimed accusingly.

"Eh?" The man's voice was muffled. "I canna see, lad, ye've got yer leg wrapped around me eyes. Aye, Simon, there's a woman in there; howe'er, *she* isna The Black Douglas, merely his cousin. Look aboot, lad."

"But I dinna see . . . Och! there he is," Simon said, his young voice suddenly hushed with awe. "There, sitting upon the floor. Is he really The Black Douglas?"

Ella grinned, nodded, and took a step toward

the door. "Aye," she said, "look yer fill, lad. 'Tis The Black Douglas in the flesh."

"Are ye sure? He doesna look so fierce."

"And what were ye expecting him tae look like?" she inquired haughtily.

"Could ye move yer leg, Simon? I canna see," the man grumbled, but if the boy heard, the lad paid him no attention.

Simon pursed his lips, his red brows drawing into a scowl. " 'Tis rumored The Black Douglas stands o'er seven feet tall."

"An exaggeration." Ella shrugged. "Suffice tae say that Connor Douglas is taller than maun. And a good few inches taller than that despicable twin of his. Nay, ye canna tell it at a glance, lad. 'Tis impossible tae predict how tall a mon stands when he's scrunched down so."

"And wide," the boy said as he scrutinized Connor. " 'Tis said The Black Douglas's shoulders are so wide that Bracklenaer's doors had tae be widened tae allow him tae pass."

Ella snorted and clucked her tongue. "Tsk, tsk, tsk. Do ye believe e'erything ye hear, lad?"

"Aboot The Black Douglas, I do," Simon announced proudly. Ella was sure she heard more than a smidgen of admiration in the boy's tone, and saw more than a wee spark of admiration light the gaze the boy ran fondly over Connor's supposedly sleeping form. " 'Tis exactly like him I want tae be when I'm a mon full grown. 'Tis exactly like him I *shall* be."

"Does that mean we can look forward tae seeing ye warming the dungeon in Bracklenaer in, och! say another score or twa?"

"Nay! A Maxwell isna caught so easily by their enemies. The ballads praise The Black Douglas's cunning and quickness, but I'm of a mind that if such were true, I'd nae be looking at him now."

"Och! lad, believe me, if the fight were a fair one, 'tis true, ye'd nae be having the pleasure of seeing him now. Unfortunately, such wasna the case."

Simon's frown deepened thoughtfully. The man upon whose shoulders he perched again demanded he move his leg, but Ella did not think the lad heard, so intently was he looking at Connor. "Are ye telling me The Black Douglas was taken unarmed? He dinna e'en put up a fight?"

"How could he? He was ne'er given a chance. E'en the fist of The Black Douglas's is nae match for Gordie's broadsword, lad." Ella took a step toward the door and, lowering her voice as though afraid she'd awaken her cousin, whispered confidingly, "They dinna tell ye? Yer brothers Gordie and Roy took Connor prisoner whilst he slept."

Ella suppressed a smile; the boy's horrified expression did not disappoint her.

"Nay!"

"*Aye!*"

Connor stirred, and the cell grew abruptly silent.

Through the shield of his lashes, Connor watched the boy slip his right hand through the bars. The lad's knuckles looked youthfully pudgy as his fingers opened.

Ella, God bless her quick-thinking Douglas heart, coughed noisily to mask the sound of the object the boy dropped clattering atop the hard, cold stone.

"Ne'er let it be said that a Maxwell won unfairly," the lad said with a maturity that belied his bairnishly rounded cheeks.

"Fair or nay, that a Maxwell *did* win this day is all that matters now," the man holding the boy grumbled. Simon had only a fleeting second in which his glance volleyed meaningfully between Ella and the object hidden by the shadows near her feet before the man stepped away from the door, hauling his youthful burden with him. "Now, get ye down, lad, a'fore I end up with me shoulders permanently stooped from bearing ye."

"A Maxwell has nae need tae cheat, don't ye ken?" the boy argued, his voice fading a bit as the man set him down on his feet. "We can win against the Douglas fairly. Just ye wait and see."

"What's that ye say? Lad, have ye learned so little from yer da? There's naught unfair or shameful aboot finding yer enemy's weak spots and taking him down by them."

"Mayhap," the boy murmured. "But there's much tae be proud of in taking yer enemy a'ter a fair fight. For example, were *I* the one who'd come upon The Black Douglas this morn instead of Gordie and Roy . . ."

The boastful ring of the boy's words faded. A pair of receding footsteps—one's stride long and sure, the other's short and quick as it hurried to keep step—indicated the man was escorting his young charge away from the cell door and down the shadow-strewn hallway.

Connor forced his suddenly alert muscles to keep their reclining pose when he would rather have bolted to his feet and satisfied his curiosity by inspecting the object the youngest Maxwell had left behind. Prudence held both his and Ella's impatience in check until they heard the thunk of a door closing in the not too far-distance.

Assured they were alone, Connor opened his eyes and pushed to his feet. By the time he reached his cousin's side, Ella had already retrieved the object.

"Och! Connor will ye look at this. 'Tis a *skean dhu,* and quite a fine one." She turned the small dirk this way and that, holding the weapon up as though trying to get one of the dreary gray rays of sunlight that managed to sneak in through the window to glint off the small emerald embedded in the short, thick hilt. The steel blade was squat, but sharp and nonetheless deadly.

Connor's gaze shifted between the dirk and his cousin. Did she have any idea the value of the object she held? Nay, he doubted it. Gently, as though reaching out to take the hand of a long-lost and treasured friend, he took the weapon from her. "Show some respect, lass. 'Tis not just any *skean dhu.*"

"Surely ye dinna mean . . . ?" She tipped her red head and looked at him quizzically.

"Aye, surely I *do,*" he said, and as his gaze lifted from the dirk to meet Ella's, he grinned broadly. " 'Tis the one Colin stole from me near a half score ago. The one our da gave tae me upon his deathbed."

Connor held the dirk up, his gaze admiring it respectfully even as his brow frowned with the memory. The weapon was small, but the symbolism of it was weighty indeed. The dirk was a weapon the real Black Douglas, James, friend of Robert the Bruce, had taken into many a battle with him, a weapon that had been tucked into the boots of all the lairds of the Douglases of Bracklenaer since.

Until the weapon had been entrusted to Connor's care, that is.

Colin had stolen the precious dirk the night their father died . . . and in so doing launched a blood feud that almost rivaled in violence the one between Maxwell and Douglas. Almost.

Connor ran the calloused tip of his thumb over the flat surface of the emerald. After all these years, the stone was still smooth and fine. The weight of the dirk felt comfortably heavy in Connor's hand. Finally, it was back where it belonged. Now, if he could only set to right the rest of his world so easily.

His gaze shifted to the door, and his grin broadened as a plan began to form in his mind . . .

Eleven

"Yer kin doesna treat ye ver well, lass. I hope for yer sake the ones ye have back in England treat ye better."

"I've no relatives in England," Gabrielle answered the man who looked like Connor, but who most certainly was not Connor. "If I did, I'd not have been at Elizabeth's court . . ." She paused, frowned. "I *probably* would not have been there," she corrected hastily. "And had I not been at Elizabeth's court, I'd not have been ordered to marry Conn—Coli—er, *you,* and therefore would not be in this despicable situation now."

Gabrielle's gaze shifted, scanning the room. Not an easy feat since the night was closing in and no candle had been left for them.

Three hours—and what had felt like several dozen staircases—ago, they'd been led here by a gloating Gordie Maxwell.

The room was small and dank, the only furnishings a bed and a chair; neither had weathered the years kindly. It was on the former which Gabrielle sat, and the latter upon which Colin Douglas sprawled. Outside, a harsh wind whipped

over the Borders, howling over craggy hills and
valleys. Even in the vague light of dusk,
Gabrielle's discerning eye couldn't detect a single
tapestry lining the walls to block out the cold,
seeping draft.

The mattress was straw-stuffed, and felt as
lumpy and as stiff as a gnarled slab of oak beneath her. It gave a token crunch when Gabrielle
shifted, so she sat further up on the bed. Since
the relic possessed no headboard, she leaned her
shoulders back against the bare wall. The cold,
damp feel of the stone soaked quickly through
her tunic, into her skin, making her shiver. A
sneeze tickled the back of her nose. Her eyes watered as she sniffled it back.

"Och, dinna fash yerself, lass. Dry yer tears.
We'll be rescued. Eventually."

His voice, she thought as she stared dejectedly
at a point where age-darkened mortar converged
the corners of four stones on the opposite,
shadow-strewn wall, did not sound very much like
Connor's. While Connor had a deep, husky voice
that washed over her like sun-warmed honey and
made her feel tingly and vibrantly alive, his twin's
voice was rougher, cloudy, and left her feeling
nothing at all.

Gabrielle's attention moved to her reluctant
companion, and she frowned when a sharp, tingly
bolt of awareness shot through her. It was as unexpected as it was intense. The dim lighting combined with the way the man's large body lounged
in the chair and dominated, while at the same
time ate up, what little space the small room provided, made her think of Connor. A stab of longing pricked at her heartstrings.

She quickly suppressed the emotion. This man might look like Connor but he was *not* Connor.

"Your men will be here soon?" she asked, and noticed that her own voice was only slightly higher than normal, only sightly breathless. "You're confident of that?"

"My men? *My* men?" His chuckle was harsh and short, not at all comforting. "Nay, lass, I dinna think so. I've nae men tae be here. Soon or otherwise."

Colin's eyes were now firmly shut. His dark head was pillowed against the chair back's meager padding. The fabric—so frayed that the stuffing beneath exploded from countless moth-eaten holes—might once have been a fine gold brocade. Might. There was no way to tell for certain. Age had faded the color, while a score or two of hard use had worn the threads and tattered them until the material was unrecognizable as anything but unforgivingly old, coarse of texture, and vaguely dark yellow in some spots, dirty brown in others.

"If you've no men, then how can you say so confidently that we'll be rescued?"

" 'Tis a matter of reasoning." His left shoulder rose and fell in a shrug. "Gilby."

Gabrielle shook her head, trying and failing to follow his logic. "Gilby?"

"Aye. The mon willna allow his laird tae stay in the Maxwell's keep a second longer than is necessary. Either a ransom will be demanded, and paid promptly, or an escape attempt launched. Mind ye, me guess would be the latter. Have ye nae heard any of the ballads they sing aboot The Black Douglas, lass? Me brother and his men have been in and out of Caerlaverock so many times

they maun ken the layout of the keep better than
Johnny Maxwell himself.''

Gabrielle's hopes plunged with all the speed
and surety of a stone being tossed into a deep
lake. Shaking her head, she said sharply, "Your
confidence is misplaced.''

"Mayhap ye'd think so—and truly I can see why
ye would—but I ken better. Yer a Sassenach,
therefore yer ignorance can be forgiven; ye simply canna be expected tae grasp the way of things
here. I, on the other hand, am a Border reiver
born and raised. Trust me when I say we'll be
rescued, and rescued soon.'' He wrinkled his nose
distastefully. "Connor's men are loyal to a fault.
And maun reliable. Especially his clan captain.
I've nae doubt Gilby will be along shortly to fetch
his laird . . . and us along with him.''

"I have doubts. Quite a few of them.''

"Aye?'' Colin grumbled and shifted, seeking a
more comfortable position. "Och! well, 'tis yer
right, I suppose. Just keep them tae yerself.
There's a good lass. I've need for a wee bit of sleep,
ye see. I was up all last eve raiding. 'Tis exhausting
work.''

Gabrielle stared at the man, and for the first
time in a long time found herself speechless.

How could he talk about last night's raid so
casually? She was sure she'd fight nightmares for
months to come, remembering how two men had
tried their best to kill each other right before her
eyes. In those long, dark hours of the night, she'd
seen more blood spilled than she had in her entire lifetime. Good Lord, she'd even watched
helplessly as Gilby clung to a tendril of life as
Mairghread and Ella diligently nursed him.

Yet here was Colin Douglas, sprawled haphazardly in a chair, referring to the incident as though a bloody midnight raid was so common an occurrence as to be insignificant. A minor inconvenience, an annoying interruption to his sleep.

She remembered the way Mairghread's eyes had glittered; the woman's ancient face had actually been lively and animated as she'd led Gabrielle through Bracklenaer's twisting hallways. She remembered also the way Ella had watched the violent swordplay taking place just outside the mouth of the tunnel with no more concern than she'd show one of the fox hunts Queen Elizabeth was so fond of. Gabrielle herself had literally become ill at the thought of participating in fox hunts!

Perhaps here on the Borders such activity was common?

Was that possible? And was it also possible for something so gruesome and horrifying as last night's raid to become so commonplace as to fade in people's minds before twenty-four hours had elapsed?

The gentle snore emanating from Colin Douglas's direction told Gabrielle that, detestable though the thought was, not only was such a thing possible, it was probable.

She'd heard the tales and many of the ballads. She'd known before leaving London that the Borders were barbaric in both landscape and inhabitants. Yet never in her wildest dreams could she have imagined exactly *how* barbaric.

Gabrielle shuddered and rested her head back against the hard, unforgiving stone. She didn't want to think about how the man who slept so peacefully and soundly near her was the man she should by now be wed to.

Didn't want to, but did.

She closed her eyes, that thought linking itself naturally to others. None of them had a bit to do with Colin Douglas. They had everything to do with his twin brother.

Hot, sultry memories of the night before teased her mind. Her lips burned as she remembered the feel of Connor's mouth moving hungrily on hers. Her fingers clenched into white-knuckled fists when she imagined the warm, smooth skin of his naked back gliding like silk beneath her searching palms.

The fire of passion that had burned inside her last night began to spark anew in her veins, heating the blood that was suddenly pumping hot and furious through her body. A soft, expectant sigh whispered past her lips as she recalled the way Connor's mouth had moved against the oh so sensitive curl of her earlobe, his voice hoarse and ragged as he'd called out her name the instant he'd spilled his seed inside her.

"Gabrielle?"

Her eyes snapped open. Her senses were abruptly alive and alert.

Sweet heavens, that was no dream, that *was* Connor's voice!

Gabrielle's attention jerked to the doorway. She squinted against the clinging shadows, her vision pulling into focus the proof of what her body already told her; that Connor was nearby.

A sconce in the corridor had been lit; the flickering orange backdrop cast his virile body into sharp silhouette. Although she couldn't see his face clearly in such dim light, Gabrielle knew for certain it was Connor Douglas who stood there. No one else had shoulders so wide, hips so hard and lean.

The hem of Connor's kilt brushed his knees as he took a step into the room.

Gabrielle's heart staggered a traitorous beat. The breath she'd been in the process of inhaling clogged in her throat.

She froze, a frown creasing her brow. How strange. In one blink she'd been reclining against the stone wall, thinking of Connor, in the next he was here and she was sitting on the edge of the bed. How had she gotten there?

It took Gabrielle a second to understand that, at the first sight of him, she'd instinctively straightened, scooted to the edge of the bed, and swung her legs over the side. It wasn't until the soles of her too-large boots hit the stone floor that she realized what she was doing. Without her mind giving her body permission to do it, she'd been in the process of standing up and running to him.

She held herself in check, but it wasn't easy. Harder still was her ability to ignore the way her body ached for her to carry the motion through.

Oh, who was she trying to fool? Gabrielle knew exactly what kept her sitting on the edge of the bed instead of surrendering to the urge to run to Connor. It was pride, pure and simple. The thought that he might turn his back on her, might reject her in the same callous way so many others had in the past, stopped her cold. Nothing else had the power to keep her feet rooted to the floor, or to counter her almost overwhelming need to feel Connor's strong arms wrapped around her, holding her so wonderfully, protectively close. The need was so intense it felt like a raw, physical ache clawing her up on the inside.

The cushions in the old chair crunched as Colin moved, walking with slow reluctance. Gabrielle's attention shifted to him in time to see the thick, inky fringe of his lashes flicker upward. The irises were a wee bit darker, a shade or two bluer than Connor's. Why hadn't she noticed that before? she wondered as his gaze met hers. His eyes were narrow and guarded, lacking even a glimmer of compassion, reminding her again of how very dissimilar the brothers actually were.

"Dinna tarry, Cousin. The guard willna stay unconscious fore'er."

The voice was Ella's; it floated into the room on the soft, flickering glow of sconcelight, coming from the direction of the open doorway behind Connor. Gabrielle couldn't see her, but judging by the nearness of Ella's voice, she decided the girl must be just around the corner, probably keeping a watchful eye on the corridor and the aforementioned guard.

Colin's attention left Gabrielle. He leaned to the side, glancing back over his shoulder, past the tattered wing of the chair. His face hardened when his gaze met his brother's, the corners of his lips quirking downward. That he'd been expecting Gilby was evident in his unwelcome expression and the way the disappointed crease carved harsh brackets on either side of his mouth.

Gabrielle's attention shifted cautiously between the Douglas twins.

Connor looked equally displeased to be facing his brother. His gray eyes were narrow, and as he took another step into the room she saw they glittered dangerously. The dagger, which she only now noticed he was holding in his right hand, inched higher. It was poised at striking level. The powerful fingers clutching the hilt tightened until his knuckles were white from strain.

"Gabrielle," Connor said again, his untrusting gaze never leaving his twin. He angled his head, issuing an unspoken command that Gabrielle could not resist.

She stood. Her steps measured, forcibly slow, she crossed the room.

Weeks ago, safe at court, Gabrielle would have sworn this wasn't possible. Imagine, Gabrielle Carelton, ward of Queen Elizabeth, seeking comfort and protection from the likes of Scotland's most notorious reiver, The Black Douglas!

Perhaps the concept wasn't as ludicrous as it might once have been. Aye, she had an unsettling feeling such was the case. Though she was wont to admit it, Gabrielle couldn't deny the hungry feeling that tightened in her stomach, nor the tide of longing that swept through her as she continued to grapple with the potent urge to throw herself into The Black Douglas's arms.

And if, in deed or expression, he'd made even the slightest indication she'd be welcome there . . . ?

He didn't.

Still, the sheer magnitude of the feelings bombarding her was frightening. It made Gabrielle stop an arm's length away from Connor. Where it was safe. She might have erred on many counts since her arrival in Scotland, but she wasn't so foolish as to draw too close to him for fear his tantalizingly familiar scent would invade her, fill her, overwhelm her . . . that the warmth of his body would seep into hers, melting away her defenses until she had no choice but to surrender to the impossibly strong yearning to again feel the safe haven of his arms enfolding her.

In this harsh, savage country that Gabrielle had been unwillingly thrust into, the shelter of Connor Douglas's embrace was the only warmth and security she'd known. Oh, but how it beckoned.

From the corner of her eye, Gabrielle saw Colin push himself to his feet. The suppleness of the movement drew her attention, jarring her from her thoughts and back to her surroundings.

Colin's spine was straight, his shoulders—almost but not quite as broad as his twin's—squared, his stance stiff and tense. The line of his jaw was hard. The dimpled square of his chin jutted at a stubborn angle as his eyes narrowed. Like a freshly honed dagger, his gaze cut through the shadows, stabbing into his brother. " 'Tis past time ye showed up, *cuilean.*"

"If ye call me 'puppy' one more time, ye'll be finding out how deadly this dagger can be, Brother. The blade may be old, but 'tis still sharp." Connor pushed the words through gritted teeth, even as he raised the dagger in question. A sound rumbled in the back of his throat; it resembled a feral growl.

Colin glanced down, his attention focusing on the dagger. A shard of sconcelight winked off a stone embedded in the hilt. The color drained from Colin's face. Suddenly, the hollows beneath his cheeks looked unnaturally pronounced, the cheekbones above high and rigid. His voice, when it came, was a combination of disbelief and outrage. "Where did ye get that?" he demanded.

"Does it matter?" Connor asked, and his voice

was as chilly as the draft leaking in through the thick stone walls that surrounded them.

"Aye, *cuilean*, it matters a great deal tae me."

The weathered creases shooting out from the corners of his eyes deepened. "And *only* tae *ye*," he said, his voice too low and even to be anything but furious. "What matters tae *me* is that the weapon is back with its proper owner. Finally. 'Tis enough."

The twins exchanged a brief glare. Gabrielle's gaze volleyed between the two brothers; so intent were they focused on each other that she might not even have been present for all the attention either paid her.

"Connor!" Ella hissed from the hallway.

Connor angled his head, his eyes shifting to Gabrielle. Was it her imagination, or did his expression soften as he looked at her? Nay, it was nothing more than an illusion of light and shadow, she decided . . . even as her heart skipped a beat and a breath caught painfully in her throat.

"Come," Connor said, and his free hand lifted, palm up, extended toward her.

Gabrielle looked at that hand. Without warning, her mind was again flooded with memories, with brief, titillating images of last night. She remembered in vivid detail how his big hand had felt as he gently caressed parts of her body that no one else had touched before. Remembered also her own wild, wanton reaction to that skilled caress.

A hot wave of color burned in her cheeks. Dear Lord, what was she thinking? She shook her head, trying to clear it. Considering the circumstances, now was surely *not* the time to be basking in intimate memories! Still, even though she forced the memories aside, her body's response to them, to Connor Douglas's touch, lingered and burned all through her body.

Gabrielle hesitated, then swallowed hard. Finally, she placed her hand in his. A jolt sizzled up her arm, quickly seeping to every part of her. The heat of his touch seeped to her very core, banishing the chill and warming her instantly.

Gabrielle could no more deny the sheer intensity of her response to even this innocent contact than she could stop breathing.

Connor flexed his fingers, curling them around hers. His grip was firm, insistent, but not painfully so. If he noticed the trembling of her fingers, he gave no outward indication. A sigh of relief whispered softly past her lips.

"Footsteps!" While Ella spoke the single word softly, the cry of alarm echoed through the room, and off its three occupants, like a resounding clap of thunder.

A movement at the door attracted Gabrielle's attention. Glancing in that direction, she saw Ella.

The girl's slender back was to the room. She was hunched over, grunting as she struggled to drag the unconscious guard's body over the shadowy threshold. "Och, Cousin, dinna stand there gaping, get o'er here and help me."

Connor thrust the dagger at Gabrielle. Without thinking, she took it, and watched him cross to Ella's side. His greater strength made dragging the guard inside a simple feat. With the sole of his boot, he sent the door careening shut behind them.

The carved steel hilt of the dagger retained the heat of Connor's palm. The stone embedded in the hilt bit into her tender palm, yet Gabrielle refused to allow the prick of pain to make her loosen her grip.

Connor had entrusted her with the only weapon among them, a weapon that meant their only chance at freedom. Gabrielle felt a surge of confusion, countered by a much stronger surge of pride. She would do her best not to disappoint him, or betray his unexpected trust.

Her attention shifted to Colin. Even in this dim light, his expression was unmistakable; he was relieved to see the weapon transferred to a less skilled hand.

The line of Gabrielle's jaw hardened. The man was in for a surprise. Little did he suspect her determination to see to it that his relief was to be painfully short-lived. Her spine stiffened, her green eyes narrowed rebelliously.

Could she use the dagger if need be? Aye, she thought she could. Especially if it meant proving to Connor that his trust in her had not been misplaced.

A small portion of Gabrielle's mind acknowledged that although violence was uncharacteristic for her, it was well in keeping with her barbaric surroundings. A larger portion of her mind refused to acknowledge the same, and indeed refused to do anything but focus intently on Colin Douglas.

She watched, waited.

Colin would make his move and make it soon. She knew it, could sense it.

And when he did? What then?

Gabrielle wondered if she would have the courage and strength needed to commit a violent act. Oh, but how it went against her upbringing. In the end, she could only hope and pray that, if and when the time came, she would find the inner strength needed to do what was necessary.

The time came more quickly than she'd anticipated.

No sooner had the thought entered Gabrielle's mind than Colin Douglas grinned and lunged for her.

She reacted swiftly and on instinct. In a quick, jerky motion, she lashed out with the dagger. The blade sliced through Colin's tunic, carving a bloody arc into his shoulder as she ducked out of his reach and scooted to the side.

Toward Connor.

Toward safety.

In the second it took to reach Connor, she was shaking and breathless. Ella was staring at her with an expression akin to awe. Behind her, Colin Douglas howled in pain and clutched at his wound; ribbons of blood streamed past his fingers, the drops splashing on the cold stone floor.

The footsteps in the hallway quickened, drawing closer; their beat was out of time with the wild thumping of her heart in her ears. A voice called out in alarm as the first man reached the door and thrust it open.

"Douglas!" The intruder was Roy Maxwell, and his furious roar demanded attention. As Gabrielle watched, Roy's green eyes narrowed and his gaze swept accusingly from an ashen, wounded Colin to an ashen, defiant Connor. "Dinna be a fool, mon. The castle is full of men. There'll be nae escape for ye this night."

"Aye," Connor agreed tersely, "men who are nae doubt celebrating their victory down in the hall. How many of them are sober enough to come to yer aid?"

From the corner of her eye, Gabrielle saw Ella inch slowly toward Roy. The man, intent on Connor, seemed not to notice. Gabrielle held her breath expectantly.

A grin curved over Roy's lips, while a glint of confidence sparkled in his eyes. "It takes but one Maxwell tae do the job, Douglas. Have ye nae learned that? 'Twas the same amount that took ye prisoner."

"Wrong. There was nae one abductor, there were o'er half a dozen. And *they* were armed," Connor reminded his adversary coldly.

Roy's grin disappeared as quickly as it had formed. His right hand reached for the hilt of his sword, but his reaction time was leadened, as though the men below weren't the only ones deep into their cups.

His fingers grappled with air. The sword was not there.

"Looking for this, *fule?*" Ella asked. It was her turn to grin as she pricked the nape of Roy Maxwell's neck with the tip of his own sword; the hilt was warm in her palm, for it was a mere second ago she'd cannily slipped the weapon, unnoticed, from where it nestled in the sheath at his side.

Roy stiffened perceptibly. He started to angle his head to look behind him, but the blade nipping at his skin must have made him think better of it because he stopped abruptly.

"Call me a fool if ye'd like, lass," Roy spat through gritted teeth, "but 'tis *ye* who be a fool if yer thinking tae get out of Caerlaverock alive. Me clan willna allow it."

"Yer clan willna have a choice," Connor inter-

vened, his alert gaze volleying between Roy and
his wounded twin. The latter had stumbled backward and was now leaning against the far wall,
inspecting his wounded shoulder. Connor tried
without success not to notice the way Gabrielle
clung to his arm, the way her ripe body shuddered violently against him, the way his body—
good Lord, even *now*—responded to her
closeness, her touch.

"There are always choices, Douglas."

"Are there?" Connor countered. "E'en when
a Maxwell's life is on the line?"

"Do you dare threaten me? In my own home?"
Ray's nostrils flared indignantly. "Make no mistake, Douglas. Killing me will gain ye naught."

"Mayhap." It was Ella who answered, and her
voice was equally as cold and hard as her cousin's.
"Whether honored to commit the deed or only
watch it, either would give me pleasure. Or do ye
forget so soon the way ye dragged me tae me
horse this morn? Me shoulders still ache from yer
roughness, and I'm of a mind that these scratches
and burns from the rope ye bound too tightly
around me wrists might ne'er go away. Och! aye,
seeing ye suffer is something I willna deny I've a
yearning for."

The man winced when, to emphasize her point,
Ella flicked her wrist and lightly jabbed the sensitive nape of his neck with the tip of the sword.

A few drops of blood trickled under the collar
of Roy's shirt; they felt discomfortingly warm and
sticky. His jaw hardened as he gritted his teeth,
waiting for the blade to sink deeper or lift to
strike the killing blow. As the girl had so arro-
gantly stated, he'd tested her mettle earlier and
not found it lacking. Oh, nay! Just the opposite.

Her sweet face and meager size was woefully deceptive; Ella Douglas easily possessed both the strength and stamina for committing such a deed. Then, of course, there was the matter of The Black Douglas. If his cousin did not do the job of ending Roy's life, surely that man would.

Two dozen heartbeats slipped past with torturous slowness. The blade did not move.

Roy relaxed . . . not a lot, but a wee bit. His gaze shifted, locking on to the room's only occupant who, he hoped, might be sympathetic to his cause. His attention focused on Gabrielle Carelton. She was standing beside Connor, her full, round cheeks as pale as a bolt of undyed linen. In the shadows that cloaked her, her green eyes looked wide and alert.

That a Maxwell was being forced to look to a Carelton for aid was not something to take pride in, nor something Roy dared allow himself to contemplate too closely. "Mistress, please, ye've a drop of Maxwell blood in yer veins, therefore ye maun be able tae see reason where a Douglas is blind. Canna ye somehow convince these devils what I say be true? That there is nae way out of this keep alive?"

Gabrielle hesitated thoughtfully, then shook her head. "How can I convince them of something I'm not convinced of myself?"

"But—"

Colin grunted and lurched away from the wall, drawing attention to himself and abruptly cutting Roy Maxwell's words short. "There be many ways in and out of a keep, it doesna matter on which side of the Border the keep rests. *If* one kens the way."

Connor's attention sharped on his twin. "Especially when one is a traitor to his clan and has spent many a night, as ye nae doubt have, within the keep in question's walls. Is that nae so?"

"It is," Colin agreed unabashedly. If he was offended by Connor's accusation, it didn't show in either his expression or his tone. Both remained level, although the former did tighten a wee bit when he lifted his wounded shoulder and rolled it gingerly back and forth in its socket, testing its flexibility.

"And . . . ?" Connor prompted when the other did not immediately continue.

"And . . ." Colin echoed as a slow grin tugged at his mouth, the gesture deeply creasing the corners of his shrewd gray eyes, "when it comes to Caerlaverock, I happen tae ken several. I'll be maun happy tae share them with ye, *cuilean*. For a price."

Twelve

Gabrielle's body ached for every laboring hour she'd spent on horseback, and there had been quite a few. The last time she'd ridden so hard had been on her trip to Scotland.

The ground beneath her bottom felt unyielding and cold as she shifted; the rough bark of the tree trunk she rested against scratched her skin through the thin covering of her tunic.

How far away was Bracklenaer? Gabrielle had no idea. She'd need to know where she was in order to gauge the distance to their destination, and she was lost.

An hour earlier, as they'd eaten a makeshift dinner of berries and nuts in the dark—Connor had not allowed them to light a fire for fear it would draw the Maxwell and his men—Connor had admitted that they ordinarily would have reached Bracklenaer a handful of hours after leaving Caerlaverock. Unfortunately, almost as soon as Colin had led them through and out of an escape tunnel that uncannily resembled the one Ella and Mairghread had hustled her through under Bracklenaer, Connor began detecting telltale signs of ambushes. Either Roy had not known of his father's lack of confidence in Caerlaverock's ability to house such illustrious prisoners, or Johnny Maxwell had not trusted it himself. Either way, he'd gone to a great deal of trouble to take precautions that would, should his prisoners find a way to escape the keep, assure him they did not have their freedom for long. If one ambush did not recapture them, surely another would.

Had he been dealing with any other man, Johnny Maxwell's flawless theory and traps would have served him well.

He was dealing with The Black Douglas.

There lay the crucial difference.

What Johnny Maxwell could not guess was Connor's ability to detect the subtle signs of a trap leagues before he fell into it. Several times, the tired, ragged-looking band of five had been forced to detour from a direct course to Bracklenaer and circle far around the men who lay in wait for them. Then, too, there was time consumed with erasing their tracks as best they could, or in laying out a false set that evaporated in a blink and led nowhere.

Because of the necessary delays, reaching Bracklenaer in the normal amount of time became impossible.

They'd stopped only when night had fallen and the darkness had become so inky and thick as to make the going treacherous. Even then, Gabrielle harbored an uneasy suspicion that the reason behind the much-needed respite was herself. Ella seemed capable, no make that *adamant,* in her desire to continue; Gabrielle hadn't missed the glares the girl had shot her while balking to Connor about the delay. The men, seasoned Border reivers all, were each capable of picking their way over the rough terrain, no matter how dark the night.

It was only she, the Englishwoman, the unwanted Sassenach, who risked stumbling her horse and maiming it by not being able to see where she was going.

Gabrielle glanced at the girl who sat beside her. The back of Ella's bright red head rested against the tree trunk, her gaze fixed on some unknown point in the darkness, a thoughtful frown furrowing her brow. The girl's enviously slender legs were stretched out and crossed at the ankles; the top foot tapped the cool night air with an impatient beat. If she was tired, it didn't show. Ella looked annoyingly alert and anxious.

What had they been discussing before Ella glanced away and the conversation lapsed? Gabrielle trapped a yawn in her throat and strove to recall. Ah, yes, now she remembered. It was her turn to frown as she addressed Ella. " 'Tis a foolish reason for brothers to fight. Surely you must be mistaken."

"Nay, what 'twas was a maun serious offense. Clans have feuded for centuries o'er less."

"Less than a dagger? I'll not believe it."

"Think ye I care?" Her sharp tone attracted the attention of Roy Maxwell, who was tied to a thick birch trunk on the opposite side of the small clearing. Colin was secured to the opposite side, but he'd fallen asleep shortly after they'd eaten. Ella scowled at Roy until the man grimaced and looked away, then lowered her voice. "Believe what ye like, lass, it matters naught to me."

"Two brothers fighting for years over a mere

dagger . . . ?" Gabrielle shook her head in weary disbelief. "I'm sorry, but it sounds ridiculous."

"Tae a court-raised Sassenach, mayhap 'twould seem so."

"I suppose next you'll have me believing that the Maxwell-Douglas feud started over something even more trivial?"

"Dinna be telling me ye ken nae the reason for that one."

"Fine. I'll not tell you then." Gabrielle glanced at the girl skeptically, a feather of curiosity tickling her. "But I don't know," she added despite her resolve not to. "How would I?"

"The feud started o'er a woman." Ella clucked her tongue and shook her head. " 'Tis surprised I am ye dinna already ken it, especially since the woman in question was *yer* ancestor. And me own."

Gabrielle blinked hard. "I beg your pardon?"

"Aye, lass, she was a Carelton."

"Ailean Carelton, to be precise."

These last words did not come from Ella.

Gabrielle's attention jerked past the girl. Her gaze pulled into focus the night- and shadow-hazed but unmistakable form of Connor Douglas. Her heart skipped a traitorous beat. How long had he been standing there? How much had he heard? She shook her head, clearing her abruptly tumultuous thoughts. While she tried to concentrate on the topic of conversation, it was not easy. Not when the wonderfully virile sight of The Black Douglas filled her vision and her senses.

"A-Ailean Carelton?" Gabrielle stammered finally. "I've never heard of her."

"Never?" Connor asked as he crossed the clearing. Twigs snapped beneath his bootheels, moss crunched. He stopped in front of them.

The soft night breeze sent a waft of his sharp, spicy scent over Gabrielle. Her breath caught and she shivered in response. "Nay, never."

"I have," Roy Maxwell said, and his words captured their attention. "She was me great-great aunt," he explained as his eyes shifted to Gabrielle. His expression softened a bit. "And yers, lady. Dinna anyone e'er tell ye of her?"

Gabrielle shook her head.

Roy chuckled derisively. "I'm nae surprised. When she married Lachlan Maxwell near on twa centuries ago, her kin considered her dead. Mind ye, the Maxwells werena tae pleased with the matter either, but there was naught tae be done aboot it. The deed was done. Besides, as any Maxwell worth his salt can tell ye, 'twas nae the woman, but her *horse* which caused the conflict."

"Hush up, mon," Ella hissed. "I'll nae be letting ye fill her head with yer nonsense. If 'tis the story she wants, 'tis the story she'll get. But *nae* from *ye.*"

"The devil you say!" Roy looked offended. "I speak the truth, and well ye ken it."

"So far as a Maxwell is able," Ella countered as she shoved herself to her feet. With tense, jerky motions she brushed the leaves and dirt from the front of her trews. " 'Tis common knowledge that a Maxwell and the truth are soon parted when the purpose suits."

"And what purpose would it suit me to lie aboot such a thing?"

"I fear 'twould take a better mind than mine to discover why a Maxwell does aught."

"Why, ye little . . . !"

Gabrielle shut out the bickering and turned her attention to Connor. He was staring at her, and staring hard. A spark of awareness fired in her blood. It took all of her concentration to return his gaze with an unflinching one of her own.

Before she realized what she was doing, Gabrielle had pushed to her feet and took a step toward him. He stood an arm's length away. Oh, but how she yearned to move closer. A minute ago her muscles had been stinging from exertion, yet now she barely noticed the deep, throbbing ache. It had been replaced by a deeper, more insistent ache . . . an ache she refused to recognize let alone acknowledge.

Keeping her voice low, so only Connor could hear, Gabrielle asked, "Will you tell me the truth of this story, m'lord?"

"Aye, if ye ask it of me, I will."

"I do." She nodded faintly. "And I am."

"So be it. But nae here, lass." Connor's gaze left her to trace over the others. Ella and Roy were still arguing, but Gabrielle didn't pay attention to a word of it. When his gaze returned to her, his eyes were narrow; the gray depths burned through the shadows of the night. He lifted his hand, palm up. "Come."

Gabrielle hesitated. She tried to swallow, but her throat was suddenly too tight and dry for it. Had she thought her heart pounding fiercely only a moment ago? How foolish, for 'twas nothing compared to the way it hammered beneath her breasts now. Her fingers trembled when she placed her hand in his and allowed Connor to lead her out of the clearing.

His fingers loosened, slipped upward, curled around her wrists. His grip was a firm, warm, thoroughly distracting pressure as he led her deeper into the woods. She told herself that his reason for not relinquishing his hold on her was the same as the reason he'd stopped for the night; he feared she'd stumble in the darkness and harm herself. It was a logical, albeit shallow, reason. So why couldn't she make herself believe it? Oh, aye, the night was, by her own estimation, too dark to be traveling, but it was not so dark as to make the simple feat of *walking* dangerous.

They passed towering, shadowy oak and birch trees, and others she didn't recognize. The bristly needles of a fir tree scratched at her sleeve as they skirted by it. The back of her hand grazed a clump of tall plants bearing clusters of tiny green flowers.

Gabrielle stopped short. A gasp whispered through her lips when something brittle pricked the knuckles of her free hand. "Ouch!"

"What?" Connor stopped, turned back toward her. Was it her imagination, or was his voice tight with concern? In this light, there was no reading his expression, but she thought that also looked unnaturally taut.

"I don't know. I think something stung me." She shook her hand vigorously, as though the gesture would help the bite of pain there. It didn't. It made it worse. "Blast it, but that hurts!"

"Let me see."

"Nay, m'lord, I'm fine. Truly I am."

"Saints alive, dinna argue with me, wench. Let me see yer hand." His tone left no room for argument. Nor did his swift reaction.

Before Gabrielle could stop him, Connor closed the step that separated them. He stood unnervingly close as he reached for her hand, cradling it in his much larger ones. His skin felt rough and warm, such a striking contrast to her own softer, cooler flesh.

Connor lifted her hand in a way that mockingly reminded her of the time the Earl of Essex had affectionately kissed the back of it before moving his mouth up to hers that long-ago night in Queen Elizabeth's garden. That incident felt like a lifetime ago to her now.

Gabrielle steeled herself against the expected— longed for?—feel of The Black Douglas's lips brushing hotly over her stinging flesh. The contact did not come. Why oh why did she feel such a bitter stab of disappointment?

Holding the back of her stinging hand close to his face, Connor scowled at it in the darkness. " 'Tis naught but a nettle."

"A . . . what?"

"A nettle." He nodded to the clump of prickly-leafed plants beside her.

Connor released Gabrielle's hand and leaned to the side, plucking the leaf off another, smaller plant. How did he know which was which? In this light, all the plants and trees looked much the same to her. He held the leaf out to her, and on closer inspection Gabrielle saw that, unlike the nettle's prickly leaves, the leaf he'd picked was softer in texture and wavy.

"Use it, lass," he said when she didn't take the leaf. " 'Twill help take away the sting."

Gabrielle glanced skeptically between the offered leaf and Connor. "How?"

Connor grumbled something under his breath. Since the words were in Gaelic, she'd no idea what he said. His tone, however, suggested he was questioning her competency.

Gabrielle bristled. She opened her mouth to debate the unspoken issue, but Connor stunned her silent by lifting the leaf and spitting on it.

"What are you doing?" she demanded warily.

"Helping ye, ye stubborn wench," he growled as he again lifted her injured hand.

"That's very kind of you," she murmured sarcastically, "however, I'll have you know I can take care of myself. It may come as a surprise to you, but I've absolutely no need of your—*Ouch!* Curse you, Connor Douglas, stop that! It *hurts!*"

He was rubbing the leaf with what Gabrielle considered undue vigor over her stinging knuckle. Gritting her teeth against the pain, she tried unsuccessfully to wrench her arm free . . . then just as quickly wondered why she'd bothered. Connor's grip was uncompromisingly firm; the fingers of his free hand were coiled around her wrist like a sturdy iron shackle. The only sign he gave of noticing her struggle was a slight flexing of his fingers against her tender skin.

Did he realize he was hurting her? Did he care?

Gabrielle's mind flashed her an image of how effective Ella was at getting The Black Douglas's attention. Unorthodox though the method might be, surely if it worked for Ella . . . ?

Before she could think the urge through—let alone consider the consequences of carrying it out—she lifted her right foot and swung it with all her might. The toe of her boot collided with Connor's shin in a teeth-jarring kick. Gabrielle winced. The impact was jarring; it rippled up her travel-sore leg, reverberating all the way to her hip.

Unprepared for the attack, he stumbled backward a stunned step. Instead of his fingers releasing her wrist, as Gabrielle had expected him to do, they tightened. She opened her mouth to again demand that he release her, only to have momentum drag her body in his wake before she could get out a word.

Her breasts hit his rock-solid chest with enough force to shove the breath from her lungs. Their thighs slammed together, their hips met.

Knowing what was to come, knowing also that he didn't stand a prayer of stopping it, Connor nevertheless tried. He reached out with his free hand, fumbling blindly to grab hold of the nearest tree trunk. It was too late. His fingertips scraped against rough bark, but found no purchase.

Connor plummeted backward. He wrapped his arm around Gabrielle's waist and shifted his weight to cushion her fall.

Tangled together, they tumbled onto the moss- and leaf-strewn ground.

His back landed hard against cold, unyielding ground, and his teeth clacked painfully together when the back of his head also hit the ground with a resounding whack. A fist-size rock gouged into his shoulder. A jagged corner tore through his tunic, slicing as easily through the material as it did through the sensitive flesh beneath. Connor grunted.

The sound was echoed by a kindred one from Gabrielle as her body settled with force atop his. Her legs had parted as they'd fallen; she now straddled his hips. Her elbows and knees throbbed, for the awkward position had caused her knees to be first to hit the ground and absorb the brunt of the impact. Her head snapped forward on her neck, and her brow crashed into Connor's shoulder. She gasped when a bolt of pain exploded in her temples; if she'd not known better, Gabrielle would have sworn she'd just run head first into a thick stone wall.

They lay like that for what felt like forever but what was in reality only a few short, breathless minutes. A crow circled in the midnight sky, then dipped to perch on one of the branches overhead. Its caw sounded loud and, to Gabrielle's ears, faintly mocking.

As the pain in her body gradually receded, a different yet equally as strong sensation trickled in to take its place.

Gabrielle slowly became aware of the virile male body that lay beneath her. If she concentrated on it—*good Lord, even if she* didn't *concentrate on it!*—she could feel Connor's heart pounding against her breasts. Her scalp burned with the feel of his ragged breaths washing over the top of her head. His hips, wedged intimately between her thighs, felt hot and hard and—

"C-Connor?" Gabrielle stammered finally, hoping to break the tension that stretched taut between them. She shifted, levering herself up on her bruised elbows to look at him.

"Aye?" he asked, returning her gaze. His gray eyes were narrow, shielded by the night's shadows and the curl of thick, inky lashes. His jaw was clenched hard; he pushed the single word through gritted teeth.

"I'm not exactly sure what you did with that leaf, but . . . well, it worked. My hand feels much better." What Gabrielle didn't say, but thought, was that the rest of her felt—

She pinched off that thought before it had a chance to blossom. It would be best not to think about how the rest of her felt right now. Letting her thoughts stray in such a wayward direction could be dangerous, especially when she was oh so excruciatingly conscious of every hard, masculine inch of the body stretched out beneath her.

Connor trapped a groan in his throat. At some point his hands had slipped downward, his open palms settling on the generous curve of her hips. Quite low on her hips, in fact. He realized this fact only now, and the knowledge cut through him like a lightning bolt. His palms burned to feel the soft heat of her beneath the coarse, tight-fitting trews. It was all he could do not to flex his fingers, to test the warm pliancy of her softness beneath his hands.

Last night there'd been no barrier of cloth between them. It had been skin against skin, and it had felt so very good and right. Was it wrong to wish the impediment gone now, so he could once again feel her silky flesh gliding beneath his fingertips, once again feel—?

" 'Twould seem I owe you an apology as well as my thanks, m'lord," she said, her tremulous voice snagging his attention even as she averted her gaze contritely. "I am in your debt after all."

She shifted as though preparing to push to her feet. The feel of her inner thighs grinding against him was an unparalleled delight. Vivid memories of their previous, mutually gratifying night together whirlwinded through Connor's mind. Before he'd realized what he was doing, his hands lifted, encircling her upper arms.

His lips parted, and while Connor knew full well that he was about to say something, his mind was such a jumble that he'd no idea what the words would be . . . until he heard them echoing in his own ears. Was it his imagination, or did his voice sound unnaturally low and husky? "She looked like ye, mistress."

"Who did?"

"Ailean Carelton," he replied. "Yer great-great aunt. The one who started this feud between Maxwell and Douglas. Ye bear a powerful resemblance tae her."

"I do?" A frown furrowed Gabrielle's brow as she gazed down at him. "How do you know?"

"There's a portrait of her at Bracklenaer." Connor swallowed hard and tried not to think about how much he wanted to cup her face in his hands, how much he ached to pull her down to him and smooth away the delicate creases of her scowl with his mouth and tongue.

"I've seen no portrait."

"Nor would ye, considering where it hangs. Dinna look so surprised, lass, I've made nae secret of keeping yer movements aboot Bracklenaer restricted, for obvious reasons. Ye've seen scarce little of the keep, naught that I didna want ye tae see." Connor's eyes narrowed still more. His expression became tense, guarded. "That, of course, will nae doubt change . . . once we're wed."

There was no need to watch closely for her reaction since Gabrielle made no attempt to conceal it. Her green eyes widened, and her jaw went slack. Her lips parted in a silent "Oh!" The full curve of her cheeks went dark with a flush, then just as quickly drained of color. While she didn't move, he detected an undeniable stiffening in the body atop his.

"You're still of a mind to wed me?" she asked. To his keen ear, her voice for sure sounded under her strict control.

"Was there e'er a doubt of it? Dinna I make my intentions clear the morn ye arrived at Bracklenaer?"

"You did, and at the time I thought you serious, but then time passed. And more time still. You left me to cool my heels for well over a fortnight in the company of only your aunt, your cousin, or your guards. Truth to tell, m'lord, I thought you'd changed your mind on the matter." What Gabrielle didn't add was how badly it stung, even now, to think he'd changed his mind about wedding her only after seeing her in the flesh. It shouldn't matter—she'd not wanted to marry to begin with, and she'd no desire to marry a heathen Scot . . . or so she told herself—yet it did. It mattered a great deal more than she cared to admit.

"Ye were sick," Connor offered by way of explanation, yet inwardly he had to admit the explanation sounded pitifully lame. Mayhap there was a reason he'd delayed the wedding? A reason he hadn't admitted, even to himself?

"I was not sick for *that* long!" Gabrielle countered tightly. "Look at me, m'lord. I'm young, I'm strong, I'm quite sturdy—er, that is to say, I regained my health quickly enough. Yet even once I was well again, you kept me prisoner, never visiting me, never revealing what your plans for me were. Surely you can see where, under those circumstances, I would think you'd changed your mind."

She needn't have instructed him to look at her, for Connor was having the devil's own time looking anywhere *else*. The inky shades of the night cast her hair a velvety shade of black, the shadows playing over her features, softening and defining them to a breathtaking degree. The weight of her was a deliciously tempting burden atop him. His hands still cradled her hips; his palms itched to slip upward, to peel off her clothing and explore again the full, ripe curves of her body, the way he had last night.

Too well he remembered her wild response to his touch.

Too much he craved to experience her uninhibited response again.

And again.

Their lovemaking was unlike anything Connor had ever felt before in his life. Somewhere deep down in his soul he was positive he would never, *never* experience anything like it again. Not with another woman. Not with any woman but Gabrielle Carelton. And, och! but didn't that make the thought of wedding her, of taking her into his bed every night thereafter, all the more appealing? Aye, for certain it did.

"I havena changed my mind, lass," he said, his voice thick with conviction. "I vowed tae wed ye afore e'er setting eyes on ye, and wed ye I shall. 'Twas a marriage between Carelton and Maxwell that started this bloody feud, and a marriage between Douglas and Carelton that shall put a stop tae it."

She glanced away quickly, before Connor could determine the emotion that suddenly clouded her expression. He watched her nibble her full lower lip between her teeth. He refused to surrender to the urge that was abruptly clawing inside him . . . the urge to pull her face down to his, to replace her teeth with his own.

"When?" she asked, and her voice cracked.

"The banns were posted a fortnight ago."

"I was still sick then."

"Aye. As I said, 'tis why I waited. Ye're nae longer sick, howe'er. We'll wed as soon as we reach Bracklenaer."

Her gaze returned to him; her eyes were narrow, the green depths guarded and unreadable. "And if I say I'll not marry you? What then, m'lord?"

"On either side of the Border some things dinna change. Wenches are nae given the luxury of making such a choice, lass, and well ye ken it. And e'en if they were, e'en if ye could choose to wed me or nay . . . would ye go against yer Queen's orders?"

"I'd be doing no such thing. Elizabeth ordered me to wed *Colin* Douglas," she replied, her chin lifting stubbornly, *"not* his brother."

" 'Tis Colin ye'd rather have, then, is it?"

"I-I didn't say that."

Before Connor could guess what she was about to do, Gabrielle pushed to her feet. First her hips, then her thighs, skimmed beneath his palms, then they were gone. Cool night air rushed in to chill him in all the places where her body had kept him warm.

Moss and leaves crunched under her bootheels as she took a few steps away from him. Her arms encircling her waist, she hugged herself tightly.

Pushing himself to a sitting position, Connor bent his right knee and cushioned his elbow atop it. He didn't follow her with anything save his gaze. He didn't dare. The temptation to pull her back into his arms—to rake his fingers through her hair, to feel her mouth opening beneath his—was still overpoweringly strong.

"Tell me, m'lord, was Ailean Carelton also forced to wed, or did she go to her marriage b-bed willingly?" She hesitated, cleared her throat. "And how does your Douglas ancestor fit into this feud? I'm a bit confused on that score. From what you've told me, 'twould seem the feud should be between Maxwell and Carelton, not Maxwell and Douglas."

"The past repeats itself, lass. My great-great grandfather planned tae wed Ailean. And so he would have . . . had Lachlan Maxwell nae taken a liking tae the lass's horse, then tae the lass herself. He kidnapped her, ravished her, and wed her afore the Douglas had the chance."

"The horse?" Gabrielle asked, a playful grin tugging at one corner of her lips.

"Ailean," Connor hastened to clarify. "Mind ye, 'tis ne'er been entirely clear in which order those events—the kidnapping, wedding, and bedding—took place."

"Does it matter?" One dark eyebrow rose in question. "The end result, the feud between Douglas and Maxwell, remains the same."

"A feud that's been tae many decades in the making, one that has caused nothing but destruction for both sides." Raking his fingers through his hair, Connor shook his head and sighed. "As 'tis, half the Douglas men I questioned a fortnight ago dinna even remember the cause, nor did they seem tae care o'er much what they be fighting aboot. Och! I'll nae be sad tae see it over. The joining of Carelton and Douglas can do that. It can put an end tae the feud once and for all."

Gabrielle grimaced. She did not look pleased to hear it.

Why, Connor wondered, did her displeasure gnaw at him ever so much?

His voice softened when, after a moment's hesitation, he asked, "Is the thought of wedding me truly so horrible?"

"Aye, of course. You are The Black Douglas,"

she replied, as though that explained everything. Didn't it?

"God's blood, lass, how many times do I have tae be telling ye? I'm nae *The* Black Douglas! 'Tis merely a silly nickname. It means naught."

"On the contrary, m'lord, it means a great deal. What may be a silly nickname to you also inspires fear on both sides of the Border. Did you know that in England mothers use your name as a threat to get their children to behave? More than that, did you know the threat *works?*"

"Surely ye jest, lass."

"I do not. Many's the time I've heard it used. 'Tis a common threat." Gabrielle wrinkled her nose, her voice rising to an unnaturally shrewish pitch. " 'Don't tarry on your way back,' they say, 'or The Black Douglas will get you. He thrives on young English boys, don't you know? He likes to eat them for breakfast and pick his teeth with their bones come noon!' "

"The devil you say!" Connor stormed to his feet. In two sure strides he crossed the distance separating them. Her upper arms felt soft and warm beneath his palms as he coiled his fingers around them, tugged, forced her to face him. The muscles in his jaw bunched hard when he gritted his teeth, unable—or unwilling?—to believe what she was telling him. His gray eyes flashed angrily as he glared down into her speculative green ones. "I've ne'er hurt a bairn in me life! Many's the time I've gone out of me way tae *spare* them!"

"Really?" Gabrielle asked. She surprised them both by the level way she met his glare and the calm timbre she injected into her tone. " 'Tis not what they say."

"They say a lot of things aboot me, Gabrielle. Just because they say it doesna make it true."

"Then it's not true that you snuck into Caerlaverock in the dead of night aided by a mere one hundred and fifty men? That you stole two hundred of the clan's livestock, took another half that amount in prisoners, and snuck out again, with Johnny Maxwell none the wiser until morn. Even then the poor man only realized what happened because no one was there to fetch his morning meal. Apparently, you'd kidnapped his cook."

"Johnny Maxwell is *nae* a 'poor man.'" Connor's grin was wicked and quick. "As for Siobhan . . . truth to tell, I was after the beasties. Howe'er, had I known the lass was so gifted with a skillet I'd have made her my goal instead."

"You admit it?"

"Aye. *Nay!* I mean . . . Och! lass, ye've got me so rattled I dinna ken what I mean." His grip on her arms loosened but didn't drop away. "There's nae shame in admitting that the last time I heard the tale, the amount of beasties I pilfered, nae to mention the amount of men who helped me pilfer them, was only a fraction of that."

"Then you *do* admit it." Her voice was as suddenly as stiff as her spine.

"Admit what? To riding against a rival family? I took from the Maxwell in the spring what the Maxwell took from the Douglas last autumn. Aye, I admit it. Open yer eyes, lass. Take a good look around ye. I ken ye've been on this side of the Border but a short time, but 'tis long enough to see the way of things here. Good God, wench, reiving is our way of life! How else would we get blankets to survive the winter? Without stolen beasties, how could we feed the children and old people through the long, snowy months? Compared tae most raids, the one you speak of was tame."

"M'lord, have you not thought of weaving your own blankets? Of breeding your own cattle and sheep? There's no need to steal from your neighbor that which your clan can provide for itself."

"Provide," he countered, "only tae have it stolen by others."

Gabrielle didn't need to think about what he said for long. Reluctantly, she had to admit he had a very good point. Raising their own livestock, making their own cloth . . . while the solution *sounded* good, in practice it would be another matter entirely. It was only a patch remedy, one that couldn't hope to solve the underlying problem: that anything the clan Douglas provided for themselves they would have to provide in profusion, for it would be just as quickly stolen by rivals who didn't share the same values. From what she'd seen, no family on either side of these disreputable Borders shared such exalted values.

Connor released her arm. With the tip of his index finger he traced the soft, full line of her jaw, the curve of her chin. His fingertip hesitated, then turned upward, skimming the sensitive bend of her lower lip.

The flesh beneath his touch trembled and, God help him, he trembled himself in response. His mind flashed him an image of her nibbling the skin he now touched; her lip was still temptingly moist from it. The muscles in his stomach knotted as his tongue ran restlessly over the backs of his teeth. Had the urge to kiss her diminished at all? Not that Connor was aware of. It still raged hot and fast in his blood.

He tipped his head to the side, lowered it slowly, his eyes blazing with hungry intent.

There was more than enough time to stop him. The fingers gripping her upper arm had loosened, now merely draping over her sleeve instead of holding her in place. Little effort would be needed to break the contact and step away from him. Gabrielle considered doing exactly that, but only for a moment.

Her attention lifted . . .

And she saw the passion shimmering in his piercing gray eyes . . .

And she was lost . . .

The topic they'd been discussing dashed from her mind with all the speed of half-starved hounds catching the scent of a nearby fox. The nearness and the heat of Connor's body suddenly consumed her thoughts. The night sounds, indeed the very night itself, seemed to close in around her, tunneling down until all she was aware of, all she *wanted* to be aware of, was Connor Douglas and the way his mouth inched ever closer in its path to claiming hers.

Her lips tingled with the promised contact. Dizzily, she swayed toward him. Her chin rose, her eyelashes flickered shut. Her right hand opened, lifted, splayed over the sculpted plane of his tunic-clad chest. His heart pounded wildly beneath the ball of her palm; the rhythm matched the one drumming loudly in her ears.

Connor's breath whisked warmly over Gabrielle's face an instant before his mouth settled hungrily over her own.

Thirteen

His arms stole around her waist. A hot shiver skated down his spine as he dug his fingers into her bottom. He pulled her close, grinding their hips together in a rhythm that was older than time. Her breasts pushed against his chest; they felt deliciously heavy and full. Even through the barrier of cloth separating their flesh, he could feel her nipples bead into mouth-wateringly rigid peaks.

He swallowed her moan of pleasure.

His tongue skated over her parted lips, then plunged into the hot, moist inner recesses of her mouth. Her teeth felt like warm, slick pearls as they skimmed beneath his searching tongue. Her taste was more intoxicating than all the whisky in Scotland.

Connor groaned and angled his head, his tongue stroking deeply, teasing and tasting. The sensations that built inside him were overwhelming in their intensity. Desire sizzled through him like a lightning bolt. It was all he could do to hold himself in check and not surrender to the urge to strip off their clothes and spread her naked body down on the ground, covered by his own.

Soon, he promised himself . . . Very soon. But not now. First he wanted to savor the thrill of longing, prolong the tingling anticipation of what lay ahead until neither of them could stand waiting a second longer.

Gabrielle's response was as immediate as it was brazen and bold. Her hands, restless for the feel of him, shifted their attention.

Her fingers clutched at the sleeves covering his upper arms. Nay, in truth she clutched at the muscle playing beneath. She could feel the hard bands of sinew bunching beneath her touch. Her breath caught at the sensations that thundered through her. Last night she may have been a stranger to desire, but no more. Connor Douglas had taught her the ways of a man and a woman, and taught her well. She knew exactly what she wanted. And she was not at all shy about obtaining it.

Deepening the kiss to a frenzied pitch, she arched her spine. The front of her body rubbed provocatively against his even as her tongue met and matched his rhythm, then in turn demanded and coaxed and increased it.

The hard, intimate length of him throbbed with need against the front of her hips. A hauntingly familiar ache pulsed in the juncture of her thighs. The sensation magnified, channeled throughout the rest of her body with a speed and power that both frightened and astounded her.

Gabrielle's knees felt weak and watery, alarmingly unsubstantial. She leaned against him, breathless and shaken. The virile cushion of his chest absorbed the tremors that wracked through her even as it offered a supportive brace for her abruptly precarious balance.

The need to feel him, skin to hot, sensitive skin was overpowering.

Gabrielle's fingers unwrapped from around Connor's arms, opened and strayed inward. The laces beneath his throat felt rough to the touch as she fumbled with them, finally undoing the knot and spreading open the plackets. Thick, inky curls tickled her fingertips as she slipped her hand beneath the cloth and stroked his skin.

The sound that came from between Gabrielle's lips was half inhalation, half gasp. The smell of leather and horse mixed with a rich, spicy scent that was entirely, provocatively male; the aromas meshed, weaving around her, engulfing her. Her senses spinning, she used her free hand to unfasten the clan brooch on his left shoulder. Free, the clasp tumbled from her fingers to the moss-strewn ground. The plaid slipped down his thickly muscled arm as her attention detoured. She tugged at the hem of his tunic until it slipped free from beneath the waist of his kilt.

The back of her knuckles skimmed the hard, flat plane of his belly as she dragged the tunic up. Higher. Abandoning the ravenous kiss, she went up on tiptoe and pulled the garment off over his head. Like the brooch, it slipped from her hand, floating unnoticed to the ground at his feet.

Her fingers combed through his dark hair, twisted, fisted the strands close to his scalp as she angled his head up and back, exposing the thick expanse of his neck.

Her lips felt dry as, green eyes narrowing, she watched the shadowy pulse beating in the base of his throat.

Gabrielle groaned. Surrendering to temptation, her mouth mirrored her gaze. His skin felt hot, and tasted salty sweet beneath the darting strokes of her tongue.

While one hand continued to cup and knead her deliciously supple bottom, the other slipped upward. Hooking his fingers over her shoulder, his forearm supporting her back, he leaned into her, forcing her to arch backward.

His legs opened, his knees vising her thighs. Effortlessly, he lowered her onto a mattress of night-crispened leaves and moss. Her silky black curls tickled the underside of his jaw as he spread himself out atop the soft bed of her curves.

Despite the change in position, her mouth never left him; she'd suckled a patch of his skin into her mouth and now teased it with her teeth and tongue in a manner that was thoroughly distracting and extremely arousing.

It was Connor's turn to shiver. The tremors rocked through his body, starting on the inside and working their way out. He would have liked to blame the shiver on the cold night air, but knew damn well it would be a lie. Had the flesh on the side of his neck ever been so sensitive? Not that he could recall.

It wasn't until he felt her fumbling at the waist of his kilt that Connor slipped his hand from beneath her. His palm slipped over the generous curve of her hip, brushing her own hands aside.

"Nay, firebrand," he murmured against the side of her head. "Nae yet."

He captured her wrists and dragged them up over her head. The brittle end of a twig scraped the back of his knuckles as he pinned those wrists in one fist. It was a double-edged form of torture, Connor realized too late. The gesture made her breasts push up into his chest more fully, until he couldn't help but be excruciatingly aware of every voluptuous inch of their firmness.

His free hand shifted to where his mind had locked, and locked hard. He'd been in the process of inhaling; his breath caught in the throat she continued to nibble as his open hand settled over one plentiful breast.

Her nipple had begun to soften. He felt it grow instantly rigid beneath his palm. As much as the weight of him atop her would allow, she arched up into the touch. A sound that was one part moan, one part whimper, skimmed past her lips.

Anchoring his weight on the elbows flanking her ribs, Connor levered himself up a fraction. Not far, yet enough to allow him to gaze down into dark green eyes that were glassy and heavy-lidded. The color in her cheeks was high, awash with a telltale peachy flush. Her lips were parted, the rosy skin there damp and still a wee bit swollen from his kiss.

"Tell me, lass," Connor said, his voice low and controlled, revealing nothing of the anticipation that raced through him as he wondered what her reaction to his words would be, "is the idea of becoming my bride, of spending the rest of yer nights entwined with me thus, truly so unappealing tae ye?"

A frown flickered over Gabrielle's brow. Good heavens, why would he ask such a thing? Could he not tell from her lusty response that she found his touch anything *but* unappealing? She shook her head. "Nay, m' lord, not unappealing," she murmured, and again arched so that her breast pushed fully into his hand, as though to prove the sincerity of her words. "Not unappealing at all."

"Yet still ye resist the idea of wedding me?"

"I'll admit I'm not as opposed to the idea as I once was." Gabrielle blushed and glanced quickly away when he grinned down at her.

Connor's hand shifted. Through the thin cloth of her tunic, he circled her passion-hard nipple with the edge of his thumbnail. "Then ye've nae objection to me doing this . . . tonight and all the nights after?"

Gabrielle lifted her chin, luxuriating in the sizzling bolt of sensation that shot through her. "Nay," she whispered hoarsely. Her voice, she noticed as though from a distance, sounded oddly low and rough. "No objection at all."

"Or this?" he asked as his hand strayed downward. Gathering the folds of her shirt in his fist, he dragged it upward. The cloth bunched around her middle, just beneath her breasts. His hand snuck beneath. "Still nae objection, lass?"

The tip of his index finger dipped into her navel, circled, then slowly, slowly, began a breathtaking ascent. His bare hand cupped her aching flesh as a sort of pleasure-pain sizzled through her.

"None," Gabrielle rasped breathlessly.

"And now?" he asked as he caught her nipple between his index finger and thumb and gently rolled it back and forth.

She clenched her teeth together hard, completely without words. She knew she wouldn't have been able to utter a syllable even if she could think of anything to say. Lucid thought was beyond her right now. It simply wasn't possible to think of anything beyond Connor Douglas's rough caress, beyond the hard warmth of his body pressing her down upon the ground.

He scoured her nipple with his battle-calloused palm.

Her back came up off the forest floor. A moan, breathless and husky and fervent beyond reason, rushed past her lips. She turned her head, trying to bury the sound in her shoulder, but already it was too late. Worse, she was beyond caring. While the knowledge that her response was wanton in the extreme played in a small corner of her mind, the knowledge that she wouldn't stop him for the world so long as he continued to make her feel so magnificent was stronger still.

Oh, nay. She wasn't so fickle or so short of memory that she'd forgotten last night. It was a memory that would follow her to the grave!

The fact of the matter remained that it was their lovemaking that had decided her fate. What good would resisting Connor now do, aside prove that she could? And even then, to what end? What could she possibly hope to gain but leave them both filled with frustrated desire and sharp longing? The damage, after all, was done. It had been done last night and, truth to tell, Gabrielle doubted if, even given the impossible chance, she would change it now if she could.

Body and soul.

The words echoed through her mind.

Last night Connor Douglas had claimed her as his own, body and soul, and she'd given herself, all of herself, to him freely.

The balladeers may have labeled this man a devil, but he made love like a fiery angel. One kiss, one touch, and her senses spiraled until she could think of nothing but here and now, of forgetting who he was, who she was, and of only laying in his arms . . . ah, yes, forever.

How could she think of aught else when he held her this way, caressing her just so, his touch lingering, teasing, promising still more intimacy. He'd learned her body well, as though he'd mapped her curves and valleys and now knew them equally, if not better, than he knew the craggy landscape beyond the night-inkened forest. His hands were sure and skillful; he knew the exact spots to stroke, the exact pressure to apply, for her ultimate pleasure. Effortlessly, he aroused within her a deluge of white-hot, tumultuous sensations . . . sensations that, until last night, were beyond anything she'd imagined, unlike anything she'd dared to dream existed.

His hand left her. A slice of disappointment stabbed through her. Cool night air washed over her passion-fevered skin. The chill lasted but a second; Connor's fingers were soon replaced by the delicious, moist heat of his mouth.

Gabrielle sucked in a ragged gasp, her body shuddering violently. Her lashes flickered down. Fingers convulsing reflexively, she gripped his sinewy upper arms, clinging to him blindly. Her back arched as she strained up, up, up into the intimacy that made her body melt and her thoughts scatter.

Or was it the feel of his open mouth covering her nipple—the sizzlingly erotic pressure he applied as he suckled the sensitive bead of flesh into his mouth, circled it with his tongue, teased it with his teeth—that made her senses spin?

. . . ye've nae objection to me doing this . . . tonight and all the nights after?

The words tumbled through her desire-fogged mind. She'd meant every word she'd said; she truly had no objection. What Gabrielle hadn't said, what she indeed had trouble acknowledging even to herself, was that she could not in her wildest dreams imagine another man touching her the way Connor Douglas did. She didn't even *want* to imagine it.

The last time she'd felt desire build inside her like this she hadn't known the emotion, had been so stunned by the force of it she'd been frightened. She knew what it was now, knew the throbbing ache deep inside her was nothing to be afraid of, that Connor would know exactly how to ease it, and when he did, she'd experience sensations equal to none.

Gabrielle wanted to feel those sensations again. She wanted to feel them again now, with an intensity that knocked the very breath from her.

Her hands slipped up his thickly muscled arms, over the broad width of his shoulders. He tensed beneath her touch as she stroked a sizzling path down his back. Her fingers curled into white-knuckled fists as he tugged at the coarse material of her tunic.

Gabrielle aided him to pull the garment up over her head by shifting her weight from one arm to the other. She tossed it aside, her hands once again hungrily caressing his back and waist before the cloth could flutter to the ground.

He lowered himself atop her.

Gabrielle pulled in a shaky breath and released it in a long, slow, gratifying sigh. Ah, yes, this was what she'd wanted, this was exactly the feeling she'd been searching for. His bare flesh against hers was shockingly wonderful. She wrapped her arms around his waist and pushed up against him, wriggled, luxuriated in the unique feel of his hot, naked skin rubbing against hers.

The throbbing between her legs magnified, piercing her to the core, then quickly whirlwinding throughout the rest of her body. Need built, focused. Tunneling down to an all-consuming, driving ache that begged to be satisfied.

She whimpered softly when his mouth left her breast. He shifted attention, sipping at the full under-curve, dipping lower.

Lower.

Lower still.

His teeth nibbled the soft skin of her stomach. Hot and wet, his tongue circled the nook of her navel. Her fingers curled inward, the nail raking the tender flesh on his back as his mouth slipped lower still.

Gabrielle stilled, and her breath wedged painfully in her throat when she felt first his chin, then lips, graze the triangular nest of thick, silky black curls between her legs. The muscles in her arms and legs pulled taut with anticipation as he eased her thighs open.

His attention traveled slowly up the soft, lush, naked length of her body.

Her attention started downward.

Their gazes met and held for one throbbing heartbeat.

"Wh-what are you do—?"

His head dipped, and suddenly Gabrielle had no breath with which to finish the question.

The first stroke of his tongue was intimate and quick; the contact surged through her like a bolt of lightning. Her hands were on his shoulders; they lifted, her fingers curling around handfuls of his thick black hair. She'd thought the feel of his breath arousing as it wafted over her naked belly, yet the sensation was nothing compared to the feel of where his breath caressed her now.

She moaned, low and deep. Her hips came up off the ground.

Seizing the advantage, Connor slipped his hands beneath her, his palms cupping her bottom, his strong fingers kneading her pliant softness as he levered her up.

The strokes of his tongue became longer, fast, bolder.

"Dear God," Gabrielle rasped, her lower body moving in time to the rhythm his devouring mouth set.

It was happening too fast. Gabrielle longed somehow to slow down the frenzied pace of their lovemaking, to prolong and to enjoy to its sweet fullness each fiery sensation. Yet the exquisite things Connor was doing to her with his mouth and hands prevented that. His darting tongue was persistent, driving her insane, pushing her closer and closer to the edge of ecstasy.

Like a fragilely built dam threatened by a tumultuous flood, weakened and ready to explode, the now familiar feelings quickened in Gabrielle's loins, hot and insistent, demanding a natural, breathless culmination. She tried to resist, tried to hold back, tried to make the moment last, but it was no use. She might as well try to make her heart stop pounding, she'd have equally as much luck. In mere seconds, the tidal wave was upon her.

"Connor!" Gabrielle cried out as the pleasure overtook her, spasmodic surges of release washing all through her body, tightening her muscles in pulsating tides that carried her under and away on the deep, blissful undertow of raw sensation.

Connor gritted his teeth. With effort he trapped a rough groan in his throat. Her knees were bent, and the inside of her thighs cupped his ears, blotting out the sounds of the night, blotting out everything except the sound of his own heartbeat thundering in his ears.

The oh so sweet smell of her, the potently unique taste of her, the moist feminine heat of her surrounded him, engulfed him, threatened to drown him. His resilience was tested in a nerve-shattering way it had never been tested before. His scalp burned from the way she tightly fisted his hair, holding his mouth to her as though afraid he would divert his attention elsewhere. The sensation served to heighten his desire. It was all he could do not to surrender to the urge to cover her body with his, to thrust himself inside her, possess her.

And then, over the din of his heartbeat echoing in his ears, he heard her call out his name and his mouth and tongue felt her body convulse with the first spasms of release . . . and he knew he could not hold back a second longer.

Lowering her writhing hips to the ground, he eased his body on top of hers. The tip of his hard, throbbing shaft did not have to search long before finding its mark.

As one, their hips pushed forward simultaneously. A shudder rippled through Connor when he felt himself gloved by her gloriously tight, wet heat.

He stilled instantly, suddenly afraid to move. He wanted the moment to last for an eternity, yet if he moved now, it would be to plunge into that abyss of fulfillment. Dear God, nay, not yet!

Again, one palm slipped under her bottom, only this time it was to hold her to him as his other hand cradled the small of her back. He shifted, rolled, until it was he whose back was cradled against the leaf-strewn forest floor.

Her legs straddled his hips. Her full, ripe breasts were plastered to his chest; he was aware of every voluptuous curve of her. How could he not be? His fingers trembled as one of his hands slipped downward, the other up. Cradling the sides of her hips, he used his thumbs to lever her up until she sat atop him.

As he watched, her lips parted in an unspoken "Oh!" Her lashes flickered upward, her green eyes narrow and dazed with passion as her gaze met and held his.

Slowly, slowly, he guided her hips forward and back, lifted her gently, then pulled her down on top of him with a wee bit more force. She was an apt pupil; she learned the rhythm well and quickly put it to use by increasing the speed and variance to a dizzying pitch.

Connor swallowed hard. Had he really thought this position would delay his own release? More the fool he; he should have known better. Not only did it increase his own pleasure, but rekindled hers as well. Gabrielle had soon set a pace that had him gritting his teeth against the flood of sensations that rushed through him.

A fine sweat beaded on his brow and upper lip. More moistened the thatch of hair pelting his chest. His hips rose when hers came down, and he buried himself inside her as deeply as he could go.

Again.

And again.

And again.

One of them groaned, the sound deep and feral. Connor thought the sound came from himself, but truth to tell he had no time to analyze its whereabouts.

His skin tingled as her hands swept over his chest, down his arms. Her fingers opened, entwining with his as she moved frantically atop him.

The fringe of her long inky hair tickled his upper thighs as she tossed her head back, exposing the creamy expanse of her neck. Her breathing came hard and fast, the ragged give and take matched by his own as he again felt the ripples deep inside her that signaled another, stronger release.

She moaned something, the words slurred and her English accent so thick as to make them momentarily unintelligible.

He was lost. His fingers gripped her hips, pulling her down on top of him, guiding her hips in breath-snatching circles as he arched up into her, finally allowing himself to surrender to his own hot surge of completion.

The contractions went on and on, longer than he could remember them ever lasting before. They drained him dry, leaving him weak and depleted, as though he'd spilled not only his seed into her, but his very lifeforce as well.

Weakly, Gabrielle collapsed atop him.

And then Connor found himself again doing something he'd never done with a woman before.

He wrapped his arms about her and, cradling her close, their bodies still intimately joined, he eased them onto their sides, facing each other. Her right leg draped his naked hip, her hand rode the slight indentation of his waist. At another time, he might have found the gesture one of entrapment. Now, he did not.

Her head nestled perfectly in the crook nature had carved between his neck and shoulder. Dark, fragrant curls teased his neck, their texture and scent a cool, soothing balm to his passion-burnt nerves. Breathing a sigh of raw contentment, he let his eyes flicker shut.

Connor knew the exact moment she fell asleep. It was the instant when her choppy breathing leveled out, when the muscles beneath his palms loosened. Although their lovemaking had left him equally depleted and drowsy, it took much longer for him to surrender to the heavy tug of sleep.

Instead, his mind played over and over the words Gabrielle had murmured at the moment of her release. Without passion driving him hard, blotting out everything else, he could now remember and understand exactly what it was she'd said.

She'd whispered huskily, "Connor, I love you . . ."

The words both shocked Connor to the core, and pleased him immensely. A strong surge of . . . *something* sparked in his blood, a need to shelter and protect that, oddly enough, did not stem from physical desire, but from something infinitely stronger and more enduring.

By her own uncoerced admission, Gabrielle Carelton had lost her heart to him.

And, sweet Jesus, but that changed *everything!*

Fourteen

"He was looking at ye again, lass," Ella said as she sidled her mare up close to Gabrielle's. "Should I ask what transpired between ye last night when ye both left camp? Or do I already ken the answer?"

Gabrielle's attention had been focused on the craggy ground that passed beneath her mare's hooves. At Ella's words, her gaze lifted, shifting forward, past the swaying backs of the two prisoners tied securely into the saddles of the pair of mounts positioned in front of her and Ella and behind Connor. The bits of both captives' horses had been tethered to Connor's saddle with a thick length of roughly hewn rope.

Connor's back was straight and proud, his attention focused determinedly forward. The ends of his hair brushed the broad shelf of his shoulder with each jostling stride of his horse. If he'd glanced back at her, as Ella seemed to think he had, there was no sign.

Shifting her attention, Gabrielle frowned at the girl. Perhaps she had meant one of the other men? "What are you talking about? Who is looking at me?"

"Connor," Ella answered promptly and honestly. A sly grin tugged at her mouth. "Who else?" A frown creased the creamy skin between her coppery brows. "I've been thinking on the matter, ye ken, and I canna remember a time when I've seen me cousin look so . . . aye, confused. 'Tis the emotion I see in his eyes whene'er he glances at ye. If I dinna ken better, I'd think ye've bewitched him."

"I could say the same for you and Roy Maxwell. The man has barely taken his eyes off you all morning."

Ella wrinkled her nose in disgust. "Nae doubt if the looks he's casting me were daggers, as he nae doubt wishes they were, I'd be dead right now. The mon isna happy tae find himself being ill-treated by a mere slip of a lass."

"Most men would not be, Ella."

The girl gave a shrug of her delicate shoulders, as though dismissing the thought, and quickly changed the subject. "Colin told me earlier that Mairghread broke free only a few hours after she was taken."

Her knees gently nudging the mare's side, Gabrielle slowed the horse's pace. She had to squint against the bright March sunlight to survey Ella closely. "Are you trying to tell me—?"

"Aye," Ella replied gravely, and nodded. "I'm telling ye that e'erything we'd set out tae do was for naught. E'en if we'd been lucky enough tae reach Gaelside, we'd have failed in our mission. Mairghread wasna there. Apparently me aunt can take care of herself, aye?"

"Must be the Douglas in her," Gabrielle remarked, her attention on Connor's back.

Ella was right, he *did* keep glancing back at her. She'd been too distracted with her own tumultuous thoughts—hot, vivid memories of their love-making kept playing with drumming persistence in her mind—to notice it before. Until Ella had drawn her attention to the fact. Gabrielle noticed it now, however, and noticed it with her entire being. Her blood warmed and she felt a tingle of awareness fire in her veins.

Her gaze met Connor's for only a beat, yet even in that short space of time, volumes of unspoken words passed between them.

His expression unreadable, Connor shifted, again facing forward in his saddle.

Gabrielle sighed and turned her attention back to Ella, only to find that the girl was no longer paying her any mind. Instead, she was staring at a different male back, and staring at it hard. The back was that of Roy Maxwell. Her expression was guarded, her forehead furrowed in contemplation.

Gabrielle shifted uncomfortably in her saddle, wondering how much longer it would take for them to reach Bracklenaer. How far away were they? They'd been riding most of the morning, surely the keep could not be too far away now?

And once they arrived? What then? she wondered. Would Connor keep his vow to see them wed posthaste? Would he—she gulped—insist the makeshift ceremony be held today? He'd admitted the banns had been ready. There was no valid reason for any delay.

Another question surfaced, this one stronger, more insistent, teasing at her unmercifully if only because there was no ready answer.

Had Connor heard what she'd said to him last night when they'd made love?

There was no way to be certain.

The only thing Gabrielle could be sure of was that she *had* confessed her feelings for him. Unintentionally, aye, but confessed them nonetheless. That the proclamation had slipped out, uttered in a moment of unbridled passion and weakness, mattered not at all. If given the opportunity to take the words back, she would not seize it; the circumstances surrounding them could not make the statement any less true.

Heaven help her, she *did* love Connor.

When had the emotion surfaced? How had it flourished? She didn't know, but surface and flourish it had, without her knowledge or consent. When she glanced at him, or he at her, her senses tingled, her thoughts spun, the world tunneled down around her until no one but the two of them existed. When he touched her, kissed her, or merely hinted at doing either, she was lost.

Those symptoms could be attributed to lust, pure and raw, except for one important fact. Aye, lately when her musings had turned to the future, she thought as automatically as breathing of Connor, of Bracklenaer, of a castle full of babes with inky black hair and piercing gray eyes. Like their father.

Had a child been conceived by their lovemaking last night or the night before that? Was Connor's babe even taking root in her womb?

The idea was thrilling beyond reason, and at the same time inordinately dispiriting.

He'd not made a similar confession, nor had he given even a curious acknowledgment of hers.

That he'd not said he loved her back cut Gabrielle to the quick.

"Och! are ye crying, lass?" Ella asked as, sitting forward, she inspected Gabrielle's face.

Gritting her teeth, Gabrielle quickly averted her attention, dipping her head so the thick, dark curtain of her hair shielded her profile from the girl's eagle-sharp gaze. With the back of a tightly balled fist, she whisked a drop of moisture from where it clung to the dark curl of her lashes before it could splash warmly onto her cheek.

"Nay," Gabrielle answered a bit too quickly for her words to carry the tone of sincerity she strived for. " 'Tis simply exhaustion coupled with this rough spring breeze. It makes my eyes water, is all."

"Is that the way of it?" Ella asked, her tone as doubtful as her expression.

"Aye, 'tis." Gabrielle shrugged vaguely. Of course the reason she'd given Ella was the true cause behind her burning, watering eyes. What other reason could there be? Surely it wasn't the way Queen Elizabeth's words, spoken long ago yet never quite forgotten, chose that untimely moment to ring a haunting chord in her mind. Words that harshly predicted Gabrielle's bloodlines would someday win her a husband, there was never a doubt of it, but her plain face and stout form would never win his singular devotion and love . . .

Bracklenaer's courtyard was alive with activity. Groups of servants clustered in stone wall-shaded corners, talking animatedly among themselves. Some of the Douglas men had led their horses from the stalls and were now busily preparing their mounts to ride.

Connor's eyes narrowed as he guided his horse to a stop. Gaze narrow, his attention swept his surroundings. The hair at his nape tingled with awareness, for the excitement permeating the cool, late-morning air was almost tangible enough to touch and taste.

What was happening? What could have taken place during his brief absence that accounted for such an unusual commotion? Had the Kerrs finally carried through on their threatened raid, or had something unexpected and dire happened?

An uneasy feeling trickled like a drop of ice water down Connor's spine. Aye, something was definitely amiss. He could *feel* it. He wished Gilby was up and about, for that was one man who would have greeted Connor with the necessary news and explained the situation in precise measure.

Gilby, however, was not about, which meant Connor would have to seek out the source of the disturbance himself.

With a quick gesture Connor indicated that Ella and Gabrielle should remain mounted and in place guarding their two prisoners. Dismounting, he crossed quickly to the nearest group of men, who were tossing saddles over the backs of their stocky, shaggy mounts and hastily securing the leather strips that held them in place.

Gabrielle watched Connor closely as he angled his head and drew into conversation the two men who continued to ready their horses as they spoke to their laird.

Frowning at Ella, she leaned closer to the girl and whispered, "What is going on here?"

Ella shook her head slowly, thoughtfully. "I

dinna ken. Something's happened. Something isna right. I can feel it. And look o'er there." She nodded in the direction where Connor stood. "See that horse? The one the towheaded lad is leading intae the stable? It doesna belong tae a Douglas. I've ne'er seen it afore."

"I have," Gabrielle said softly, and her heart skipped a beat. Could it be . . . ? The question had no sooner crossed her mind than the answer to it stepped out of Bracklenaer's door and into the bright golden sunlight.

It had been almost two years since the last and only time Gabrielle had seen Robert Carey, warden of England's East March. So little did the man she saw now resemble the man she remembered visiting Queen Elizabeth's court that it took a second for her to recognize him.

Mud smeared his clothes, plastering them to his body. Dried blood clotted and caked around a nasty gash on his forehead, the wound caused by a recent fall. Apparently he'd been in too much of a hurry to properly attend the injury. Dirt and sweat marred his cheeks and chin and brow. Dark circles bruised the thin skin below his eyes. In the unforgiving sunlight, his cheekbones looked unnaturally high, the hollows beneath unnaturally pronounced. Exhaustion pulled his features taut and shadowed his dark eyes with a weary glaze.

His steps seemed to drag, as though his boots had been chiseled out of lead, when, catching sight of Connor, Robert waved a weary greeting and made his way over to the trio. He spotted Gabrielle, and although he inclined his head politely in her direction, when he made no attempt to approach her, her curiosity grew.

"What is *he* doing *here?*" Ella asked coldly, unintentionally voicing the question that was at the same time playing in Gabrielle's own mind. The girl's gaze sharpened on Robert Carey as the man joined in the conversation with Connor and the other two men.

"I've no idea." It was Gabrielle's turn to shake her head. An excellent question, that. Exactly what *was* Robert Carey doing here, at Bracklenaer? The keep, after all, wasn't even located in the same jurisdiction as the March which Robert oversaw. And didn't that make his unexpected presence all the more mysterious? "Unless . . ."

Icy fingers of dread curled around Gabrielle's heart, tightened, squeezed with painful tightness. Apprehension settled in her stomach like a chunk of ice. She shuddered, unwilling to give credence to her suspicion, yet at the same time unable to think of a more plausible reason for Robert Carey to be at Bracklenaer.

The explanation she'd come up with made her blood run cold.

Despite Connor's unspoken instruction that she remain where she was, Gabrielle swung her leg over the saddle and slid to the ground. She hurried over to where the men stood, and her consternation doubled when, upon seeing her, the two abruptly stopped talking.

Connor glanced at her, and while he looked a bit irritated that she'd not obeyed him, he looked more upset about something else. That he wasn't chastising her lack of obedience was telling in itself.

Gabrielle mustered her courage and turned her attention to Robert Carey. Her smile faltered. "Greetings, m'lord. You look, er . . ."

"Like bloody hell, no doubt." Robert tried to

smile and failed. "Most men who'd left London the morn before last would, I've no doubt."

Left London the morn before last? For what purpose? Gabrielle was afraid to ask for fear he would tell her the answer, and that the answer would be something she did not want to know. "Still, it's good to see you again."

"And good to see you, m'lady," he responded stiffly but politely as, with a grimace, he cut a weary bow. "I wish only that our second meeting could take place under more pleasant circumstances."

Gabrielle's hand fluttered to her throat; she felt the pulse there accelerate to an anxious pace. Her palms were clammy, her muscles tense. Was it the sun beating down upon her head that set her temples to pounding, or the way she gritted her teeth in nervous anticipation? Robert's words had not eased her fears, they'd increased them twofold.

"What is it you mean?" she inquired finally. While it was true she might not be entirely prepared to hear the answer, dreaded hearing in fact, her curiosity was nonetheless great; it gnawed at her, growing more persistent with each heavily expectant second that ticked past with torturous slowness. Her ignorance of the reason for Robert Carey's presence frayed her already tattered nerves. The need to learn once and for all why he'd come to Bracklenaer so she could set her fears to rest was greater than her reluctance to hear any bad news she suspected he carried.

"Gabrielle, Carey is here only long enough to fetch a quick meal and fresh mount before—" Connor's mouth snapped shut when his words were cut short by Robert himself.

"Queen Elizabeth is dead," Robert blurted, too tired and in too great a hurry to waste time imparting the information gently. "I ride to Edinburgh with the news that James has been named her successor. Gabrielle, the day no one thought would ever come is finally here. Scotland and England are united under one crown!"

Gabrielle gasped and staggered back a shaky step, as though she'd been delivered a powerful blow. Connor, prepared for her reaction, quickly stepped to her side. His strong arm coiled about her waist and he drew her close to his side, lending her support and strength.

Gabrielle's cheeks drained of color. Her lips moved, yet no words came out; her voice refused to budge past the lump of emotion suddenly wedged in her throat.

Elizabeth was dead?! She shook her head, dazed. "Nay, 'tis not possible! Why, just last month, I—"

Robert softened tiredly. He reached out and placed a hand on Gabrielle's shoulder, his fingers squeezing gently. " 'Tis not only possible, 'tis true. I was with her just before she died, and saw her body afterward. Elizabeth is dead, dear lady."

Gabrielle stifled a sob behind one tightly clenched fist. Her knees felt treacherously shaky; she leaned gratefully against Connor. His support helped immeasurably, both physically and emotionally. Surrendering to it, she turned her head and buried her face against the hard strength of his shoulder. A tear spilled over her lashes, splashed warmly on her cheek, rolled down her neck, then disappeared beneath the limp, soiled collar of her tunic.

The tear was followed by another.

And another.

Connor cushioned his cheek atop Gabrielle's sun-warmed head and drew her fully into his arms. Had he ever felt so helpless in his life? Nay, not that he could recall. He'd no liking for Elizabeth, nor could he honestly say he would mourn her death, yet he could feel Gabrielle's pain as though it was his own. Her grief sliced through him like a sharply honed dagger, tearing at the strings anchoring his heart and tugging at it in a way he'd never suspected was possible.

Gabrielle Carelton wasn't a delicate woman, yet he felt a surge of protectiveness swell up inside him. He wanted to shelter and protect her, to absorb her with his body, to sip away her tears with his mouth . . . he wanted to make her pain go away. He would take on her anguish himself if he could, if it meant she would be spared feeling it.

He had close to forgotten Robert's presence, and he turned in his direction. The man's expression was grave, befitting the occasion, yet there was a sparkle of enlightenment in his eyes, as though he saw what others did not—the reluctant, unspoken emotions Connor harbored for the woman who stood crying in his arms—and was pleased by them.

Connor's arm tightened around Gabrielle. The fingers of his free hand opened, tunneling through her silky hair as he cradled her head against his chest. The damp heat of her tears soaked through his tunic.

Dear Lord, it felt as if her tears were seeping straight into his skin, branding him.

The afternoon and early evening had passed by in a blur.

Once she'd calmed, Connor had left her to seek out news about Gilby's condition while Ella took care of the prisoners. Feeling oddly lost and alone, Gabrielle retreated to her room—nay, *Connor's* room.

Forgoing the evening meal, she'd instead preferred to closet herself away with her confusing thoughts, wrapping herself in a blanket of grief.

It wasn't until the rest of the castle's occupants had retired to their beds that hunger finally got the better of her and she snuck out of her room and into the great hall below.

She rumbled absently around the kitchen, but her meager appetite deserted her without warning and she retreated to the hall. Sitting at the table atop the dais, she stared pensively at the flames snapping and popping in the huge stone hearth.

One of the hounds chained nearby whimpered and rolled sleepily onto his side when Connor Douglas entered the room. Gabrielle didn't notice his presence, so caught up was she in her thoughts.

Connor came upon Gabrielle quite by accident. Thirst had prompted him to enter the hall in search of ale. What he'd found instead had been an unusually silent Gabrielle Carelton.

She seemed oblivious to his presence when he crossed the room and filled a tankard from one of the large wood barrels tucked in a shadowy corner of the hall. Nor did she notice when he approached the table.

"Drink this, lass, 'twill help warm ye." Connor eased himself onto the bench across from Gabrielle. Age-chipped pewter scraped against the scarred oak tabletop as Connor slid the half-filled tankard of ale across the table to her.

"Thank you, but I'm not cold," Gabrielle murmured dispassionately, even as she wrapped her fingers limply around the tankard.

"Nay? Then what are ye, lass?"

"I don't know." She shook her head vaguely and a thick lock of raven hair fell forward into her eyes. She brushed it back, her gaze lifting to meet his. "I know this may sound strange, m'lord, but I'm not cold, I'm not hot, I'm not . . . well, I'm not anything. I feel numb."

" 'Tis tae be expected. Ye've suffered a shock."

"You mean Elizabeth's death? 'Twas not *that* much of a shock. The woman was old, and 'tis common knowledge she ailed on and off for most of her life. There are many who predicted she'd be dead decades ago." She shook her head. "Nay, her death was not unexpected to most, and anxiously awaited by many."

"I sense ye arena one of the many."

"You're correct," Gabrielle confirmed with a sigh. "I'm not." She lifted the tankard; the pewter felt cold against her lips as she tipped it and swallowed the yeasty-tasting brew. Unlike the whisky she'd drunk before, the liquor did not burn her tongue and throat, but slid with deceptive ease down to her stomach. "Elizabeth had her faults— I'd be lying if I said otherwise—yet there was also much about the woman to admire."

"She took care of ye well, then?"

Stand up straight. I said straight! *Shoulders back. Oh, for God sakes, girl, suck in your stomach, you look like an overstuffed goose!*

Gabrielle hesitated. A frown creased her brow as she thoughtfully nibbled her lower lip. A half dozen years of Elizabeth's harsh words played in her mind. While she was accustomed to the sting of humiliation the thoughtless comments brought, she'd never become immune to them.

"She took care of me," Gabrielle said finally,

flatly. "For a girl of my station, orphaned as I was, her thoughtfulness and care were greatly appreciated. I was young and alone, grieving over my father's death, frightened for my future. Elizabeth took me into her court, she fed and clothed me and asked only for my loyalty in return. It was enough. More than I could have hoped for." She took another, deeper sip of ale then, placing the mug on the table, slid it back across to Connor.

The pewter retained the heat from her hands, Connor noticed as he wrapped his fingers around it. The rim also felt warm as he turned the tankard around and, meeting and holding her gaze over the upturned bottom rim, placed his mouth in the same spot where hers had been only a moment before. The aroma of ale assailed him, engulfed him. As he forced himself to swallow a mouthful of the brew, all he could think of was the sweetly intoxicating flavor of Gabrielle Carelton's mouth, and of how very much he ached to stand up, lean over the table, capture her lips beneath his own and taste her again. Deeply. Dear God, the need to slide his tongue over her temptingly full lower lip, to savor the essence of her mouth, was impossibly strong. He trapped a groan in his throat when he imagined her thoroughly feminine flavor mixing to absolute perfection with the rich flavor of the ale . . .

'Twas a heady combination. One to die for.

"And now James has united the kingdoms," Gabrielle said, feeling the need to say something to break the sudden tension crackling between them. "Scotland and England are at last one."

Connor nodded. "Aye, for what it's worth. We shall see how long the union lasts, shall we nae? I'm thinking 'twill nae last o'er long." He lowered the tankard onto the table with more force than was intended. "We Scots dinna take kindly tae being ruled by ye Sassenach, as the past has proven, and the future will again."

"James is not English."

"For all intent and purpose he may as well be. 'Tis nae secret Jamie harbors a fascination with Sassenach ways. How long do ye think 'twill be afore he has taken himself off tae London and embroiled himself in English politics, meanwhile forgetting all aboot his own country's troubles? Nae long, I'll wager, as will many men who live on this godforsaken side of the Border. Under James's united rule, Scotland is destined tae be absorbed by England and governed by an absent monarch." Shaking his head, Connor fingered the cold pewter handle of the tankard. "Troubled times are afoot, lass, mark me words."

"From what I've seen, your precious Borders could not possibly get *more* troubled than they already are, m'lord. For centuries now, two sovereigns at a time could not tame them."

"The time for taming has come and gone. Och! but if that was the only problem with this union, I'd be of the same mind as ye."

"Then you think—?"

"Nay, I dinna ken what I be thinking right now, Gabby. I only ken that these Borders have always separated two warring factions. Aye, those factions are now one. *In name.* The Border and the wild Border ways remain the same and will nae die easily. So long as there is English and Scot, there will be differences. So long as there is a Border between the two, Sassenach and Scot will fight. Sometimes I think 'twas what we were born for. With Elizabeth's death and Jamie's ascent tae

the throne, the Borders are going tae be pried
loose from their mooring. Dinna misunderstand
me, I'm nae fortune teller. Where and how it all
will end 'twould take a better mon than meself
tae predict. Right now, howe'er, me mind is on
another matter, one closer tae home."

Gabrielle had leaned forward and was reaching
out, about to reclaim the tankard. His words
made her freeze. No longer paying attention to
what she was doing, her fingers grazed his. A bolt
of awareness shot up her arm, wrapped warm fingers around her heart. Her gaze shifted from
Connor's hand, skated up his muscular forearm,
over his broad shoulder, the sunkissed side of his
neck where his pulse hammered, along the hard,
stubbled line of his jaw . . . higher.

Piercing gray meshed with inquisitive green.

Her fingertips trembled against the back of his
knuckles as she arched one dark brow. "And what
matter would that be, m'lord?"

"That of our wedding, lass. What else?" His attention darkened and dipped.

Earlier, Gabrielle had changed into one of the
gowns from her paltry wardrobe, this one, a loose,
high-waisted garment of rich rose brocade. Without the customary farthingale beneath, the skirt
felt comfortably loose around her hips and thighs,
much less restrictive than the trews that had pre-
ceded it. She'd used a scrap of ivory lace to tie
back her thick, wild black curls. The dress's neck-
line—etched with a thin, matching strip of lace—
was scooped; it revealed the ripe curve of her
breasts.

Her skin felt hot and tingly under the touch
of Connor's gaze. More so when she saw the way
his expression grew dark and hungry. The gentle

play of firelight sculpted and defined his features, made his gray eyes gleam as his gaze raked her from the waist up.

Gabrielle shivered. Her fingers curled around the tankard, and she dragged it toward her gratefully. It felt heavy as she lifted it, tipped the rim against her mouth, drank deeply. On her empty stomach the brew hit her hard, making her head feel light and dizzy.

Or mayhap 'twas The Black Douglas's intense gaze, not the sting of ale that made her senses spin?

Gabrielle cleared her throat. Keeping her voice level took intense concentration. Was she the only one to notice that her grip on the tankard had grown so tight that her knuckles were white with the strain of it?

"Our wedding?" She forced a chuckle as she also forced her grip to relax, forced herself to put the tankard down carefully upon the table. "Connor, please, rest assured that your obligations have been met, albeit not in the way anyone intended. Now that Elizabeth is dead, the Maxwell and Douglas are united under the reign of your young King James. What need is there of a union between us?"

Perhaps it was a trick of firelight and shadows, but for a fleeting second, she could have sworn Connor looked uncomfortable. His gaze shifted thoughtfully, then just as abruptly returned to hers; the gray depths were as masked and unreadable as his harshly sculpted features.

Gabrielle watched closely as he lifted the tankard. Again he turned it so that his lips covered the spot where hers had been. This time there was no fooling herself, no pretending the gesture was anything but what it was: intentional. Arching one dark brow high, he tipped the tankard, swallowing down the rest of the ale.

A shiver skated down Gabrielle's spine. A burning tingle of awareness sparked in her blood; the fire crackling in the hearth felt chilly by comparison. It took a mighty surge of concentration to muster the flagging remains of her courage, to return his stare with one she hoped boldly met the unspoken challenge that sparkled like molten-gray fire in his eyes.

"There is a need," Connor said finally, firmly.

The husky timbre of his voice made Gabrielle wonder exactly what sort of need he referred to? Did she dare hope it was more than a physical yearning? Dare she wonder, even for a second, The Black Douglas could come to care for her? And if she did allow herself to believe it, what kind of pain would she endure if she were eventually to discover he truly didn't care for her at all . . . the way Elizabeth had always predicted would be the case? It would tear her apart from the inside out to learn such a thing. She knew it, could *feel* it deep down inside her, in that dark, lonely place where she kept her emotions carefully hidden.

Lacing her fingers in her lap, Gabrielle averted her gaze to the flames snapping in the hearth and asked as dispassionately as possible, "What need is that, m'lord?"

"My need for a son."

Her gaze jerked back to him, her eyes widening in surprise. "I beg your pardon?!"

"Ye heard me right, lass. I've need for a son. Ye be young and strong, of . . . er, more hardy stock than I'd dared hoped ye would be. Mairghread says yer wide hips were made for birthing and—"

The sound of her open palm colliding with his whisker-shadowed cheek was loud.

Gabrielle's palm stung from the force of the blow. She didn't acknowledge the pain as, already leaning forward, she stood abruptly. Wood scraped against stone as the back of her knees slammed bruisingly against the bench, in turn forcing the bench to slide backward.

The urge to slap him again was strong, countered only by the gleam in his eyes that dared her to repeat the gesture, and that promised a similar retaliation if she tried.

Instead, Gabrielle bunched her hand into a tight fist, held rigidly at her side as she glared down at him. The imprint of her hand lingered an angry shade of red on his cheek. "You miserable bastard," she hissed, the glint in her green eyes murderous. Her cheeks flamed with furious color. "How dare you suggest that the only thing I'm good for is bearing children?"

"Och! calm yerself down, lass, I dinna mean—"

"Of course you did! What else *could* you have meant?" A part of Gabrielle was aware of, and embarrassed by, her high, shrewish tone; a larger part of her was too furious to care, let alone make an attempt to correct it. "I know full well that I'm not beautiful, but you do me a grave disservice to suggest by your words that I am stupid as well as plain."

"I meant only—"

"Quiet! Please, do not insult me further by lying and saying you think me comely. I know better. No man with eyes has ever mistaken me for that. 'Tis a fact I learned to accept long ago. However, no man with a grain of compassion has dared say as much, and in so crass a manner, to my face.

Methinks there's a reason they call you Scots barbarians, and 'tis for more than your tactics on a battlefield. The ballads say The Black Douglas is a cruel man, but I'd no idea *how* cruel."

"Gabrielle—"

"Be quiet, I tell you! I—"

"Lass, are ye crying?"

"—don't wish to discuss the matter further. And I most certainly am *not* crying. As for what you've said . . . your opinion of anything—least of all your opinion of me!—means less than nothing." Gabrielle bit down on her lower lip until it stung and she tasted the sharp tang of blood on her tongue. The lie tasted sour in her mouth, but pride forbade her to take it back. She dashed a hot, traitorous tear from her cheek with her fist and, gathering up her skirt with her free hand, turned to leave the room.

Connor was on his feet in a heartbeat, and across the room in two. He caught up to her just as she was about to disappear into the shadowy corridor outside the arched stone doorway. Curling his fingers around her upper arm, he tugged, stopping her short.

He heard her try, and fail, to suppress a choked gasp of surprise. Beneath the brocade sleeve, he felt a tremor ripple through her.

"If I've said aught tae offend ye, lass . . ." Connor's words trailed away when he noticed the way Gabrielle strained her neck to keep her face turned away from him. The jerky lift and fall of her shoulders told him that indeed she *was* crying.

The muscles in Connor's stomach fisted. God, how the sight tore at him! He longed to enfold her in his arms, press her cheek to his shoulder, stroke her soft, inky hair and croon soothing words in her ear. He'd no practice comforting teary-eyed women, but for this one, heaven help him, he would make that attempt.

If Gabrielle allowed it.

The rigid set of her spine and shoulders suggested that she would not. The stiffness of her posture also suggested that, if Connor so much as thought about trying to soothe her, she would slap out at him again. Blindly, wildly. His cheek still stung from her first blow; fierce Douglas pride forbade him from giving her another opportunity.

Gabrielle muffled a sniffle with the back of her hand and cleared her throat. She would have wiped the tears from her cheeks, but there were too many and they refused to stop falling. Her voice shook only a bit as she said, "Unhand me, please. You're hurting my arm."

Connor's fingers loosened, but he did not let her go. "Why? So that ye can run away? I dinna think so, Gabby."

"I am *not* running away."

"Then what would ye call it?"

"I'm"—*sniffle, sniffle*—"simply retiring for the night, is all."

"Do ye always run tae yer chambers when ye retire for the night, lass?"

"Only when I've been gravely insulted and wish to be alone with my thoughts, m'lord."

Connor sucked in a choppy breath as the pad of his thumb traced small circles against her sleeve and the warm, soft skin beneath. "How many times do I have tae say it? Nae insult was intended."

"Mayhap a part of me believes you, but a larger part most certainly did take insult."

"Is it yer habit tae take insult whenever a mon offers tae wed ye?"

"I wouldn't know, the offer has never been made before." Gabrielle dashed the tears from her cheek and, finally managing to gain control over her emotions, craned her neck to glare hotly up at him. "Heathen Scot though you are, surely even *you* cannot be so ignorant as to think that your offer is what I find so insulting. 'Tis not, 'tis the *reason* for it. Obviously you think of me as nothing more than a brood mare. *That,* I find insulting in the extreme. What woman with even a tattered scrap of pride would not?"

"Ye arena making any sense." Connor shook his head, confused. "Arranged marriages are an age-old custom in yer country as well as mine. A marriage based solely on begetting heirs is nae unusual. Och! but 'tis a maun honorable reason to wed. I ken few couples on either side of the Border whose marriage is based on—"

He gulped, his throat closing tightly around the word.

Gabrielle's gaze sharpened on him when Connor stopped speaking abruptly.

"On what, m'lord?" she prodded coldly. When he still refused to finish the sentence, she determinedly finished it for him. "You know of few couples on either side of the Border whose marriage is based on . . . *love?* Is that the word you're having so much trouble saying?"

"Aye," he growled, his gray eyes narrowing angrily. He hated the way his tongue tripped awkwardly over the word, hated, too, the way his mind tripped even more awkwardly over the prospect of voicing it.

"Have you ever been in love, Connor?"

He gritted his teeth, making the muscles in his jaw bunch hard, and shook his head. "I've nae time tae waste on such silly emotions."

"You think love silly?"

"Quite."

Gabrielle opened her mouth to say something, but abruptly changed her mind; the glint in her green eyes suggested that the words she settled upon were not the ones that originally entered her mind. "I pity you, Connor Douglas. Not only can't you say the word, you can't even feel the richness and depth of the emotion."

"I dinna lack for feelings, lass. Ye be wrong aboot that."

"Mayhap, but you obviously lack the most important one. Love. Methinks 'tis what the term 'barbarian' truly means."

That said, Gabrielle reached up and untangled her arm from his shock-slackened fingers. Turning her back on him, she quit the hall without a backward glance.

That he'd been insulted, Connor did not doubt. Exactly *how* the insult had come about, however, he wasn't so sure of. He knew only that without her presence to warm it, the great hall felt suddenly chilly and . . . aye, lonely in its vast emptiness.

Connor stared at the empty spot where Gabrielle had stood for a full two minutes after the clipped echo of her footsteps faded away. He might have stood there a good deal longer if not for the two sudden, sharp pains in his shin that snagged his attention.

His gaze jerked down and to the side, colliding with one that was a bit bluer, wider, and fringed by long, thick copper lashes.

"So help me, Ella," he snapped, "if ye dinna cease kicking me, I'll see ye wed tae—"

"Ye be a real charmer, Cousin," Ella said sarcastically, ignoring the threat he'd been about to voice. "I canna remember the last time I heard a mon turn a woman's head with such honey-sweet words." Crossing her arms over her waist, she met Connor's glare with a steady one of her own. "Tsk, tsk, tsk. Even Roy Maxwell has a smoother tongue than yers, and that mon was *purposely* insulting me. 'Tis wondering I am, why ye dinna ask Gabrielle tae open her mouth and show ye her teeth. Indeed, ye might as well have asked her tae bare all. A Douglas ne'er does anything by half measures, don't ye ken? If ye're bound and determined tae treat the lass like ye're doing nothing maun important than buying a horse, ye may as well do it right."

"If Roy Maxwell has insulted ye . . ."

"Roy Maxwell isna the point. Gabrielle Carelton *is*. I'll thank ye tae be sticking tae the subject at hand. Dinna be trying tae change it again."

"Have a care, Ella, I'm in a foul mood and of a mind tae take ye over my knee."

"I've just come from the dungeon, and Roy Maxwell's voice is still ringing in me ears. Since me mood isna any better than yers," she gave a careless shrug, "I'm almost of a mind tae let ye try. Almost."

Connor clamped his teeth around a terse reply. Spinning on his heel, he retrieved the tankard, left the table long enough to fill it to the cold, pewter brim, then returned. Thinking only of turning his back on his annoying cousin, he sat where Gabrielle had sat . . . then instantly wished he'd chosen another spot.

Was it possible for the bench to radiate the

woman's heat, even now, or was his imagination getting the better of him?

Connor swore under his breath, then lifted the tankard and gulped down half its contents in two huge swallows. Perhaps whisky would have been a better choice? The potent liquor would be more numbing to his senses, something he could most certainly use just now.

An uneasy feeling settled in the pit of his stomach. Complete intoxication would be the only way he'd be able to chase wayward thoughts of Gabrielle from his mind, he realized. Even then, the remedy would be temporary. Aye, he could get blindly drunk, mayhap even forget about the lass for a wee bit, but as sure as the sun would rise come dawn, he knew that when he sobered, his traitorous thoughts would stray right back in that woman's direction.

Gabrielle Carelton was like a fever in his blood, one that ran strong and deep, one he could not seem to shake himself of. When he wasn't with her, he thought about her. Who was she with? What was she doing? Was she happy or, at the very least, content?

And why, *why* did the answers matter ever so much?!

Bloody hell!

When he was awake he fantasized about her, when he was asleep he *dreamed* about her. More provocative dreams he'd never in his life experienced, yet he had to admit that only a small portion of those dreams centered around the tantalizing memory of their lovemaking. Equally as many left him to wake with the lingering impression of Gabrielle's smile, or the bittersweet trill of her laughter echoing a haunting melody in his ears . . .

". . . Alasdair Gray."

The name broke into Connor's thoughts and caught his attention. He focused on his cousin and demanded she repeat herself.

"I said only that the last time I saw such a ridiculous expression on a mon 'twas on Alasdair Gray, when he took Vanessa Forster to wife."

"And what expression is that?"

"I may be wrong," she replied, and grinned impishly, "but methinks the kitchen wenches call it 'lovesick.' "

"Och! Cousin, I'm *nae* lovesick! Curse ye for e'en suggesting such a thing!"

Ella's lack of a verbal response made her arched copper brow all the more compelling.

"Ye dinna believe me?" Connor growled as he slammed the tankard down on the table. With his free hand, he plowed his fingers through his dark, shaggy hair. "I'm *nae* in love."

"If ye say so." A grin tugged at one corner of Ella's mouth. The gesture suggested that she didn't believe him for a second, as did the flicker of amusement he saw flash in her wide blue eyes. She gave his shoulder a light slap. "Och! Connor, dinna look so distraught. Truly, it nae longer matters if ye love Gabrielle or nay. Ye made such a disaster of proposing that there isna a chance she'd consider wedding ye now." She pursed her lips and frowned thoughtfully. " 'Tis a stroke of luck that Robert Carey had tae stop here on his way tae Edinburgh for a fresh mount, aye? If he'd passed us by, ye'd ne'er have learned so quickly of Elizabeth's passing, and by the time ye did find out, 'twould have been too late, ye'd already have been wed tae the cursed Sassenach wench."

The fingers of one hand curled around the bowl of the tankard while the finger of his other tightened around the handle. Had the molded pewter been made of less sturdy stuff it would have snapped off with the force of his grip. "Ye forget me reasons for wanting tae wed her in the first place. I want a son. An heir will assure that Colin can ne'er get his conniving hands on Bracklenaer."

"I forget naught," Ella replied, ignoring the reference to Connor's twin instead of allowing him to change the subject, the way she'd a feeling he'd intended it to do. "And I'm of a mind that neither will Gabrielle. Especially after ye explained it tae her in such"—*cough!*—"succulent and gallant terms."

"I was being honest with the lass, 'tis all."

"Were ye?" Ella rested the knuckles of her fists on the table and leaned toward Connor until they were on eye level. "Were ye really?"

"Are ye suggesting otherwise?" he asked tightly.

"What I be suggesting is that there's a fine muckle of good, healthy Scotswomen who'd be overjoyed tae share yer name, yer bed, and yer bairns. Gabrielle Carelton may have been needed tae settle our feud with the Maxwell, howe'er she isna the only woman who can supply ye with an heir. Since yer qualifications are so ver basic, would nae any woman do the job nicely?"

"I dinna want *any* woman, I want—!"

"Exactly." Ella's smile was irritatingly broad, the gleam of triumph in her brilliant blue eyes unmistakably bright.

The thickly uttered Gaelic curse that he tossed at his cousin's glorious red head was much more colorful.

Fifteen

"Colin? Colin Douglas, are you down here?" Gabrielle called out as loudly as she dared. She stood poised in a doorway that, from what little she could see, led on to a dark, narrow hallway. How far the hallway extended, she'd yet to discover. The light from the sconce she'd stolen from an upstairs hallway extended only so far and, first, she wanted to be sure the man she sought was even down here before searching further.

She hadn't retreated to her room—nay, it was not her room, it was *The Black Douglas's*—after quitting the hall, but instead had roamed aimlessly throughout Bracklenaer's twisting corridors. Her thoughts had been focused inward, tumbling painfully over each other as she replayed the encounter with Connor in every minute, painful detail, not on where she was going. Without intending it as her destination, a moment ago she'd arrived at the narrow, steep stone steps leading down to the dungeon.

It had taken less than a minute for her to come to a hasty decision, and barely thrice that to retrace her path, retrieve one of the wall sconces, then hurry back and carefully navigate the treacherously steep stone stairway.

Gabrielle now stood at the bottom of the stairs. She leaned forward, straining to hear a reply, even a distant one. She heard naught but the clatter of her own heart pounding like thunder in her ears.

A frown creased her brow and her fingers tightened around the sconce's chilly metal handle. If Connor hadn't dispatched his twin and Roy Maxwell down here to the dungeon, where *would* he confine them?

The question had no more entered Gabrielle's mind when it was chased away by a sudden, unexpected flicker of movement.

Her attention jerked in that direction. The movement had come from in front of her, from somewhere down the narrow, pitch-black hallway. In the twisting shadows, at a point just beyond the flickering bath of sconcelight.

She heard a faint rustle of sound, then . . . aye, right there, it moved again!

Her knees rattled together beneath the rose brocade skirt; they felt weak, watery, threatening to buckle from beneath her as she lurched back an instinctive step. Her fingers trembled around the sconce's handle. Squinting, her gaze tried and failed to pierce the thick, concealing shadows.

"Hello? Is someone there?" Gabrielle called. She winced to hear the high, shaky quality of her own voice bouncing off the hallway's chokingly close stone walls.

Without warning, a man stepped from the clinging darkness and into the shimmering ring of pale, orangy-yellow light. The *click* of his bootheel atop ice-cold stone sounded startlingly loud.

The breath Gabrielle had been holding rushed past her lips in a sharp exhalation.

"Ye look shocked," Roy Maxwell observed as he hoisted higher the plaid strip tossed over his left shoulder. His green eyes sparkled in the flickering light. She detected an insolently mocking grin cutting between the thick fullness of his red mustache and beard. "Were ye nae looking for me?"

"No, I— Where's Colin?"

"Och! lass, cease yer search. The mon is long gone."

"G-gone?"

"Aye. He left the second we broke out of that thing The Black Douglas calls a cell. Truth tae tell, the door was as flimsy as the guard who stood outside it. Neither proved a worthy match for the likes of a Maxwell, don't ye ken?"

The fingers of Gabrielle's free hand fluttered nervously at the base of her throat. "You're escaping!"

"Nay, nae yet." Roy shook his shaggy red head. "Colin, now *he* has escaped. Me, on the other hand, I thought 'twould be only fitting tae delay me own escape until I found something here worthy enough tae take back tae Caerlaverock with me. Ye ken, I'm looking tae procure compensation for all the time and trouble Connor Douglas has caused me. Something . . . Och! aye, something the mon shall maun sorely miss."

Gabrielle's eyes widened. Gulping, she retreated another step. A grimace furrowed her brow when her back came up hard against the craggy stone corner of the doorway.

Surely Roy Maxwell did not mean . . . ?

She shook her head determinedly. If he was of

a mind to take her with him, he'd best think
again.

Bloody hell, she would not allow it!

In her short time on this cursed Border she had
already been kidnapped thrice. That was three
times too many. Nay, nay, *nay.* Gabrielle vowed that
she would *not* allow herself to be so mistreated
again, no matter what grisly atrocities Roy Maxwell
used to threaten her into compliance.

Gabrielle's tongue darted out to lick parched
lips. Her thoughts raced, tripping over themselves. Roy Maxwell was almost twice her size, his
body solid and well muscled. How on earth could
she stop him from kidnapping her, if kidnapping
her was indeed what he had in mind?

Like a dog chasing after its own tail, the question circled dizzyingly in her mind, the answer
tantalizingly close yet always a teasing fraction out
of reach. The solution was a good deal murkier
than Gabrielle's resolution that, somehow, stop
him she most certainly *would.*

"Surely you aren't so foolish as to think The
Black Douglas would let a prized possession slip
from his grasp so easily, sir," she said finally, her
words more an effort to stall than anything else.

"Och! lass, who's tae say I'd be giving the mon
a choice?" His green eyes dancing with mirth, Roy
tipped his red head back and laughed. The sound
was hearty, deep . . . and woefully short-lived.

"I do."

The answer came from a voice located so
closely behind Gabrielle that she felt the hot,
misty rasp of the speaker's breath filter through
her hair and graze her scalp. Her scalp, in turn,
tingled in warm response. The voice did not belong to Roy Maxwell; it was too resonant, too rich,

and far too tight with fury. Her attention jerked over her shoulder to confirm the intruder's identity, even though deep in her soul she knew there was no need. The voice could belong to none other than The Black Douglas himself.

Connor's gaze raked Gabrielle. A sigh of relief hissed past his lips when he saw she was unharmed. Och! if he'd been a few minutes later, if Roy Maxwell dared to hurt her . . . !

His fingers clenching to white-knuckled tightness around the hilt of the broadsword sheathed at his hip, Connor abruptly swerved his thoughts from that dangerous course. He turned the full force of his attention on his rival.

Roy Maxwell had the good sense to squirm. While the echo of his mirth still ricocheted off the cold, confining stone around them, he was no longer laughing. The man's expression sobered instantly. A glint of nervousness flashed in his shrewd green eyes as his gaze shifted past Gabrielle to meet and hold Connor's.

"The lass has been shifted from hand tae hand long enough," Connor said. " 'Tis in my hands she is now, and in my hands she stays."

Roy's face reddened with an impotent fury that was reflected in his terse tone. His fingers clenched and unclenched at his sides. "Situations change, Douglas, especially on these Borders. Ye should ken that well enough. Whether I take her back with me tonight, or take her back a fortnight—two fortnights, more—in the future, rest assured that the Maxwell *will* take her back. Eventually."

"Ye and yers can *try*," Connor snapped as he stepped out from behind Gabrielle and into the flickering ring of sconcelight. In one confident stride, he moved to protective position in front of her. Roy appeared to be unarmed, yet Connor refused to rely on appearance and chance. He couldn't. Not where Gabrielle Carelton's life was concerned. "Howe'er, ye'll have to go through me tae get tae her, and I'll warn ye now, I'll nae give ye an easy time of it. I'll defend the lass with my life's last breath if need be."

"Och! mon, she's hardly worth *that* maun trouble."

"I disagree," Connor growled, the words punctuated by the steely rasp of his sword being drawn from its hilt. He felt Gabrielle stir behind him, but resisted the urge to glance back over his shoulder at her.

"Ye joke!"

Connor's glare was hot enough to melt stone. "I've ne'er been more serious. While her looks may nae rival that of the Blessed Virgin's, I'll grant ye that and nae more, the lass is sweet-tempered—Och! well, normally, when she's nae riled—gentle and maun loving than any woman I've e'er kenned." The tip of the blade lifted, coming to rest on the place in Roy Maxwell's neck where his blue-veined pulse throbbed and the lump in his throat bobbed with a dry, nervous swallow. "Och! aye, she's worth that. And more. Maun maun more. There are few men on either side of the Border who would ride in the dead of night to rescue an old woman from the enemy's clutches; Mairghread, a woman she'd barely met. Yet she did. At least, the wench tried. The action speaks for itself, would ye nae agree?"

"Well, I'll be guddled! Siobhan tried to rescue yer aunt?" Roy asked, his eyes widening as he pursed his lips and scratched at the furry underside of his jaw. " 'Tis maun unlike the lass. The last raid on Caerlaverock—ye remember that, do ye nae?—she was the first out the tunnel. Mayhap the ver same tunnel yer twin escorted ye from. Nary a soul was surprised by it. 'Tis well kenned that Siobhan be a fine muckle fond of staying close tae her kettles and herbs . . . and as far from danger as she can get." He scowled and shook his shaggy red head. "Yet she tried to rescue yer aunt, ye say? Och! I'm surprised."

Roy Maxwell wasn't the only one.

Realization hit Connor like a fist colliding solidly with his belly. An icy wave of shock washed over him, punching the air from his lungs and . . . aye, there was no mistaking and less denying it, he *did* feel the heat of a blush—the first in his life—flood his cheeks and seep slowly, slowly down his neck. If his air-hungry lungs had the breath to spare for it, he would have groaned.

Good Lord, the man was talking about Siobhan, the Maxwell's *cook, not* Gabrielle Carelton!

Connor's mind raced and his spine went rigid. Was there a chance, even a wee one, that Gabrielle had somehow missed hearing his incriminating words? He closed his eyes, sighed. Nay, no chance at all. It would take a good deal of luck for such to be the case, and as the ballads were fond of saying—and he was equally as fond of arguing—what need did the notorious Black Douglas have for luck when he possessed the cunning and skill of ten seasoned reivers combined?

Were the situation not so infernally dire, he might have laughed at the irony.

Pity take it, it would require the shrewdness of three times that amount of men to maneuver his way out of the mire he'd just unwittingly created for himself.

As suddenly as Connor's embarrassment came, so did it ease. Deep down he had to admit that if given the chance to take the words back, he would not do it. Oh, aye, he'd known when he spoke the words that they were the raw, unornamented truth. Yet not until this very second did the full depth of understanding pierce him with a tip more sharp and deadly than the one he held poised against Roy Maxwell's throat. A bevy of strange yet oddly comforting emotions coiled like gossamer-thin threads around his heart. Threads of emotion that, for all their fragility, twisted and linked into tight, unbreakable knots.

Nay, even if he could, he would not take the words back. He was a Douglas to the core; his tenets ran deep and true. It would be a formidable lie indeed to rescind the most sincere words he'd ever spoken in his life.

Gabrielle's grip tightened around the sconce's handle, and the fingers of her free hand shook when she wrapped them loosely around his upper arm. Connor felt the warm fullness of her breasts as she leaned to the side and peered at Roy from around Connor's shoulder.

Cloth rustled.

Unbidden, the image of rose brocade skimming soft, creamy thighs sprang to mind.

Connor's eyes snapped open. Had they only been closed for a fraction of a second? It seemed much longer. His slitted gray gaze locked on his adversary.

Roy Maxwell grinned knowingly, his attention shifting to Gabrielle. Her grip tightened. Connor felt her fingertips digging into his upper arms as she seemed to instinctively press more closely against him.

"Am I right in assuming 'tis a cook you're after, not a captive?" Gabrielle asked. Her voice was husky and low, cracking with an emotion Connor couldn't decipher.

"Aye," Roy answered. "What else? Unless . . ." He paused then, after a thoughtful second, his grin broadened. "Och! lass, surely ye dinna think—?!" He shook his head. "Dinna mistake me, lass, I mean nae offense when I say I've naught against ye—except mayhap that large dollop of Carelton blood flowing through yer veins. Howe'er, 'tis nae *ye* I'm wanting tae take back tae Caerlaverock with me. Good Lord, nae! *I* dinna want ye there in the first place. Kidnapping ye was me da and Gordie's idea. A nae so brilliant one, I might add. I was against it from the start. And with good reason, so 'twould seem. Truth tae tell, lass, ye're a fine muckle more trouble than ye're worth—e'en if stealing ye did irritate the clan Douglas better than anything the Maxwells have done tae them in the past. Nay, nay, I'm through with such foolishness. The only wench I'm wanting tae bring home with me this night is Siobhan. Da would ne'er forgive me were I tae seize the plainest lass in all Scotland instead of the best cook this side of the Esk, don't ye ken?"

The threads around Connor's heart tightened and tugged when he heard Gabrielle's swift intake of breath. Turning her head, she cushioned her cheek against the back of his shoulder. A steamy patch of moisture there suggested she was quietly crying. Her grip on his arm tightened, her nails biting into the tender skin beneath his sleeve; oddly enough, he did not complain or entertain the notion of pulling away.

The emotions churning inside him were as foreign as they were intense. It came as no small surprise to discover that he felt Gabrielle's pain as though it was his own, slicing deep and raw. But why? A month previous, Roy Maxwell's callous remarks would not have bothered him a bit. Surely there were worse atrocities to be withstood in these parts than to have one's looks glibly criticized and to be slighted in favor of a cook. Now, however, Connor heard the words as though they'd been filtered through Gabrielle's ears; coldly spoken, callously disrespectful, and delivered with utter disregard for how they'd be interpreted.

Unfortunately, he knew there was a time not so long ago when he might have said those same unfeeling things himself and not thought twice about it. If he'd wondered before, he wondered no longer. It was obvious how Gabrielle had come by her impression that Borderers were a crude, unfeeling lot. Instead of basing her opinion on hearsay and ill-concocted ballads, as he'd at first presumed she'd done, he now realized she'd come by it all-too honestly.

With a flick of his wrist Connor exerted pressure on the point of his sword. Not a lot, but enough to make a few drops of blood bead against Roy's throat. "If yer ancestor's tongue was as honeyed as yer own," he growled, "there can be nae doubt as tae why me great-great aunt chose a Maxwell o'er a Douglas."

"Aye," Roy agreed, and his grin was back with annoying force. "For all that she was a Carelton, the wench had maun distinguished taste."

The insult had the desired effect; it rubbed raw a centuries-old wound.

Connor didn't think so much as react with all his well-honed instincts. His sword arm drew back, his muscles pulling taut, his gray eyes narrowing and glinting with deadly intent.

Too late, Roy sensed the grave mistake he'd made. Only a fool issued such openly challenging words when he'd no weapon to back them up with . . . and only an insane man did so to a reiver like The Black Douglas. That Connor was going to run him through, of that there was no doubt; Roy would do the same were the situation reversed. With that thought in mind, he started to duck, his arms lifting, crossed at the forearms, forming an ineffective, makeshift shield as he prepared to rush Connor and, with luck, tackle him in the stomach. Gritting his teeth, he mentally readied himself to feel the sting of The Black Douglas's blade sinking into his flesh.

The feeling never came.

Gabrielle assessed the situation in a blink. Connor's anger was palpable, crackling in the air like the tingling spark of static before a storm. The way his arm pulled back—his elbow jabbing into her rib cage hard enough to make her gasp—told her all she needed to know.

"Nay!" she cried as she shoved the sconce at Roy. Grabbing Connor's arm with both hands, she planted her feet apart for balance and yanked. Hard. Rather, she *tried* to yank him backward, hoping that in so doing she would foil his aim before the deadly point of his sword could find its mark . . . and give this asinine feud reason to continue for still more senseless decades.

The muscles in his upper arm were hard with

the tension that twisted through him; it felt as though the bands of sinew had been molded from unyielding steel. There was no give in either Connor's arm or his stance. However, Gabrielle knew her unexpected action must have startled him, for he paused abruptly, just shy of completing the thrust.

"Don't do it, Connor," she pleaded breathlessly. "Please, I beg of you."

"Unhand me, wench, 'tis none of yer affair. The mon insulted me family. Nae Douglas worthy of the name listens tae such slurs without exacting flesh in retribution. Well Roy kenned that when he uttered the insult."

" 'Twas an insult, but *nothing more*. They are words, *only* words."

"Words that deliver grave insult to me ancestor and me clan."

"But words all the same. Surely words alone are not a good enough reason to commit murder!"

"There's many a mon on this Border who'd disagree, many a mon who's killed for less."

"Must *you* be one of those men, Connor?" Gabrielle's grip on his arm tightened. Her green eyes were wide and pleading as she looked up into eyes that were as gray as they were guarded. "Elizabeth sent me here in an attempt to end this feud once and for all, something James seemed equally as eager to see happen. I confess, at the time I'd severe misgivings that any family dispute could be as critical as she indicated. Now I know she was right. Connor, don't you see? The feud between Maxwell and Douglas has gone on long enough. Decades too long! It *must* end, and that ending *must* start somewhere."

A muscle in the left side of Connor's jaw ticked

spasmodically when he gritted his teeth. "Then
let a Maxwell make the first offering of peace between our families."

"Och!" Roy piped in. " 'Twill be a cold day in
hell afore ye'll see a Maxwell—"

Gabrielle glared the man into silence, then
quickly shifted her attention back to Connor. She
was getting through to him on some level, she
could sense it, yet why couldn't she make him see
reason on the most crucial aspect of what she was
trying to convey, that the Maxwell/Douglas feud
had to end? Surely there must be some way to convince him that the important issue wasn't *who*
made the first gesture in that direction, but the
end result of it: a cessation of bloodshed and
peace—nay, at this point she'd settle for reluctant
tolerance!—between the rival clans?

Surely there must be a way to make even a man
as single-minded and stubborn as The Black
Douglas understand the importance of her reasoning. But how?

An idea occurred to her. It wasn't a brilliant
one, but it was the only one she had. Tilting her
chin up, Gabrielle glanced at Connor from down
the length of her nose and said, "Only two hours
ago you accused me of running away. Now who is
doing the running, m'lord? Which of us is truly
the coward?"

The barb had its desired effect. Connor's eyes
narrowed and an angry red hue suffused his brow
and cheeks. The muscle in his jaw ticked harder.
" 'Tis ne'er cowardly tae fight."

"Mayhap. However, 'tis *most* cowardly to refuse
to perform a simple conciliatory gesture when
the occasion arises. Especially when your sole rea-

son is that you're much too childish to be the one to take the first step toward peace."

"Beware, lass," he hissed. "Yer sharp tongue has ye treading on yer thin ground."

"Is that so? And if I refuse to shush? What do you propose to do about it, sir? Turn your blade on me and extract silence by spilling my blood? That does seem to be your natural way of settling disputes, does it not?" Gabrielle gulped; for a flickering instant Connor looked as though he intended to do exactly that. Thankfully the moment passed. She sucked in a relieved gulp of musty-smelling night air.

"This conciliatory gesture," Connor said, and the flaring of his nostrils suggested the words were uttered with great reluctance. "What would it be?"

Her gaze shifted between Roy and Connor, settling finally on the former, who was watching her with grim amusement. "Release Roy Maxwell. Let him ride back to Caerlaverock unharmed and let him bring Siobhan back with him."

"Nay!" Connor's dark, thick brows drew together and his expression grew stormy.

"Aye!" she countered just as hotly. "What better way to show the Maxwells that the feud is over, that you'll shed no more blood over it, than to provide him with such an outstanding peace offering?" Her attention turned to Roy before Connor had time to answer. "Would such a gesture not sway your father, even a little bit, to consider ending this senseless fighting?"

Roy shrugged uncertainly, his expression bewildered as he scratched at the underside of his bearded chin. It would seem the idea of ending the feud was not something he'd seriously contemplated . . . until now. His lips pursed, and the glint in his green eyes evinced that the suggestion was not unappealing. "I canna say," he admitted after a thoughtful pause. "Howe'er, considering how me da feels about Siobhan—Och! but his feelings for the lass and her cooking be a fine muckle strong!—methinks returning her would be a grand start. Johnny Maxwell wouldna argue with the gesture, for certain."

The smile that had been tugging at the corner of Gabrielle's lips now blossomed as she returned her gaze to Connor. "Well?" she prompted. "Do you not think 'tis at least worth a try?"

"Mayhap," Connor replied with a vague shrug.

"If you'll not do it for your clan, then do it for me. You once said you'd do anything if I but asked . . ."

Connor groaned. "Dinna say it, lass. Please."

"Don't you see, Connor? I *have* to." Gabrielle hesitated, licked her lips nervously, wondered if perhaps she'd pushed the matter too far, then just as quickly decided it was too late to drop the matter now. The subject of ending the feud had been broached, a suggestion as to how to end it had been offered . . . nay, fear of The Black Douglas's reputed temper aside, the matter was simply too important to her not to pursue. Her fingers loosened, trembled slightly as her open palm stroked the hard muscles of his upper arm. "I'm begging you, please, let Roy go. Take the first step in ending this feud by sending Siobhan back with him."

"Do ye ken what yer asking of me, Gabrielle?"

"Aye, I do." She nodded firmly. "I'm asking far less of you than Elizabeth asked of me."

"A feud generations strong doesna end so easily, nae merely by returning a cook."

"I'm not so foolish as to think it will. What I

am is smart enough to realize that the feud will not end at all if one family does not stop the fighting. M'lord, you vowed a few moments ago that you would defend me with your life's last breath if need be, did you not?"

"I did," Connor admitted grudgingly.

"I'm not asking that of you, I'm not asking of you anything so exalted. All I ask is that you take this one small step in trying to bring peace to the Maxwell and Douglas. That's all, I'm simply asking you to *try.*"

Connor's indecision was as tangible as the dark wisps of smoke curled up from the sconce Roy Maxwell held and twisted toward the low stone ceiling. She trapped her breath in her throat as she watched a variety of emotions play in Connor's narrow gray eyes. Suspicion. Reluctance. Caution. Then, in the end, resignation.

"Ver well, lass," Connor said tightly. He lowered his sword, hesitated, unwillingly resheathed it. Roy's sigh of relief was audible. " 'Twill come tae naught, I vow, but a Douglas is a mon of his word." He shifted his attention to Roy, and his expression hardened. "Go. Take Siobhan with ye. And whate'er ye do, mon, take pains once you're back at Caerlaverock tae tell Johnny Maxwell exactly why the wench is being returned and what is expected of him. Make sure yer da understands the magnitude of what accepting such a gift means. Och! what are ye waiting for? Get ye gone!"

Roy didn't need to be told twice. After hesitating only long enough to send Gabrielle a thankful glance, and Connor one that questioned his sanity, Roy bobbed his head and dodged past them. In mere seconds he'd disappeared up the steep, narrow stairway, the only indication of his nearness the receding click of his bootheels atop bare stone.

Connor waited until he heard the doorway at the top of the stairs slam shut before turning his attention back to Gabrielle. He'd no idea what he planned to say to her, and the second their gazes met, he no longer cared.

The lass was smiling up at him and . . . Och! but he'd never felt his heart speed up and somersault against the cage of his ribs this way in his life!

Had he once thought her smile beautiful? Aye, he had. Now, Connor was forced to reassess. It was not beautiful, for beautiful was too mild a description. The way her green eyes crinkled at the corners, appealing dimples bracketed the sides of her mouth, and her full cheeks flooded with happy pink color . . . Och! aye, 'twas most devastating, is what the sight was!

So captivated was he that Connor didn't at first realize he was returning the gesture. Until he saw her smile widen, and realized it was in response to his own grin.

The strings around his heart twisted into yet another mind-numbing, soul-binding knot.

"The feud will nae end so simply, lass," Connor said. Yet even as he heard the words bouncing off the cold stone around him, heard them echoing roughly in his ears, he found himself doubting their sincerity. Was he wrong? Could a feud that had started so simply, over a woman and a horse, end with equal ease? There was but one way to find out. As Gabrielle had so wisely pointed out, all he could do was try. He had. Grudgingly, aye, but he had. In the end, only time would tell if his meager effort would be successful.

Gabrielle's smile faded and she looked suddenly uncomfortable. Letting her hand drop to her side, she averted her gaze and, her voice soft and shaky, asked, "What you said earlier about me, m'lord, did you mean any of—?"

A commotion sounded from above, halting her words. Feet stomped, male voices roared. Apparently a Douglas had spotted either Roy or Siobhan and assumed the pair was escaping. A natural assumption, one he would have made himself under similar circumstances. While he longed to linger and offer her an abundance of comfort and reassurance, there was no time for such luxuries. His attention was needed above.

Connor's gaze dipped, fixing on her mouth. Nay, more precisely it fixated on the small, moist tip of the tongue that darted out to lick her full, perfectly shaped lips.

He swallowed a groan and leaned toward her, his mouth brushing over hers. Back and forth. Gently, gently. Her breath smelled sweeter than wine as it washed over his skin, seeping deeper and deeper into him. "Aye, lass," he whispered huskily against her mouth, his gaze holding hers ensnared. Now that they'd been voiced once, he was surprised to discover he'd no problem saying the words again. They felt almost natural as his tongue curled around them. "I meant e'ery word and more."

"H-how much more?" The crack of anticipation in her voice was nearly missed to the escalating noise emanating from the floor above.

Curling his left hand into a fist, Connor stroked the back of his knuckles over her softer-than-velvet cheek. "Lass, I've made ye a promise and I intend tae see it kept. I maun go above and escort

Roy Maxwell safely out of Bracklenaer afore me men kill him and worsen the feud ye've tried so hard tae end. Once that chore is completed, with yer permission, I'll happily prove tae ye exactly how ver maun I meant what I said. I'll prove it all night, if ye like."

This time the grin that tugged at Gabrielle's lips was one steeped in pure feminine mischief. She cocked one dark brow at him. "All night, you say?"

"And then some if ye insist."

She shivered in hot anticipation and her voice dropped a throaty pitch. "Then you'd best be about it, m'lord. The night grows late, and this is one promise I've no wish to see The Black Douglas break."

"Nor I," he agreed with a rakish grin.

Connor planted a sound kiss on her lips, then turned his attention toward the stairs and the commotion to be settled above. Knowing the unmatched pleasures that awaited him when the chore was over made him impatient to see the task completed with speed.

Sixteen

The loch, calm and clear, with nary a breeze to ripple its placid surface, was located within walking distance of Bracklenaer. Gabrielle was surprised to find that by the time she reached the wooded clearing bordering the water, her breath came almost as easily as when she'd left the keep.

Her weeks on this tumultuous side of the Border had been fraught with one adventure after the other. While her several escapes hadn't seen her lose so much as a quarter stone in weight, spending more time in a saddle than out of one—or so it seemed—had relaxed joints unaccustomed to such strenuous exercise, defined and toned muscles in her arms and legs and back, muscles she would never have guessed even existed upon leaving London.

The Black Douglas had once described her as a "maun healthy, sturdy lass." As she stepped into the clearing, that was exactly how Gabrielle felt. At some point the words had lost their bitter sting. They no longer felt like an insult, but something to be proud of.

The circle of branches and leaves above revealed a hazy, pink- and gold-tinted sky. The bellies of the two slim clouds that hung suspended there were a singular, pale shade of lavender.

The air was sweet with the rich perfume of the dew-kissed, vibrantly colored wildflowers growing in profusion on the low bank of the loch, the scent mingling with the crisp, sweet scent of grass. Her sense of hearing must have been inordinately acute from a night of sleepless anticipation, for Gabrielle could have sworn she heard the soft buzz of a bee as it flitted hungrily from one pollen-rich petal to the next. High up in the trees, birds chirped as though singing out a welcome to the newborn day. Somewhere in the woods behind her, the snap of twigs and hushed rustle of leaves marked the passage of a red deer.

All those sounds were overridden by another, more subtle noise: the gentle tinkle of water being cupped in a big, hard palm and splashed over broad shoulders and a wide, sinewy chest.

Gabrielle stopped on the edge of the clearing, her ears filled with the sound, her dazed green eyes filled with the sight that created it.

Connor Douglas stood waist-deep in the frigid, mountain-fed loch, the water lapping against the tight indentation of his waist. She blinked hard, thinking again that her senses were deceptively acute this morn—or her imagination entirely too overactive—for she knew that from this distance and angle it simply wasn't possible to see the tiny rivulets of water trickling down his sunkissed flesh.

Possible or not, imagined or not, her body flooded with a warmth to chase away the dawn's chill. Her right elbow was invisible beneath the folds of her black cloak, hiding the way her fingers balled into fists as her palm itched to run over the slick surface of his skin. Her fingertips tickled with the equally strong and impulsive desire to caress him all over.

A soft, pleasant rumbling sound reached her ears. Gabrielle frowned. It took her a moment to place the noise, and when she did, she gaped, then smiled.

Connor was humming. While the melody was wincingly off-key, she eventually recognized it as a song her mother had often sung to her when Gabrielle was a child. A song about a knight, a war, and lady fair.

She was surprised a Scotsman could hum with such easy familiarity a song that, until now, she'd considered a completely English one. That it was a song with blatant romantic overtones, and that it was being hummed with such husky intensity by the likes of The Black Douglas, a notorious reiver whom many on both sides of the Border had written songs *about*, was more surprising still.

Most surprising of all, however, was that while Gabrielle found herself mouthing the familiar lyrics in her own language . . . she couldn't help but wonder how the words would sound in Gaelic. A bit harsher, yet she'd a feeling the no-longer-so-foreign tongue would add a harshly passionate texture to the complex ballad of love, deception, and bittersweet reunion.

Connor's arms were lifted, his hands smoothing water from the dark hair plastered to his scalp and the back of his neck. What was it, she wondered, about the nape of a man's neck, that gently curved expanse between shoulder and hairline, that displayed vulnerability in even the fiercest warrior? Or Border reiver?

Gabrielle's mouth went dry as she watched the

water sluice down Connor's spine. His skin was slick, his flesh a shimmering shade of bronze in the early-morning light. If he'd been close to her, she would not have been able to resist the temptation to angle her head and lick off the silvery droplets of water beading on the shelf of his shoulders. They would taste crisp and sweet, she knew; her tongue curled against her palate in thirsty anticipation.

The humming stopped abruptly. His hands, which had been working the excess water out of the shaggy fringe of his hair, stilled. Awareness pulled taut the rigid sculpture of muscles in his back and shoulders.

Connor turned his head, his neck craning as his gaze sliced through the hazy morning. He didn't scan the bank. It was as though his gaze was a magnet and she a motionless chunk of steel standing on the edge of the clearing; his attention was drawn to her with a force that astonished them both. And once there, it refused to budge.

The chirping of birds overhead receded, the sound chased away by a loud thumping.

Curious, Gabrielle traced the noise back to herself; it was the throbbing of her heart in her ears. Her vision darkened around the edges, tunneling down until all she could see, all she *wanted* to *see*, was a wet, naked Connor Douglas: his gray eyes, piercing and narrow and intense . . . his dark hair slicked back against the cup of his scalp . . . the morning light kissing each angle and plane of his harshly carved face. His skin was a wet temptation to her palms; her fingers ached to find out if his flesh really felt as wonderfully warm and slippery as it appeared.

Everything around her faded to insignificance.

She felt as though her entire world consisted of herself and Connor Douglas, and nothing else.

Gabrielle's lips parted. She'd sought Connor out to tell him something, something important, yet the words she'd been about to voice died on her tongue unspoken when he lifted his arm and extended his hand to her. The sound of water drops falling from his skin and back into the glossy loch trickled in her ears like the first refreshing splashes of a gentle rain falling on a scorching summer day.

Her attention fixed on his hand. While she couldn't see it from this distance, she remembered each thick, powerful finger, remembered the short, springy dark hair on the back and between the first and second knuckle, the way it teased her fingertips. It was a hand capable of wielding a broadsword with deadly precision: *'Tis in my hands she is now, and in my hands she stays.* A hand also capable of caressing a woman's body with a gentleness that was soul-shattering: *Ye've nae objection to me doing this . . . tonight and all the nights after?*

Her gaze traced the length of his forearm, up over his shoulder, past the hard, darkly stubbled square of his jaw. Higher. His attention narrowed. This muscle in his jaw ticked. His gaze was intense and . . . aye, it hadn't been a trick of the hazy morning light, there really *was* a glimmer of uncertainty in his penetrating gray eyes, a flash of vacillation that tightened his expression as he watched her.

The sight touched her, way down deep, in ways a curtly uttered command for her to come to him never could have done.

Gabrielle's legs moved of their own accord, carrying her past the place where he'd carelessly tossed his clothing in a wrinkled heap upon the grass. Her feet felt heavy, her knees weak and shaky, yet somehow the latter found the strength to support her and keep her upright.

Rose brocade dragged over the grass as she took one step.

Two.

Three.

She stopped hesitantly on the bank, so close to Connor now that she no longer had to imagine each droplet of water clinging to his skin—she could *see* them, if possible her gaze could *feel* them. The sight made her stomach do strange little flip-flops, made her breathing uneven and shallow, made her heart pound hard until her head felt dizzy, her senses spinning crazily from the sudden onrush of blood, lack of oxygen, and the tidal wave of raw sensation that being within touching distance of this man always seemed to cause.

Relief seeped through her. Up close she could see that no fresh wounds marred his skin. No trace of blood, dried or fresh, clung to his wet body. It wasn't until Gabrielle had assured herself that Connor was unharmed that she realized how very worried she'd been that he would somehow get hurt while returning Roy Maxwell to his family.

She breathed in a deep sigh of relief. It was then that a new scent reached her, mingling evocatively with the fresh morning fragrance of wildflowers and grass and pine sap. It was the unique, musky male scent of Connor Douglas, and it was a scent to savor.

His arm was still raised, his hand palm up—the skin there puckered slightly from the water—and extended toward her. It was a conciliatory gesture, yet at the same time a beckoning one. It tugged at a place deep down in her soul that she found almost impossible to resist. Almost.

If she reached out—as she was oh so tempted to do—her fingertips would graze his. Connor's would feel warm and wet, Gabrielle knew . . . even as she commanded her hand to stay exactly where it was, hidden beneath the thick folds of her cloak, so he couldn't see how much he affected her, how badly she was shaking.

The memory of why she'd sought him out came at her in a rush. Her breath caught, for as the reason played in her mind, it was easily recognized for what it was. An excuse to see him.

She'd not come to tell him anything he wouldn't have learned from one of his men upon returning to Bracklenaer—probably from Gilby, who was now up and about and, when not complaining about his wound, was busy practicing on anyone who'd tolerate it the cusses he'd learned from Mairghread that fateful night in the tunnel.

The reason Gabrielle had given herself for being here, she realized now, was a deception, and not a very good one at that; the reason was embarrassingly shallow, flimsier than a battle shield constructed of a material no more substantial than a strip of diaphanous gauze. Only now did she understand that she harbored more deep-seated and intense reasons for disturbing Connor's bath. And only now, slowly, slowly, did she begin to realize exactly what that reason was and, more importantly, what it meant.

When she'd approached the edge of the loch, she had been dazed and only partially aware of what she was doing. Now, when she slipped her hand from beneath the warm folds of her cloak and lifted it, the motion was done with silent intent. Gabrielle knew exactly what she was doing.

Her trembling fingertips brushed Connor's. She was right, his skin felt every bit as warm and wet and wonderfully slippery as she'd imagined it would.

Because she was standing on the bank and he in the loch, he had to tilt his head in order to continue holding her gaze as he turned and took one small step in her direction. The concealing surface of the water rode temptingly low on his hips as his wet palm slid along the length of her dry one.

Then, suddenly, with a flick of his wrist they were palm to palm, the pulses in their wrists beating against each other as though vying for speed. One by one his fingers curled inward, linking and weaving with her own.

Connor's grip was possessively firm, but not painful. Gabrielle could easily have pulled away from him . . . if she'd wanted to.

She did not want to.

What she *wanted* to do was move *closer.*

Connor's voice, when it came, was throaty and low, no more than a hoarse whisper. "I'm a mon of me word, Gabby. While I still dinna think 'twill do much tae end this cursed feud, Roy Maxwell is safely back with his kin. Nae doubt Johnny Maxwell is e'en now rejoicing in the return of his treasured cook. Methinks he will be tae busy celebrating and feasting for the next fortnight or so tae ride against us or any other clan."

"Thank you," Gabrielle said, her voice equally as soft and husky. She was having trouble concentrating on the subject at hand, however. The feud between Maxwell and Douglas suddenly seemed very far away; her thoughts had latched on to something else, something more immediate.

Gabby.

No one else called her that. While the nickname sounded foreign to her ears, at the same time she found she liked very much the soft, guttural way the two syllables rolled off Connor's tongue.

Warmth radiated from his fingertips, sinking into her skin, heating her blood. Waves of awareness radiated from that spot and out to the rest of her body. Her breath caught and her fingers flexed convulsively. His gave a reassuring squeeze in response.

"Ella's gone again," Gabrielle said, because she felt the need to say something, and her reason, no matter how feeble, for being here seemed as good as any.

"Aye, and well I ken it."

"How did you find out?"

"She did what any Douglas would do. There wasna a need tae be told the obvious."

"If you knew," she countered, her green eyes widening in surprise, "then why didn't you stop her?"

The hint of a grin tugged at one corner of Connor's lips. The tip of his thumb was stroking a leisurely path up and down the length of her index finger. "Me cousin has a mind of her own, as ye've nae doubt discovered." He muttered something under his breath about finding Ella a husband, but Gabrielle couldn't make out all of his rumbling since a goodly portion was in Gaelic. "Had I tried tae stop her, she'd have kicked me in the shins, cursed me blue, then set off after him no matter what I said tae her. Since arguing with the stubborn wench is maun the same as arguing with a lifeless pile of wool—and comes to maun the same—I thought it best tae save me shins the bruising, don't ye ken?"

She blinked hard. "You didn't stop her for fear she'd *kick you?*" she asked, then tipped her head back and laughed. She couldn't help it. The thought of this man—the infamous Black Douglas, the stuff of Border legends and ballads—being in any way afraid of a wee slip of a lass like Ella was so preposterous it was comical. Gabrielle laughed until her sides ached and her cheeks hurt.

" 'Tis nae *that* funny," Connor said, but his mind was only partially on the words his tongue formed. A bigger part of his concentration had been snagged by the sound of her laughter, and the way her pretty green eyes and softly rounded features seemed to light up the morning.

The gentle trickle of her laughter was mesmerizing in a way he'd never known before. It took effort to continue speaking, and not drag her down into the water with him so he could feel her body pressing against his again.

What had they been discussing? Ah, yes, he remembered now, vaguely. "In case ye've nae noticed, me cousin is stubborn tae the core and has the kick of a spoiled thoroughbred."

"Ella is a Douglas born and bred."

He thought about that for a second, then, his grin broadening, beamed proudly up at her. His thumb continued the hot, lazy strokes that made her skin tingle. "That she is, Gabby. That she maun definitely is! One of the rare facts those cursed Border ballads have gotten right is that a Douglas is relentless. Once we set our mind tae something, anyone with a scrap of sense stays out of our way. Ye could say 'tis unhealthy tae try tae stop us. One way or another, we get what we're after."

Connor was no longer referring to Ella or Roy Maxwell or anything so simple. Gabrielle could tell by the way his piercing gray eyes narrowed and his expression sobered.

As though she was hearing it from the opposite end of a very long tunnel, her voice seemed to come from a distance when she asked, "What is it *you're* after, Connor Douglas?"

"Ye don't 'ken?" he counted huskily.

"I think I do, but I want to hear you say it."

"Och! Gabby, I can do better than that. Come closer, lass, and I'll *show* ye."

"Don't be silly. I can't. I'm already standing on the edge of the bank. Another step and I'd—"

Connor's grin was wicked and quick. A flick of his wrist saw what she'd been about to describe happen.

Gabrielle gasped when she felt her hand jerked suddenly forward, felt herself tip precariously in the same direction. Her toes curled within her shoes, as though trying to claw through the hard soles and dig into the earth beneath in an effort to find some purchase.

The chilly water of the loch loomed closer, then receded somewhat when she flailed her free arm. Unfortunately, that arm was still buried beneath the thick folds of her cloak; moving it about did precious little good to stabilize her wavering balance. If anything, the panicky gesture had the opposite effect.

She could feel herself again lurching forward. In a final attempt to save herself a frigid dousing, her fingers tightened around Connor's. She pushed with all her might against his hand. It might have worked, had Connor not been prepared for it. She'd intended to use his resistance as leverage, but there was no resistance to use. Instead, he let her push his hand backward even as his fingers meshed more tightly with her own.

"Connor!" she cried, and in the same instant the ground beneath her feet disappeared. The pressure of his grip pulling her forward made Gabrielle helpless to stop her body from following.

The last sound she heard before hitting the water face-first was the deep, rich sound of Connor Douglas's laughter.

Gabrielle's belly took the brunt of the collision; her cloak and gown provided precious little padding against the slap of pain as she hit the water. Momentum, coupled with suddenly drenched, water-heavy clothes, dragged her under. Her breath burst from her lungs in a rush that made an explosion of bubbles scurry to the surface.

Connor had not let go of her hand. Gabrielle clung to his grip as she willed her quickly numbing feet, snarled in the folds of her saturated skirt and cloak, to find the soft, muddy bed of the loch.

The water had only been up to Connor's hips. She knew that if she could only find her footing, she'd be able to push herself to the top. Unfortunately, her feet were hopelessly ensnared; it seemed like the more she kicked and tried to work them free, the more tangled they became.

Panic, dark and blinding, clawed at her insides. With effort she swallowed it back.

C-c-cold! My God, she was soooo c-c-cold!

The frigidity of the water made her limbs feel unnaturally heavy and unresponsive. Just when she thought her lungs would burst from their burning need for oxygen, she felt a strong arm slide around her waist and haul her upward.

She broke the surface with several loud, choked, shuddering gasps that supplied an abundance of blessedly sweet morning air to her deprived lungs. Her teeth chattered against each other so violently that the clicks of them knocking together filled her head and drowned out the panicky throb of her heartbeat.

A tiny portion of her mind recognized the hard, strong body she was being held tightly against. A much larger portion recognized, and appreciated greatly, the heat that body emanated. It was a heat that washed through her, seeming to chase away the most desperate part of the cold that felt as though it had settled right into the marrow of her bones.

Gabrielle's eyes were closed. She opened them now and blinked away the droplets of water clinging to her lashes.

Green eyes narrowed, her gaze fixed with furious disbelief on a smugly grinning Black Douglas. Her lips were blue from the cold. She could barely feel them, and could move them only by exerting extraordinary effort. "W-w-why did you d-d-do that?!"

Would she understand if he told her? Nay, Connor thought, she would not, especially not in her current, indignant frame of mind. *Showing* her, however, as he'd promised before dragging her into the water with him, was something else again . . .

Connor angled his head, his mouth swooping down hungrily to cover hers.

Gabrielle's lips felt icy cold and, at first, unresponsive.

The heat of his passion soon thawed them.

Connor groaned low and deep in his throat and dragged the tip of his tongue over the crease separating her upper lip from her lower. Her mouth opened for him, and he delved inside the sweet inner recesses, darting and stroking and driving the chill from her with an intensity that stunned them both.

She squirmed against him, her feet finally finding their way free of her skirt and touching the floor of the loch. She stood on her own now, leaned forward, pressing her upper body against his.

Her arms stole about his neck, her splayed fingers combing through his wet hair, clenching, fisting it in handfuls so close to his scalp that the roots of his hair stung. Soon the gooseflesh-prickled skin on her forearms and shoulders was also warming as she drained the heat from his body and drew it into her own.

It was only as Connor began to slip his other hand around her waist, yearning to pull her temptingly soft body closer still, that he realized their fingers were still entwined. Without missing a beat, he diverted the course of his arm. Water dripped down his forearm as he lifted their linked hands, turned them at the wrists, then slowly, slowly stroked the quivering line of her jaw with the back of his knuckles.

"Beautiful," he whispered hotly against her lips. "Och! but ye be so ver beautiful."

"You're blind to even think it," she replied shyly, and with equal huskiness against his mouth. A blush warmed her cheeks, the pinkness creeping up to her hairline, washing down the length of her neck.

"I dinna *think* it, I *ken* it." Connor pulled back and looked down into her eyes, breathtaking green eyes that swam with confusion and . . . aye, a hopefulness that yanked at the strings of emotion this woman had somehow, without his knowledge and certainly without his consent, wound in a complex web he'd never be able to untangle around his heart. "I be many things, but blind isna one of them. I see ye for exactly what ye are. And I like yer maun what I see."

"Are you saying that you meant those things you said to Roy Maxwell about me? Truly?"

"With all my heart, Gabby." His voice rang with a sincerity that was echoed in the flash of candor sparkling in his eyes. "I meant e'ery word."

Gabrielle's mouth gaped open. The question hovering in her mind slipped off her tongue before she could stop it. "Then mayhap you like me well enough to . . . ?"

The words trailed softly away. Her head spun and she leaned weakly against him, positive she would have collapsed without the support, her knees suddenly felt that weak and shaky.

Had she gone insane? Aye, Gabrielle thought, she must have. What other reason explained why she'd just come so perilously close to asking this man to—?

"What?" Connor prompted when she blushed and glanced away. He slipped his hand reluctantly from around her waist. Applying the crook of his index finger to the wet, silky underside of her chin, he nudged her mouth shut and at the same time brought her gaze back to his. He wanted badly to kiss her again, but sensed this wasn't the time. Later, he vowed, he would kiss her until they were both breathless and wanting. Right now, however, he'd a feeling she needed something much different from him. "Enough tae . . . what, lass?"

"T-to . . ."

"Tell me, please."

"Enough to *wed me.*" She wrenched from his grasp and, clasping her arms tightly about her waist, turned her back on him. The motion wasn't easy, especially considering the way her water-heavy dress and cloak hung from her shoulders like lead, pulling at her and making her movements awkward, but she managed it. It was either that, or let Connor see the humiliation she knew must be evident in her gaze and her expression. "There, I've said it. Are you happy now?"

"Nay, lass, nae yet. But almost."

Gabrielle closed her eyes briefly. The vision of Elizabeth Tudor's pinched, mocking face floated in the blackness behind her tightly scrunched eyelids. Harsh, hurtful words echoed in her ears. She tried to chase the memories away, but they refused to go. Were it not against her nature to hate a woman so recently dead and buried, Gabrielle might finally have allowed herself to feel the animosity for her former Queen that had been slow-simmering inside her for so many years.

Releasing a shaky breath, she used one hand to smooth her wet hair back from her brow. Her fingertips strayed to her lower lip. Her mouth still felt hot and swollen from Connor Douglas's kiss. If she dragged her tongue over her lips, would his taste linger there? Gabrielle didn't dare try it to find out. Surely the sweet, musky flavor of him clinging to her skin would be her undoing.

A heavy weight settled upon her shoulder.

Connor's fingers dug lightly through the soaked cloth, into the tender skin beneath. There was a leashed strength to his touch, a barely restrained impatience that was mirrored in his voice when he spoke. "I dinna find the idea of wedding ye unappealing."

"Really?" The fingertips against her lips felt icy again as they trembled against the kiss-swollen skin there. "Aye, I suppose that's true enough. The chance is good our marriage would give you the heir you so desperately want. I can see where you wouldn't be too opposed to the idea. After all, Mairghread says—"

"Please, Gabby, dinna—"

"—these repulsively wide hips were made for birthing and—"

" 'Tis nae *all* Mairghread said about ye." The grip on her shoulder tightened, his fingers biting into her skin now. "Och!, lass, she *dinna* use the term 'repulsive,' nor will I let *ye* use it tae describe yerself. Nothing could be further from the truth."

"Don't lie to me Connor. Not about this. Don't you dare! I'm not blind. I know the truth when I see it, and I see it every time I look in a mirror." *And every time Elizabeth's cold, cruel words come back to haunt me.* "Believe me, m'lord, I suffer no delusions about how I look."

"What do ye see when ye look in that mirror, Gabby?"

"An overstuffed goose," she replied automatically. Biting down hard on her lower lip, Gabrielle swallowed back the sob that wedged tightly in her throat. Unshed tears stung her eyes, but she refused to let them flow. She would not cry in front of Connor, not about this. If nothing else, she still had her pride.

His hand left her shoulder. Gabrielle waited to hear the telltale splash of water that would signal

Connor had turned his back on her and walked away in disgust. What happened instead was so unexpected it surprised a gasp out of her.

A splash did reach her ears, but it was closer than she expected, close enough to make the surface of the water ripple around her. Connor must have bent at the waist, for suddenly he slipped one strong arm beneath her knees and coiled the other around her back.

Gabrielle felt his muscles bunch and strain as he hoisted the burden of her weight, which was added to considerably by her water-soaked gown and cloak.

"What are you doing?!" she cried, even as she wrapped her arms around his neck and shifted her weight, trying to spread it more evenly in his arms and make her easier to carry. Telling him to put her down never once crossed her mind; she enjoyed too much the hardness and heat of him pressing against her to willingly relinquish the feeling.

He didn't answer, but instead turned toward the bank and started walking. By the time he reached dry ground his breathing was a bit labored. She thought the dampness clinging to his upper lip and brow had more to do with the effort he exerted than any remnants of his bath.

Stopping in the middle of the small, dawn-lit clearing, he sat her down upon the ground and knelt beside her. He was gloriously naked and wet and . . . aye, he was aroused.

Gabrielle's heartbeat stuttered beneath the cage of her ribs. Suddenly, Connor wasn't the only one having trouble breathing.

"What are you doing?" she repeated when his fingers went to the laces beneath her chin, laces that held the plackets of her wet cloak securely together.

"Plucking you," Connor replied as he deftly untied the water-tightened bow, then eased the cloak off her shoulders. That done, his hands slipped behind her, his fingers working free the tiny seed-pearl buttons that trailed down the spine of her bodice. "I promised ye last night I'd show ye my true feelings for ye. I can think of nae better time and nae better way."

"Surely you don't intend to . . . ?"

Their gazes met.

Determined gray meshed with shock-widened green.

"Aye," he replied, his voice low, deep, and husky with raw conviction, "I do."

"Now? *In broad daylight?*" A blush warmed Gabrielle's cheeks. The two times they'd made love before had been at night, amid the comforting shield of darkness. Panic bubbled up inside her. Daylight would expose the many flaws in her plump figure, flaws that she could pretend the cover of night had so graciously concealed. "Nay, Connor, please don't."

"Why nae, lass? Do ye nae want me?"

Gabrielle almost laughed. How could he think such a thing? Her fingers rested limply in her cold, wet lap; she twisted them nervously together. "You know I do. It's just that . . . truth to tell, m'lord, I'm not entirely sure that *you* want *me.*"

Connor cocked one dark eyebrow, his gaze leaving hers only long enough to shift briefly down to the part of his anatomy that gave hard, vibrant proof that he did indeed want her. So badly he ached from it. "Does it look like I dinna want ye, Gabby?"

Her attention shadowed his, and her blush deepened to a hotter shade of pink. "Well, no, but—"

"Nae 'buts' aboot it. I want ye, Gabby, and nae for the reason ye think. Aye, I'll nae lie and say I dinna want an heir, several of them in fact, because I do. Howe'er, if ye said ye dinna want tae carry me bairns, it wouldna change the way I feel for you. I'd still be wanting tae lay ye back against the cool, sweet grass, strip ye bare, and make love tae ye until neither of us could think straight."

She didn't want to ask. She *had* to ask, *had* to know. The uncertainty of his motives was gnawing at her insides, creating doubts where, perhaps, there should be none. "Why?"

Connor's fingers left the buttons at her back. His hands shifted, his open palms gently cradling her cheeks. His expression didn't blanch, nor did his gaze waver as, without missing a beat, he replied, "Because I love ye, Gabrielle Carelton. Why else?"

The sincerity with which he uttered the words made her spirits soar higher than the eagle that circled the sky above. She was torn between a strong sense of disbelief and an even stronger sense of unadulterated joy. Had she misheard? Had he really said he loved her? Dare she hope it was true? "But how can you? I'm not beautiful. I'm not—"

"Ye are tae me," he corrected her firmly. "Ye're maun than beautiful. 'Tis all that matters, dinna ye ken?"

Gabrielle blinked hard, her senses spinning. The Black Douglas loved her? He thought her beautiful? Had she really drowned when he'd pulled her into the water? Died and gone to heaven? She thought she might have, for never in life had she known such elation.

"I'm not dreaming, am I?"

"Nay, lass, yer nae."

"And you really do mean it, don't you?" Her voice was edged with disbelief.

Connor nodded, the gesture making his dark hair sway wetly against his shoulders. "I do. It may take me a lifetime tae prove it to ye, but . . . Och! lass, I've ne'er meant anything so maun in me life. Why do ye think I'd have tried tae end the feud between Douglas and Maxwell? Do ye think I'd do that for anyone else but ye? Nay, I would nae have. But *ye* were the one who asked it of me and, try though I have, I canna deny ye anything, e'en that."

Gabrielle unlinked the fingers clenched tightly in her lap and, his words filling her with a heady burst of confidence and boldness, splayed her open palms against his naked chest.

He felt hot and damp to the touch.

He felt oh so very wonderful.

The smile she bestowed upon him was so radiant that at first Connor was too entranced by the sight of it to realize she was speaking. Even once he did realize it, her words did not register in his mind and he was forced to ask her to repeat them.

"I simply pointed out that there's another feud in need of settling, m'lord."

"There is?" he asked, dazed by both her touch and the intense desire it aroused within him.

"Aye. The one between you and your twin."

Gabrielle's hands were not content to remain still. She began stroking restless, distracting paths over his hard-muscled chest and belly, his shoulders and arms. He groaned when her water-wrinkled palms left a blazing trail of molten fire in their wake.

"Later, Gabby," he said throatily, his mouth dipping with slow intent toward hers. "We'll discuss it maun, maun later."

His mouth carried through its promise and was on hers, his tongue urging her lips apart. His kiss was ravenous; it obliterated all thoughts of family and feuds and weddings from her mind.

Connor's arms stole around her, holding her impossibly close, and Gabrielle decided abruptly that later would suit her fine. There was no rush . . . now that she knew there would *be* a later. A lifetime of them. She looked forward to each and every one.

JANELLE TAYLOR

ZEBRA'S BEST-SELLING AUTHOR

**DON'T MISS ANY OF HER
EXCEPTIONAL, EXHILARATING, EXCITING**

ECSTASY SERIES

SAVAGE ECSTASY   (0-8217-3496-2, $4.95/$5.95)

DEFIANT ECSTASY   (0-8217-3497-0, $4.95/$5.95)

FORBIDDEN ECSTASY   (0-8217-5278-2, $5.99/$6.99)

BRAZEN ECSTASY   (0-8217-3499-7, $4.99/$5.99)

TENDER ECSTASY   (0-8217-5242-1, $5.99/$6.99)

STOLEN ECSTASY   (0-8217-3501-2, $4.99/$5.99)

FOREVER ECSTASY   (0-8217-5241-3, $5.99/6.99)